An Anthology of Short Stories

 Look What I Found

Compiled By NorGus Press

ISBN-10: 0615460275
EAN-13: 9780615460277

An Anthology of Short Stories

Look What I Found

Compiled By NorGus Press

Table of Contents

The Maestro Signal

BY WILLIAM R.D. WOOD

"Let me go, Mommy."

Claudia squeezed her daughter to her chest, letting her long coat wrap around the preschooler like the wings of a mother bird protecting her young. Tears flowed down her cheeks, mingling in the coarse white strands of her little girl's hair.

Ashley stood still in her mother's embrace, arms at her sides. "Mommy, I need to go."

"No, honey." Claudia's voice cracked as she tightened her hold and shut her eyes. Maybe if she held her baby long enough, when she opened her eyes, the girl would be normal again. Maybe she wouldn't want to leave. *Please, God…oh, please, just let her be my Ashley again.*

"But, Mommy…the music…"

"Hush, now." Claudia placed a finger across Ashley's mouth. Her four-year-old lips felt hard and cool. Claudia sat the girl on the couch behind the sales counter and knelt, stifling a new wave of tears.

The media had dubbed the transformation the Medusa Plague. Her little angel's skin shimmered in the fluorescent lighting like fine porcelain. Most unnerving were her eyes. Like polished stones, they swiveled to follow Claudia as she turned and looked out the storefront's plate glass window. The only people on the street were the infected, their gleaming white arms swinging oddly out of time with their steps. Each swayed in a slow, individual rhythm, as though the laws of physics and physiology now tailored themselves to conform to a whole new set of paradigms. To Claudia, they were a jumble of random movements that should have sent each of the afflicted people tumbling to the pavement, but the sum of their movements combined--resonated even--defying reason and keeping them upright as they walked on their northward trek: some serpentine, some insect-like, but all *wrong*.

Claudia shuddered, triggering her guts to tightened, small stabs of pain reminding her she'd been crying far too much in the last few days. She clenched her teeth and forced her best *all is well with the world* look onto her face and looked into Ashley's eyes for a trace of her chocolate brown irises. The pearly, pupil-less marbles stared back and all Claudia saw was the girl's gentle question.

Can I go, Mommy?

A week ago, she and Ashley had sat upstairs in front of the television eating chicken nuggets and watching Nickelodeon. The boy band on the screen ran around, screaming and singing their way through their latest ridiculous adventure. Claudia could barely tolerate the show herself, but she melted every time Ashley doubled over in giggles. Just as she'd stood to get more honey mustard for Ashley's nuggets, the screen had darkened to the red, white and blue Seal of the United States as a high-pitched hum filled the air. The dial tone of the end times, her father had always called it.

It's okay, she had started to say to Ashley. They do these tests during the day so they don't interfere with the prime time money-maker shows. Then the seal faded to a podium clustered with microphones.

A grim-faced woman, her face cinched tight by the bun of black and gray hair behind her head, stepped into view. She began by reminding everyone of the ruins recently discovered off the coast of Africa by a private deep sea oil exploration team. Under a mile of water were thousands of structures buried in the sediment. Soon after the first pictures were circulated to the awe-filled world as recovered artifacts were brought to the surface. Then the spokeswoman produced a single photo of a girl stricken with the Medusa Plague. Holding up a hand to silence the burst of questions from the press, she stated simply that the President and other world leaders believed the two events were connected. She assured the nation and the world that the world's top scientists were working in conjunction with the CDC and the UN to contain the situation but, as she put it, the genie might already be out of the bag.

A shadow passed over them and Claudia looked up into the unshaven face of Rolpho, the shopkeeper who rented them the studio apartment upstairs. "You should let girl go."

Claudia stared at him for a moment.

Rolpho pointed at the shop window. Beyond the glass, three of the infected—two women and a small child—had stopped in the middle of the street and were looking in their direction. The child could have been a boy or a girl, Claudia couldn't tell. The corners of the child's lips turned up as both women began to wave their hands, beckoning. Claudia felt Ashley lean into her, her small body wavering in time with the hands of the infected trio.

"See," said Rolpho. "I decide this. You let her go."

Claudia spun and rose to her full five-foot-two, blood boiling. Fists clenched at her sides, shaking visibly, she took a step toward the dark, Mediterranean immigrant.

Rolpho backed away, hands raised. "I'm just saying…"

"Who the hell do you think you are?"

He shrugged. "You look like you need someone to make hard decision for you is all."

"It's okay, Mommy," said Ashley. "I want to go."

"American women like strong man to make decision. Internet says so."

Claudia glared at the man and dropped onto the couch and pulled her daughter close. "No, honey. You're staying right here with me until they figure out how to cure this…"

"Plague," finished Rolpho.

"It is not a…it's just a *condition*." Claudia wanted to protect Ashley from the *p-word*. Herself too, for that matter. Besides, plagues had some vehicle of transmission between people. Medusa sprang up on four continents within hours. What could cause that?

"Condition, sure. Whatever you say." Rolpho pulled a shotgun from the cabinet beneath the register and walked to the window. "Crazy grave robbers should have left ruins alone."

Claudia looked at the flickering flat-screen on the wall. She'd lowered the sound when she and Ashley came downstairs this morning. She glanced quickly at the news ticker along the bottom. *Medusa Rages Across Globe. Atlantis Excavation Halted in Wake of Plague. Dow, Nikkei, Hang Seng Plunge to All Time Lows.*

Rolpho gazed out the window at the distant spire growing above the city's skyline, a gleaming alabaster structure that looked like a three dimensional graph meant to show geometric growth:

ever wider at the base and ever taller at the center, like a giant fang bared to heaven.

"Plato wrote much about plague," said Rolpho. "On Internet, I saw—"

"Plato wrote no such thing." Claudia shot the man a withering look. Since the DHS press conference had thrown the idea out to the world, Medusa and Atlantis had become forever fused together in everyone's mind. Every crackpot was reading Plato now and claiming to be an expert on the only two writings in which the ancient philosopher even mentioned the lost continent.

"Internet does not lie—"

An infected man stepped in front of the window. Startled, Rolpho swore in his native language and brought up the barrel of his sawed-off shotgun to point directly at the glistening face on the other side of the glass. The man was fully transformed, like a marble statue straight from the Museum of Art. His lips stretched thin in a closed-mouth smile and he peered over Rolpho's shoulder at Claudia and the girl. His porcelain eyelids blinked at slightly different speeds as his head rocked back and forth like a metronome, personified.

"Mommy." Ashley pushed herself to the edge of the couch, leaning forward to get a better look at the man.

Claudia shifted her body to block Ashley's view. The infected man gestured to her with both hands like a minister calling his flock to the altar.

"Mommy?"

"No." Her voice sounded flat in her own ears, drained of emotion from exhaustion, though her heart swelled with love for her baby girl. She should feel afraid, Claudia knew, but the human mind could only take so much stress and right now, she knew her mind was denying her the luxury of fear.

"But I can hear the song now too, Mommy! Not just the music—"

"No, angel. You belong with me."

The man outside the window stopped moving and Claudia could feel his icy gaze rake across her. Her heart crept into her throat and she froze too. She'd thought their asynchronous swaying had been disturbing, alien even, but to see one go completely motionless was terrifying.

She'd heard no reports of violence by the infected but saying something had not happened was no real reassurance that such a thing *could* not happen. Everyone assumed these people were diseased, but what if Medusa was not a disease at all. Suppose the *infected* were simply something new, or something unseen for millennia, or longer? Regardless, no one could honestly say what they were capable of.

The infected man's head pivoted to take in Rolpho who had taken a step back from the window and lowered his shotgun to waist level, now aiming at the man's chest. The porcelain man opened his mouth as if to speak, seemed to think better of it, and smiled instead, soft white light oozing between his teeth. And then he was gone, turning away and moving on in ill-measured steps as he rejoined the migration toward the spire.

Rolpho exhaled audibly, shoulders slumping as he lowered the shotgun. "I don't like sick."

Claudia didn't think she could pull her daughter any closer, but she tried. The television was showing the same video again. The triggering event, according to some United Nations think-tank in Switzerland. A smiling scientist stood flanked by oil company executives, their crisp suits oddly out of place aboard the merchant marine ship they'd gathered in. The scientist gestured at the object on the table the way a game show host's assistant might ham up presenting a winning letter in a word puzzle. Two white softball-sized spheres, fused in the center rested in a cradle of padded metal struts. The surface was intricately etched with overlapping lines and blocks, reminding Claudia of the foil runs on a circuit board or magnified views of microprocessor chips. The scientist released a latching mechanism and opened the box. An impossible clockwork of multicolored glass and light shimmered inside.

"Sooner... later... she joins them," Said Rolpho, causing Claudia to jump. "Really. Don't you think?"

"No. I don't." Claudia stroked her daughter's cheek. Hardly a square inch of untainted skin remained. Had only a few days passed since the excited preschooler charged into the kitchen? *Look, Mommy, I'm crying milk!* Claudia had wiped away the viscous white tears and watched as they hardened into glassy chips and tinkled to the floor like tiny wind chimes.

Even then, the top news stories centered on the plague. All around the world, in a grand synchronized exodus, the infected had politely excused themselves from hospitals, from their families and jobs, and began moving into the cities.

And began to build the spires.

Claudia could see the structure in the downtown metroplex through the window. It had to be a mile high now and still growing. A group of healthy people fleeing the bay area had passed by the shop just before noon headed south and told them thousands, maybe even tens of thousands, of the infected were crawling over the spire like bugs. And as they did, the spire grew.

Claudia stifled a yawn. She'd not allowed herself to sleep for days, afraid she'd wake to find her arms empty and Ashley gone to join the migration. "Do you have more coffee?"

The moment hung heavy and still with only the mindless drone from the television reminding her time had not collapsed to zero.

"Coffee all gone." Rolpho pulled on a new filter mask and adjusted the rubber straps. He'd worn the flimsy paper safety precautions on and off all day, since she'd brought Ashley downstairs. "You *and* girl...should go."

"Go?" Claudia snapped fully awake. Rolpho held the shotgun, muzzle down, but pointed in their direction. "Go where, exactly?"

He nodded his head toward the window and the street beyond. A few infected wandered by.

Panic rose in her stomach. "You can't be serious."

"Girl is sick." The nose of the shotgun rose an inch. "You won't let girl go alone...so..."

"B-but...we can't—you can't make us leave."

Rolpho pursed his lips and nodded his head, an answer to some internal dialogue. "No. I decide. You leave now."

"But we have a lease—"

"Tell to the judge." He raised the gun a few more inches. Still not pointed directly at them but his message was clear enough.

Claudia rose to her feet, placing herself in the line of fire. Without looking, she reached back to touch her daughter, but Ashley was gone. The couch was empty. She let out a cry and spun back to face Rolpho. Ashley stood between them, her right hand outstretched to the armed man as if she expected him to lead her across the street to preschool.

His eyes widened in terror. He raised one hand and pressed the paper mask tighter against his face. With the other hand, he swung the shotgun toward the girl.

Claudia screamed and dove across the open space.

Thunder erupted in the small store as pain tore into Claudia's neck and shoulder. Her feet lost their grip on the floor and she slammed hard to the tile, cracking her head. Her eyes lost focus in the fog of pain and the roar of her own pulse slamming against the inside of her skull, perhaps for the last time. She flopped her head left and right, neck unable to respond as it should. Deep in her mind, she realized that her muscles were ripped apart and her precious blood was splashing in gushes to the floor. Her daughter--her precious angel--lay in a heap a few feet away and Rolpho stood, his back against the wall, his face stretched in horror.

Ashley's body twitched several times and she pushed herself to her feet. A dark stain spread across the back of her Disney Princesses t-shirt where her left shoulder blade should be, only her shoulder was a chewed mess of white and red. She steadied herself a moment and stepped toward the armed man.

He swung the gun around for a second shot. Ashley touched the end of the barrel. Light flashed and a white film formed along the muzzle, advancing like frost in a time-lapse video. With a gentle swat from her right hand, Ashley shattered the weapon, sending a spray of crystal fragments over the man as he dropped to the floor and backpedaled into the wall.

The light in the room faded and Claudia wondered if the mist swirling in the air was real. If the melodic rhythm of her heart beating in her skull was growing stronger or if she were living her last few seconds, her senses failing and feeding her impossible information? Ashley knelt over her and passed her palms lightly over the wounds. Claudia looked at her daughter's left arm and shoulder. A moment ago, she'd been sure the girl was permanently maimed at best, but more likely, dead. Blood streaked the front of Ashley's shirt, but through the gaping hole, Claudia watched the girl's flesh knit together, tug itself tight, and harden into gleaming marble. Within seconds, all that remained of the damage were a few small cracks in the porcelain complexion of her face.

"I… love you… angel." Warmth spread across Claudia's neck and shoulder as Ashley stroked her skin. The pain faded and she found herself struggling once again against the urge to sleep.

Ashley hugged Claudia, her tiny white arms cold like stone against her skin. Then she stood and moved back to the shop owner.

"Don't hurt people, Mister Rolpho." Her unblemished brow wrinkled and she pointed a single finger at the cowering man. "Be nice."

Rolpho pulled his legs against his chest and buried his face in his arms, shielding his eyes from the girl.

"Mommy?"

Claudia nodded, tears welling in her eyes. She couldn't contain this divine little creature any longer. Amazing things were happening out there and her daughter was a part of them. "Yes, angel."

Ashley's eyes widened and she smiled, her expression a white-washed version of the one Claudia had seen countless times when the girl got an eagerly anticipated treat.

Claudia choked back the sobs growing in her chest. "You can go."

Ashley kissed her on the cheek. Her lips were cold and Claudia felt static dance between them. Then her little girl turned and walked away.

Claudia's chest tightened, her heartbeat pounding in her chest and she could contain her sorrow no longer. A broken wail rose in her throat and she cried.

The door opened, jingling the bell hanging from the frame, and cool night air poured into the room. Seconds passed and Claudia looked up through bleary eyes to see her daughter standing at the threshold.

"Come with me, Mommy."

Claudia wiped her eyes. "Wh-what? I can?" She crawled across the floor and sat next to the standing girl, wrapping her arms around her shimmering form.

"It's okay. They're ready to show us."

"Show us?"

Ashley nodded. "To show us how."

"How to what, angel?" Images flashed in Claudia's head. Gleaming white cities reaching skyward beneath crimson sunsets. Multi-spoked spires drifting in the darkness of space like dandelion seeds. Men, women and children, hands joined, strolling the beaches of alien seas.

Claudia shook her head to clear away the vision and dabbed at the corners of her eyes. Faintly, just above the level of hearing, she heard the music.

Ashley's skin glowed with light from within. "How to… *everything.*"

Claudia's lips quivered and she felt tears rolling down her cheeks, tinkling like glass as they struck the tile floor. She held up her hands, ivory fingers glistening in the fluorescent light from above and the few street lights working outside. She tentatively reached into her blouse and felt her injured shoulder and neck. Perfectly smooth.

"You made me like you?"

"No, Mommy."

"Then—"

Ashley placed her finger across her mother's lips and smiled. "We've always been us. The deepest, bestest parts have just been waiting."

We are the song.

Claudia's lips thinned in a smile and she nodded to the man huddled in the corner. Small flecks of white glinted in his hair. Change was painful and terrifying and not a single soul was to be spared this one. Like it or not, the whole human race was on the verge of waking.

The sun would rise in the morning.

And the world it rose on would be a new one.

One last tear rolled down Claudia's cheek and she stood. Taking her daughter's tiny hand in her own, she walked through the doorway into the cool night air.

The Curious Case of Josiah Mint

BY SEAN T. PAGE

The sight of young Robert Carfax returning in triumph from his well-publicized military adventures in the West Indies was enough to make the ashen-faced lawyer, Josiah Mint, turn green in the shadows of his oak-paneled office.

He watched the farcical theatrics through the soot covered sash windows of his busy central Bath office, as the handsome heir dismounted his horse to the great acclaim of waiting family and a clutch of well-meaning onlookers. Each delicate step the jubilant young prince took drove dark splinters of hatred deep into Josiah's heart, adding more black coal to the hidden fire raging within the jealous lawyer's calculating mind.

Josiah slumped back into his faded leather chair, still watching the sickening scene on the street below. Forty years old, as yet unmatched in marriage and an over-looked junior partner at the provincial law firm Arbuckle, Grant and Peabody. This was hardly the great destiny he had dreamt of as a boy, and all the while Robert Carfax had seized all that life had so generously bestowed on him: a wealthy family, a royal commission in the guards, good breeding, and an apparently open pass to all the bounties that society has to offer.

Watching Carfax in his sparkling guard's uniform, complete with wildly exaggerated military decorations, Josiah moved his hand, almost passionately, over the bulky, red leather-bound volume on his desk. A lucky find perhaps, or maybe some leveling by fate of an unsustainable imbalance created by both fortune and misfortune-- whichever it was, powers had conspired to present Josiah with the opportunity to replay the hand he believed chance alone had dealt.

Josiah had made his lucky find during one of his frequent forays to re-stock his legal library along the bustling bookshops of Charing Cross road. Attracted by the deep red cover and faded gold-embossed spine, he clawed the book down from a high shelf, only to be covered by a thick layer of grey dust – it had clearly been there for some months, if not years.

Curiously titled "The Cult of the Dead," he had presumed it a supernatural work, akin to the gothic epics of Mrs. Radcliffe so fashionable in good society. On closer inspection, however, he discovered that it was no such story. In fact, it was no novel at all but rather one twisted man's night-visions of true evil.

Written by a mysterious gentlemen called Rudolf Versant and dated barely a few decades before the turn of the century, the devious volume lied about its age, as it appeared at first glance to a far older; although in truth the author did claim in the forward that he himself had translated extracts of it from a far older text. It was, by the author's own admission, "a mere shadow of the power which once was known."

Purchased along with several other legal journals of note, Josiah had the books delivered to his chambers the next day. An inquiring luxury perhaps, as the staid lawyer had never been one taken by either art or literature, something his few friends had often said explained his very poor notions of polite conversation with the fairer sex.

However, in this instance, Josiah devoured the volume, marveling at its intricate text and the complex, sprawling diagrams within, some of which purported to represent the fabric of the universe and its abstruse inner workings. But the echoes within the book were not of Wicca or Celtic witchcraft, they were much older and ancient than this, dark knowledge from many generations past. It took the fearless reader on a true voyage of the damned and into the temptation of pure evil – that is, the hidden knowledge which true deities had never intended man to have.

The text was truly an abhorrence, an antithesis to the selfless love of the Abrahamic God, revealing, and therefore gifting, imperfect mortal man with both the power and the means to fulfill his heart--something he was never meant to possess.

The first chapters of the fearful volume pulled back the covers of the universe to reveal the structural ley-lines, last touched by the creator at the beginning of all things. These invisible strings bind all matter together as a wooden frame underpins the new construction of marble-faced building: never to be seen by those who dwell within, but vital to the creation of a measured institute.

The later chapters taught Josiah how to harness the dark energy which passes along these unseen conduits and how to focus this untapped, immortal and inexhaustible power. He learnt of the cosmic balance which always, according to the dark text, tips slightly in favor of evil, held in check only by the essentially good nature, thoughts and deeds of all the creatures which dwell within its confines.

In the weeks before Robert Carfax's reveling return to England, Josiah was absent from his chambers of law, self-imprisoned in his adjoining rooms, the only outside contact being through his dull Irish housekeeper, who feed him with copious quantities of stew and broth. Day after day he sat in the moody darkness of his room, with the curtains partly drawn, deep in meditation and only occasionally breaking the silence with mystical chants in a long-lost language or to frantically consult some section of the obscure text.

The truth he had discovered during his long hours of study, or the mistruth revealed to him by this most malevolent of authors, was that he could truly channel all of his dark energy and draw in negative power from dimensions as yet undiscovered by man towards the object he hated most in the world: the lean, youthful figure of Robert Carfax, soon to be the Lord Wessex.

The mysterious death of Carfax was all he needed to change his luck, to even the unbalanced credit and debit column that was his tired life. As the appointed legal representation to the Carfax family, he knew the delicate workings of the will, the weak mental state of the current Lord Wessex, and how easily it could all be taken from the young heir: his money, his life--even his fiancée, the society beauty Amy Hardcastle, fresh from Cheltenham Ladies' College and with her rich father's legacy in tow.

So, on a brisk October morning, as Josiah watched through the window at the ceremony below, he began a deep guttural chant, slowly at first, then rapidly building up into a twisted crescendo of wicked chorus.

There was a large china jug of water next to him from which he took regular sustenance to maintain the flow of words directing the inhuman power. The faint smoke in the room was evidence of his opium pipe which he had used as was recommended in the text to heighten his awareness of the other realms.

He continued to chant, his faint grey eyes leaking into black, pupil-less orbs boring into the young captain on the street, as he funneled the untold power of the universe through his body and out towards his unsuspecting target.

During his long hours of meditation and transcendental movement, he created the perfect vessel to hold the non-corporeal essence of what was once Robert Carfax: a solitary confinement in the nether dimensions of the universe where he would suffer in silence and alone.

Josiah's shadow-soul lifted and as he connected to the mysterious ley lines of the universe, he thought he saw the young Carfax falter and slip as he greeted his fiancée. It was working, it was truly working.

Josiah sped up his wicked dialogue, all focused on the man he hated most in the world and a blue haze started to appear around them both, although for the moment only Josiah could see it. This was the break though point described in the text, the crossing of realms and the merging of energies. He channeled power untapped since the start of time at his unsuspecting rival.

Suddenly, Josiah felt tightness in his chest, as though a dark hand was reaching in and squeezing his black heart. He slumped to the floor but continued to chant, more weakly now, driven to finish his contorted prayer.

As he struggled for breath on the wooden floor of his room, he drifted into a deathly haze, quietly muttering over and over again – "The man I hate the most. The man I hate the most," in the mysterious new tongue he had mastered.

Josiah Mint's mortal life expired that morning, his cold body lying undiscovered until the next morning when his housekeeper returned to air the rooms. Robert Carfax suffered no great ill-effects and continued his celebrations through to the fine dinner which had been planned that evening at the famous Belfry Hotel in Maningbridge. The only absence from the meal was the family lawyer but few noticed this. Indeed, by unlucky chance, Josiah Mint's colleagues at the law firm misplaced his obituary and his untimely death was not announced in the Bath Times for a further month.

But Josiah's being survived, his essence--or spirit, as the psychics would say--trapped in the empty prism of hell he had created for the object of his envy, the young Mr Carfax, now forming an unbreakable, endless prison which held only one prisoner for all eternity, the man he truly hated the most: himself.

Jacob and Larry

BY ROBERT FREESE

"Mom," Jacob hollered excitedly as he rushed into the kitchen through the side door. "Mom, come quick!"

Gayle Fanning responded to the cry of her only child with a look of concern.

"Mom, you won't believe this." The boy's eyes were big as pie pans.

"Stop," Gayle commanded with an upturned hand. "Look at the mud you're tracking in."

Jacob looked down at the floor and for the first time noticed the clumps of red mud caked onto his ragged sneakers.

"Take them off."

"But Mom."

"Don't 'But Mom' me, Jacob Michael. I get one day off a week and I don't want to spend it cleaning the house twice. Take them off right now."

"I'm going right back out." He glanced at the kitchen door leading outside. "That's what I called you about."

"Were you up at that pond behind the Gardner's farm again?" She studied the mud on her son's sneakers with a skeptical eye.

"Yeah," Jacob responded in a rush. The boy then tried to back-pedal when he realized what he had just confessed. "No, uh, but…"

"I don't want to hear 'No, uh, but,'" she said in a stern tone. "How many times do I have to tell you to stay away from that filthy pond? There's an old, rusted car in the bottom and the river empties into it. There's no telling what sort of nasty stuff washes into it. Not to mention those two boys who drowned there a couple summers ago."

"But, Mom, you're not listening."

"Jacob Michael Fanning, you are the one not listening. Take those muddy sneakers off right this very instant."

The nine-year-old became frustrated. He rolled his eyes and made a face that looked like he had just been tricked into eating a mushy vegetable. Gayle wanted to snicker at the exaggerated look of pain on her son's face, but as a single parent she had to adhere to some semblance of parental authority.

"You're not listening," he repined, stringing his words together and stretching them into a long, nasally whine. "I really found something."

"Found something," Gayle responded. She was becoming irritated with her son. She hated when he started to whine; it reminded her of his father. "The only thing you're liable to find in that dirty pond is a tetanus shot."

"No, I found something really cool," he insisted.

"Something really cool," she repeated, trying not to lose her temper. "Like when you found the nest of mini dinosaur eggs that turned out to be blue bird eggs? When you went to snatch them the momma blue bird attacked you and pecked your forehead. You almost had to get stitches."

Jacob looked sheepishly at the floor.

"Or how about the time you found that rusty, old lock-box and you convinced yourself it was full of pirates' treasure. You cut your hand wide open that time and really did have to get stitches, and all it had inside was a bunch of moldy postcards."

"You got to believe me, Mom. This time is different."

Gayle watched her son shuffle from one muddy sneaker to the other. The way he looked up at her with his round little brown eyes made her feel like a monster for not listening to him. She knew her son had a wild imagination. It was surely the product of being an only child and not having any kids his own age in the neighborhood in which to play. She squatted down so they could look at each other eye to eye, and put her hand on his shoulder.

"Look, kiddo, I know you get bored because there's no one around here to play with, and you pretty much have to always entertain yourself. You have a terrific imagination and I encourage it. You can be a very strange boy at times, but you come up with some really wonderful stories. I hope one day you use that imagination to be the next Steven Spielberg, and you'll make millions of dollars and buy me a little house and let me retire young. But I'm too tired to play today. I'm sorry, Jacob, I love you but I'm too tired for your stories today."

"But this is not a story," he said exasperatedly. "I really found something!" Gayle gave her son a tired smile and kissed his forehead. Her knees popped as she stood up. "Go play a little longer and I'll make some lunch, but stay in the backyard."

"No," he exclaimed. He grabbed her by the arm and pulled her toward the kitchen door.

"Jacob!" Gayle barely kept herself from falling over from the sudden tug on her arm.

"I've got something to show you and I'm gonna show you." He fumbled with the doorknob and swung the door open. "You'll see it's not a story."

"Wait a sec, Jacob." Gayle stopped long enough to slide her bare feet into a pair sandals by the door. Then she was pulled through the door.

The screen door snapped shut behind them. Outside, pulling his mother along the side of the house toward the backyard, Jacob became animated and rattled on excitedly.

"This is so cool, you're not gonna believe it. I hope he's still out here. He followed me all the way home. He was just out by the pond sleeping when I found him. He scared me at first, but he turned out to be really nice. I thought since you said I could get a dog this summer and we haven't gotten one yet I could just keep him instead. I don't know what he eats, but we can figure that out. He's a lot cooler than a dog anyway."

As soon as she was led around the corner of the house and they entered the backyard, Gayle was aware of being swallowed up by a huge shadow. She suddenly stopped where she stood, her breath catching, her blood running cold, and her heart skipping a beat.

"Pretty cool, huh, Mom?" Jacob was beaming.

Resting on its haunches, the creature was easily ten feet tall. It stirred as the chattering boy approached. Its tail whipped from side to side and it flapped its leathery wings. Sunlight reflected off its scaly body.

"I wonder if he can breathe fire too. That'd really be cool."

Gayle stood frozen in fear as the beast stretched its long neck to inspect the woman and the child. Up close, its teeth seemed like ivory daggers, each a foot in length. She could smell the cloying scent of blood and meat on its breath. The dragon sniffed her up and down.

"I think I'll call him Larry," Jacob said with a big, rosy smile.

The Strange Affair of Silas Heap

BY SEAN T. PAGE

It is rare, in the life of a hardened thief and criminal, for an opportunity to arise which may, without recourse to murderous business, lift the life of the villain beyond his ill-gotten days and into an existence so very different from his own.

This, however, is exactly what happened to the coarse Bristol-born rogue, Silas Heap, as he completed his fourth burglary of an, up to then, fruitless night of criminal endeavor. With a conviction already marking his card and with the great suspicions of the local police as to his nocturnal activities, the experienced thief Silas could ill-afford to throw caution aside, so his targets were, for the time being, lowly ones–his villainous travels taking him to the poorly protected homes of the rich elderly, to the vacated second homes of wealthy country dwellers, and then to his particular macabre specialty: the residences and offices of the recently deceased.

So it was that Silas Heap, without so much as a slight tilt in his significantly weathered moral compass, came to the wood-paneled chambers of the recently deceased lawyer, one Josiah Mint, at the influential Bath law firm, Arbuckle, Grant and Peabody.

"Last one of the night, my son, last one," whispered Silas to himself as he moved cat-like through the downstairs window and into the converted city centre townhouse. The place already smelt of damp musk and the unfortunate lawyer, who by all accounts had died in these very rooms and in some discomfort, had only been dead a month or so.

The light from the gas-lamps in the deserted street was enough for the keen eyes of Silas Heap as he scanned the office, assessing with the clarity of an experienced Sotheby's auctioneer the relative worth of the objects scattered around the room. He was no amateur in this grim business of looting the possessions of the dead and he knew well which were highly-prized on the seedy black market of Tatton Street and which were the shiny trinkets unlikely to turn the head of any pawn-broker of note in the city.

Josiah Mint's legal chambers had been hardly touched since the lawyer's untimely death but still seemed at first glance to offer Silas the prospect of a poor return. The few paintings on the red velvet-paper covered walls were of poor quality, most likely student daubs and very much a mediocre man's copy of the great artists of the day.

Suddenly, Silas's ears pricked up like a cat in a haunted house. Sensitive to any sound or movement and with the threat of deportation hanging over him, Silas had become a very cautious thief indeed and so he quickly looted some items from the desk drawer and stuffed the batches of papers on the desk into his brown sack. With his meager pickings for the evening, and in his final assault on the possessions of the deceased lawyer, he reached across the desk and lifted a single leather-bound volume, weighing it carefully in his hand–its size alone hinted at value. Silas was unable to make out the detail in the shadows but the cover was certainly of quality, so he added it to the swag and made his way downstairs. There is a saying amongst thieves that only old thieves are cautious thieves and on this particular evening Silas Heap stayed true to this mantra and left the spooky chambers, a trifle unsettled, feeling less than rewarded for his full night's villainy, but, nonetheless, still a free man.

The room Silas rented for a shilling a week from his hawk-like landlady, Mrs. Mayweather, was a claustrophobic single box-room, roughly wall-papered with a faded pink floral design and decorated with patches of ever-present damp coving in each corner. But a man in this line of work needs a secure location, away from prying eyes, where he could sort the booty of a villainous night's work and settle the eternal question of every thief across time: to the pawn shop or the more risky, but rewarding, direct sale on the black market. With one son in prison on the isle of Sheppey and one already transported to Botany Bay, Mrs Mayweather was worldly enough to know Silas's line of work with the strange hours he kept and wise enough not to ask any unnecessary questions.

As dawn broke over the regal city of Bath, even in the sprawling slums where Silas sat pawing through his meager catch, a glimmer of light broke through his soot-encrusted window panes. A few silver candlestick holders (plated), some brass fittings he had levered from the wall in the old man's house, and a small crystal decanter (top missing). Then, from the bottom of the sack, he lifted out the heavy leather-bound volume he had taken from the deceased lawyer's chambers. In the darkness he had thought it a ledger of sorts, possibly containing the confidential details of some great society case–well-to-do families would pay good pounds to prevent scandalous information reaching the press. However, Silas's plans for blackmail were soon scuppered as the elegant red book was found to be nothing of the sort. Deeply engraved with faded gold lettering along the spine, the title read "The Cult of the Dead" and a cursory examination of the preface revealed the author to be a Rudolf Versant. A queer, ghostly work, thought Silas.

"Never 'eard of em!" muttered Silas as he flung the book to the floor.

Without changing, he lay back on his small bed and pulled a coarsely woven sheet over himself. Sleep comes quickly to an evil man, his conscience long since abated and buried deep within his blackened heart, but it was not a restful slumber for Silas. His dreams were roving, full of confused and disturbing images, scenes dominated by dark shadows and pages of written script corkscrewing into the air as if caught in some kind of vortex-gale, so that no single page could be read—what were they saying?

Silas awoke with a start and, checking the fine brass pocket watch he had stolen from a wealthy Jewish trader last year, he realized he had been asleep for less than two hours. The morning bustle and noise of the busy street easily permeated his small second-floor room, the ill-fitting windows barely keeping out the elements, let alone the loud voices of the traders and hagglers below.

Wide awake now, Silas sat up in his rickety, iron-framed bed. He heard a faint scratching in the walls–the rats were back. Nothing untoward in a slum dwelling such as this, but Silas, like many, had a mortal fear of these devious and scavenging rodents, who had been known to even feast on sleeping humans if their hunger pangs were strong enough. Unable to sleep further, he reached over and picked up the faded red-leather bound volume and, for the first time in his adult life, Silas Heap opened a book with the intention to read it.

The product of a charity Methodist school in the centre of the city, for a rogue of the lower-classes, Silas had a reasonable command of both reading and writing, something his teaching pastor had always hoped would keep him on the honest path. Like most people in modern times, he had read the garish advertising posters dotted around the city selling everything from palm oil hair cleaner to vibrant redwood tonic for the constitution, but he had never attempted to read a full book, and his limited literary talent had hardly kept him from a life of crime.

Still, something drew him to this volume, and even as he flicked through the weighty cream pages, the passages of text and complex diagrams dancing in front of his eyes, he could neither look away nor completely understand its meaning. It had no story and was certainly not a work of historical adventure such as the colorful and exotic tales he had so loved as a child.

Slowly at first, he picked passages from the text and read, word by word, paragraph by paragraph. He sat for four hours pawing over the curious volume; for the first time in his short and hard life the hardened criminal Silas Heap was absorbed in a work of letters.

To describe the mystical text is a challenge beyond any writer other than, it seems, the mysterious original creator of the volume, since even the acknowledged author, Rudolf Versant, referenced that he himself had openly plagiarized parts from much older and ancient source material.

The book Silas held in his guilty hands, for hour after hour, was an epic work combining pseudo-science, myth, and dark legend. It described, in some detail, the nature of the forces which created the very fabric of the universe, the unseen underpinnings of its construction, and, most frightening of all, the volume offered the fearless reader a path to access the immortal power which had been used to construct matter and life itself.

Fiendishly complex on paper, the script was imbued with an almost supernatural ability to communicate with its reader and invariably the temptation of untold power lead even the most ardent and grounded of men–a category into which Silas Heap does not fit–towards their darkest fantasies. It is, it would seem, not just absolute power which corrupts absolutely but rather any deviation one way or the other which can turn a wicked man's heart.

Silas did not leave his damp room for days, instead, he could be heard talking and chanting a fanciful dirge through the thin walls, as he followed the wicked text of the book.

"You got someone in there?" screamed Mrs. Mayweather at one point, something her few house rules forbad. "Is it that woman?"

Silas did not answer and his landlady shuffled away to continue her eternal cleaning duties elsewhere. He simply silenced himself for an hour or so before once again beginning his unholy chanting and his intense self-conversation.

For the humble burglar it was as if the entire universe had been opened to him through these pages. He had scraped an illegal living from a cruel world by taking from others and somewhere in his mind this promise of new power could equal out the terrible imbalance in human life, where he could be born into freezing, desperate poverty whilst others lived lives of privilege, comfort, and plenty. Over his years of struggle, one man in his mind had come to represent the inequity of this life, and that man was Richard Haversham, a wealthy and successful investment banker who Silas had watched many times as he strolled in the financial quarter with, it seemed, not care in the world. Never brazen enough to pickpocket or even rob this ideal of a gentleman, Silas had watched with admiring and envious eyes as the merchant financier made his way in good society

Although not obvious to any casual observer, of which there were none in the small room save the occasional looting rodent on the search for stray crumbs, the reader should be aware that despite reviewing the whole diabolical volume, Silas's focus was on a specific chapter, curiously entitled "Transmortification". It outlined the process, well known to certain Eastern mystics, of astral travel– that is, the spatial movement of the mind alone, cutting lose any ties to the physical body. The chapter referenced a work by the great Hindu guru, Manskrit Than, in which the mystic claimed to have traveled to other parts of the world and beyond, despite his fasting body never leaving its position, seated in the shade of a banyan tree at the Virshu temple in northeast India. The polluted work of Versant, however, went far beyond the achievement of these sagely monks; it revealed how through specific chants and incantations even the novice could tap into the immense energy involved in the creation of this and other dimensions of existence. It offered Silas the chance, not just to astral travel in spirit but to transmogrify–or as his old Methodist teacher would have said, possess–if only briefly, the body and mind of other beings. The final chapters counseled that if induced by an alternative chant this transference or transmortification could be made permanent, thus transferring the target's mind and sanity back in the body of the originator of this transcendental exchange.

Exhausted after an eight hour reading session, Silas's body finally surrendered to sleep but even in slumber, his subconscious continued to formulate criminal schemes with the powerful new forces that had been placed at his disposal by his lucky find. Despite being worldly and cunning in character Silas Heap was, like many men born into the criminal lower-class of society, a man of modest and limited ambition; not for the likes of him were there dreams of Alexandrian conquest or immortality. Even when offered the opportunity to travel to realms truly beyond the imagination of man, his narrow daydreams fell much closer to home, and that night he conceived a devious plan to change forever his unequal lot in life. It was a scheme that was intrinsically linked to the rich merchant banker he had frequently observed and on which, as is oft the case when men inherit dark powers never meant for human hands, would end in cold unimaginable terror for the unsuspecting Silas Heap.

Whilst his mental onslaught into the contorted world of Versant's book continued and his plan to take over the very life of Richard Haversham progressed, Silas used his new powers to continue his underworld activity. Even though his current endeavors were entirely metaphysical in nature, his pale body needed sustenance. With this in mind, he completed a few minor break-ins on sites he considered safe. He needed to raise a few shillings for bread, dripping and gin – little more, except possibly a few coins to keep Mrs. Mayweather from poking her noise into his business.

But these few petty crimes were merely a distraction from his real focus, which was the book and in particular transmortification, and following a few nervous out-of-body experiences, at his ninth attempt, and using a more advanced sequence of complex chants, he achieved his objective—that is, complete astral travel and the transmortification of another man's faculties. The mental power required was exhausting but gradually he learnt, using Versant's twisted guidelines, how to tap into the eternal lay-lines of the universe. These were the hidden conduits holding the very fabric of time and space together.

His first victim was a modest, or so he had believed, hardware merchant he had seen several times along the High Street. Tentatively at first, then more confidently, the thief had invaded the mind of his victim, taking control of the businessman's movements and thoughts. Silas's plan was cunning and direct. He led his victim right into the West Counties Deposit Bank and withdrew the man's life savings and investments, in this case a surprising booty of over 600 pounds, quite a small fortune for a seemingly humble merchant of iron and tools.

Unable to keep his ill-gotten gains in his own room without raising the undue suspicions of both his land lady and equally villainess fellow lodgers, Silas happened on the idea of setting a nest egg as it were, squirreled away in a secret location and of which his future-self, once permanently transmortified into the person of Richard Haversham, could take full advantage. So, before the tall white stucco Haversham townhouse in Mayfair Street, Silas directed the unfortunate hardware merchant to hide his fortune in faded grey sack under the servant's stairwell.

Whilst the selection of his first victim was somewhat random, Silas soon found that observing the bank gave him access to a whole procession of eligible and wealthy targets. He became familiar with the structure and operation of the bank, and with invasive access to the minds of his victims he was easily able to steal from their suppressed sanity any account numbers, codes, or other protections required to withdraw the funds.

Silas repeated his transmortifying process on a couple of gentlemen of some distinction in the city, once more completing a daylight robbery by stealth and deception, for to all others, there was no robbery at all, simply their banked assets were drawn and subsequently vanished. Typically, the victims of the transmortifying process recovered their senses some day or so after the intrusion, and so by the time both men reported events into the local constable their stories sounded even more fantastical. Both were left nigh on penniless and surely the walls of Bedlam called them as they tried to explain to the police how they had, in person, withdrawn all of their monies, only to return with complaints of foul-play a few days later. The authorities and the banking ombudsmen suspected foul-play, certainly, but rather some scam of their own creation to claim on their investment insurances.

But these affairs scarcely troubled a man with the scruples of the gutter and after his second 'job', by crude reckoning, Silas estimated that he had over 1000 pounds securely hidden under Richard Haversham's Mayfair Street home, and a further 900 pounds with addition of further teleporting scams. Each time the trick worked effortlessly, for such is the process that once in the body of his victim, he was also able to access their character and thus flawlessly imitate their actions, conversations, and even signatures. It was truly the most perfect of crimes.

However, Versant's volume, the Cult of the Dead, was merely a vessel for knowledge on the dark sides of creation; it could not, despite the power of the chants it contained, re-write the rules of the universe, and even the process of transmortification had its limitations, something Silas was fully aware of and had planned for. It was written in the text that whilst matter may be moved at will by this power, living tissue, and thus man, could only complete the transmortifying process five times before such a change became fixed and their consciousness implanted permanently to over-write that of the host. The significance of the number five was lost of a man of poor education such as Silas, but anyone familiar with the world's great religions will instantly recognize the divine significance of the digit in the faiths of this planet, including the five books of Eli in the Gnostic gospels, the five pillars of Quershi in Islam, and the sanctity of the Dravidic number in the life of Hindus.

For Silas it was a very practical matter. His four transmortifications up to then had been all about resource collection and building up a suitable reserve to see him comfortable—or one should say, more comfortable–in his new and final host, the young Richard Haversham. Already an accomplished man in his own right, nevertheless, Silas wanted to ensure that his every need would be taken care of, and knowing little of business, he thought it prudent to build up this reserve as bulwark against trouble in his new life. In this measure, he had had greater success than he realized, for he had amassed a stash of coins, including pieces of bullion, untraceable bonds, even property deeds from the Americas–all in all, assets worth nearly £300,000, more than enough to fund a life of luxury.

The preparations for his final transmortification needed to be more thorough than his previous efforts, and so he fortified himself in the grubby Duke's Head with several pints of thick, creamy black stout before retiring to his room. The chants in this particular process were more advanced than his other attempts; he needed to transfer his entire spirit-essence into Haversham or risk a fusing of the minds and a cruel insanity for both, while their two egos collided within the limits of one man's brain. Also, as this process in effect involved an exchange of consciousnesses rather than the temporary residence of a villainous intruder, Silas would become Richard Haversham and poor Haversham would become the penniless thief and low-life Silas Heap–ample reward in Silas's mind for his life of excess and plenty.

And so, the final journey of Silas Heap began, as he started a particularly long sequence of chants in a language unknown or long forgotten. He had discovered early on the importance of pitch and tone in these incantations, and it was as if these varying levels of sounds helped to unhinge, if only for an instant, the binds of time and space. Silas sapped up the power coming from the unknown and it built in his small frame until, unbeknownst to himself, he began to effervesce a faint blue glow; he was connected to the infinite lay-lines of the universe and was tapping into the vast power he would need to complete his vile exchange.

The exhausting process continued for several hours but Silas was unable to interrupt for fear the process be broken and his sanity scattered across the ether of the universe. Like any man with nothing to lose, he fought long and hard, carefully following Rudolf Versant's wicked text, word for word.

Suddenly, he felt the tingling in the hands that marked the beginning of the transmortifying process; excited, he increased his volume and rate. As before, his consciousness lifted from his puny body in its tired rags and surged out into the cold night and across the city, towards Mayfair Street. Silas was briefly confused when his spirit soared past the street and deep into the Dorset countryside, only then realizing that Richard Haversham must have been weekending at his country estate in Wellingborough.

The journey of three score miles took less than a few seconds and soon the disembodied Silas spiraled down towards a dark unlit house. As was the case on previous occasions, it was customary to lose some awareness of events during this part of the process and then to awake, as it were, in the body of occupation. Being on this occasion a permanent transmortification, this stage took slightly longer as Silas's mind rampaged over what had been Haversham. After a minute of this invisible battle, it was over and the thief's mind, his very life substance, had been successfully transfer into the object of his jealousy, Richard Haversham.

During any process of transcendental travel, it is typical that it may take a few seconds for the invasive traveler's eyes to adjust in a new host and so Silas was not unduly panicked to awaken laying on a soft surface, he presumed a bed, in the pitch darkness of a curtained room. But as his breath was fully restored to vigor in his new body, he felt a closeness that instinctively told him that he was not in the open space of a bedroom. As he leant forward to get up, his head connected sharply with a solid wooden board. He frantically felt around, there were wooden walls on each side of him. With no light, he could not make out the detail but he was most certainly trapped, sealed inside a quilted wooden box. The cold terror, which will haunt the reader's dreams, dawned upon Silas Heap as he desperately thumped to escape his confines, kicking only weakly as he could not fully angle his legs to deliver maximum force.

He was trapped, sealed alive inside a solid mahogany casket of the finest quality, set deep inside the ancestral vault in a disused church on the once great estate of the Haversham family, the entirety of which was now locked in probate with London's most senior lawyers, engulfed in a legal battle on behalf of distant relatives, which would last a decade, leaving the home and grounds vacant and the tomb undisturbed.

The power of the transmortification process had supernaturally re-invigorated the corpse of Richard Haversham, driving life-force into every dead sinew and muscle and Silas's had, unknowingly, cemented his mind into a vacant and rotting, but now living, human shell. He screamed to no effect, and tried to recall the chants, but, alas, without view of that cursed book he could only mutter snippets and several disjointed passages.

The savage disregard of Silas Heap for the consequences and victims of his transcendental crimes had most wickedly caught up with him. Richard Haversham had died by his own hand on the 4th of February 1803, after much of his fortune and his entire reputation had been destroyed by the collapse of the hideously over-subscribed West Counties Deposit Bank, of which he was principal underwriter and guarantor. Indeed, the institution had recently been the object of a string of fraudulent withdrawals which had seen the business ruined after rumors of liquidity problems had caused what is known in the city as a 'run' on the bank by its panicking depositors. Richard Haversham had taken his own life by poison when he realized he was finished, unable to face the public humiliation and tarnished reputation of a bankrupt charlatan.

Death and misfortune frequently follow those who possess this most devious of books but in this case, it also granted a ruined man a second chance as it were, for as Silas transmortified into the re-corrected body of his choice, so cosmic forces conspired to return the eternal essence of Richard Haversham into the weak body of the thief in his shabby room. He awoke with a start and stared through the window into the wispy clouds far beyond the smog of the city. He was alive.

Dazed, confused and completely unaware of the dark forces to which he had been victim, Richard Haversham, now, as he soon discovered, one Silas Heap, tried to rebuild what life he could in his new and quite desperate circumstances. It is frequently said that a near-death experience can change forever an outlook on life and in truth, this force is so much stronger when the essence in question has not only faced death but overcome it, like Lazarus in the Gospels–albeit with the addition of an element of mystical body transference also involved.

Life was hard for the former gentleman and his sanity remained fragile, his memory incomplete as he nervously made his way in new world, blissfully unaware of the devilry to which he had been subject, but he labored honestly and no doubt raised some queer remarks from his landlady and others who gossiped of the remarkable changes in the man they believed to be the petty thief Silas Heap.

Occasionally, he returned to his former townhouse in Mayfair Street, now standing dark and vacant, to glance longingly through the boarded windows at the remains of his furniture and artwork. It was on one of these nostalgic night time expeditions, as he stared through a basement window at what was left of his billiards and smoking room, that he discovered a grubby grey sack, hidden just under the stairwell. Always hungry, he quickly searched through it for any scraps of food, possibly stale seeds, anything to steal the hunger pangs which always torture the poor. The sack did not contain food, instead, it yielded gold and silver coins, far more than he could ever have believed, a veritable fortune if truth be told.

Fate had truly given the new Silas Heap a second chance at life, whilst the former Silas Heap was entombed, buried alive and trapped in the dry husk of a rotting corpse, which the mysterious powers described in the Cult of the Dead would keep alive for decades, maybe even centuries to come.

Shimmer

BY JUTTER CAIN
(For my friend, Clive Barker)

It was a cold November day, walking through the park. You know, it's funny, I remember that with crystal clarity. The cold, numbing wind that pierced my coat. The sky, overcast and dark. The clouds billowed, as dismal as grey slate. I even remember how loudly the park swings creaked: that loud, high pitched keen that sends shivers down your spine. I think it was when I watched the swings move in the breeze of that deserted park, that I first felt uneasy. It wasn't anything I could explain you understand, just a feeling, a sense that something wasn't right.

I taught English at the local university; my house was just the other side of the park from the school, so I always walked to work. I had gotten a call from my friend Bill–he was an archaeologist at the college. Bill had found something and wanted to show it to me, so I was meeting him at the lab on Saturday.

* * *

The detective took a drag on his cigarette. Smoke curled past his blue eyes. He watched the man. He said, "was that something unexpected?"

"What?"

The detective studied the way the man sat, then pressed, "That Bill Harriman would call you about a find?"

"Well, not exactly. Bill knows that I am a linguist and from time to time we worked together transcribing things."

The detective watched the man's hands. He didn't like the man's eyes, they seemed wild–not like the effects of drugs, but strange and insane. He said, "I see. Go on please."

**

As John walked through the park, a strange, eerie, creaking sound split the silent morning. John paused, looking up at a swing. It gently swayed in the breeze. Now and again a loud squeak came from the rusted hinge. The wind tasseled his short blond hair. He checked his watch, and hurried down the path toward the college.

The door opened in the lab. "Bill, I'm sorry I'm late–"

"Oh, enough of that! Come and see–you have got to see this." Bill tugged John into a side room and sat him in a chair by a table. Sitting in the center of the table was a large golden box.

"Good Lord, Bill, is that–"

"Yup, solid gold and one heavy son of a bitch, at that."

"I bet it is. Looks about two feet square and two feet high."

"Two and three quarters actually."

"Where did you find it?"

"As you know, I was in Mexico studying some ancient Aztec ruins. I was wandering through an ancient temple when an earthquake trembled through the forest. A section of floor collapsed–and nearly took me with it–but underneath was this huge chamber. This box was sitting on some sort of altar."

John listened, studying the box. It was made of gold, with ornate symbols sculpted along it; here and there small, faceted gemstones were fitted into the sculptures. The sides were covered with strange symbols: insects, flowers, and plants. The top of the box was carved with a spider, a web, and a very beautiful woman. At the rear of the Gold Box, just under a lady bug, was a small hole. The hole probably used to hold an emerald or ruby that had long since fallen away.

"But, John, this isn't what I wanted to show you. Look at this." Bill very carefully released the top's locking mechanism and opened the box. Inside was a large book. Bill, using great care, took the book out of the box and closed the lid.

"It is perfectly preserved, like it was made yesterday. The pages are some sort of leather or hide, I think, I've never seen the like, and, I think, the language is some sort of Portuguese."

"Let me see."

John took the book from Bill and started to read. "Your right Bill, this is Portuguese, though a very old dialect. This first part reads like a log: We the chosen ones, having been exiled from Portugal, spin our webs to float on the breeze. Shimmer will protect us; she is the warmth of the womb, she protects her children.

Bill, I've never heard of Shimmer."

"Neither had I till now, but we know that the Aztecs assimilated Gods and Goddesses from others. I think we found a new cult–isn't that exciting?"

"Truly exhilarating."

"John, your knowledge of Portuguese is better than mine, so you could probably translate it far better than I can. What I've managed to decipher is that Shimmer was a Goddess of beauty, love, poison, death, nature, and pestilence. At least that would explain all the various insect carvings."

John nodded and said, "Yes, that follows. It reads like a Bible."

Very slowly, small black legs flexed, and crept from the hole.

"Hey, Bill, listen to this:

'In the beginning, Shimmer plucked us from the sea and delivered us to a land of plenty, Praise be Shimmer. The land was a lush garden, a paradise. There were many people of a primitive tribe. The harvest would be bountiful, Praise be Shimmer. They soon became eager to worship her glory. As was foretold unto me, I would become a high priest and led the primitive toward salvation.'"

"It sounds to me John, as if our new cult came to the Aztecs and took over."

Testing the surface with each step, a small black spider, with a white tiger stripe and red hourglass pattern on its back, emerged from the hole. It crept to the table top.

John said, "they are starting to sound aggressive. Perhaps that is why you found the temple underground. Maybe this Shimmer cult took over the Aztecs and were later conquered themselves, the new city having been built on top of them."

Bill tapped a finger to his cheek and said, "That's possible and would certainly explain why that chamber and this book seem to be the only remaining evidence of the cult." Bill walked across the room to a coffee pot and filled a mug. "John, would you like a cup?"

"Yes, Bill, thanks."

Bill handed John the first cup and poured a second. Bill returned to his chair, placing a saucer on the table near John. The spider froze. Bill then set his cup and saucer down on the table.

John looked up and noticed the saucer–"Oh, thanks"–and placed his cup down on it.

The spider scuttled across the table. It paused at a pen, then crawled over the pen and in between some lose pages of notes.

"Bill, tell me more about the chamber."

"Well, there isn't much to tell at the moment." Bill ran his fingers through his black hair. "There were some strange carvings all over the room. Some odd artifacts–I'll show you later. What I found strange is that every entrance–except the hole in the ceiling–had been walled up. Impossible to tell what else is down there, without mining or blasting, and I'm not sure how safe that would be."

"Ground sensing sonar?"

"Yeah, but that costs more money than I have right now, John. I took everything in the chamber that I could reasonably remove. Of course, I photographed everything, but the film won't be developed until tomorrow. That is where you come in John."

"Of course, you want me to translate what I can so that you can be convincing enough to the board to get a grant."

Bill smiled, his blue eyes looking down at the closed book.

The spider crawled along the paper and stopped. Its small front leg explored the smooth plaster wall, and then walked along the edge of the table next to the wall.

John glanced at the golden box. "You said it was on an altar of some sort?"

"Yes, I think so. To be honest, John, I don't know what else to call it. I made a sketch of it, somewhere." Bill stood and reached behind the box to the pile of paper. Pulling out a sheet, he looked back at John. "Here it is."

"Bill, that looks like a table made from human bones."

"Yeah, John, I know–but, the strangest thing is, it was made of gold."

John's eyebrows rose, "Gold?"

"Yeah, but unmovable, attached to the floor somehow. I'd swear, John, it was as if someone piled a bunch of skulls, bones, sticks, and animal parts suchlike, then poured molten gold over the sculpture and allowed it to fuse to the floor."

The spider glided across the table top and stopped under a saucer. Bill picked up his cup of coffee, took a sip, and set it back down on the saucer.

"John, you've been awfully quiet with that book in your lap. Read me some more."

John flipped a few pages, saying, "Bill, this is a bit disturbing."

"John, read. You're talking about the Aztecs, the people who believed in eating the heart of the enemy to gain their strength, and shrinking heads. What about them isn't disturbing?"

John picked up his cup, took a sip, and placed it on the saucer. The spider crawled to the table leg and started to climb down.

John's brown eyes scanned the page as he spoke.

"'The Rite of the Harvest. Shimmer the blessed Goddess of beauty requires the stamina of young men. Men full of vigor, to withstand her insatiable lust. It is written that if the harvest be small, Shimmer the Goddess of Pestilence shall smite thee with her army of the insects. Twice each year, on the solstice, shall we reap the harvest of flesh for her glory. Never less than fifty young men in their prime shall be gathered. They shall be staked, bled, and skinned for her beauty and lust. The blood of the fallen shall be mixed with wine and drunk by the faithful. The meat shall be given to Shimmer so the insects can devour it. Grieve not for the fallen, they shall be made love to by the Goddess till their souls die.

'The Rite of Passage. Twice each year, on the equinox, shall be the offering of flesh. No fewer than eleven young men and fifty virgin woman shall be infested with the eggs of living spiders and maggots. The chosen of the offering shall be possessed by the Goddess as a servitor. Her avatar shall be among us, and judge us, as long as the body of the host shall live.

'The Orgy of Lust. Once a year for the span of the rainy season, all of the faithful shall have their fill of lust from the fold.'"

Bill picked up his cup, took a sip, and placed it back on the saucer. "Wow! How do I become one of the faithful?"

John snickered.

"Well, John, it beats being one of the fold, fallen, or passage people any day."

The spider crawled down the shadowed side of the leg, until it reached the floor. It scurried across the floor, then crawled up a long loop of white shoelace. Its legs tested the surface of a red sneaker and spun a web to the white cotton sock above. Dangling from the thread it reached the sock. It paused, then edged its way underneath a denim pant cuff. It crept to the top of the sock, its eyes fixed on the bright heat source. Then it reached a pink ground with a forest of fine black hairs. The spider paused, sinking its mandibles into the pink skin, cutting, and injecting venom.

"The Ritual of the Great Summoning-"

"Oh shit!" Bill vigorously tried to stamp his foot.

"What, Bill, what happened?"

"I'm sorry, my leg fell asleep. God, I hate that. I'm sure it will work out the pins and needles shortly. What were you saying?"

"Not much, this next part is hard to read. Seems to be some sort of ritual and spell to call forth insects, but I can't make out how to pronounce some of it. It's like the author was writing down a guttural chant."

The spider pealed back a section of flesh and crawled in, its rear legs weaving a web around the blood, sealing the cut. The spider moved through the calf muscle, laying small egg sacks in the weave of the muscle.

Bill picked up his cup and sipped some coffee. "As you said, it's like a Bible. Skip a bit, John, see if they wrote hymns and psalms too, or if the religion is more primitive than our own."

John flipped a few pages.

"Bill, looks like more ritual, sacrifice, and horrible artwork. I mean look at this: a picture depicting a woman in some sort of torture. God, this thing is sick sometimes."

"Well John, what have we learned?"

John picked up his cup, took a sip, and said, "I'm out of coffee."

Bill smiled, taking the empty cup. "So am I." He rose and walked over to the coffee pot, then returned with two steaming cups of coffee.

"Well, Bill," John took his cup, "thank you. We can tell the board that you've uncovered some sort of devil cult that indulged in human sacrifice. They came from Portugal and were probably exiled due to their practice of sacrifice. They found an Aztec culture and enslaved them. We know that they were eventually overthrown, and sealed away. Probably, the Aztecs wanted them forgotten, and to learn more we simply have to get more money and go back."

Bill absently scratched his wrist.

"I think that will be compelling enough–that and the gold artifacts. I mean, my God, Bill, you've already pulled out enough gold to finance a dig and you even left some behind. And, Bill, if they don't go for it, I'm sure you could take that Box and get a loan. I can't even think about how much that thing is worth. As horrible as that altar is, I think you should go back with a team, the proper equipment, and pull it out of there: be far better behind glass in a museum exhibit than collecting dust in a ruin–or worse yet, melted for gold and stolen by a pot hunter."

"I agree, John, but keep looking in that book. I'm sure there is a clue as to why they disappeared or whatever happened to them– maybe even why the room was sealed."

"Okay, Bill, let's try the old mystery reader's trick, and flip to the end and find out how the book ends."

"Like it's going to end happily ever after."

The last few pages were filled with highly detailed drawings of the human body that showed how to cut the skin in such a way as to skin the living victim. It also told of the various procedures for storing and preserving human skin. The last page ended with the words:

Four thousand souls gave themselves to the forging of this book.

John closed the book and dropped it on the floor. "Bill, these pages are not leather or animal skin–they are human skin."

At that very moment Bill started to scream and thrash about wildly.

"Bill? Bill! What is it? Oh, my God!" Blood sprayed out of Bill and he slammed his body against a wall, screaming. Small worms burrowed out of his skin and then sank down into him again. His screams were cut off as he choked on his own blood, his vital organs being eaten from the inside. Silence filled the room.

**

The detective closed the book and left the room. John stood at the Plexiglas window watching him walk away.

"Well, detective?" an orderly said.

"Gold artifact worth, if melted down and barred, one billion dollars US. One victim, and only one person alive in the building. Case is closed. Autopsy report says it all: partially eaten corpse." The detective stopped and turned back toward the door. "He's blaming it on invisible insects."

"Was there any trace of insect in the corpse?"

"Of course not. Fucking cannibal, I hope they gas him."

John absently scratched his wrist.

Shimmer has cursed us.

Skin Deep

BY ALLAN IZEN

Janelle glanced down at the magazine laying open by the sink. Marilyn Monroe was smiling up at her with that steamy, insinuating look she had: eyes half-closed with lush, lipsticked lips lasciviously parted as if maybe she was a little tipsy.

Janelle leaned close to the mirror, examining her makeup. She had penciled copies of Marilyn's lovely gull wings over her own meager eyebrows and they actually looked pretty good. But her lashes–they were dreadful– looked like centipedes had crawled into her eyes. And her mouth was worst of all: how could she ever transform her little coin-slot of a mouth into Marilyn's wide, generous one? She had tried to paint a "Marilyn mouth" over her own, but the attempt only made her look clownish.

And her hair. She would never be able to match Marilyn's alabaster wave; not while she was stuck with such an unreasonable, out-of-control mother who wouldn't let her color her hair. Wouldn't even discuss it. Not even a lemon rinse.

Annoyed and exasperated, Janelle squinched her eyes shut and pulled off the fake eyelashes. Angrily she scrubbed the makeup. When she'd dried her face, she lowered the towel and gazed sadly at herself and sighed: horsy face, freckles, bulgy eyes, lumpy nose, snaggle teeth – she could hardly bear to look.

"Jaa-aan?" Her mother called from downstairs.

"WHAA-aat?" she yelled back.

"Dexter's here."

"Be right down."

Janelle and Dexter had been friends since elementary school. They'd always been easy with each other but lately Dex had been acting kind of strange, as if she were his girlfriend or something.

She pushed open the front door and saw him on the porch, staring moodily into the yard, hands stuffed into the pockets of his warm-up jacket.

He heard her come out. "Hey, Jan," he said over his shoulder.

"Hi, Dex."

"Yeah," he said.

They stood together for a while, looking out into the front yard. Finally he said, "Me and Tommy went to the Mansion after school."

"The Mansion" was their name for the empty house at the end of Innis Street: a sagging, out-of-plumb Victorian ruin with boarded up windows, peeling paint, an out-of-plumb belfry, and a reputation for being the site of gruesome atrocities committed against children in days gone by.

The inside of the mansion was dark and shadowy, even in daylight. There were cobwebs everywhere, it smelled like a toilet, and was littered with fast-food wrappers and old newspaper blankets used by the bums who slept there. Only the bravest boys in the neighborhood ventured into the Mansion. Occasionally one would emerge with a relic from the house's mysterious past; in fact, it was the possibility of finding such artifacts that made the house exert such a powerful draw on the neighborhood kids. Generations of boys had been sneaking into place in defiance of the horror stories, which everyone thought were bull. But, maybe not.

Like the one about the kid who stayed in the Mansion all night on a dare: he came out the next morning stark raving mad, his hair white as snow and he never uttered a coherent word again in his life.

But still, Dorry Andrews had found a grimy old nickel with a buffalo on it. Morley Soto came out with a rusted cloisonné pin and Brendan Scully brought out a tiny paper parasol with Japanese letters. There was supposed to be a trove of cool stuff in the basement, but not many had the courage to go down there. Not many would even go near the cellar door, for that matter.

"Did you go down to the basement?" asked Janelle.

"O yeah," Dex answered with a nonchalant shrug. Janelle sensed his quiet pride. He dug in his pocket, brought out a small, mud-crusted object and held it out to her. "Brought this out for ya."

Janelle took it reverently – it had some weight to it.

"What is it?"

"I dunno, but smell."

She took a sniff and said, "Wow." It had a dank, musty odor, but beneath that, a faint hint of ancient perfume. "It smells awesome."

"Yeah."

"Thanks, Dex."

Dexter shrugged. No big thing.

They stood around awkwardly, watching shadows creep across the yard.

Dexter said, "I gotta go."

"Awww."

"Yeah, my mom gets weird if I get home too late."

Janelle took the gift upstairs to her room for a closer look. It was a teardrop-shaped metal bottle crusted with mud and topped with a brass stopper. She tried to pull it open but the stopper was stuck tight. She chipped away the mud with her thumbnail and flakes of filth fell on her bedspread. Mom was going to love that. She swept up the flakes and threw them away.

She brought the bottle into the bathroom and held it under the faucet. The mud washed off easily, revealing tiny, loopy designs etched into the metal. When she'd scrubbed it clean, she wrapped it in the hand towel and dried it.

Suddenly, the stopper popped out and clattered into the sink. A sudden gout of thick purple smoke surged out.

"Yow," Janelle cried, startled. She pitched the bottle into the sink and jumped back. The smoke was billowing out, filling the small bathroom and making her cough. She turned the faucets on all the way, but the smoke kept pouring out.

Janelle shut the door and locked it. What was going on? An amazing quantity of smoke was pouring out. It was like no smoke she'd ever seen: dark purple, shot through with glittering sparkles and spangles. How could so much smoke come out of such a small bottle?

Finally it stopped. The smoke coalesced, gathered itself into a huge plume and slowly evaporated to reveal a tall young man in a turban, vest, baggy pants, and embroidered elf shoes. He stood next to the toilet, muscular arms folded, looking haughtily down at her.

Janelle's looked at him, her eyes the size of dinner plates. What a major babe!

In a surprisingly deep voice, he intoned: "May the manifold blessings of eons, epochs, and ages rain down upon you."

"Huh?"

"I am Hasheed and you have freed me from captivity. For this I will grant the most treasured wish of your heart."

"Huh?"

Hasheed steepled his hands and bowed. "Yours is to command; mine to obey."

He talked kind of funny, Janelle thought, but jeez, the guy was such a Clydesdale.

"Where – where did you come from?" Janelle tried to keep the warble out of her voice.

"I was imprisoned in the bottle by Maktorak. Rubbing the bottle broke the enchantment."

"You mean drying it with the towel?"

"Towel, yes, that is the word."

"And . . . what was that about a wish?"

"Anything your heart desires, anything at all."

"Just one?"

"Alas, only one. I am merely an imp, you see, not a genie. I lack the authority to grant the traditional three."

A parade of wishes marched through Janelle's mind, each more seductive than the last: "a million dollars", "a horse", "peace on earth," "three more wishes." Her eyes fell to the magazine, still open on the sink. One of Marilyn's eyes seemed to wink. Janelle made her decision: "I want to look like Marilyn Monroe."

"Easily done," smiled Hasheed, making magical passes in the air.

Janelle felt her face grow warm. She turned to the mirror and tried to scream.

She tried and tried but could not.

Hasheed's eyes fell to the magazine. "Oh, you meant as she looked then? I am so sorry."

And with an impish grin, he vanished.

Shallow

BY D.G. SUTTER

From dust colored ash, there rose the bones
of memories long gone, forlorn.
Inside a mausoleum's walls,
where death is king and life is none,
the creatures known as Sclezekmoors,
formed finely from a hellish floor.
They crawled until they learned to walk,
and dually learned to soar and stalk.
They filled the sky with wings of bats,
and found a place to rest at last,
amongst the trees and worm that crawl,
until the servants come to call.
Then it is they'll rise once more,
those creatures known as Sclezekmoors.

I recall how hot it was that day, the air more humid than a Florida hurricane. It was impossible to escape from the perspiration which stuck to your skin like condensation on the outside of a bottle. It was typical of New England to be exceedingly rainy one moment and desperately arid the next. School was out and relaxation was in. A pool would have been ideal had any of our families been able to afford one.

What is a youth to do for relief from the sun, but find a watering hole in the heart of the woods and proceed into it? So we swam and dunked and splashed, and submerged ourselves in the algae surfaced body clad in our underclothes.

There were three of us impartial to the detail that the water was most definitely unsanitary for swimming. Youths tend to grow into hygiene and dirt almost always finds its way into the hair and cuticles by the end of the day. It was almost dusk when James found the shallow sand bar.

"Hey, guys!" Instead of using his arms as oars his hands hailed us as he stood waist deep. James moved freely until his knees showed above the surface. His shout warranted our attention, thus we paddled over to the shallow bar. It was actually quite like mud, the hole that James pointed out to us. It was four feet wide and severely darker than the surrounding liquid. "I dare you to put your foot in there," Mark said to James.

James peered into the blackness. Slowly, as if he might fall in, he dipped his foot into the hole. "I don't feel a bottom." I thought of it at the time like one of those fabled tunnels to China. One could enter this side and fall off the opposing side of the world. Bubbles rose from the hole. It signaled either fish or oxygen far below. I sat on the edge and let my feet dangle down there. "Anything?", asked James. Like James, I could feel no bottom to the pit. The water was much cooler where my feet kicked in the emptiness. Then, I scootched off the edge. My head bobbed slightly above the surface. "What are you doing?", James marveled.

"What does it seem like?" I wanted to know how deep that hole went. I had swam through underwater tunnels before and knew they usually shot off to the sides. I held my breath and propelled downwards. I floated down, down, down, but did not feel a bottom. The walls fell away. Then, I had to come back up for air.

"Did you feel bottom?", Mark asked, curiosity alight in his eyes.

I couldn't speak for the others, but at the time I felt an undeterminable specialty for the hole. If I could possibly find the bottom, something spectacular would be there, like gold, fairies, a world all of its own.

"I didn't but I'm going to try again." Mark pushed me forward, always the antagonist. "Do it! Go all the way to the bottom this time. Don't come up till you've touched."

"Here goes nothing." I used the crust of the Earth to push myself faster. I tried to keep my eyes open but the mud clouded the water. It fell with me and I could feel the muck embedding in my hair. Then, I could see. I looked up and what seemed miles above my head was a pinhole of light. Hovering above the hole were two shadows. I dug my hands into the sides of the tunnel to prevent myself from floating up to them. I pulled my hands out and shoved them back in like reverse ladder rungs. Sludge filled my fingernails until they were full of Earth. Eventually, my hands hit rock and just as I was about to give in and file for oxygen, so did my feet. I looked up once more. This time the light was less than available, just a shimmer, a far off star. My lungs stung from the lack of air.

I almost concluded the hole as an unused well. Except my right hand found a tributary to the oddity which was a vertical river. It was three feet wide and as I felt inside, the top announced a pocket of air.

I shoved my face into the sweet pocket gulping greedily. The molecules bounced around inside my head. It was euphoric and all at once, necessary replenishment for a fasting body. Breathing had never felt so good.

So far below the ground one would assume total darkness. Oblivion, a void almost created from the complete absence of life. Yet a brilliant glow hailed from above. I grabbed at the ledge which protruded into the tunnel and pulled my weight up. All one hundred pounds of wet cloth. The space I came into was a rock closet filled with an abundance of sharp points and sulfurous stink.

I wished that Mark and James could have seen the place for surely they would have appreciated it. I crawled hand over hand, knee behind knee unknowingly. For all I knew it could have led to the land of the dead, but either way it didn't stop me. I reached a fork. The path left curled downwards and intuition told me to stay true to the path which forked on an even plane.

Being underground was not a pleasant feeling. I could feel the actual weight of the dirt above me, weighing on my aura and at the same time I prayed it not to collapse. If it were to fall, only two would know I was down there. And how long before they decided it was time for rescue?

Just as I thought the route would indefinitely transport me to the center of Verne's Earth, I was contradicted. My head grew tight, if not from the pressure, from the nervousness displayed from the consequences. What if water filled the tunnels? What if rocks fell in front of my exit?

However, had I not gone against better judgment, I never would have stumbled upon the marvelous world I had. The ground of the larger chamber I was spat into was covered with red powder and stalagmites. I felt as though I were on Mars. The stalagmites reminded me of the canine teeth of a wolf. I touched one of the rocks and it was sticky wet. Also around the chamber were columns where the stalactites had decided to touch hands with the stalagmites. I wiped my hands on my pants.

There were thousands of stalagmites and stalactites in the room, like giant never-melting icicles. There was no pattern to them. The stood in various spots guarding an unseen treasure. As I walked through the columns and freestanding cones I pictured the water markings as taking on human features and it made me shudder. Their stone characteristics were oddly human, or something close to it.

I fell further into the chamber, my footsteps pleading echoes for me to stop and return from whence I came. Somehow the temperature rose as I proceeded. It very well could have been from anxiety. I blew all the air from my lungs. There was yet another tunnel in the underground labyrinth. I feared loss of direction.

This passage was twelve feet tall and like the previous rooms illuminated by a subtle green glow. Along the walls were markings like cave paintings. It was much brighter and I could see the paintings on the wall almost clearly.

They showcased an ancient hunt progressively. The first was of men on horseback, then a group of riders with their spears raised and ready to throw. Next shown was the animal, something of the buffalo sort, with the spear in its' side. Finally, I rested my eyes on the last drawing. It was seemingly disconnected from the previous ones. There were two groups of men. The group on the right were pointing their fingers at the left group. The indicated party was cowering as if sentenced to a horrible end. I couldn't make complete sense of the painting, but it deeply disturbed me.

The hall narrowed ahead. At the end it became a bolt of lightning, crooking left, right, left, right. My legs pulled me through a jagged exit. The green light was dimmer in the next cave. It made no sense where the light was coming from. There was no space above from which it could radiate and hang in the air from particles of dust. I could tell this room was the end of the road. It was a large cave, which was round and had no exits.

Again with the wolf teeth. In this place there were *thousands*, though. I stopped and rested my hand on the top of a point. The same as before a humid sludge coated my palm. The cavern was gigantic. I didn't know the formations grew so closely together and so plentifully!

The ground quaked. It was ever so subtle, yet I knew I was more sensitive to it. My heart felt tight and my hands sweat cold water. Beneath my hand the rock cracked. It split the stalagmite asymmetrically. I stepped away from it.

Further it split like a shell. In the hollow center I could see a face, its eyes closed and lips pressed together in anguish. Then the eyes shot open.

They were similar to that of a bat, round and black, with no iris. They looked around, maybe adjusting to the light or lack thereof. It had a head of hair, bristly like a pig. The thing, for it wasn't human, looked ready to cry. I decided it was a baby. I shuddered at the size of an adult.

Finally its gaze locked on me. The mouth opened to reveal shark teeth and it screamed the most ear piercing sound I've ever heard. The rock cracked lower, revealing a body which was dark brown and skeletal. Out of the crack dripped a liquid I assumed was the placenta. *They are eggs!* I panicked. The other "shells" were hatching. I bent and slipped back through the jagged crack I had come.

Running now I could hear the things hatching, pieces of rock bouncing in the acoustics of the cave. I navigated the crooked path with dexterity. The cave paintings flew by through car windows of my eyes. When I reached the initial chamber the light was blinding compared to that of the "breeding chamber". The only prayer I continued was *I hope they can't swim, I hope they can't swim.* I risked a glance back and saw that the things were lurching in my direction.

They weren't moving very fast, but I gathered their speed would increase once their footing steadied; they were just born. Like baby chicks their feet wobbled and threatened to fail.

The leader of the pack, who was the initial one hatched, pitched its head back and let out another shrill cry. It was then I became worried for my existence. All around the rest of the eggs started to hatch. I took off at full sprint, fully aware that it could be my last minute alive.

As I passed one of the stalagmites a wing shot out from inside. Extended from the end were razor sharp claws which did not catch me, but raked across my exposed bicep. The pain was deep and intense but it didn't stop me. I covered the wound with my healthy arm and spun toward the exit. It was suffice to say there was a decent amount of blood relieved from the wound and it disgusted me to witness the winged creatures stop to lap it up.

I released the wound to crawl into the tunnel. Halfway down I looked over my shoulder. The pack leader was attempting to squeeze his enormous body into the smooth circle. "It's just a matter of time," I thought, "until one of them small enough can fit through." The hand soaked in blood was caked with dirt and pebbles that dug into it.

My head spun from blood loss. Then I was in the water rising, rising, rising toward the surface. The pinhole grew larger until I blacked out.

* * *

I awoke to two boyish faces staring down at me. Mark said "Well. What happened?"

There was absolutely no way for me to explain to them the gravity of the situation. They would have had to witness it firsthand. How could I possibly define the creatures? "There was a cavern down there."

Jimmy piped in. "What about your arm?" I told them it snagged on a rock and left it at that. Both glanced at each other in disbelief; the claw marks were distinct. "We better get you to the hospital," James worried. I told them I would live.

We three walked home and parted ways. I hid the arm from my parents as long as I could, until one day when I stepped out of the shower. My mother fretted, but by the time, the scrape had healed enough to look like a gravel scar–and it was a scar. Sometimes it kept me up at night, thinking of those things beneath the ground. I feared they would find a way out. Once escaped, they will hunt me down and kill me. I will always live in fear of that day and that place, when a simple summer day turned into a nightmare. I hope I'm dead when they rise. For who knows how many chambers lay dormant? I'm glad I didn't take that downward tunnel.

Dad's Secret

BY BRANDON CRACRAFT

The last thing I expected to find hidden in my father's closet was a package of disposable diapers. I imagined my father keeping some bastard little brother a secret. My parents never wanted to talk about why they were getting a divorce. I knew that they could no longer look at each other, and my older sister refused to talk to him on the phone.

"Probably just babysitting for someone while I'm at school," I assured myself, trying to cram the diapers back into the grocery bag.

"What are you doing in my closet?" I heard my father bellow. I instantly jumped at his tone and the diapers spilled onto the floor.

"Um. . .I'm. . .sorry," I said, stumbling over my words.

Dad looked terrified. When I was a little kid, he used to kill all the bugs, or at least, command our cat to kill them. Even though I was sixteen, I still kind of thought of my father as being fearless. The more scared he looked, the more I felt horror twist at my spine. "I'm sorry, Dad. I told you that I need to borrow a tie and some nice shoes for the school play. You said I could. I wasn't trying—"

"It's all right, Trevor. Let's just put them back into the closet and forget you ever saw them."

I didn't know what to say, so I just nodded.

"Thank you," he said, forcing a smile and blink away the sweat that stung at his eyes. "Let's find you a nice tie." He cleared his throat, and his fear suddenly vanished. "I feel like I've already seen the play with the way that you've been rehearsing."Dad gave me a playful punch on the shoulder. "Don't worry, I'm still going to see your play. I don't care how many times I've heard recite the lines."

After he closed the closet door, he turned toward me suddenly. The threat in my father's eyes made me take a step back. "Next time you need something from my bedroom, Trevor, I'll get it. I don't go through your stuff. I know a lot of parents that do, but I respect your privacy." His tone lowered. "Respect mine."

"I'm sorry," I said, probably for the tenth time.

Dad squeezed my shoulder gently, and I let myself relax. "Don't be sorry, Trevor. You have nothing to be sorry for. We all make mistakes. Just don't make that mistake again." He continued to glare at me, and I wasn't certain if he was pissed or scared. "Do you understand me, Trevor? Never go into my room without permission again."

"Yes, sir," I said.

Dad grabbed my hand like I was a toddler and pulled me out of his bedroom, locking the door behind us. His hands kept shaking, so he thrust them into his pockets.

"I think I'll make us some lunch." he said, practically running into the kitchen.

* * *

My father worked as a freelance colorist for several comic books, allowing him to work from home and keep his own hours. The sounds of him on his computer or the canvas lulled me to sleep every night. I expected a couple nights a week to wake up just before he pulled on that old Pima Community College football jersey and stumbled into his bed, occasionally missing and crashing on the floor.

Every squeak and crack Dad made that night made me wake up again. The soft sounds of the Indian flute he worked screamed in my ears. A couple of times, I tiptoed out of bed, cracked the door open, and watched him.

I just about convinced myself that I was being an idiot when I heard a very unexpected sound. Dad pulled down the door to our attic and began to climb up the rickety ladder. I heard the door slam behind him.

"It's none of your business," I whispered to myself. "He's probably just storing some paints or old pictures up there." I tried to convince myself that it was nothing even as I snuck down the hallway and ducked into the bathroom where I could get a better glimpse of the attic. I crept into the shower and pulled the curtain, peaking over the rings with one eye.

My father stayed in the attic for the better part of hour, before he made his way back down with the package of diapers under his arm.

When he rushed into the bathroom for a quick drain, I felt pressure in my bladder. I held my breath, certain he knew I was there.

I didn't breathe until he returned to his work. When I was certain he was engrossed in mixing the absolute perfect shade of purple for a super villain's cape, I tried to make my way back to my room.

"Trevor," my father screamed. I stumbled on my feet, guilt written all over my face. "What are you doing out of bed? It's almost three a.m., and you've got school tomorrow."

My father strode over to me. The look on his face told me that I was in trouble. I swallowed, pointing to the bathroom and looking like a moron as I tried to come up with the perfectly logical explanation of needing a late night leak.

Dad face softened. "I woke you up, didn't I?" Before I got a chance to respond, he nodded at the reason. "I should be in bed; we both got a lot to do tomorrow." He talked about a picture he was doing for the historical society of territorial Arizona. I nodded, keeping my mouth shut for fear of revealing anything.

"I should get some sleep," I finally said. He nodded and escorted me to my room and tucked me in. When he shut off the light, I got the distinct impression he was trying to keep me in my bed for the rest of the night. I think he would have locked me in if my door had a lock.

My body refused to let me sleep, even as I heard the sounds of my Dad snoring in the next room. "It's nothing," I told myself as I snuck back out. My body acted on autopilot, even as my mind tried to convince me that nothing was wrong.

My arm reached up to pull down the ladder before I realized that I was back in the kitchen. My father's door remained closed and the buzz saw continued to run. Letting out a huge sigh, I scurried up the ladder and pulled the door shut behind me. My mind raced as I contemplated a million excuses why I went up to the attic just before dawn. None of them made the least bit of sense.

"What are you expecting to find up here?" I said. "What? You think your father hid your little brother in the attic?" I laughed at the prospect, but an irrational part of me believed something like that. "You think your little brother was born deformed or something?"

I closed my eyes as I pulled on the chain for the light, wondering if I would open them to a playpen, a cage, or some sadistic combination of the two.

The first thing that caught my eyes were two bright blue baby bottles filled with milk.

"What's going on in here?" No signs of an actual baby, but a black, velvet tarp covered most of the north wall. "I'm sure when you pull off this tarp, you're going to realize that you've been a huge idiot."

Instinct forced me to close my eyes as I yanked on the tarp. After a few seconds, I convinced myself to open them. I stared at a giant dollhouse that took up most of our attic. My stomach burned when I realized that it was an exact replica of our house when it was built in 1916. All of the modern additions had been shaved off.

"Just another one of your dad's historical projects," I said, forcing myself to relax.

I opened up the dollhouse, expecting to see replicas of the old rooms, but the entire doll house had been gutted. The cuts were swift, almost angry. The only thing inside were two life size boy baby dolls.

The first one looked like it had been designed after me. It even wore a karate uniform like I did. I remembered running around in it, pretending to be Bruce Lee. It never occurred to me that I was wearing that exact same outfit to bed.

The second doll disturbed me more than the first. The eyes matched my father's grey eyes. He managed to find some kind of fake fur that matched my father's graying blond hair perfectly. I picked it up slowly, expecting it to attack. It wore the same community college jersey my dad always slept in. A quick check revealed that Dad freshly diapered that thing.

Looking around me, I felt my heart thunder and pound against my chest. "Every night, he changes, cleans, and dresses these dolls." Small hair combs and toothbrushes hung on the wall.

I couldn't stand to hold my father's doll anymore, so I picked up the one based on me. "What did he use for hair?" I asked, wondering how long it took him to match all three shades of red in my hair. When I ran my hand through the doll's hair, I thought I was gong to vomit. Mom forced me to cut my hair earlier that year, and Dad sewed it onto that doll.

The worst shock came when I pulled back the fabric lips to reveal a mismatched set of teeth. He pulled out the teeth from various animals at the roots and sewed them into this miniature monstrosity.

I no longer cared about being quiet. I wanted to get downstairs to my cell phone and call my mother or the police. I remembered all those shows where the kids said that they never knew that their father was some kind of insane lunatic until they found where he hid the bodies. Everything about the situation drove me to the same conclusion. My father was a psychopath.

I jumped down and ran into my father. I let out a scream, and pulled away. I fell over my own feet and tried to crabwalk away from him.

"You found the dolls," he said, his voice completely and terrifyingly calm. I was completely freaked out, and Dad didn't even seem to care. Who was this person? It all seemed so impossible and surreal. The fact that aliens replaced my father made as much sense as any other reason.

"Don't kill me," I begged. I tried to say more, but it came out garbled from all the hysterical sobbing. "Why did you make those horrible things?"

The madman left the room, and I saw my father again. "You know that I would never hurt you, son." He leaned down and gave me a tired smile. "I don't blame you for being scared son. I was terrified the first time I saw them." He helped me back onto my feet, casting a worried glance back toward the attic. "I didn't make them, Trevor. I really hate those things. I hoped you would never find them."

"What are they? Where did you get those teeth? Who made them if you didn't?"

My father ignored all my questions and simply said, "If I don't take care of them, something horrible will happen."

"Something horrible? Are we being blackmailed by a psychopath or something?"

My father shook his head. "They're like voodoo dolls, Trevor, except much, much worse."

"You don't really believe that, do you?"

"I made a mistake, Trevor. I was a complete idiot. Something happened to your sister, and I'm going to spend the rest of my life paying for it."

"What happened to Amanda?" I asked.

Dad swallowed audibly. "Nothing happened to Amanda. Something happened to your other sister, Claire."

I stared at him in confusion, uncertain what to ask. He was talking nonsense. "I don't have a sister named Claire."

Dad escorted me back into the room, shutting out the lights and hoping that I couldn't see that he was crying. "I know." When he thought he couldn't hear me, Dad added, "Not anymore."

* * *

For the next few days, I pretended not to notice that Dad went up to the attic to dress them exactly the way we dressed that day. I tried not to wonder about where he even got the replicas of all our clothes, because I was tired of being scared all the time.

When I caught him dressing the doll in my costume for the school play, I decided I had enough. My father had a meeting with his publisher that promised to take up most of a Saturday. I decided it was time to make my move.

Even though touching the doll disturbed me, I grabbed the one dressed in my father's suit and dragged it down the stairs. "You're a stupid doll. Some crazy person made you. He screwed with my dad's head, maybe even with mom's head. You're just a doll."

I ripped off the dolls clothes and tore out its stolen hair by the roots. I thought about taking a wrench and pulling out its teeth, but I couldn't bring myself to touch them.

After I was done, I put the cell phone in my pocket and set it on the loudest ring. An illogical part of me expected my dad to call me and say that he was suddenly bald and naked.

The phone never rang. At first, I felt more confident. The confidence melded into blind fear when I realized it was seven o'clock at night and my father still hadn't called to tell me that he was on his way home.

"Maybe he's running late," I said, knowing that dad checked in every couple of hours.

I dialed his cell number, and I got a message telling me that it was out of service. Shaking my head, I dialed the number four more times.

"Where are you, Dad?" I whimpered.

I thought about Dad's regret over a sister I never remembered having. When my father hadn't returned at midnight, I called the cops. I begged them to tell me that they found some unknown accident victim out on the highway. I fantasized about my dad trying to call my name but unable to talk because of a broken jaw and unable to write because he lost his hands in the accident.

I spent the rest of the night staring out my window, convinced that every car meant Dad was about to pull in the driveway.

I thought about calling the cops several times, but I was afraid of what they would say. At eight o'clock in the morning, I bit the bullet and called my mother. A part of me expected to hear her tell me that she never heard of "Scott Blankenship." I wanted her to tell me that I was being an idiot.

She said the last thing I wanted to hear when I told her that Dad went missing. I cried for a few moments, barely able to say hello to her. Mom waited patiently for me to gather some composure before calmly asking, "You found the dolls, didn't you?"

"Dad's missing," I said. "I got upset—"

I heard my mother take a deep breath. Despite her soft tones, I could hear the crack of terror in her voice. "Tell me that you didn't destroy the doll."

"No," I whined.

"At least you're not as stupid as your father," she said under your breath.

"What would have happened if I destroyed the doll, Mom?"

"Tell me everything that happened," she said, using the firm no nonsense voice she normally reserved for her clients. She listened, offering quick responses to get me to continue.

"I need you to be very strong, Trevor," she said. I took a few breaths. "If you want to see your father again, you're going to have to do something a little. . ." she paused for a moment while she figured out the proper word, "disturbing."

"What do I have to do?" I said, pretending to be tougher than I was.

"They like it when we treat the dolls like normal babies. Your father changes them and dresses them like you boys. They seem to like that."

"So I should—"

"No!" Mom shouted, and I jumped at the sound of her demeanor breaking. After a moment, the calm returned to her voice. "First off, get the doll back into his clothes—"

"What about the hair?"

"Don't worry about the hair, Trevor. They will sew it back on."

I bit my lower lip. "Who are 'they'?"

For a moment, she contemplated telling me more. "It's best that you don't know. If your father wasn't such a moron, you never would have known about the dolls in the first place."

I winced at the sound of her criticizing Dad. "What do I have to do?"

"Feed the doll. I think your father keeps a bottle for them in the attic. He did when we were together."

I thought back to the attic and told her that I knew what she was talking about. "What do I feed them?" I said, looking at its yellowed, rotting teeth.

"Just a bottle of milk," she said, letting fear creep back into her voice for a moment. "Boil it until it's so hot that it boil the innards of a normal baby. Once you've got it hot enough, add some of your blood."

"Mom?" I started, "who's Claire?"

"They don't like it when we talk about Claire," she said with a sigh. She hung up before I could ask any more questions.

**

I went into my father's room and discovered that most of his clothes were missing. The antique pipe his father gave him seemed transparent. Whatever controlled the dolls was trying to erase my father.

"I'll feed your stupid doll!" I screamed. On my dad's now stripped bed was an old fashioned straight razor. Dried blood gone purple and black dulled the blade.

I dressed the doll back into my father's suit while the milk bubbled up. "What a good boy you are," I told the thing, feeling stupid until its head twisted and the grey eyes focused on the straight razor.

"You'll get your food!" I shouted.

I knew kids at school that cut their arms for attention or out of some compulsion to hurt themselves. I always thought it would be easy, condemned them as cowards. Holding the blade against my palm, I realized it took a lot of willpower to slice yourself on purpose.

The sound of the dolls stomach growling made me jump. "You'll get your blood." I closed my eyes and sliced. My palm burned and itched as pain shot through my entire arm. Blood spilled on the floor as I held my wound over the open bottle. A few drops turned the mixture a sick purple. The grotesque mixture swirled in the bottle, and I stopped it with a nipple before it could bubble over.

"Have to do to this," I reminded myself, wrapping my wound. "I need my dad back. I screwed things up. I'm the only one who can–" I stopped talking and shoved the nipple at the doll's cloth lips. The mouth parted and the animal teeth opened to reveal an engorged, grey tongue that happily lapped at the bottle. I rammed the bottle the rest of the way in, knowing I couldn't choke the thing. The doll twitched and contorted as it drank the vile stuff with loud slurping sounds.

"Just give me Dad back," I demanded.

The sound of the key in the lock almost made me drop the doll. I placed it gently against the floor where it stopped moving and making sounds. The milk returned to a normal color.

When Dad appeared in the doorway wearing a thrashed version of his suit, I threw my arms around him. He looked like he had been mauled by a large animal. I saw huge bite marks on his shoulder.

"Where have you been?" I asked. "What happened to you, Dad? What did this to you?"

Dad held me for a few minutes, crying without sound. "It doesn't matter. I'm home now." He pulled away from me slowly, eying the doll like it could attack at any moment. He leaned close and whispered, "They want us to pretend like nothing happened."

After hazarding a look at the doll, I nodded. I knew better than to question them again.

Clock Watchers

BY LACHLAN DAVID

Lewis stood at the open window of his father's tiny bedroom and filled his lungs with the cool night air. The air in the room had been thick with the scent of his father's sickly breath for weeks, but recently it had taken on a new quality. It was death. Lewis didn't know how he knew it; maybe it was some lingering primal instinct that caused him to recognize the aroma. But whatever the reason, he had no doubt what it was. He had avoided the room almost completely since he first noticed it, knowing the morphine would prevent his father from ever knowing the difference. It was his wife, Marie, who tended to him when the nurse went home for the evening. On this particular evening, she noticed his father's breath was more labored and irregular than usual, even with his oxygen. They called his doctor to see if anything could be done for him, but after a brief exam and checking to see whether the medical equipment was still working as it should, he told them sadly that Anson Straub's time had come. It would only be a matter of hours, maybe minutes, before his body gave up.

Marie called Lewis's family immediately to give them the news and an opportunity to pay their last respects. They each offered their condolences, but they were either too far away or too inconvenienced to come at a moment's notice and spend the evening with a dying man. Meanwhile, Lewis wanted to wake up their 11-year-old son, Michael, so he could say good-bye to his grandfather. But when he opened his bedroom door and saw the boy's peaceful face lying on the pillow, he decided to let him sleep. Lewis could tell him in the morning and save him the trauma of seeing his grandfather die. That left only Lewis and Marie to sit in the oppressive room and wait for Anson's final breath. They barely spoke a word to each other during those last hours. The only sounds were the beeps and whirs of medical machines and the raised floor creaking beneath Lewis's feet as he slowly paced between his chair and the window.

As Lewis stared into the darkness of night and contemplated returning to his seat, the clock on the wall struck 1 AM. A jovial, unidentifiable tune broke through the monotonous noise of the medical equipment and flooded the room. It was the cuckoo clock Lewis's grandfather Günter Straub had built soon after his escape from Nazi Germany. The clock was the first of three he made for each of the firstborn sons in his family, and Marie had recently hung Anson's next to his bed at his request. Every hour on the hour, little hand-carved woodland creatures danced and twirled in front of it as the tune played in the background. But this time, Marie and Lewis were both startled by its intrusion on their somber moment.

Lewis turned away from the window and watched the macabre irony play out in front of him. "Why is that thing still going?" he asked. "Who wound it up?"

"Your father told us to keep it running. He loves that clock," Marie said.

"But he can't even hear the damn thing!"

"You don't know that."

"I'm telling you, the first thing I'm going to do..." He stopped when Marie's words sank in, but it was too late by then. Marie knew exactly what he meant to do, and if Anson had been able to hear and comprehend, he would have figured it out too.

"You're not doing anything," Marie told him. "That clock is an heirloom, just like the ones your grandfather made for you and Michael. They're the only things we have left from his days as a clockmaker in Germany, and I think we should keep them. They might even be worth something by now."

"All the more reason to get rid of it. God knows, we need the money." He walked up to the clock to take a better look at it.

"That's enough." Marie jerked her head toward his father. "Don't you think we should talk about this later?"

"Yeah, you're right. I'm just not in the mood for dancing animals right now, that's all."

The song and dance had ended by now, and Lewis reached up to touch one of the little wooden rabbits. The details that were carved into his grandfather's clocks were amazing. Even the fur was given texture, and he could almost single out the individual needles on the evergreen trees and garlands. But there was something else unusual about Grandpa Günter's clocks besides their superb craftsmanship. They had a fourth weight. Not only did his clocks keep track of the hours of the day with a charming little animal show, they also kept track of the days of the year. Birthdays. His grandfather's cuckoo clocks were the only ones he knew of that were set to go off once a year on the hour in which his son and grandsons were born and put on a special presentation just for that occasion.

Lewis looked at the fourth weight on his father's clock and saw that it nearly reached the floor. The other end of the chain had almost run out of length, so he grabbed onto the ring and pulled it down, just like he would do to wind up the other weights, but it didn't stay. The weight fell right back to its previous position until the ring stopped just short of hitting the base of the clock. Lewis expected that. The fourth weight had always behaved that way, same as the ones on the other clocks. Once a week, they pulled the weights to wind up their clocks. Each time, three weights stayed at the top and restarted their invisibly slow decent, but the fourth weight always fell. It was dedicated to counting down the years and never turning back. It was an unsettling thought, even when there was plenty length left on the chain. Now, seeing the ring so close to the top at the same time its owner was ready to pass away gave Lewis an eerie feeling.

"I wonder what Grandpa Günter was thinking when he made these for us," he said while tossing the weight in his hand.

His words woke Marie out of a daydream and she looked up at him. "What?"

"What was he thinking? Why did he make a clock that counts down birthdays?"

She still didn't completely understand the question, but she took a shot at answering it. "I don't know. He probably just wanted to make it special. I know Michael goes in at six o'clock in the morning to watch his clock on his birthday. It's kind of cute."

Lewis picked at the edge of a little door in the front of the clock to try to open it, but the door fit too tightly for him to wedge a nail under it. "It's a fun idea, I guess, but think about that. You got a wolf that comes out of this door, and some guy with a horse and spear who comes out of that other one," he pointed to another door on the other side of the clock, "and it looks like the damn wolf is attacking the him. What the hell kind of a birthday show is that?"

"I never thought about it."

"Well, think about it the next time you see it.

"Then there's this middle one here, too, that never opens." He tapped on a third door in the middle of the clock. "Who knows what's behind there? I mean, really, what was he thinking?"

Marie rubbed her face in her hands. "I have no idea what Grandpa Günter was thinking, Lewis, but maybe you should sit down now and worry about that later. You're all upset about a clock, and you should be thinking about your father."

"That's right, I'm upset. I'm upset about this clock going off every hour and dancing around like it's Christmas. I just want to turn the damn thing off!" He yanked the chain on the fourth weight, violently this time, and nearly pulled the clock off the wall. The other three weights swung around, bounce against each other, and tangled their chains, but the fourth one dropped toward the floor again and swung hypnotically all on its own. The jolt caused the pendulum to stop, and once all the weights had stabilized, the clock was still. "There you go," Lewis said. "It's stopped."

"Okay, whatever. Just sit down." Marie was tired by now, and as much as she wanted to be supportive of Lewis during this difficult time, she didn't have the patience to deal with a temper tantrum over a cuckoo clock.

Lewis returned to his chair, and they sat quietly at Anson's bedside for a long time without saying another word to each other. Every now and then, the dying man would let out a groan, move slightly, or stop breathing for an extended period of time. Lewis and Marie watched him closely each time to see if the end had finally come, but Anson always resumed his breathing.

After a while, Lewis got up to pace again, taking the opportunity to get more fresh air at the window. Marie left to use the bathroom, then came back with a book and read quietly. A little while later, Lewis came back to his chair and picked at his fingernails until his head jerked forward suddenly, and he realized he had nearly fallen asleep. As he stretched and shifted in his chair to keep himself awake, he looked up at the cuckoo clock to see what time it was. The clock hadn't moved since 1:04. He glanced over at the watch on Marie's wrist and saw that the time was 2:12. The clock had ceased to strike the hour, and it made Lewis smile. He leaned back in his chair, clasped his hands over his chest and listened to his father's irregular breathing, barely audible over the sound of the medical equipment in the room. The man looked peaceful, there was no doubt about it. There was no expression on his face to indicate that he felt any pain. He was already out of touch with the world around him and for all practical purposes, already gone. It was just a matter of waiting for his body to accept the fact and wind down.

A few minutes later, his body did just that. The heart monitor, which had been beeping slowly but steadily, suddenly became as irregular as Anson's breathing, and he began a series of weak coughs. Lewis and Marie knew this was it, and they rose from their chairs to be at his side. Lewis took one hand, Marie took the other, and they held onto him while he struggled to take short, shallow breaths, then one final gasp.

"Gong! Gong! Gong!"

Marie let out a small scream.

"That fucking clock!" Lewis yelled, but his voice was overcome by the dreadful music that filled the room. It was a tune the clock had never played before. The melody was chaotic and rife with minor chords, and the animals danced and twirled in celebration as two doors on the clock opened, the one with the wolf and the mysterious middle door. The stunned couple watched to see what would come out of it. It was a man in a large pair of boots wielding a sword. He glided out and met the wolf in the middle of a platform where they performed a choreographed battle. They circled around each other, dipped and twirled until finally, the man tipped forward and the wolf tipped backward in a pose that made it clear who the victor was. The wolf stayed in place while the man returned to his place behind the door.

The clock went silent. The only sound left in the room was the heart monitor alerting them to Anson's flat-lined condition. Even it had not been able to compete with the commotion of the clock.

Marie rushed over to turn it off, but Lewis stood still, trying to make sense of what had just happened.

When the monitor was finally silenced, Marie returned to Lewis and placed her hands on his shoulders. "Are you going to be okay?" she asked and gently guided him back to his father's side.

Lewis followed, but reluctantly. He definitely wanted to say good-bye to his father before they called the coroner to take him away, but he was still stunned by the clock. "How did it know?" he asked her.

"Lewis, I don't think it knew anything. It's just a clock. Come here and say a prayer for your father."

He wanted to argue with her, but now wasn't the time. He lowered his head and said a prayer.

* * *

It had been just over a week since his father's death, and Lewis sat at the kitchen table with a set of screwdrivers and his father's cuckoo clock sitting in front of him. Even though Marie insisted that the timing of the clock's presentation was no more than an unfortunate coincidence, he knew there had to be more to it than that. The clock had stopped running. He was sure of it. How could the weight continue dropping when the gears were no longer turning? Marie reminded him how roughly he had handled the clock earlier that evening and suggested the chain might have just slipped. But to Lewis, that only confirmed his suspicion. If the chain was going to slip due to rough handling, it would have happened right away, not more than an hour later. No, it was something more deliberate, and he was going to find out what it was.

He started by just opening the back of the clock housing to look inside. He traced the path of the gears, and with a little bit of patience, he was able to see which gears caused which movements, and which weight was responsible for what functions. There didn't appear to be anything unusual about the fourth weight. It was controlled by a set of gears just like the others, which meant it moved at a set pace dependent upon the spacing of the teeth. When Grandpa Günter built the clock, he would have to already know when his son was going to die and cut the gears accordingly. That was impossible, unless the man was some kind of a psychic or magician. Lewis wasn't the type to readily believe in that sort of thing, but there was really no other explanation. It was either that, or it was a coincidence just like Marie had said.

"No, there's no way. It was too perfect," he muttered to himself. He turned the clock around and looked at the woodland scene that framed the front of it. His attention was immediately drawn to the wolf that still sat on the platform after its final battle. Its back was arched, its fur was bristled, and its snarling face revealed long, sharp fangs. It was definitely something to be feared and probably not intended to entertain a child. Then he pried at the small doors with one of his screwdrivers, this time chipping away at the wood until he could work the tool's edge underneath. They popped open to reveal two little men, one on a horse with a spear and the other with a sword and oversized boots. He removed them from the clock by force and looked at them. It was clear by the fierce looks on their faces that they intended to kill the savage animal, but only the man in boots had prevailed. Why would his grandfather would create such a sinister piece of machinery, Lewis wondered.

Marie and Michael came home from baseball practice while Lewis was examining the wooden figures. "What are you doing?" she asked when they entered the kitchen and found him there. Before Lewis could answer her, she was already heading toward the table to see for herself. Michael followed close behind. "No, you didn't!" she said when her suspicion was confirmed.

"I had to figure it out," Lewis confessed.

"Your grandfather made that. You'll never get it back together again. It's ruined!"

"We'll take it to another clockmaker."

"They won't know how to fix something like this. Do you know how much it will cost to find someone who can fix it right?" She started picking up some of the pieces and looked at them as though she might be able to repair it herself.

"What's inside the clock?" Michael asked as he looked at the back of it to see.

"Pretty interesting piece of work, ain't it?" Lewis held up the man on the horse so Michael could see it.

Michael took it from him. "Can I keep this one?"

"No, you can't keep it," Marie said. "You're going to put it down and leave it alone so it doesn't get lost."

Michael set the piece down on the table.

"Now, go to your room so me and your dad can have a talk."

Michael looked at his dad, hoping he would say he didn't have to leave, but Lewis pointed toward his room.

When Michael was gone, Marie turned to Lewis. "I can't believe you destroyed this clock. It was a *beautiful* clock."

"Yeah, but there was something strange about it. Always has been."

"Why? Because it counts down birthdays?"

"No, because it counts down doomsday. I'm telling you, Marie, it was no coincidence. Do you know what happened when I tried to wind it back up today?

Marie rolled her eyes. "No. What?"

"Nothing. Nothing happened. I pulled the chains, and they fell right back down again, just like that other weight used to do. Then I tried to get this pendulum swinging again, and it won't go. Sure, it'll swing back and forth a few times, but then it stops. This clock was broken way before I got hold of it. It broke when Dad died."

"That's probably because you yanked on it. You know better than to treat a clock like that."

"You think so?"

"Yes, I do!"

"Here, let me show you something." Lewis stood up from the table. "Come on, let's take a look at the other two. I didn't yank on those clocks, so you tell me what's going on with them, okay?" He motioned for her to follow him into the living room where Michael's clock hung next to the television. "You don't know this," he said as he led her in there, "but the day after Dad died, I marked on the wall how far down the weights had gone." He stood under Michael's clock and pointed to a fine pencil mark just next to the bottom of the fourth weight.

Marie had to squint to see it. "Okay, so?"

"I put that there a little over a week ago, and look. I don't think it's moved since. Now, look at mine."

Marie followed Lewis into the den where his clock hung next to the fireplace, and he pointed to the mark he made on the wall. "I marked this one at the same time, and it's gone down a full quarter inch since then."

Lewis's weight was lower than Michael's, and Marie had to stoop down a bit to see the mark. "I don't get it," she said when she stood up again.

"Think about it, Marie. The clocks are identical, but mine's moving faster than Michael's. Why would that be unless they were set to go off at different times?"

"Maybe because they're all handmade, one-of-a-kind clocks, and they're not as identical as you think," she suggested.

"That could be. Or maybe it's because I'm not going to live as long as Michael, so mine's moving faster."

Marie looked at the length of chain that hung from the back and saw there was only about a foot left before the ring reached the top. She shook her head and laughed a little. "Well, at this rate, you'll be dead in about a year."

Lewis's face went pale at the thought, and she suddenly realized just how seriously he was taking all of this. At that moment, she caught movement out of the corner of her eye and thought it might have been the weight dropping just a little more. Lewis hadn't noticed, so she hoped it was only her imagination.

"This is too much," she said. "Maybe you're taking your father's death a little harder we thought."

"You're right." Lewis ran his fingers through his hair nervously.

"Okay. Good. So, if you like, we can find someone to talk to about it. Do you think that would help?" She tried to place her hand on him, but he broke away from her.

"No, I mean about the clock," he said. "It's moving too fast."

"Lewis, no! Stop it, now!"

Lewis bent over to look at the mark and gasped. "Look at it! It moved again."

"It did not!"

"It did. Look!"

Just as Marie turned to see what he was talking about, she saw it move again. She was sure of it this time. The weight was nearly two inches further down the wall than it had been only minutes before.

"It's still moving!" he shouted. He reached up to grab the clock from the wall and managed to get his hands on it, but Marie jumped in front of him and pushed him away before he could get a good hold of it. The clock swayed back and forth then hung crooked on the wall as the weights danced around beneath it. He couldn't say for sure while it was still moving, but Lewis thought the fourth weight had dropped again.

"I want you to stop it!" Marie shouted at him. "You're going to drive yourself crazy with this and take me with you. That weight doesn't mean anything. It's *just* a clock!"

Michael came and stood in the doorway. "Is Dad all right?" he asked.

"Your dad's fine. Now, go back to your room!" Marie shouted over her shoulder.

Lewis took advantage of the distraction to reach around Marie and grab the clock again. She tried blocking him, but this time, he was able to knock it to the floor. He attempted to stomp on it, but Marie kicked it out of the way before he could. They both dropped to the floor and scuffled for it.

"Dad, what are you doing?" Michael said and ran to join his mother in keeping him from destroying the clock, but the boy wasn't large enough to be any help. In the struggle, Lewis pushed Michael away and sent him tumbling across the floor, knocking over the fireplace equipment and causing him to hit his head on a nearby table. The move surprised even Lewis and made him stop.

"See there?" Marie said. "Look what you did."

She turned to Michael, who was nursing the back of his head. "Are you okay?" she asked. Michael nodded, but his eyes were red and watering.

Marie picked up the clock and hung it back on the wall. "I'm definitely calling a doctor. I'm not sure how you got so caught up in this thing, but we need to..."

"My God!" Lewis shouted and pointed to the fourth weight. It was hanging about six inches below the mark on the wall.

Marie grabbed the ring on the other end of the chain and gave it a tug, but the weight fell right back to where it was.

"That doesn't work. It never works. You know that!" Lewis reached over and pulled the ring. Once again, the weight fell. He pulled it again with more force. It fell again. He tugged the chain back and forth several times before letting it loose. It fell further down the wall, leaving only about two inches of chain before the ring hit the base of the clock. "Why is it doing that?" Desperation was thick in his voice and his eyes were becoming moist.

Marie tried to calm him down. "I think you're breaking it. If you'll just leave it alone, it'll be fine."

"It won't be fine," he insisted.

"Why don't you lie down for a little bit, okay?"

"It *won't* be fine! That damn clock is still counting down!" He reached out and yanked the chain so hard this time, it pulled the base of the clock from the housing and several gears fell out. The momentum of the pull sent Lewis stumbling backward where he tripped over a piece of scattered fireplace equipment and fell on top of it. He lay on his back, and his eyes rolled back into his head. His body began jerking violently.

"Lewis!" Marie and Michael both ran to him and Marie sat him up. The handle of the fire poker bobbed up and down from where it was lodged in the base of his skull, then it fell to the floor. Blood spilled out onto the carpet, and Lewis's body went limp.

"Gong! Gong! Gong!" The chaotic music played again, and even though several gears were laying on the floor, the wolf and the man in boots came out from behind their doors and engaged in battle.

"No!" Marie screamed as tears streamed down her face. She ran to the clock and began pounding on it frantically. Several pieces broke off and the wood became smeared with red as splinters jabbed into the sides of her fists. After several blows, the clock fell from the wall, and Marie slid down with it, sobbing and crying out, "You killed him! Damn you! You killed him!"

Michael ran to his mother's arms, and they cried together until the tears ran out and they had no more strength. Then Marie let go of Michael and picked up the phone to call the emergency line.

"What's your emergency?" the operator said.

"My husband was killed." Her voice choked up as she spoke.

"Is there someone in the house with you? Are you in danger?"

"No."

"We're sending someone down there. Tell me what happened, hon."

Marie paused for a moment. What did happen? "He fell."

"Is he breathing?"

"He's dead."

"Do you know how to perform CPR?"

At that moment, Michael's clock struck two, and music poured in from the living room as the little woodland creatures performed their hourly dance. Marie didn't hear the operator anymore after that. She took the phone into the living room with her, set it on the television, and watched the animals twirl. When the music ended, she picked up the chain on the fourth weight and tied it in a knot just beneath the base. Then she sat down and waited for the paramedics to arrive.

Montgomery

BY JEREMY BUSH

A25. Montgomery stares down at the number on his ticket, then squints through his spectacles at the cabin doors as he shuffles by, reading each number to himself under his breath. One wrinkled hand holds the railing that runs the length of the hallway in the train car, while the other grasps tightly onto a cane and his ticket.

Montgomery stops. He holds his ticket up to his face, cane dangling down from his wizened hand. He tilts his head forward. If he gets just the right angle for his weak eyesight and just the right amount of light, he might be able to read his ticket.

A25. "Yes, of course. Now I remember," Montgomery mumbles. "A25. A25. A25."

Montgomery looks at the number on the door across from him.

"C…4…2. C42. I thought I was in car A. Oh no, I'm not even in the right car. Nothing to do but keep goin'."

And so Montgomery travels through the entire length of Car C, stopping occasionally to first check his ticket and remember that his cabin number is A25, and then to stare at the doors around him and recall that yes, he's still in the wrong train car.

Montgomery slowly shuffles his way out the door of Car C, into the howling outside air between train cars. Then he opens the door to Car B, leaving the rushing night air behind and continuing his journey.

"A…2…5. By golly, I knew that. Don't know why I just can't remember it anymore. Silly old fool." Montgomery drops his hand, which he had brought up close to his face to see his ticket, back down, and the bottom of his cane bangs lightly on the ground. He peers at the closest door. "Why, I'm still in the B's! I have a whole 'nother car to get through." He shakes his head in dismay as he starts back into his tortoise-slow walk down the hall.

It takes ten more minutes and several more stops to stare at his ticket and the surrounding cabin doors, but Montgomery finally discovers his room. At first try the knob won't turn, but with a few judicious strikes of the cane, the door springs open.

Montgomery wearily lowers himself onto the seat, letting his head fall against the back of it, and closes his eyes.

"I can't even find a cabin on a train without tiring myself out anymore." Montgomery sets his cane beside him on the seat and rests the ticket in his lap and runs his fingers through the small remnants of his white hair. "Can't even do that without needing a nap afterward." He continues to rub his head, thinking back through his day up until now and just how it was he came to be here.

Montgomery's life for the past years had been routine—the perfect dictionary definition of routine. He was prepared and given the same foods for the same meals, served at the same time each and every day. And the same people came to pay him visits on the same days that they always came to pay him a visit. And the same radio programs were played loudly each night. And there were the same activities. And the same pills. And the same nurses. Each and every day.

And Montgomery had never really minded, not thinking much of it. Until one day, and for no apparent reason to himself, Montgomery had suddenly had an itch. An itch to do something— anything—different than what was always done. And Montgomery had pulled himself up out of his wheelchair and found his cane in the corner beside the bed and slowly walked to the elevator. He had ridden down to the ground floor, politely chatting with the nurses riding with him, and walked to the front door. There he had waited until one of the families who had come to visit a relative left and he walked out just behind them, barely reaching the door before it shut and re-locked.

Then he had slowly shuffled down the driveway, away from the home to the sidewalk. He had expected that at any moment someone would come running after him, calling for him to stop. "Now, Montgomery, you know better," a nurse would politely say while pulling him back down into his wheelchair and wheeling him back inside the home. But no one did notice and he had been able to amble all the way down Main Street, stopping to stare in the windows of so many shops that were new to him and that he had never seen before, and on to the train station on the other side of the village. When he went up to the ticket counter he momentarily panicked, thinking he hadn't remembered to grab his wallet and money and put it is his pocket before he left. But then his hand had jumped down and felt the rectangular bump in his back pocket. The panic took a minute to dissipate and he had to step away from the counter to calm himself. When he walked back up, he had asked the man behind the window which was the furthest stop that this train went to, and had then ordered a ticket for it. The train had started up before he had been able to find his cabin, and the constant swaying movement and the noise of wheels hammering on train tracks had disoriented him just enough to make it that much harder for him to try and find his room. But he had found his room in the end.

And so here Montgomery sits, not knowing this place (he doesn't even recall ever hearing the name of this town before) that he has bought a ticket for and travels ever closer to, and not knowing why he must travel, why he felt the sudden urge, not knowing what made him just get up and leave.

But Montgomery isn't scared, or worried, or anxious (well, maybe just a little, just a little of each of these things). Mostly though, he is brimming, overflowing with excitement. An excitement he hasn't felt in years, not since he was a young man. An excitement he can't explain really, and that he knows in his head doesn't make any sense.

Montgomery smiles, just not able to help himself. He raises his head off the back of the seat, his tiny crop of hair sticking out in all directions, and opens his eyes. There, on the opposite seat from him is a black briefcase. A briefcase he didn't see or didn't notice when he first came in. Montgomery's brows furrow for a moment, then he picks his cane up and, after a brief struggle, raises himself out of his seat. He slowly–even more slowly now after all his day's trek–plods over to the briefcase, and holding onto the wall with one arm uses the other to hook the handle of the briefcase with the end of his cane, and drag it forward to the edge of the seat where he can grab it easily.

His fingers run over the clasps that hold it shut tight, as he wonders what's inside, what it holds. But then he resolutely walks to the door, opens it, and stands waiting. After a few minutes one of the train attendants comes by and Montgomery waves to him.

"This briefcase was in my room. I think whoever had my cabin before me must have forgotten it and left it behind. I just want to make sure they get it back."

"Oh no, sir. No one left it. That's your briefcase."

"What? What are you talking about?"

"That's your briefcase, sir."

"It was here when I got in the room. It's not mine. Somebody must have left it behind."

"But sir, it has your name on it. Look."

"What? What are you talking about?" Montgomery brings the briefcase up closer so he can see, and there in gold letters just above the handle where he could have sworn it hadn't been when he was looking at it only seconds before, is spelled out "Montgomery C." The briefcase clangs down on the floor as Montgomery hugs the door frame trying to steady his swirling head. "There must be a mistake. That isn't my briefcase.

That's not mine. I swear."

The smiling attendant picks up the briefcase and lightly dusts it off and holds it out to Montgomery. "Oh no, sir. I'm positive it's yours. It's ok to take it. Really. Here." He puts it back in Montgomery's hand and gently ushers him back into his cabin.

"But… but there must be a mistake. I know I didn't bring this with me. Well… I don't think I brought it with me…" Montgomery's voice slowly trails off as the attendant smiles again and shuts the door to the cabin, leaving Montgomery alone in his room.

Montgomery stands staring down at the briefcase in his hand, the bright bold sun-gold letters staring back up at him. His knees feel weak beneath him and he lets himself slowly drop down onto the seat behind him. He pulls his handkerchief out of his front shirt pocket and dabs the drops of sweat off his forehead.

"Must be a mistake," he whispers to himself. "Must be."

Montgomery cradles the briefcase in his arms, and then presses it tightly against his chest, wondering what to do. He knows it's not his… but then again it does have his name on it. And the attendant said it was ok. And what *is* inside?

Montgomery, the curiosity eating away at him, finally gives in. He lays the briefcase across his lap and undoes each of the side clasps. When he goes to open the middle one–the one with the keyhole–it won't budge, locked in place.

Montgomery, after the initial disappointment, chuckles to himself. "My own briefcase and I can't even get it open. Locked myself out of it. Too bad I don't have the key, either."

He lets the case lay there on his lap, his hands resting folded together on the top, gold-leaf letters shining brightly up at him.

"I do wish I knew what was in it." Montgomery sighs, and then shrugs his shoulders. "Oh well."

Itch. Montgomery's hand convulsively shoots up to his chest to scratch a spot where it feels like the hairs are standing up and his skin is tingling. It takes a minute of scratching before the nerves in his fingertips can relay to his brain that they are touching something. Something hard. And thin. And smooth. No. No, not completely smooth. One side has small jagged teeth all along the edge. It's so familiar… ah, a key.

Montgomery hurriedly reaches in his shirt and pulls out a key attached to a gold chain hanging around his neck. Montgomery stares down at the key in disbelief, positive he had never seen it before this moment.

"Now I know that hasn't been there. It couldn't have been. They never would have let me have this chain at the home. My gosh, what's happening to me? I must be losing my mind!" Montgomery brings his hands up and covers his face while the room begins to twirl before him. When the spinning stops he takes his spectacles off and sets them on the briefcase and rubs his eyes with his bony gnarled knuckles. "What's happening to me?"

Eventually though, the curiosity overtakes Montgomery, overpowering all his other emotions of fear and confusion and worry. He takes the key and turns it in the lock and the middle clasp pops up. Montgomery carefully opens the case and peers in. Nothing but a large manila envelope with "Montgomery C." printed in black letters on it, with a slight bulge at the bottom of it. Montgomery lifts the envelope out and peeks inside. Then he turns the envelope upside down and out slides a black stone, flat and perfectly circular. A good stone to try and skip across a creek, Montgomery thinks. He stares down at the stone, something feeling so familiar about it to him. Then he picks it up and holds it up close to his face, turning it in his fingers. Yes, there is something, something about it that Montgomery just feels is so familiar to him… but he can't quite place it.

As Montgomery studies the smooth palm-sized rock, his vision slowly begins to blur. He brings the rock closer and closer to his eyes, and then stretches it out at arm's length. "I can't see it…" Montgomery pauses, his voice sounding suddenly odd to him, familiar but changed somehow. Montgomery removes his spectacles and rubs his eyes again, "I must be going mad." He opens his eyes. The black stone, the manila envelope, the briefcase, his hands, the entire cabin—all are crystal clear.

His hands! No longer his wrinkled arthritic fingers before him, but young unbent strong hands. "What!" he cries out, again hearing that odd voice. His voice, only younger and stronger. His voice fifty years ago when he was a young man. His whole body feels different, all the aches and pains from all the long years of life gone and an energy like he hasn't felt in decades. He springs out of his seat and rushes into the restroom in his cabin. There in the mirror he sees a smiling face, eyes twinkling, looking back at him. Montgomery runs his hand over his head, the young man in the mirror mimicking him. Smooth unwrinkled skin. A full head of chestnut brown hair.

There is a light knock on the door of Montgomery's cabin. He runs to the door and flings it open. The same smiling attendant is there.

"Sir, I just wanted to let you know that we'll be coming up on your stop in a minute. I hope you've had a good ride with us today. Anything I can get you, sir?"

"No. No, thank you," Montgomery hears his still-odd sounding voice reply.

The attendant smiles at him and walks away. Montgomery can feel the train slowing, while the racing wheels get quieter and quieter. Holding the rock grasped tightly in his hand, he looks around the cabin, then decides to leave his cane and spectacles behind, and walks down the hall toward the exit. As the train comes to a stop he hears the whistle blow a long, high-pitched squeal.

He lightly bounds out of the exit and down the steps into the first rays of a new day. He stops. Before him is a small village, a village that, like the stone in his hand, he knows and recognizes without remembering how it is he knows it. He hears the whistle sound again, and the train quickly starts back up and chugs away down the track. Montgomery watches it as it leaves him behind, and waves back at the smiling attendant who is standing on the back platform of the caboose waving goodbye to him.

"Montgomery!"

Montgomery turns back to the village, and there strolling toward him is a beautiful young woman in a pink dress, with a small child holding onto her hand.

"I know her. I know that woman," Montgomery thinks to himself.

"How was your business trip?" she asks as she hugs him tight, holding the small child up so it can wrap its arms around him too.

"Why, what's that in your hand? Where did that come from?" The woman smiles up into his face. "Why, it's our stone that we found on the beach on our honeymoon. I thought we had lost it forever…"

Soul Property

BY JEFFREY A. ANGUS

Prigs Point wasn't difficult to get to. Northwest Territories Highway 5 ran close by, making it an easy trip for two seasoned treasure hunters who were used to difficult terrain. Of course John and Mary hadn't been this far north in a few years and there was always the risk of roads becoming impassable in October.

"Last time the museum needed something from the Great White North it was a bust," John commented as he drove along the cold, abandoned logging roads to reach their destination.

"I know," Mary nodded, remembering well.

"I still don't like the way that went down," he added quietly.

"We have a couple solid leads this time, and the money will be good if we do come back with evidence of the burial site."

"At least the weather's holding up. National Weather Service doesn't predict any big storms over the next week. Maybe some light snowfall."

Each of them had logged extensive time in the Northwest. Hiking trips, camping, mountain climbing excursion, the two spent more time with nature then in civilization. They understood the rules of the wilderness in this part of the world. You were at the whims of the weather. It could turn bad without notice. You had to be prepared or your trip ended in tragedy.

"Still, it's not going to be a walk in the park," Mary sighed. "But hey! It'll be better than that last ghost hunt in Afghanistan!"

"That wasn't my fault! I closed the lid! That type of ghost wasn't supposed to do that anyway!"

Mary laughed at him. He shook his head with a smirk.

"I'm never going to live that one down, am I?"

"I was just kidding," she slapped his leg.

"Yeah... yeah."

John turned on the radio and fiddled with the buttons looking for something suitable to drive to. He paused on one station and out of the speakers blasted "Who you going to call, Ghostbusters"

"Are you freaking kidding me?" John flipped a switch on the side of the radio.

"Thank god for Satellite Radio," he mumbled, finding a station.

Mary settled into the passenger seat for the long haul. It would take the better part of the day to get to the town near the abandoned mine. As she watched the winter-ravaged land fly past the window, she drifted in and out of her daydreams, remembering every detail of the past three months that led to this day.

It started with a book they had found on an expedition to New Mexico three months ago. There was an entry about an ornate wooden box that was discovered many years ago at Prigs. The box was a coffin said to hold the bones of an unfortunate miner who died in the mine. He was buried in one of the disused veins and sealed off from the world. Reports mentioned a small locket and a red stone cross. The person who discovered the box held the cross and locket in his hand. He died the next day from a strange illness, the cross clutched in his hand. The locket at his feet was onyx black. They reburied the dead with all its possessions at an undisclosed location. Within two years, the other members involved with the unearthing died of a mysterious illness.

Mary reached out to people in the area surrounding Prigs Point that she'd met on earlier expeditions. All reports suggested the tale was true. The locals said strange things had been happening at the mine for years. They were too scared to go up to it anymore. Even the Mounties suggested they avoid the place.

The details played over and over again in her mind until she jolted out of her trance by John, who was singing - very loudly and very badly - with the tune on the radio.

"What are you barking on about?" she stretched.

"Look who's back with us! Enjoy your nap?"

"Nap?" She looked at the clock on the dashboard to find she had slept over three hours. "Shit. I'm sorry."

"No problem. It was boring going anyway. But now the fun begins."

"Why?"

Just then the GPS sang out, "You have reached your destination."

"In the middle of nowhere," John added.

Sure enough it appeared they were at the end of the world with a crooked red sign that read ROAD CLOSED in front of them.

"Okay, I guess we go it on foot from here. We can't be more than a couple miles from the mine at this point anyway."

From the back of the Range Rover, Mary opened her pack and strapped on her pistol. Grabbing a short-barreled shotgun, she slipped it into her back holster. A small explosive pack was safely stowed in her hip pouch.

"Expecting trouble?" John smiled as he watched her suit up.

"Always, Johnny-boy. Besides, I've worked with you enough to know that a girl should always be prepared."

They joked about it but John sensed she was a bit more nervous than normal. He decided to let it go for now. It was probably just the adjustment from being in a warm car moving to the zero degree cold.

"Ok then. I suggest we get a move on it."

He locked the Rover and they headed down the mine road. They paused just before the bridge and looked over an old map John had printed and laminated. They agreed that their destination should be North East and went into the forest.

"Prigs Point was a mining town that was abandoned in and around 1938 when the mine collapsed."

John would go on and on with facts and information on the region. He tended to research every little detail and share all of them whether you wanted to hear it or not. There were many times that Mary wanted to throw him off a cliff rather than listen to him prattle, but today she was glad to hear every word that came from his mouth.

After about two hours of walking through dense forest they came across some old foundations. Signs that some kind of civilization had been here at one point and the map and John's research told them they had reached their destination. It was starting to get dark and they needed to find shelter for the night fast.

"Head for that cave up ahead and we can make camp."

With a firm grip on the handle, Mary slid the pistol out of its sleeve. She readied it for action, and made her way towards the same dark opening. John stopped and turned, looking at her.

"What are you doing?"

"It could be occupied. You never know."

She continued to peer past him into the dark entrance. Her free hand traveled near her neck and wrapped around a necklace with a red stone in it.

John smirked as he shook his head, "You are wearing that old locket, and you are expecting trouble."

She smiled and tucked it back into her shirt. "Well, it's good luck, you know.

"Women. Always have to be so melodramatic." John turned back toward the cave.

Mary noticed his hand now hovered over his pistol on his hip. She smirked as they continued towards the cave.

The cave was dark and smelled musty. Evidence that this was one of the entrances to the long abandoned mine lay strewn about near the walls outside the entrance. A few boards still covered the mouth of the cave, but looked easy enough for John and Mary to remove. A tattered sign read *danger unstable mine* was tacked to one of the boards.

"Well we are unstable minds so how fitting." John was still aware that Mary seemed a bit nervous and was trying to loosen up the tension.

Mary shook her head, and John took a little extra time looking around the entrance.

"Looks like this will be a good spot to camp for the night and start fresh in the morning." Mary started to pry the boards off the entrance.

With the day getting old and the weather starting to turn they paused just long enough to pull their lights out of the pack. Together they stepped into the dark; on guard in case something was waiting, they allowed time for their eyes to adjust.

Their small beams of light not doing much to penetrate the ink black darkness, they slowly made their way into the cave. They worked their way in a bit further, checking the floor and walls for any sign of life. They found nothing but strange drawings on the wall.

"What do you think of that, Mary?"

Mary got a little closer, smiled, and turned to John.

"I think we are in the right place; it looks like a Shaman has been here."

"Do you know what it says, or can you read any of it?"

"I can make out some of it, *the birthing of our divinity and blossoming of our caretaker souls lay here until…*" Mary stopped.

"You okay? Does this mean something?"

"I can't make out the rest, but let's get a picture of it and bring it back so we can give it to Turner."

"Sounds like a good idea. I'll get a few pictures and you start setting up camp." John reached into his pack and pulled out his camera and Mary set about making camp. The two spent the next few hours getting firewood and setting up the rest of the campsite. They decided not to go too far into the cave; it was getting late and they were tired from the trek.

They got a fire going, helping the mood and warming them up after the day's cold march. They ate and talked and Mary, ever the cautious one, set up two lanterns, one in the back of the cave and one in the front. She also hung a few cooking pans and utensils on string near both the entrance and the back of the cave in case something decided to visit them in the night.

"Really, do you think we need all that? We have been here for some time; if anything was in here it would have made its presence know." John shook his head.

"I plan on making it back alive; I don't want to take any chances and we are so close." Mary continued her work.

It didn't take long for Mary to fall asleep and as John was starting to drift off, out of the corner of his eye he thought he saw something move. He propped himself up on his elbows and starred into the darkness. He stayed that way for a few minutes, watching and waiting. He settled back down but kept an eye towards the back of the cave. The day's trip got the best of him and soon he was fast asleep.

From the back of the cave a dark form lurked and watched as the two slept. It was able to blend into the dark, being black and tucked against the wall, out of reach of the intruders' light. Two red dots appeared from the blackness as it opened its eyes. It was smart enough to know to keep them closed when John had been looking in its direction, helping it remain hidden in the black recesses of the cave.

The blackness started to tear apart and a ghostly mist began to appear on the surface. The mist struggled, trying to break away from the blackness. As the tear widened and more of the mist hissed out of the opening, it started to take shape. Like a caterpillar's cocoon, the spirit made its way through the black membrane. The mist now floated near the blackness.

"I see we have visitors," the ghost whispered to itself.

The mist stretched and transformed into a shape it had not taken in many years. It changed into a man-like form. It paused and allowed itself to acclimate itself with its surrounding. No longer in the protective blackness it would be more vulnerable until it was able to harvest the living soul and become one with the husk that lay near.

"I smell the presence of another, but it matters not, I will claim this one they call John."

It descended down from the ceiling and slowly made its way. It moved cautiously and deliberately as it took its time and floated above John, making sure the firelight was dim. It lost control on descent and came close to the light of the fire. It shot back up towards its black cocoon like shell. The light caused it obvious pain and discomfort, and it hid within the protective shadow.

"Mitch Browning is weak in this form; I must be more cautious." The ghost of Mitch paused.

It stayed near the ceiling for around an hour before it attempted to float down again. It had been waiting for years, wondering when it would get a chance to walk among the living. It hovered and slowly made its way until it was above John. John turned over; the apparition froze in place. John rolled back over and looked to be in a deep sleep.

Mitch had a chance; it was going to be able to be whole, and it was going to be able to walk among the living. The spirit of Mitch Browning had waited years for this. The spirit shimmered with excitement and drifted down towards John. It started to mold around John's form; it made no noise and John's expression never changed. The mist started to seep into John's body, his skin turned pale as it slowly worked its way in like a burrowing animal.

It was half way in when a log on the fire fell and the light in the cave flared bright. The mist sputtered and popped and John's body was lifted ever so slightly off the ground as the corporal form of Mitch Browning hastily retreated back to the ceiling.

As the form left John's body, he dropped and awoke with a start. He felt like he was falling, that feeling you get when you are just starting to fall asleep and something jerks you awake. He sat up and looked around, eyes blinking in the firelight. Nothing looked to have changed, the alarms and early warning devices that Mary had erected had not been disturbed - he just felt as if something was not right. He decided to add a few more logs to the fire and as he did the sparks carried up into the blackness of the ceiling. The crackling and popping of the fire covered the slight hiss of the creature now forming back into its cocoon.

Morning came with John sleeping in and Mary preparing breakfast. She had made eggs and bacon and was getting ready to wake John. She looked at him and noticed a film on his skin, a strange white powder. She stopped and looked around; she had seen this before. John turned over and scooted closer to the fire.

"How did you sleep John?"

"Not real well, I woke up three or four times during the night. Guess the excitement of the discovery and the riches to be had finally got to me."

Mary watched close as John grabbed his plate and held it out. He was waiting for Mary to dish out the eggs.

"Mind if I share some of that breakfast?" John smirked as Mary just stared at him.

"Sorry, I guess I didn't sleep well either; I was just zoning out."

The two sat in silence and ate their breakfast. Mary was keeping a close eye on John for anything strange or out of the ordinary. John noticed her stare and just continued to eat. After about ten minutes John had decided to have a little fun with her.

"I do feel a little strange, like something happened to me last night," John said stone-faced.

"Go on, do you really think so?" Mary looked more intense.

"Hmm, maybe not. I think it's just your cooking giving me gas."

"You are such an ass!" Mary tossed a piece of bacon at John and stood up and walked outside the cave.

It was cold and had snowed overnight. The fresh white snow reflected the rays of the sun, causing Mary to turn back into the cave.

Mary was sure this was the right place; she could feel it. She turned back around and started to clean up the breakfast dishes. John joined her and they had the camp back in order, and once again they prepared themselves to journey forward.

"We need to look further back in the cave, I noticed about twenty yards back it was a bit darker than the rest of the wall; it's an opening, I'm sure of it." The two got the lights out and headed back into the cave.

They followed a side tunnel and found a few artifacts that Mary was sure the museum would purchase. The day was still disappointing for the duo: no sign of the box or any reason a shaman would mark the entrance. They spent most of the day exploring tunnel after side tunnel, making sure to mark each turn so as to make it easier to return to camp. Once they decided it was getting late, they headed back.

"Looks like we are still alone, nothing has been disturbed." John sat next to his sleeping bag.

"I think we should keep the fire stoked a bit more tonight, I was a bit chilly." Mary shivered for effect. John went and got a few extra pieces of firewood and set them up so they would burn a bit longer through the night. Mary made soup and the two sat and enjoyed the meal.

"We found a few good pieces, Mary, but no sign of the box or anything that looks like a burial site."

"It's not really the box they want, John. It's the soul stone locket and the cross found many years ago the museum is interested in."

"They want to rob the dead - nice!" John said sarcastic as always

"The museum wants to study the locket and then they will return it to this place. If it turns out to be what they hope, they can then protect it and stop any unlawful access to the site." Mary began to clean up and prepare for bed.

"As long as I get something out of this, I will be fine with whatever they do."

The two wanted to get an early jump on it the next day so they agreed to call it a night. John piled wood onto the fire, and both wrapped themselves against the cold and settled in for the night.

Mary waited until John was asleep, she watched until she was sure he was out. The tonic she slipped in his soup would keep him out to the early hours of the morning. She hated to do it, but this was a chance to get back what was taken from her many years ago.

Mary had given John the impression that the soul stone locket was a piece the museum requested, and when they wanted something it always paid well, but she had other reasons for this trip that she was not about to let John in on. He probably wouldn't believe it anyway, but nonetheless, it had been her secret for long enough and she was looking forward to finishing it once and for all.

She lay down and started to hum a strange tune. It filled the chamber and the air seemed to shimmer around the fire, dimming it a bit. Satisfied that the fire was under control, the tone of her voice changed.

She laid still, facing the ceiling, her body growing rigged as she stretched out on her back. The locket around her neck took on a faint glow. Mary's board-like body slowly lifted from the ground, and from her body a white mist started to separate from her still form. It seeped from her flesh and took the form of her, but as a ghostly visage. The apparition of Mary made it to the entrance of the cave and concealed itself in a far corner.

Not long after the ghostly figure of Mary had tucked itself out of sight, a shadow appeared above John. The fire was dim; at least it looked like that to the red eyes that appeared in the blackness. The glow of the red eyes increased with its excitement as it looked down on the unsuspecting man. It looked at the other body near the fire - the one called Mary. She looked to be asleep and a slight hum came from her - a snore, the blackness assumed.

The black cocoon started to tear apart. The spirit of Mitch Browning struggled, trying to break away from the blackness. As the tear widened, and more of Browning's spirit made its way out of the opening, it formed into the man. It looked to have grown more solid. With one ghostly hand then another, it used the misty appendages to pry and tear at the tissue-like membrane. Once again released from its prison, it floated not far from John.

The spirit form of Mary watched and waited; the time was almost upon her. She would have to endure the pain of the fire's light to protect John, and recover the essence that this rogue spirit had stolen and locked away from her so many years ago. If Mitch succeeded in possessing John's soul and his body, she would have a hard time taking her essence back.

Mitch worked his way down to John, watching for any signs that the fire would burst again, easily injuring his weakened form. The light was instant death if it was able to consume him, and he was so close to success that he was not about to let this happen. It floated ever-so-close and started to mold itself around John's body. John started to lift off the ground a bit as the spirit began to enter him.

Mary made her move, and with lightning speed whisked into view and over her body. She had been doing this for a long time and was much faster than the spirit trying to enter John. She entered her body and stopped the humming noise coming from her earthly shell.

The fire that had been dim flared so bright she had to shield her eyes. The painful screech from Mitch Browning told Mary she had timed it well. She could see his form sputter and pop like kernels of corn. It struggled to disengage from John, thinking of only safety and escape. Mary almost felt bad for the pain Mitch was experiencing - almost.

Mary began to chant, and the blackness above sank down and hovered above Mitch and John. Mitch was unaware, its only thought of escaping the pain, and shot up into the blackness. Mary had taken control of Mitch Browning's protective black cocoon, and as he disappeared into it, she changed her song and sealed the blackness, trapping the spirit inside.

Mary continued to chant and she held her soul stone locket to face the black cocoon. The blackness, instead of moving up, moved into the fire. Mary's song changed again and the blackness opened, allowing the firelight to assault Mitch.

The fire sparked, and the creature in the blackness writhed in pain. Mary looked over at John, the effects of the tonic she had given him still holding him in a sleep-like trance. The blackness now fully engulfed in flame the spirit of Mitch Browning shrieking.

"Mitch Browning, you will no longer cause pain as you did to me. Many years I have been searching for you, my husband. The years of torture I had endured at your hands make this ever so enjoyable."

"Mary, it was not what you think: I had to do it to preserve you - people did not understand." The voice of Mitch echoed painfully in the cave.

"I will never forgive, and you now will never forget." Mary started to chant louder as she tossed a powdery substance into the blaze. She pulled the locket free from her neck and tossed it into the fire. The fire flared, the flames now a deep black reaching for the ceiling, the black cocoon fully engulfed.

The faded voice of Mitch Browning repeated, "Mary, you witch, I should have known - dirty shaman trickery!" His screams stopped and the cocoon folded into itself.

The fire died down as she ended her chant. She grabbed a stick and moved what was left of the cocoon out of the fire. It was hard and burnt and smelled of lilacs, with an after tone of decay and rot. She grabbed her knife and cut open the burnt cocoon; the smell was enough to cause most to faint or vomit. She reached in and pulled out a slime-covered onyx medallion. She rinsed it off with water and hung it around her neck.

Once again she laid still and started to drone a tune. The fire died down to its previous state. The spirit inside Mary lifted out of her body. It hovered above Mary's shell. The locket around her neck started to glow and a misty stream flowed from the locket into the hovering spirit. It finished and the black stone in the locket turned clear. The spirit shimmered and sparkled and once again lowered itself down into Mary's still form. Mary, exhausted from absorbing the spirit Mitch had stolen from her, smiled.

"I feel whole again, Mitch; I hope you understand it is nothing personal." She turned over and slipped into a deep sleep.

John woke when the cave entrance showed signs of day. He noticed that Mary was still asleep. He stretched, feeling as if he had not slept in days. He went to the entrance of the cave and saw that the snow had again added a few inches to the surrounding area. He came back and Mary was sitting up. She looked as tired as he did.

"One more day of this and we will call it a bust. This is taking a lot out of me; not sure why, but man, I feel like I've been run over by a bus.

Mary smiled, and stood up and headed to the back of the cave. She kicked at a stone sitting on the floor. She was stretching and getting ready, and John noticed something shine when he pointed the light back towards her.

"Mary, don't move." She froze in place.

John got up and went to the spot he had seen the gleam. He bent down and picked up a clear stone locket. Mary smiled and looked at John. He wiped it off and looked in the book he had been carrying about treasures the museum wanted from the site.

"Well it's not the box, but I think this is the locket noted in the entry. Maybe this wasn't a big waste after all.'

Mary smiled and shook her head. "I think it was well worth it. Let's look around one more time and head out; I have had enough of this place."

"If we leave now, we can make it out of here before dark."

She agreed, and they packed and headed out. She stopped before she left the cave; John had gone down the hill and started into the woods. He yelled back to her to step up the pace. She grabbed a piece of charred wood and made a few lines on the wall in the shape of a butterfly.

"Let others know that a shaman has been reborn here." She smiled and turned and ran towards John.

The Pumpkin Patch

BY THOMAS SCOPEL

The bus ride from Philadelphia to Sherroldsville, a small quaint, age-old town just outside of Boston, was exceptionally long this time. Having barely enough time to get through the front door before being met, she expected it.

"C'mon, Aunt Martha, hurry up!" little seven-year-old Johnny Walker excitedly blurted out, taking hold of her hand and tugging somewhat vigorously. She bent down, sat her suitcase on the foyer's tiled floor, and placed her purse on top of it. It flopped to its side and her return ticket lingered halfway out of the full-length side pocket. She didn't care.

The boy's seven-year-old innocent looking face, coupled with an added abundance of early morning energy, clearly showed through as he looked up into his Aunt's older and just starting to wrinkle face.

"They always grow there. We never have to plant seeds or nothing like that. They just keep coming back every year. Dad says it's our special little part of the many Halloween secrets. I don't know… but it is kinda cool, I guess." He beamed proudly, as if he was one of the ancient explorers and had found a new land. His blue eyes sparkled as he rambled on, pulling her back out of the front door, across the porch, down three steps, and into the early morning sunshine.

Leading her along, Johnny was talkative and genuinely excited with his aunt's yearly visit. They went around the house into the back yard and followed the edge of the lawn until reaching a path nestled and flowing in between two good size oak trees. Each had just started to shed leaves and they were sporadically scattered about. She followed him into the high, but recently trodden down, grass that had taken on the familiar golden fall color. Martha felt her feet getting damp as the early morning dew began to saturate her shoes. Johnny's tugging decreased, allowing her to slow a bit, and she was able to appreciate the sights and smell the fall aroma that filled the air. It being a far cry from the normally acrid and manmade city smells that she typically was accustomed to, she savored the moment, smiling gently, and playfully squeezed Johnny's hand. He squeezed back.

They reached a small, shallow, trickling stream and followed alongside it. She watched a leaf gently glide and fall into it and float away.

"It's just right over there,"" Johnny pointed across the clear stream toward a very large oak tree standing majestically, but somewhat menacing, above everything else. Its large branches reached out in all directions and it reminded her of her days as a child, when she was quite the avid climber. She admired it and faintly considered attempting to get up onto the largest bottom branch. Her fifty-something year old mind applied common sense instead, quickly overruling it using the "you'll hurt yourself" argument.

Johnny let go of her hand, followed a gentle slope down the slick, muddy bank to the water's edge directly in front of five large, flat stones resting above and leading across the water's surface, forming a makeshift crossing. Looking back and making sure his aunt was following, he stepped out onto the first stone, onto the next, and continued across them, reaching the other side. He turned and looked back. "C'mon Aunt Martha," his somewhat squeaky voice echoed throughout the thin forest. Waiting, he watched as his aunt followed, gingerly placing each foot directly on each stone and being cautious to keep her balance along the way. When she reached the last stone, Johnny turned and ran through the fallen leaves gathered below the oak, scattering them in the process.

"See," he pointed, holding his pointing pose while Martha slowly made her way toward him. Standing alongside him, she looked toward where he was aiming and saw the bright orange, vine-laden fruits sparsely scattered and poking through the higher grasses and dead leaves directly below the largest branch she had initially and faintly considered climbing. She turned and gazed at the trunk of the tree, wondering silently how old it must be and how long it had been there. Carefully, she inspected the thick grayish bark and noticed a perfectly carved deep cross like scar that the bark had grown up and around. Reddish-colored sap had seeped from the bottom of it and made its way down the trunk, clumping along the way, to the ground. She wondered if it was a natural occurrence or a manmade marking and how long it had been there too. Oddly, the whole area reminded her of a time when she was young and she and three girlfriends sat around a campfire taking turns telling scary stories. Hers was one that her grandfather had told her about Halloween and children missing the following day. It seemed frightening, and even believable, at the time. Suddenly and mysteriously, she felt that familiar fright return with full force. Attempting to eliminate it from her mind, she turned her attention back to Johnny and the patch.

"This is wonderful, Johnny. You say they always grow here?""

"Yep, every year," he stood proudly by, showing off his find.

"They all look so ripe and plump. Say! Do you have a wagon Johnny?"

"Sure do; it's in the garage," he answered inquisitively.

"Why, I'll bet we could bring that wagon of yours back later, pick out a good one, and take it back to the house. We couuuuuld…" she teasingly dragged it on, pausing for a few seconds before continuing, "…carve a Jack-O-Lantern later. Afterward, we can put a candle in it and it will glow into All Hallows Eve."

"All Hallows Eve?" Johnny questioned.

"That's what it used to be called in the beginning. It was a time when for just one night spirits, goblins, and witches were allowed to roam free. And… some of the bad ones would chase and often take children." She tossed in a little Halloween scare prank, just for fun.

He looked up at her. "Really?" He seemed slightly frightened, but not quite sure of what. She took note and enlightened him a bit.

"It's just a spooky tale. Halloween is supposed to be scary anyways, right?" Johnny shook his head.

"So, would you like to carve one later?" Her eyes glowed lovingly back as she quickly changed the subject. Johnny's face lit up and she could see that her prank induced thoughts of ghosts and goblins had passed and been replaced. She chuckled quietly to herself.

"That would be great," he answered, quickly beginning a scan of the pumpkins, one by one, obviously committed to selecting the very best one. Martha wanted to get out of her wet shoes. "Let's worry about finding it when we bring your wagon back later, Johnny." He didn't argue.

When they got back to the house, she quickly replaced her shoes with a pair of slippers she had stashed in her suitcase for such occurrences. They felt warm and comforting. Prior visits with her single parent, little brother Rick and his son had taught her to be fully prepared for virtually anything, and she always made it a point to try to be.

Johnny had already placed bowls, spoons, a gallon jug of milk, and a box of cereal on the table when she entered the kitchen. Sitting and fast preparing his breakfast, he struggled with the weight of the jug, barely managing to keep adequate control while pouring it. The milk splashed off the oat rings and onto the table, forming a tiny moat ring around the base of the bowl. He sat the jug down with a slight thud that vibrated the table. Martha reached across and lifted it to her side of the table so he wouldn't have to struggle again to pass it. He took a bite and handed her the jug's blue lid. After pouring a small amount of cereal, and even a smaller amount of milk, she replaced the lid and sat the gallon jug down. All the while, she could see Johnny's growing anticipation.

Martha stood at the sink washing their few dishes and watched through the small window over it as Johnny followed the sidewalk to the garage's side door. He turned the knob and went in, closing the door behind him. A few moments later, Martha could hear the electric garage door opening. Ten seconds or so later, he emerged pulling his little red wagon behind him. She found it to be a cute sight.

The hike seemed shorter to Martha this time and before long, they were ready to cross the stream. Johnny made a valiant effort to remain on the first rock while still pulling his wagon. He slipped, and his foot submerged into the water just over his ankle. He shrugged his shoulders in an attempt to convince her that it was incidental, stepped into the water with his dry foot, and continued merrily sloshing across the stream, pulling his wagon behind him. Water flung up from the wagon's wheels and, not wanting to be sprayed by it, she waited until he was over half across before stepping onto the first stone. He was already well into the selection process with his trusty wagon standing faithfully by, when Martha caught up.

Choosing a nice round medium sized one, Martha bent down, placed the scissors she had brought around its vine and snipped, leaving a few inches of stalk for good measure. A loud scream bellowed. It startled her and she jumped. They both looked up in time to watch a loon soar by just above them. Placing the pumpkin into the wagon, Johnny stood patiently by holding its black handle. When he was sure she was finished loading it, he pulled. The pumpkin rolled toward the back of the wagon, banging into the rear lip of it, where it remained, upside down, seeping red tinged white droplets from its severed stalk.

It was dusk and getting darker by the minute when the wagon's wheels hit the sidewalk. Johnny held the door open as she carried the pumpkin in, setting it on the kitchen counter. Johnny took day-old newspapers and opened the pages, layering and spreading them across the table. "Be sure to put a bunch down," she suggested while taking a washcloth and wiping the outside of the pumpkin off.

She set the pumpkin in the center of the spread out newspaper as Johnny went to the silverware drawer and retrieved two paring knives, placing one on the table and holding onto the other.

"We'll need a spoon too," she mentioned.

"Oh yeah," Johnny blurted, "I forgot." He dropped the knife on the table, went back to the drawer and retrieved a large tablespoon.

Martha cut through the top of it. Johnny watched as she lifted it and sliced through the undersides attached white stringy moist mess of seeds and pumpkin flesh, and set it aside. ""First, it needs to be scraped out. Just pile it beside it right there, Johnny."" She pointed to the ideal location, turned, and went to the stove.

Johnny leaned across the table and looked inside the fruit. He couldn't resist reaching into the squishy mess and playing with it for a moment. He felt his hands grow distinctively warmer. It wasn't uncomfortable and he didn't think much about it.

Johnny was close to finished with the scraping when the hot water whistle began to blow. Martha turned from watching him, went back to the stove, and filled her teacup. She carried it to the table and sat down in the chair beside Johnny.

The somewhat grotesque pile of white seeds and pumpkin innards glistened and sat idly by. She handed him the dampened washcloth. He quickly wiped his hands, missing half of it in the process, and tossed the washcloth down. Together, they discussed the best location to put the face. After choosing, Johnny slid the pumpkin towards him, grasped the knife placing the point of it where he thought the top of the first eye would be, and pushed it through the firm flesh. It slid in, completely through the flesh, and came out the other side. Wiggling the knife up and down, and struggling somewhat, he managed to slice through the flesh, carefully keeping an angled line. He then repeated the other side and the bottom as well, until the complete triangle was cut. Pushing from the inside out, the loose piece of pumpkin flesh gently popped out.

Sitting back on his curled up behind him legs he inspected his work thinking it was a good job. Martha agreed. Leaning onto the table again, he began to carve out the second eye, remaining careful to stay as even as possible with the other. He placed and started pushing on the knife. It was a harder and a less forgiving area than the previous eye location. His hand slipped forward, off and over the handle of the knife, and along the edge of the blade, coming to rest against the pumpkin. He quickly let go of the knife and jerked his hand back, leaving the knife sticking out of the fruit. Martha's eyes opened as wide as Johnny's were. Blood dripped sporadically onto the newspaper. Slouching back onto his knees, he turned his hand over. Two slices were prevalent, but somewhat hidden by the constant flowing blood. Martha quickly grabbed the tossed aside washcloth, placed it over his fingers, and held tightly. Johnny's eyes were filled with fear and uncertainty. Tears began to stream down his face by the time she had gotten him over to the sink.

"It burns Aunt Martha, it burns real bad."

"It'll be better after we get it washed out," she attempted to reassure him. Turning on the water, she adjusted the temperature and placed his bleeding fingers underneath it. The warm water stung and Johnny cried out. With the water washing away the blood, Martha was glad to see that the slices weren't as deep as she had originally feared, and she sighed in relief.

Johnny looked at the cartoon character covered bandages on his fingers and waited for Aunt Martha to finish the pumpkin's carving.

"We'll need a candle," she asked, placing and aligning the pumpkin's top.

"There's some birthday cake candles in the drawer below the silverware one," he replied.

"Those probably won't last for very long, but they will work." She let go of the pumpkin's stalk, leaving the lid resting slightly crooked and went to get the candles.

Taking the Jack-O-Lantern out to the porch with Johnny closely in tow, she placed it on the wide banister sill. After lighting the candle, she replaced the lid. Johnny, his fingers still burning, quickly ran down the porch stairs and halfway out onto the sidewalk. He looked back at the glowing pumpkin's face as Martha joined him. Johnny couldn't help but feel like he had let his Aunt down, unable to finish it himself. She sensed his dilemma and patted him on the back. Standing in the darkness admiring their glowing achievement, Martha asked, "How do your fingers feel, Johnny?"

"Oh, they're alright. I can barely feel it now," he lied, holding them up and wiggling them gingerly and shrugged his shoulders. Martha hoped it wouldn't scar him towards future pumpkin carvings.

Martha opened her eyes. It was Halloween day. She glanced at the electric digital alarm clock and saw it read ten a.m. It was uncannily quiet. She had expected to awake to Saturday morning's noisy cartoons blaring and breaking the silence from the other room. Realizing that he had been up late, she calmed a bit, thinking that Johnny was still sleeping. She had stayed up even later, waiting on her brother to get home, and by the time she and Rick hit the hay, it was well past midnight. She rose, slid into her slippers, and tossed on her robe. Passing through the living room, she noticed that the television was off and she continued toward the kitchen, hoping that Johnny was awake and in there eating breakfast. He wasn't, but his father was, sitting at the table reading the day's newspaper and nursing a cup of coffee.

"Oh, you're here?" Rick seemed genuinely surprised. "I thought maybe you and Johnny were out and about this morning. That boy always hits the ground running… every single morning." He didn't seem concerned and was accustomed to his son's adventurous ways. "He's probably out in the woods… he always explores there." Martha gave a small smile and poured herself a cup of coffee.

The two sat there talking and catching up while waiting for Johnny to come through the door with his latest exploring story. Two hours turned to three, and then four. Both she and Rick began to worry.

"He's never this late… never misses lunch–especially on Saturdays. With the way I work, it's basically the only time we get a chance to spend time with one another. Something's wrong, very wrong." Concern took hold of their faces.

"I'm giving him until three," he continued. "And then I'm going to go find him."

At three o'clock, Martha quickly changed her night clothing and met her brother outside, on the sidewalk at the base of the porch stairs. Rick quickly led the way around the side of the house, through the portion of the back yard, onto the trodden path, and across the stream. Rick wasn't concerned with staying on the stones or getting wet and he stepped on the first one, missing the second one completely, and avoided the remaining few, bypassing them and quickly sloshing across the shallow brook. His wet feet slipped once while climbing up the small embankment and he almost fell, but continued on and up into the pumpkin patch without missing a stride. Johnny wasn't there. Martha caught up to him and they stood together in the green, vine-covered area, searching meticulously. Martha called out. "JOHNNY!" A loon screamed loudly. Both were caught off guard and startled by it. Martha glanced up into the massive branches of the old oak, half hoping to see Johnny stretched across a branch looking down, laughing as if to be playing some sort of demented Halloween prank. But he wasn't.

Her eyes followed the length of the bottom and largest branch, out toward its tip. Just over halfway out, and almost directly over the center of the patch itself, she noticed a groove embedded into the branch. She found it slightly strange, but quickly deduced that is was probably a rope swing at one time, and directed her thoughts back to finding the little boy.

They separated and Rick disappeared into the nearby wooded area. Distantly hearing her brother's voice calling out, echoing around her, she could distinctly hear his growing despair, but couldn't tell exactly what direction it was coming from. It made her feel lonely, completely secluded, and increasingly distraught.

She began making her way through the patch itself, making every effort to not step on any of the numerous scattered vines. At the place where she and Johnny had taken the pumpkin from the day before, she inadvertently and unconsciously started searching for the cut vine and missing fruit. But, she couldn't find it. Perplexed and becoming more frightened, she frantically continued her impromptu search, only stopping when her brother reappeared at the edge of the nearby wood line. Glanced over toward her, he shook his head. Trudging toward her through the patch, not concerned with where he was stepping, his foot became tangled. It visibly angered him and he kicked viciously, yanking his foot loose from the thick tendril. Martha noticed a nearby pumpkin move with his motions and roll onto its side.

With no sign of the missing youngster in or around the patch itself, they hoped he was waiting for them at the house, and quickly made their way back toward it. Along the way, the two were silent. Worried, Martha could clearly see her brother's face firmly held the same concerns and it added to her increasing despair.

Closing in on the porch, Rick noticed his sister and son's previous night's work, sitting on the banister in all its holiday glory. Climbing the stairs, he complemented her on their nicely carved creations.

"Carvings?" Martha thought to herself, and looked up to see two pumpkins resting silently side by side, their faces beaming away.

With the sun collapsing and sinking into the horizon, she noticed a slight flicker emitting out from the two-pronged carved teeth of the pumpkin that neither she nor Johnny had carved. Quickly, she climbed the porch stairs and went to it. Lifting its top and peering in, she watched as the same type of skinny birthday candle they had used in the other, was now all but completely burned down. She watched, as the flame lightly flickered once and went out, extinguishing itself in the liquid wax puddle that had formed below it. An eerie feeling invaded her as two simultaneously thoughts crossed her mind. "This isn't the pumpkin we carved," and "that candle should have gone out hours ago."

""We'll do everything we can,"" Mike Lement, the town's constable, reassured them. Rick nodded his head slightly and Mike could see that although Rick may have understood, he wasn't so sure that his voice of encouragement had broken through the father's growing desperation. "Trust me Rick, we'll find him," he added, patting him on the shoulder before going down the porch stairway and back toward his patrol car.

Over the next couple of weeks, Martha fought hard to remain steadfast, sturdy, and optimistic while leading many of the townsfolk-contributed searches, allowing her return bus ticket to expire. She didn't care and was more concerned with helping to find her nephew, as well as carefully watching over her now disheartened, fully depressed, and maybe even a bit suicidal brother. Frantic daily searches and inquiring phone calls would begin hopeful, but end with despair at a dead end.

Gradually, the constant chaos began to wind down and was replaced with the slow realization that the boy may never be found. In early January, both she and her brother resigned themselves to the fact that, although hope hung on by a thread, nothing more could be accomplished and it was time for her to go home.

* * *

Three Years Later

Martha sat in her kitchen eating cereal. Glancing at the wall hanging calendar, she realized that it was Halloween eve. Although it had been three years since the boy went missing, not a day passed without her thinking about him. It had been especially hard during the two previous Halloween seasons, when pumpkins were more prevalent and a constant reminder. She began literally hating the very sight of them and avoided them at all cost.

Taking a bite of the cereal, strong memories immediately flooded back, as if it was only yesterday, and she began to weep. Wiping away the tears, she bowed her head, said a silent prayer, and did her best to remain strong and fight against the sadness that invaded her heart. Not hungry any more, she stood up, carried the half-eaten bowl of cereal and spoon to the sink, and placed the carton of milk in the refrigerator. She hadn't noticed the black and white photograph of Johnny's smiling innocent face on the backside of the carton under the heading ""MISSING,"" as she allowed the door to swing closed.

* * *

October 29th, 1789

Gwendolyn Smith carefully plucked a sprig of wolf's bane, placed it in her small woven basket, and followed along her garden's perimeter, around the large oak tree, and onto the opposite side. She crouched at a cluster of plants in the corner and snipped a small piece of hemlock, taking care not to directly touch it, and let it fall into the pre-positioned basket directly underneath. "This spell is going to work well," she thought to herself, throwing her long unkempt black hair back. Rising back up, she heard and saw the mass of people, led by the Puritan preacher, William Gray, coming out of the woodwork and directly toward her.

"TAKE HER," his deep voice yelled as three men obeyed him and grasped hold of her, leaving her basket to fall to the ground, spilling most of its contents.

"NO MORE, WITCH! YOUR EVIL DAYS ARE OVER," he cried out, holding and shaking his bible high over his head. Voices praising God and agreeing with him trickled throughout the obviously bent on destruction crowd. A large man tossed a pre-noosed rope over the oak's large bottom branch and continued to wrap it three times. He then tied it off around the tree's trunk, went to the dangling end, and stood by waiting for the captors to bring the captive to him.

The men held her tightly and lifted the thrashing about woman up. The designated hangman placed the noose around the old decrepit woman's neck. William Gray read aloud from his open bible and made every attempt to avoid directly looking at the condemned woman, who continued to peer wickedly back at him.

"I will be back, heh heh heh heh, I'll always be back," She cackled loudly. "There is one single night when you can't stop me, Mr. William Gray. I *will* have my revenge… starting with you and your family." Continuing her threatening words and following them with a chilling laughter, she stopped when the captors let go of her, leaving her to dangle by her neck.

With gurgling sounds occasionally being heard, she writhed. The townsfolk, especially William Gray, watched in demented excitement, while others continued forming a woodpile directly below her. She stopped twitching and the sickening gurgling sounds ceased. A loon screamed as it flew closely by, nearly knocking the preacher down in the process. A gasp went through the congregated crowd.

William cut the rope, allowing her body to collapse onto the makeshift woodpile below her. Contorting oddly and uncontrollably, it flopped limply as it landed, remaining motionless over the top it. He tossed a flaming torch into the dry timber and it quickly caught hold. Most watched as the flames grew and fully engulfed the dead woman's body. Burning flesh filled the air and a few became visibly sick. Others chopped and raked the woman's unorthodox garden into the fire, carefully covering their mouths and avoiding any toxic smoke many of the plants created. Afterward, with the fire dying down and the old woman's body having turned to ash and gone completely, the preacher beamed with pride and accomplishment. He began to carve a cross shaped marking deeply into the trunk of the tree.

"No need to worry about her anymore, folks," he attempted to reassure them. "She can't harm us any longer. All Hallows Eve will pass quietly tonight."

With dusk closing in, the townsfolk turned away from the makeshift execution sight and began dispersing in different directions. The preacher waited until everyone left before continuing his carving. He was almost finished when the knife slipped and sliced open his index finger's knuckle. Both sap and blood mingled together and slowly trickled down, through the cross carving, giving the normally dark yellow sap a reddish tint. The loon bellowed loudly again from high above him.

The following day, Sunday morning, the congregation waited at the church for almost two hours for their preacher to appear. When he didn't, they all went to see if he was still praying at the burning site. He wasn't, and numerous rumors began to circulate. No one noticed the two tiny, freshly grown orange pumpkins, nestled in the ash and partly covered with leaves directly under the tree.

Should Have Been There

BY MATT NORD

He should have been there. He could have changed the entire outcome of events if he had just said yes to going down to the park with his son. Eric had just wanted to play catch with his Dallas Cowboys Nerf football, but Peter was too tired from work that day. Actually, he wasn't. He works in a fucking air-conditioned office, sitting in front of a computer screen all day. How tired could he really be?

And so he blew him off that day, the day he shouldn't have.

* * *

"Come on, Dad," Eric said. "I haven't seen you all day."

"Cut me some slack," Peter replied. "I just got home. Don't you have some friends to play with?"

He tossed his laptop case on the couch and pulled his shoes off without bothering to untie the laces, a testament to his laziness. He plopped his ass down next to the laptop and snatched up the remote. He scanned the channels faster than he could process the information from each.

"Please?" Eric said. "None of the guys are around. I'm bored!"

"Dude," –and yes, he called him dude– "just let me relax for two goddam minutes!"

Eric's lip started to quiver. Peter rolled his eyes.

"Look, go play up in your room for a while," he suggested. Eric shook his head. "Then just go down to the park. I don't care, just leave me alone for a while."

"You never want to play catch with me," Eric said pushing his glasses further up on his nose and acting more upset than one might have expected.

That did it, though. Peter jumped up from the couch and got in his thirteen year old face. He got so sick of Eric's attitude sometimes that he just went off.

"That's bullshit and you know it!" he shouted, shoving a finger an inch from Eric's nose. "How many other dads are out there playing catch with their sons as much as I do, huh? And how many dads play Modern Warfare 2 with their kids on the weekends?" he asked, pointing towards the large screen TV that was attached to the gaming system.

Peter's wife didn't say anything from the kitchen. She knew that Eric could often be annoying and not considerate of the fact that Peter did work. Sometimes he just wanted to come home and relax. However, the way he expressed it that today...

"What am I supposed to do, play catch with myself?" Eric asked in an attempt to stand up for himself. Peter wasn't having any of it, though.

"Take a basketball, smart-ass," Peter snapped. "It doesn't take two people to shoot around. Just go do something!"

By this point, Eric was near tears. Peter started to feel bad, but now his pride was on the line... at least, that's what he tried to tell himself.

"Look, just go down to the park," he said. "I don't feel like playing right now. I don't feel like doing anything, all right? I feel like sitting my fat ass down and watching some fucking TV, if that's not a problem for everybody!"

He sat back down and glared at the screen of the television as if it had wronged him in some way. Eric stood there for a minute, staring at him before turning around and leaving the house.

"You know, you probably..." his wife started to say as she came into the room.

"I'm not in the mood, Patricia," he cut her off. "You know how he is. I mean, you complain every day that he bugs you about being bored, whining about not having anything to do. Why the hell did we spend all that money on the roomful of shit he has upstairs?"

"I know, but he's been looking forward to you coming home all day. You didn't need to treat him like that," she chastised.

And of course she was right. His heart told him that he should go after Eric and apologize. That he should give him a big bear hug and toss the ball around with him for the half hour that would satisfy him. That wasn't too much to ask for. But his head, the ego, the proud man that he was, felt that he was in the right.

"He'll be fine," he said, looking back at the remote control. She stood in the entryway to the kitchen, her arms crossed, giving him "the look." He spared a glance at her before refocusing his attention back on the television. He couldn't even tell what was on.

Her glare burrowed into him like a drill. He started to feel about a foot tall–make that one inch tall.

"Fine, I'll go down in a few minutes," he said. "Just let me relax for a little bit."

Eventually, she turned and went back into the kitchen, leaving Peter to stew in his own shittiness. While brooding over his next mood, he got sucked into whatever was on the TV. Slowly, he forgot about Eric and the park and drifted off to sleep.

* * *

Several hours later, Patricia shook Peter awake. He rubbed his eyes in an attempt to wipe away the blurriness, and looked up into her worried face.

"What is it?" he asked, coming fully awake.

"Eric isn't home yet," she said.

"He's probably still down at the park," he said through a long yawn.

"No, he's not," she said. "I looked down there already."

"Then he probably went over to…"

"I've already called over to Adam's and Stevie's, Peter," she said, her voice raising and speeding up a bit. "He's not there either."

"Calm down, Patricia," he said, raising his hands and standing up. He stretched a bit and walked over to her, putting his hands on her shoulders.

She slapped them away unexpectedly.

"Don't fucking patronize me, Peter!" she shouted.

He backed off, shocked by the sudden outburst. He must have looked like an idiot, standing there with my mouth gaping like a dead trout.

"You get out there and find our son."

"All right," he said, going to the front door and getting his shoes on. "I'm sure he's fine."

The look he got from her then jarred him as he reached for the doorknob.

"He had better be," she said, storming away to grab the telephone again.

* * *

It was getting fairly dark and there weren't any kids down at the park. In fact, the only vehicle he saw was a van parked a little way off in the parking lot. He didn't give it a second thought.

Eric was nowhere in sight. Peter walked towards the basketball court. He noticed his basketball, lying discarded in the grass, and his blood ran cold. He picked it up and looked around again.

"Eric!" he yelled. He listened for an answer that did not come.

"Eric!" he yelled louder. Still nothing.

"ERIC!!!" He started to panic and ran towards the large group of trees and bushes that the neighborhood children sometimes used as a makeshift fort house, dropping the ball as he went.

Peter crashed through the underbrush, knocking away leaves and branches. They tore at his hands and arms, scratching every inch of exposed skin. A particularly sharp branch caught him under his left eye; a stream of blood ran down his cheek.

"Eric, are you in here!" He didn't know what caused him to behave so hysterically, it wasn't the first time Eric had been late. Usually he was just at a friend's house or had run to the library. It also wasn't unusual for him to forget his basketball down at the park; many times Peter had sent him back to retrieve it. Something about this time, though, just didn't feel right.

Then he saw it: a shoe lying on the ground about ten feet away. One of Eric's shoes. His entire body went numb and he got dizzy to the point where he felt for sure he would pass out. The feeling passed, however, and he willed himself to walk over to the discarded shoe. He bent over to pick it up and fell to his knees. Cradling it in his hands, he began to cry.

His mind was flooded with flashes of painful and hopeful thoughts. *He's fine. He's going to show up at home and I'm going to tell him I'm sorry for the hurtful things I said. I'm going to play catch with him for hours and hours. I'm going to hug him and never let go.*

He's fine, Peter kept thinking. He looked at the shoe again. Maybe he just…

"Oh God." He saw the blood on the edge of the shoe, then more on the ground and the leaves around the area–too much blood for just a skinned knee or some other small, child-type, playground injury.

He stood up on wobbly legs, Eric's shoe still clutched in one hand, and looked around in a daze. Peter saw his glasses on the ground a few feet away. Picking them up, he noticed the crack down the middle of one of the lenses. *What the hell could have happened? We live in a nice neighborhood. This wasn't supposed to happen to us.*

The dizziness came back for a moment, but quickly passed. Panic was quickly joined by sudden anger. *Who the fuck would do this? Why would somebody do this?*

When he finally got a hold of… The van! He hadn't thought too much about it at first, thinking it must have been another parent looking for their child, but something in the back of my mind buzzed like an alarm now.

He bolted back through some thorn bushes, his shirt tearing to shreds, and sprinted across the park, running over the basketball court toward the parking lot. He heard the ignition turn over and then the van peeling out, tearing across the asphalt.

Peter ran as hard as he could. His foot caught on a rock and his ankle twisted. Losing his balance, he fell forward. He felt my right wrist pop as he hit the ground. He looked up and watched as the van sped off into the night.

"Get back here, you fucking son of a bitch!" he screamed after it. "I'll fucking KILL YOU!"

* * *

The next several hours were a blur. The police were called, questions were asked, and accusations were thrown at him from his wife, all of which he absorbed without argument; it was his fault, after all. His wrist was wrapped up with an old t-shirt. He refused medical attention. In actuality, Peter couldn't even feel the pain. He answered the questions the police had then walked down to the park with them and replayed the scenario for them. They found fresh, burnt-in tire tracks in the parking lot where he told them he had seen the van speed away.

At that point he broke down, falling to the ground, weeping uncontrollably. The two detectives he was with started shuffling their feet and looking around uncomfortably. Obviously that weren't that well-versed in grief counseling. After several moments he composed himself and stood back up.

"Is there anything else you need down here?" Peter asked, wiping the lingering tears from his eyes. They glanced around at the officers and dogs that were searching the area for any other clues.

"No, Mr. Markley," one of them answered. "Why don't we head back to your house? There are a couple more questions we'd like to ask."

Peter didn't argue. He just turned and walked back toward his house. The two detectives followed at a bit of a distance. He could hear them talking, but they were too quiet for him to make out what they were saying. He wasn't paying attention anyway, lost in thought and self-loathing.

Peter's main thought was, *How am I going to get my son back?* His second thought was, *What is the most pain I can inflict on the son of a bitch that took him?* His last thought was, *If I don't get him back, what's the point in living?*

Rational thought at that point was not an option. It showed in Patricia, too; by the time that they reached the house, she had a pot of coffee on and was finishing up with sandwiches. She had obviously gone on autopilot.

Peter dropped down onto the couch and something sharp poked into his side. He reached into his jacket pocket and pulled out Eric's glasses. His eyes began to moisten with tears. He lifted the glasses closer to his face, again noticing the crack that split one of the lenses down the center. Putting them to his own eyes, he dreaded the thought of the last thing his son had seen while wearing them. And then…

* * *

He was in the van. His vision bounced a bit with the motion of the vehicle. He noticed beady eyes glancing back in the rearview mirror at irregular intervals, but he never got a good look at the whole face.

* * *

Peter snatched the glasses from his face and jumped up from the couch, spilling the cup of coffee his wife had set next to him on the arm of the couch. Tears streamed down his face. He took a swing at one of the police officers out of shear confusion. Luckily for the officer, and for Peter, he ducked it and moved away from another potential attack.

"Easy, man!" he said with his hands raised. His partner's hand moved toward the canister of pepper spray on his belt. "I told you we'll do whatever we can to find your son. You just need to calm down and answer some more questions."

Peter heard Patricia weeping quietly in the couch next to him. He looked down at her, then at his son's glasses that rested in the palm of his hands. The crack on the one lens stood out.

"Mr. Markley…" the first detective said, signaling his partner to stand down. "Please, can you sit down?"

Detective Simmonds had seen fathers and mothers alike react with anger and frustration and even violence against those who were trying to help when it came to kidnapped children. They were frustrated because the safety of their child and the entire situation as a whole were out of their control. They were angry because they felt like the police weren't doing enough. And the violence… sometimes calming them down was part of the job.

His partner, Detective Anderson, wasn't as forgiving. He didn't care what the situation was. As soon as things got a bit hairy, he'd go right for his pepper spray… or his Glock 22, depending on the circumstances.

Peter looked up at Simmonds. He had tears in his eyes, as well, and a confused but somehow hopeful look in them.

"He's alive," he whispered.

"I'm sure he is, Peter," Simmonds said. He'd found that using someone's first name could do one of two things: make them feel more at ease or make them feel like they're being patronized. Simmonds had a lot of experience dealing with people and hoped he was making the right choice.

"No," Peter whispered. "No," louder. "I saw the van."

"And we have the license plate number. They already have it tracked down to an owner," Simmonds reassured him. Unfortunately, the van had been reported stolen the prior week, so they were fairly certain the owner had nothing to do with the kidnapping. "It's only a matter of time before we find it."

He knew that didn't necessarily mean that they would find the boy. If fact, it was more likely that they would find the vehicle abandoned on some back road or side street. It was also likely that they would find Eric in the same fashion. The thought caused a knot to form in the pit of his stomach. This wasn't the first missing-child situation he had been a part of. Sometimes they were just at a friend's house and hadn't told their parents, something innocent like that. Sometimes it was bad. In this situation, they already knew that Eric had been taken. There had been blood… it was bad.

"You're not listening to me!" Peter's voice cracked with the last word. "I saw the bastard that took my son!"

He lifted the glasses toward Simmonds. Again Anderson flinched and took a step forward. Simmonds eyed him, but Peter didn't even notice. When Simmonds didn't take the glasses immediately, he began shaking them vigorously.

"Put these on," he said. One of the arms of the glasses frame made a clicking noise as Peter continued to shake them, sounding vaguely like a clock ticking away. Simmonds pulled a cloth handkerchief from his pocket, reached up, and took the glasses, being careful not to touch them. He turned them over, looking at them at different angles.

"These are Eric's, aren't they?" he asked, looking up at Peter. He nodded and Patricia's head perked up. "You know, these are evidence."

"Just look through them," Peter pleaded.

Simmonds glanced back down at the glasses again and noticed the crack in one of the lenses. He also noticed the small red dot, nearly imperceptible, in the corner of the lens while he lifted them to his eyes.

After a few seconds he lowered them. He turned slightly toward Anderson and shook his head. Then he reached into his pocket and pulled out a plastic bag, placing the glasses gently inside.

"Wait, what are you..?" Peter sputtered. "Didn't you..? You can't take those!"

He went to reach for the bag before Simmonds put them back in his pocket, but Anderson intercepted him and wrenched his arm behind his back. Simmonds had been itching for that.

"Shit!" Peter shouted as the larger man tweaked his injured wrist.

"Let him go, Anderson," Simmonds said. After a moment, Anderson complied.

"One more time and I throw the cuffs on," Anderson sneered at Peter. "I don't care what he says." He nodded toward Simmonds.

Does this fucking idiot think I have something to do with Eric getting kidnapped? Peter thought as he rubbed his wrist. After a second though, he remembered that if he had just gone down to the park with his son in the first place, it wouldn't have happened. He *was* responsible. But the good cop/bad cop bullshit wasn't helping them to find their son.

"Look, these are evidence now, Mr. Markley," Simmonds said, gently sliding them into his front jacket pocket. "Now, you need to just calm down. We're going to do the best we can to find your son and return him to you, but you flying off the handle isn't doing anything for him or for you and your wife. You need to stay strong. We've got a *lot* to work with."

The emphasis he put on the word was lost on Peter. He was too worried about losing the glasses, his connection to his son and the man who had taken him. Before he could protest any more, Simmonds pulled a card and a pen from another pocket. He wrote something on the back and handed it to Peter.

"If you have any more information, anything at all that either of you can think of that may help to bring your son home," he said, acknowledging Patricia, "let us know."

He reached for the door and turned the knob, waving to Anderson to follow him. Simmonds opened the door and let the big man pass him.

"We will do everything we can," he said before turning to leave. He shut the door behind himself.

Peter walked over to the door and looked out the window in it. The two detectives got in their unmarked car and shortly pulled away. He saw another car, a police cruiser, parked just out front on the street. It didn't make him feel any better.

He started to think about what he had seen. Had he imagined it? Had it just been his traumatized mind throwing fucked-up visions at him? He rubbed his eyes with the palms of his hands. The card he held scratched his forehead. He had forgotten that he even had it.

The front had Detective Simmonds' information: the department phone number and address, his email, his cell number and the unit number. He flipped it over and gasped, his throat tightening. He read the short line of writing over and over.

It read, "I believe you."

* * *

Detective Simmonds didn't say anything to his partner as he drove back to the station. On top of the fact that he was getting sick of Anderson's overly physical treatment of Markley, he was trying to work through what he had seen when looking through the kid's glasses.

He knew he couldn't talk to anyone about it, least of all his partner. They would think he was crazy. Well, not unless he could show them, too–but what if they didn't see anything? What if there really was nothing? But it had been so vivid.

"What's on your mind, man?"

Simmonds jumped at the sound. He'd been so lost in thought that he'd nearly forgotten he wasn't alone.

"Nothing," he said quickly.

"You're being quieter than normal," Anderson said.

"Yeah…"

"So, what's eating you?"

"Nothing," Simmonds said again, not trying to change the subject, but just trying to get Anderson to shut up.

"That guy was whacky, huh?" The big man didn't take the hint.

"His kid just got stolen, what the hell do you expect?" Simmonds snapped.

"Hey, I understand that," Anderson said defensively. He managed to keep his mouth shut for all of fifteen seconds. "But what about that shit with the glasses? I mean, if he'd just said he wanted to keep them or something, I could understand. What was he talking about, though? Seeing his kid through them."

"No," Simmonds said, remembering what he had seen. "He saw what the kid… he saw what Eric saw."

Anderson stared at him for a short time.

"Well," he said, "what did you see?"

Simmonds pulled into his parking spot at the station. He hadn't realized until the last minute that they had driven all the way across town. Taking a deep breath, he answered his partner's question.

"Nothing," he told him. "Like you said, the guy was a just whacky."

* * *

Later that night, Peter sat in the kitchen, downing his seventh cup of coffee. Patricia had taken something to help her sleep, at his strong suggestion. He glanced over at the clock on the stove, its digital display glaring back at him with its harsh green light: 01:47AM. He didn't know why he was staying up. He kept looking at the card that Detective Simmonds had given to him.

"I believe you," Peter said out loud. *Why hadn't he said anything? Why had he just left? Is he going to show someone? Is he coming ba…*

There was a knock on the French doors right next to him, making him jump up from his seat. The chair he'd been sitting in was knocked to the floor. Detective Simmonds stood just outside.

"You came back," Peter said.

"Let's go," Simmonds replied, turning and walking through the back yard.

Peter grabbed his coat and shut the door, making sure to lock it.

"Where are we going?" Peter asked.

"My car is over this way," the detective said.

"Why this way? Why didn't you come to the front door?"

Simmonds stopped. His shoulders rose, then fell as he sighed deeply. He turned around to face Peter.

"I'm not here officially, Mr. Markley," he said, taking Eric's glasses out of his pocket. "Look, when we got back to the station, Anderson looked at the glasses, *through* the glasses. He didn't see anything. Neither did a couple of the other guys at the station he showed them to. They got a good laugh out of it."

He looked them over for a second and then handed them to Peter.

"But I know what I saw," Simmonds said.

"And what was that?" Peter asked.

Simmonds looked down, back toward where his car was parked and then back up at Peter.

"Like I said, I'm not officially here. I'm not here as a cop. I'm here as a father."

Peter didn't say anything at first; he didn't know what *to* say.

"What…"

Simmonds cut him off.

"I know where he is. We need to go now."

* * *

They parked down the street from the house Simmonds had quickly seen when he had first put the glasses on. It was definitely the place: he'd eventually been lucky enough to see a magazine with an address on it on a trash-covered coffee table. Unfortunately, he'd also seen a pistol and a bowie knife lying on top of the magazine. He had also seen a set of keys.

He hadn't taken the glasses off since his shift had ended, hoping that he'd see something to give away where the boy had been taken. That had finally been it.

Simmonds wasn't sure why he'd brought Peter along. Maybe it was because he didn't plan on arresting this guy, anyway…

One town over, Simmonds had found Philip Stevens. It hadn't been too difficult to track him down. He hadn't even had to connect to the police system database. He'd popped up as a sex offender.

"Okay, this guy is a nutcase," he said.

"That doesn't make me feel any better," Peter said.

"He's been in and out of jail since he dropped out of high school seventeen years ago. He got off on charges of murdering his parents when he was eighteen because of a technicality. He went to jail for rape seven years ago. Got out early for good… good behavior. He's a known drug dealer, but again somehow he's managed to avoid arrest for the past three years."

"How the hell is this guy not still in prison?" Peter asked.

Simmonds didn't answer.

"Why is this guy allowed to keep doing this shit?"

"The system isn't perfect," Simmonds whispered.

"Yeah…" Peter said.

"Well, what are we waiting for? Let's go get your son."

They both got out of the car and walked down the street toward the house. It was the only house on the block that still had any lights on.

The plan was for Peter to make a distraction out front while Simmonds went around back to break into the house and get Eric. They knew he was being kept locked in a large dog cage in the room in the center of the house. Peter had nearly lost it when he'd seen that, but he knew now that he had to keep it together if he was going to save his son.

Simmonds had explained to him that one of the other reasons he had only come with the two of them was because Stevens was the type that wouldn't hesitate to cause as much damage as possible if he thought he were in danger of being arrested. He would have no qualms about killing Eric before they took him down.

Peter watched Simmonds go around toward the back of the house. He got a thumbs up as Simmonds rounded the back corner of the house. Looking through Eric's glasses, he saw a pair of torn jeans walk past his vision. They stopped in front of the cage. Eric looked up into Stevens' pitted, craggy face. He was saying something that Peter couldn't make out. Globules of spit formed in his mouth. He smacked the top of the cage and then stormed away.

Peter took a deep breath, took the glasses off his face and walked up the stairs to the porch as quietly as possible.

* * *

The backyard was full of trash. There was a high fence surrounding it to hide the junk from the neighbors. Simmonds had seen it before. The fence wasn't out of consideration for those who lived around him, but an attempt to prevent them from reporting him.

He picked his way through and around bags of trash, parts of a dismantled mower and a few rusty (most likely stolen) bicycles. He had to move slowly so he didn't trip over anything and give himself away. Simmonds only hoped that Peter didn't do his part before he was even able to get to the back door.

He didn't hear anything yet, so it seemed like he was in luck. Finally, he reached the door and put his ear to it. He didn't hear anything. So, he'd waited…

Before too long, he got his distraction. He heard a very loud crash come from the front of the house. He knew he had to move fast, so he checked the knob of the door and couldn't believe it when it actually turned. The door swung open with a still creak.

Shit. He froze where he was, straining to listen for anything inside the house. All he heard was Eric, weeping softly. Simmonds only hoped Peter's distraction had been enough. He pulled his handgun from its shoulder holster and pushed the door open the rest of the way.

Slowly, he made his way through the kitchen. He tried to repress a gag–the smell was so horrible. According to the records, Stevens lived alone, but he couldn't be sure that there wasn't anyone else in the house. He walked through the kitchen doorway and there in the next room was the cage that held Eric.

"Eric," he whispered, trying not to startle the boy. He held his finger over mouth, scanned the room and, once he saw the room was empty, made his way over to the cage. He grabbed the keys off the coffee table. Eric had a terrified look on his face. "It's all right. I'm going to get you out of here. Your father is…"

"Behind you," Eric said, pointing up.

A bat upside his head put him down to the floor. As he was losing consciousness, he saw Peter lying on the floor next to the couch.

* * *

Eric watched as his captor searched through the pockets of his father and the man he didn't recognize. Stevens hadn't bothered to reclasp the lock. It still hung off the door of the cage.

Looking from the lock to the coffee table, the gun caught his eye. The awful feeling that had been in the pit of his stomach all night got even worse. Could he actually do what was going through his head? If he didn't though, what was that madman going to do to him and his father?

That thought pushed him into action. He quickly and quietly removed the lock and swung the door open. He also noticed that his glasses were lying at his feet. Somehow they had managed to get into this creep's house even though Eric remembered them falling off at the playground. He quickly picked them up and put them on before rushing to the table and snatching the gun off the table.

"Stick 'em up, fucker!" he shouted, cursing himself in his head for sounding like a 1960's bank robber. The barrel of the gun shook as he tried in vain to steady it.

Stevens stood up slowly and turned around. Eric saw the evil look in his eyes. He sauntered over to the coffee table and reached down for the knife.

"Don't do that!" Eric yelled, shaking the gun at Stevens, who paused only for a second before snatching the knife. He smirked at the boy as he straightened back up and began to move toward Eric.

"You little shit, if you were going to do it, you'd have done it already," Stevens growled through rotted teeth. "I'm gonna gut your papa while you watch. Now drop the fuckin' gun and get back in your…"

BAM.

Eric's ears rang. Stevens looked down at the hole in his chest as the red circle spread across his dirty wife beater. He dropped the knife and fell to the floor.

The young boy dropped the gun and looked around in a bit of a daze, focusing on his father. He gave the body on the floor a wide berth as he walked over to him.

"Dad?" He shook his shoulder when he didn't get an answer. "Dad!"

Peter groaned as he came to. He struggled to sit up, even with Eric helping him. Peter looked around groggily. Simmonds began to stir next to them.

"Dad," Eric said, getting his attention.

"Yeah, buddy," Peter said, pulling him into a tight hug.

"Can we go home?" Eric asked.

"Yeah," Peter said, letting out a sob. He held his son, who returned the tight hug. "And tomorrow I'll take you to the park, OK?"

Peter felt his son's head nod against his chest and he hugged him tighter.

Under Pressure

BY MARC SORONDO

The craft descended through blackness, displacing the thick atmosphere of the abyss. Dr. Nathan Harpur stared through a small circular window, its thickness warring with the pressure outside the craft, while another man served as pilot.

Virginia Harpur saw this; rather, she knew it without having to see it, as if she floated beside the descending ship, intruding where water permeated and crushed all.

Outside, visible to Virginia now through the eyes of her husband, swam the impossible. Living lights moved through the weight of the darkness as they passed over alien creatures that needed no oxygen to live, impossible animals that thrived on hydrogen sulfide that plumed up like black smoke from vents that seemed to open up from a Hell that lay just beneath the crust of the Earth.

Lights outside the craft flashed and went out like an old light bulb. The once-welcomed darkness took on an ominous importance and the dread inside the small craft was nearly palpable. No longer under their control, the darkness took on the same maliciousness as the vast quantities of water that tried to crush the ship beneath its weight.

Then there was light: a rosy hue that seemed to emanate from the darkness itself before it collected in front of that thick window. It formed a vague outline that clarified into a horrible smiling face. It was that of Evil itself, amused by this intrusion into its domain, fathoms deeper than the rays of the Sun dared to venture.

Then the mouth opened as if to swallow the craft whole or to let out a boisterous laugh. The window, thick Lucite called unbreakable, cracked down the center. The crack spread, past the window and through the steel that was inches thick, circumnavigating the entire craft like a doomed explorer.

The two halves of the craft separated, as if blown apart by an explosion. For a moment the water was held at bay by some unseen force; the two men, one Virginia's husband, were exposed to the abyss, cocooned by a small bubble of air.

Then it gave up its hold. The water crashed in from all sides, pounding on them and through them, crushing them until they were one with the ocean and nothing of them remained.

* * *

Virginia woke with a jump and tried to sit up, but her belly, pregnant with their first, their future, would have none of it.

Nathan woke. With a concerned look and a hand placed just below her bellybutton, he asked, "are you okay–what's wrong?" with near panic in his voice.

The man would volunteer to explore Hell itself, but the prospect of a child scared him–the prospect of not having one even more so. His worry was charming in a vulnerable sort of way and Virginia smiled at him.

"Another nightmare," she said.

"The same one?"

"The same." She paused, uncertain, before going on. "Do you have to do this?"

"It's the chance of a lifetime. Think of how few people have even been close? It's... it's like going into space."

"But I keep having these dreams. What if something goes wrong?"

"Since when do you believe in prophecy?"

"I don't..."

"Nothing's going to happen," Nathan said, his index finger tracing the outline of her bellybutton; it stuck out from a t-shirt that hadn't really fit since her first trimester. He smiled. "Besides, a psychologist once told me that the abyss really represents the subconscious, and..."

"Don't twist my words around and use them against me, Nate." She tried not to smile but couldn't resist. "This abyss represents the real abyss that you want to play explorer in."

"I won't be playing. It's going to be for real," he said, his grin widening.

"Tell me again why I shouldn't worry."

Nathan inhaled and then, as if it had been memorized and recited innumerable times before, said, "The bathyscaphe *Trieste III* is the most advanced submersible in history. The walls of the craft are composed of steel six inches thick. Between the walls and the inner chamber, the Trieste is filled with gasoline for buoyancy. As gasoline is both lighter than water and a liquid, it will make the craft float and better resist the pressures of the Hadal Zone. The closed-circuit rebreather system is similar in design to that of the space shuttle, and an electric heating system provides a degree of warmth in the frigid depths. There are three windows, two smaller and a larger main observation window for study of the animals and conditions in the trench. Those windows are composed of polymethyl methacrylate–Lucite, or Plexiglas if you prefer–nearly a foot thick, which makes it virtually unbreakable. Nine tons of ballast are used to get the ship to sink, and that ballast is held to the underside of the ship by an electromagnet, which ensures that even in the event of a total power failure, the ballast will be dropped and the ship will ascend to the surface. The craft's interior…"

"Enough," Virginia said. "I get it: it's high tech, it's strong, you guys have thought of everything."

Nathan nodded in agreement.

"But how high is the pressure down there?"

"Eleven hundred atmospheres, give or take a few. About eight tons per square inch, but the Trieste can withstand more than that."

"And how deep are you going?"

"Thirty five thousand, seven hundred and ninety eight feet."

"What if something goes wrong? I mean, people aren't meant to be all the way down there?"

"Nothing will go wrong. The worst that could happen would be a loss of power. That would end our trip, force us up to the surface."

"And this Navy guy's good?"

"He's the best they've got, and that says a lot when 'they' is the U.S. Navy."

She sighed and said, "Okay".

"Try to get some sleep. Tomorrow's a big day," he said.

He laid his head back on the pillow but left his hand resting on her belly. She was happy he did.

* * *

Nathan sat before an audience and cameras, fielding questions from eager reporters that fought for the mediator's attention.

He was well muscled and handsome, tall, and smiled often as he answered questions. He had a good smile, not so handsome that he could be on some poster in a teenage girl's locker, but it was open and friendly, and there was a hint of youth in it.

He wore brown loafers and pale blue jeans, topped with a plain white shirt. Over this he wore a tweed blazer, like some lit professor at a liberal arts college.

He looked handsome and nerdy at the same time, Virginia thought as she sat next to him, watching him answer questions.

"We hope to collect specimens that have never been properly studied before," he was saying. "Usually, when dealing with these creatures, the pressure proves to be a huge obstacle. The species that live at these depths have adapted to far greater pressures, and often die if we try to bring them to the surface. The *Trieste III* will change that. The craft is equipped with numerous pressurized chambers. We can use the bathyscaphe's robotic appendages to catch animals and the chambers will keep the pressure stabilized as we ascend back to the surface…"

Virginia wondered how many readers of the *Times* or *Post* cared about some jellyfish that lives 35,000 feet under the water. She guessed, however, that the real story, the thing people wanted to read about, was man's conquest of nature yet again: our innate ability, skill, and need to resist nature, to overcome every challenge she set for us, whether it meant the building of houses on rivers that flood every year, cutting through whole mountains so that roads don't go interrupted, or breaking her gravitational embrace to escape her altogether. Whenever nature said no, people had a need to defy her. The deep was off-limits; Mother Nature had said so. Who wouldn't want to read about the petulant children who refused her mandates and went anyway?

Then her dream came back to her: that terrible luminescent face, the crack zig-zagging its way around the ship, the water pausing for an instant before it crushed her husband into nothing.

Maybe that's the news they want, she thought. They're hoping for something horrific to give their readers some excitement. It'll look less morbid when they report about the accident if they've been following the story from the beginning.

She forced herself to stop, knowing that she was projecting her own fears and frustrations outward, letting herself get angry at them to avoid what was really bothering her.

"Mrs.… excuse me, Dr. Harpur," a reporter said. "What are your thoughts on your husband being a part of this expedition?"

She saw a flicker of nervousness in Nate's eyes, as if he thought she would burst out crying and tell the world about her nightmares, beg him not to go in front of the press.

"He'd better come back up," she said, forcing a smile.

A chuckle spread throughout the crowd.

"My husband has told me all about how safe and advanced his *Trieste* is. They've taken every precaution."

The questions then went back to Nathan and his pilot, and only companion on his trip to the depths, Lieutenant David Helmsford.

Every precaution, her voice echoed in her head. That smiling face in her own abyss winked at her.

* * *

After the press conference, Nathan and Virginia went to dinner: a farewell dinner, as his flight left the next morning.

They went to their favorite little Italian restaurant to eat mozzarella caprese and penne ala vodka, to drink imported mineral water and talk about things other than the Challenger Deep for a little while… about baby names and private schools, curfews and birthday parties, colleges and weddings and grandchildren.

Once they'd stuffed themselves on rich sauces and richer desserts, and planned out impossible lives for their unborn child, Virginia said, "tell me the truth: am I being ridiculous for getting so worried about this?"

"I wouldn't say ridiculous," he said, flashing her a smile, "but you really don't have to worry."

Maybe it was the way he smiled with such confidence, or the warm, comfortable feeling of her full belly, but she believed him.

"Well, you'd better call me as soon as you reach the surface. I don't care what time it is."

"You're sure you don't want to come? See me reach the surface with your own eyes?"

"You know I can't. I've got too many students to skip a week's worth of classes, especially with finals in two weeks."

He reached across the table and took her hand.

"I thought it was supposed to be safe marrying a scientist. You're supposed to be boring, not dangerous," she said.

"I am boring," he laughed.

She smiled and shook her head.

"Come on, it's true. I could bore you to tears if you let me talk about whatever I want. Do you remember when I gave that presentation for your friend's ecology class about the effects of commercial fishing practices on Caribbean fish populations? Forget the students, I almost put your friend to sleep."

"I know, but this… adventure of yours? You go from that boring guy to this guy sitting in front of me beaming about a chance to go to the most dangerous place on earth."

"You have to understand a little bit. There's no explorer in you? You wouldn't say…" he grinned at her, and although she didn't know what was coming, she knew he thought it would prove his point, "…I don't know, interview a serial killer if given the chance? Try to get inside his head, poke around, figure out what makes him do what he does?"

Virginia, who read as much Patricia Cornwall as psychology journals, and could write a dissertation on Thomas Harris' Hannibal Lector, had to grin back. "That's a low blow," she said, lifting her cup to her mouth and forcing herself to look away from him.

"Besides, it's different," she added after taking a sip of water.

"How so?"

"Well, if I were to interview a serial killer it would mean that they'd been caught. They'd be restrained and I would be safe."

Nathan twisted up his smile and made it as evil as possible. He raised one eyebrow suggestively and said, "Are you quite certain of that, Clarice?"

"You could eat something with fava beans and Chianti, as far as I'm concerned, and it's not liver." She tried to look angry. She failed.

"We've been married too long to think that the fake mad-face is going to fool me."

"Fine. I give up. Go play Captain Nemo, but after that you stay on the surface… at least within a few hundred feet of it."

"Yes, ma'am."

"Let's go home," Virginia said. "If this is the last time I'll see you for a week, I want some time alone with you."

"We're alone," he said.

She shook her head. "Clueless," she noted, as much to herself as him.

"Oh," he said. "Oh," again, now smiling more as he realized what she meant. "Yes, ma'am, again."

* * *

Nathan left at eleven o'clock the next morning. It was difficult for him, but knowing that Virginia's mother was going to stay with her for the week made it a bit easier. Someone would be with her, watching out for her–her and the baby.

He had to hop on a commercial flight at two, which took him to the west coast. There he met up with his pilot. He'd met Dave a few times already aside from the press conference, and spoken with him a few more on the phone.

They had time for about three minutes of pleasantries—how's your wife, how was your flight, can you believe we're really doing this—before they boarded a Navy plane to Hawaii. From Hawaii they took another plane to Guam, where they boarded a Navy helicopter that took them out to a government research vessel, the *Benchley*, that was already at sea over the Marianas Trench.

The ship was owned by the Pacific Oceanographic Association, a privately-funded research organization. It had already been at sea for almost a year and, with the exception of some disaster, would remain there collecting data for a further three.

"That's a very old-school approach to science," Nathan said as the helicopter got close enough to bring the ship into view.

"What do you mean?" David asked. He never took his eyes from the view of the ocean, stretched out uninterrupted in all directions for as far as the eye could see, aside from the small speck of the *Benchley*. Some men joined the Navy to serve their country, while others loved the water and saw enlistment as a chance to be close to it. Helmsford was one of the latter.

"To stay at sea for years, collecting data, observing the ocean, examining it all constantly for years… a lot of people don't have that kind of dedication anymore. There was a time when men spent years at study and exploration: they suffered for it, they sacrificed for it, and a lot of them even died for it. It wasn't a job, it was a passion. I'm not saying that's totally lost, but there's a whole order of scientists out there who would rather propose theories based on other's discoveries. They'd rather shoot down new ideas or proclaim their faith in the old ones than sacrifice a great block of time on research."

"Does risking our necks down there make us old-school or part of the new breed?" David asked, watching the way the sun reflected off an ocean almost free of waves.

"Old school, I guess," Nathan said.

David pulled his gaze from the view and looked at Nathan. "Good. The way you describe those armchair explorers, I wouldn't want anybody talking about me with that kind of disdain in their voice."

"Don't worry about my disdain. You pilot that submersible tomorrow, get us down and back in one piece, and you're good in my book–Hell, I'll consider you a close friend after going through something like that together."

"I've got to be honest, doc, they could send you down there with a monkey in a tinfoil helmet manning the controls; the thing's just about foolproof."

"I know… but I hope you do a better job than the monkey."

"I will, as long as I'm wearing my tinfoil."

* * *

Sunset on the *Benchley* made you believe in God, if you didn't already, and love him a little more if you did. All those colors reflecting off the water like an enormous and imperfect mirror, the darkness and depth hinted at beneath the reflection, the complete lack of discernable horizon so that purple faded to red, which in turn faded to pink and back to purple again as one looked from above to below–it was too great and too subtle to be captured by any human endeavor, be it painting, photography, or mere description.

At dawn Nathan and David traded it in for the black abyss.

* * *

"What's the fish you want to catch again?" David asked.

"Not really a name for it. It's only ever been seen once. When the first *Trieste* reached the Challenger Deep in 1960, it disturbed a flat fish, one that looked almost like a flounder, which swam away. Before that, people didn't think anything could live down there."

They were already in the *Trieste III*, running complicated diagnostic checks on the craft as it bobbed on the surface.

It had been tested countless times already, and the crew of the *Benchley* had taken her on a few test dives, although nothing more than a few thousand feet.

Nathan was checking the robotic arms on the outside of the craft. One of the things he was most excited about was the prospect of bringing live samples back from the trench. Their bathyscaphe was the first to be armed with robotic appendages that could be used to capture live specimens. Nathan felt giddy. Everything he'd worked for was coming to fruition. Years of study and classes and sacrifice were all paying off.

They had a few more brief tests to run. Then they began their descent.

* * *

Virginia awoke with a scream ready to explode out from her, sitting up and pushing the blankets away before she'd woken. She'd had the damn nightmare again.

She ran her left hand over the part of her belly that stuck out, uncovered by her pajamas, and looked at the clock. She tried to work out the time difference and figure out how long she had before she should be expecting a phone call.

She said a quick, silent prayer, something she hadn't done in years, and tried to go back to sleep.

* * *

The light was growing dim. Nathan and David were cramped but comfortable if all the factors were considered. They were warm, but their multiple layers of clothes would be worth the discomfort once the temperature around them dropped to twenty degrees below zero. They were about eight thousand feet down, so they had a while to go before reaching the most interesting depths, but even there both men were amazed.

Though the same fish that one saw on the surface could potentially dive to a thousand or even a few thousand feet, depending on the species, in general the ocean's life fit the template of some science book illustration that divided the sea into horizontal zones of different colors, each of which was home to different species.

David kept pointing out the bathyscaphe's thick windows, exclaiming, "look at that one," or "what the hell is that thing?" Nathan was glad to see that his excitement had been contagious, and did his best to identify every species he could.

There were cameras mounted all over the *Trieste III*, some of which pointed straight out while others could be aimed by the controls that sat in front of Nathan. Many of the creatures they captured on film had never been photographed before, and Nathan debated trying to catch one or two in the pressurized chambers. He decided against it, opting to keep them all open for the real menagerie that waited below them.

Their descent continued.

* * *

"It's like piloting a spacecraft," David said as they moved through the blackness. The only light at that depth came from the bioluminescent creatures that lived there.

"Have you flown in space?" Nathan asked, awestruck.

"No… not yet, anyway. I want to, and I'm hoping that after this I might get to."

"Be the first man to ever see the highest heights and the deepest depths?"

David smirked. "Something like that."

They were at 32,750 feet, and had spent hours in the craft already.

They had lights on the craft, but opted, at least for the time being, not to use them. Instead they let the animals announce themselves with their neon advertisements.

Nathan and David had already seen some of the ugliest creatures alive, monstrous-looking fish with huge jaws larger than the rest of their bodies, teeth like ivory needles that pointed back into their cavernous mouths, and black bodies marked with small lights used to attract prey. These fish swam in perpetual night, and in that nocturnal realm they were bad dreams, ghouls twisted by childlike imagination and fear of the dark.

"God, that is ugly," David said as one such animal passed. "Should we catch it?"

"No, they've been seen before. They've got a pretty wide range in terms of depth. We've never caught a live one, but dead specimens have been examined. I want something new."

"Okay. I don't know if I'd want that hideous son of a bitch riding with us anyway."

* * *

"Explain to me how it's getting hot after it was so damn cold," David said as he wiped sweat from his brow on the sleeve of his shirt.

"Because we're getting close," Nathan said. "The hydrothermal activity in the trench heats up the water. The vents spew chemical rich water at seven hundred fifty degrees. It'd be way beyond boiling if it weren't for the pressure."

"God, I'm sweating my ass off and wearing enough layers to go snow shoveling in Antarctica."

"You've been to Antarctica?"

"No." David shook his head. "That'll have to wait until after the space shuttle," he added with a chuckle. "How many containers do we still have?"

"Most of them," Nathan said. There were a few specimens that he just couldn't pass up: a slender jellyfish that glowed pale green, a black fish with no eyes and a long, semi-translucent tail that trailed behind it, twice as long as its body.

"What's our depth?" Nathan asked.

"About thirty four thousand."

"We're going to pass through what amounts to a layer of cloud covering soon. It's going be all blackness for a little while we pass through it."

"Why's that?"

"Those hydrothermal vents that are making things so hot are pluming out what looks like black smoke. That's where the heat comes from, and the chemicals that enable a whole food chain based on bacteria that eat substances that would kill almost anything else."

"Won't the whole bottom be filled with this black stuff?"

"The superheated material rises until it begins to cool. At that point, there's a sort of canopy of it. Beneath that, it'll be even hotter."

Then the windows were darkened, blotted out by what looked like ink in the water.

"There you go," Nathan said, motioning to one window.

They descended through the darkness, the instruments in the *Trieste III* letting them know when they'd reached 34,500 feet, then 35,000, and 35,500.

They approached the very bottom, the bottom of the sea, the bottom of the whole damn world, and David was using sonar to navigate.

"We're pretty much at the bottom. You ready for those lights?"

* * *

Virginia had been awake for a while and was trying not to wait for it. She found that CNN had mentioned the expedition twice, albeit briefly, in the past few hours. Their information was hardly up to date, however, consisting mostly of clips from the press conference, blurbs said by other experts, and reminders that the Doctor and Lieutenant were in the depths even now.

Two men had gone down there before, Virginia told herself. A guy named Jacques and a guy named Don, the last names wouldn't come to her now, but they went down and came back–in 1960, no less. She figured that it was foolish to worry about it at all, considering all the technological advances since then.

But that reddish grin in her mind told her she was lying to herself.

* * *

Nathan told David to hold off on the lights for just a second while they hovered, neutrally buoyant, just above the bottom.

He closed his eyes. He'd made it: he'd reached the very deepest; he'd reached the unreachable. More people had been to space than the Challenger Deep.

Before he opened his eyes, he heard David say, "Now what the Hell is that?"

Nathan opened his eyes and followed David's gaze out one of the windows. Two small lights, almond-shaped patches of bioluminescence in a shade different from any they'd seen up until that point, sat motionless in the water.

Nathan's face screwed itself up in confusion and then he smiled. "Something new, perhaps? Something never seen before?"

"You think so?"

"Only one way to be sure."

"Light?"

"Let there be," Nathan said.

David flicked a switch to his left.

Now illuminated, an impossibility sat before them.

Nathan saw it and frowned. He found himself thinking: if the abyss represents the unconscious mind, as Virginia had said, then this was God's subconscious, and in it evil dwelled.

It looked like an old man, the skin tanned to a deep brown, the head hairless, the face weathered and wrinkled. It wore nothing. It sat with its legs crossed on the bottom of the trench. It would have looked like a Buddhist monk in meditation if not for the miles of water crushing down on it and the luminescent eyes that glowed as they stared at Nathan and David through the main window of the submersible.

Nathan bit down, ground his teeth. His brain began to list off all the reasons why this couldn't be happening: the pressure, the temperatures through which one would have to swim, the complete lack of air for miles in any direction; yet there it sat, staring at the *Trieste* and them inside it.

"How…" David started to say, but his words trailed off. His lips kept moving, silently asking all the questions no one would be able to answer.

Nathan didn't turn to look at him; he couldn't force himself to stop staring at the thing that sat before them.

Then it moved. Nathan watched the muscles in its thin legs flex as they pushed its body up against the weight of the ocean.

It stood. Its body was emaciated. Its face was placid.

"Get us the fuck out of here!" Nathan screamed. It was too much. He didn't care anymore, not about exploration or discovery; let someone else figure out what this thing was. He wanted to forget he'd ever seen it, to let the memories of this nightmare fade away, covered by those of his child's first steps, first words.

All at once Nathan Harpur decided that he no longer wanted to know everything, that if things like that existed, his ignorance really was bliss.

The *Trieste* didn't move.

Nathan turned to look at David. The lieutenant was staring, mouth agape, past him, watching the old man of the abyss.

"Dave!" Nathan screamed.

David's eyes slipped out of focus for a moment, but he was on the controls again even before he could see them clearly.

Nathan turned to the thick, Lucite window and found the old man standing just in front of it.

"Oh God," Nathan whispered.

A snarl came to its face and it lifted both hands with the fingers tensed like the talons of a bird of prey.

The bathyscaphe began to rise.

The tips of its human-looking fingers dug into the Lucite, created frosted white craters where they pushed through it.

Nathan realized that he was never going to see his child, would never know if he had a son or daughter.

The muscles in the old man's chest and shoulders flexed. A thin crack, the thickness of a hair, meandered in an erratic path from the center of the window out to the edges.

David dropped the nine tons of ballast that had made the submersible sink.

It was too late.

The back of the sub began to rise, but the front was held in place by the creature. It pulled at the window again, worsening the crack so it spread out in a spider web design that covered most of the Lucite.

It let go and the sub ascended.

"Will it hold?" David asked as the craft's buoyancy pulled it towards the surface.

"It would be a miracle," Nathan said, watching the figure of the old man disappear in the receding light of the ship, only his glowing eyes remaining visible once all else was lost in the darkness.

The window groaned. It seemed to bubble inward, and the force compressing the shards of Lucite together made them squeal.

Nathan said a short prayer for his wife and unborn child. David said a shorter prayer for his companion and himself.

The pressure finally broke through, sending bits of plastic into the small bathyscaphe with the speed of bullets that stabbed into the two men. The pressure that followed crushed them into oblivion. The darkness consumed them.

Sweet Madeline

BY STEVEN MCGUIRE

The Odd Shop was different, to say the least. Most shops in downtown Portland are a little odd to begin with, but this shop took the cake.

The shop is small, just off Burnside, and close to the Powell's City of Books. It would be easy for one to walk right by the small door. The store could be compared to that of a narrow bedroom: full from the side, and lined with glass cases.

The cases are nightmares on display: skulls, mummified hands, and odd medical tools. It's a specialty shop for those looking for the arcane, the ancient.

Max finishes a display of an iguana. It has been used for veterinary-school purposes. It has been dried and cut in half. Its bones and waxed organs are removable. The iguana is resting on a limb, completed with wax leaves. Max had purchased it two days ago from another collector.

He just received a call from a different collector who said he was interested in it. Max bought it for $100.By the end of the day, he will have sold it for just over $300.

Max finishes the display by settling the clear bubble-shaped glass dome over the wooden base. He steps back and admires his work. He pulls a microfiber cloth from a drawer, then wipes the glass clean.

The inside of the shop is dark. Max keeps the doors closed to keep the random strangers away. Really, he isn't interested in the causal shopper. Max's clients are specific: the buy and sell.

A rush of cold air wafts past Max's scraggly blond hair. He shivers and lifts his ice-cold blue eyes towards the door. A man walks in. The newcomer is wearing a black top hat and a long vibrant red cape. This is odd for even the strangest of local Portland dwellers.

You might think instantly of a vampire, yet this man looks nothing like the typical typecast. He's flush, his cheeks are rosy, and bright life fills his eyes. In this, he appears pretty normal.

Max offers a smile and a small wave. His slender bony hands are a road map of veins.

"Good afternoon, welcome. What can I do for you?" Max says in his best cheery voice.

"Hello." The strange man nods and removes his hat, placing it on the counter along with a large briefcase. Much too large for a businessman Max thinks, but says nothing.

"I have something that I would like to have you look at. I think that you might be able to help me." The stranger's voice is velvety: deep, yet smooth.

He places the case on the counter, then turns the lid towards Max, opening it slowly. Inside, there are multiple dividers and plastic bags filled with bone. Max leans in, pulling a couple of the little bags out and examining them.

"Oh! It's a skull!" His says excitedly.

The stranger smiles, pleased. "Yes, it is a completely disassembled skull, all twenty-nine pieces." He leans over the counter with childlike glee. His eyes are wide. He is getting excited.

"I heard through some friends of mine that you are a skull collector. Also, that you have repaired and reassembled skeletons."

Max leans against the counter. He flips his hair out of his eyes with a quick jolt of his neck. A shit-eating grin comes across his face. His reputation is preceding him. Again.

"Yeah, I do a lot of that. Are you looking to have me make you a Beauchene skull?"

"Yes, I believe it's called a Beauchene?"

Max smiles wide, trying to hide his excitement.

"Yes, a Beauchene skull, or exploding skull, is a way to display all of the 29 pieces of skull. The bones are held by wire and are on a metal post. The bones can be moved in and out of place." Max uses his hands like he is actually moving the parts. "They are used for medical teaching, and by the occasional odd collector." Max folds his arms across his chest. All he needs now is pipe and a chalk board.

The strange man nods and smiles bag. "Yes, exactly what I am looking for."

Max smiles, and sees the dollar signs in front of his eyes. This isn't a cheap process. He has to play this just right. Usually he gets around $3,500 for his work. He can shoot high, or let the customer make the first draw. He decides to test the customer's emotional attachment to the skull.

Max pushes to find how serious the stranger is. "This is pretty incredible; tell me about this. Usually, the owners have the parts scattered. Hell, I got a skull all in a paper bag one time. What's the story?"

The stranger smiles wide, removing the vibrant cloak, showing a fine, form-fitting suit underneath. The suit is all black, with a red tie and bright gold cufflinks. He is older, perhaps in his fifties.

"Oh, well. This… this is something special. I have had this for a number of years. I purchased this from an antiques collector. He found it at an old World War II German base. Officer's quarters. The skull, at one time, was fully formed. It was disassembled… well, that, my friend, is another story." He laughs and smiles.

"Well, how much are you looking to pay to have me set things up for you? By the way, I'm Max Erris. I never got your name?" Max holds his hand out.

"James. James Andres." James thrusts his hand out. Max half expects the hand to be ice cold, and is rather shocked to feel that it is perfectly warm. James' skin is soft, his grip firm.

James puts his perfect hand to his forehead. His eyes open wide. "Uh, I guess I would go about $10,000. That seems fair. Will that work for you?"

Max tries not to jump out of his skin. Either James is handing him the bologna for the sandwich, or he is serious.

"Uh…" Max pauses for professionalism, then purses his lip, nodding in approval. "I think I can make ten grand work."

He still waits for James to burst out laughing, but it never comes. Instead, James' eyes light up. He jumps a little, like a kid who just opened a Christmas present and found exactly what he wanted. He quickly grabs his elaborate cloak and pulls out a thick leather clutch bag. He sticks his elegant fingers in, and removes a thick stack of green bills.

Max can hardly believe his eyes. James is counting out hundreds. A hundred of them, total. Max's heart is bouncing like a cartoon across the shop. At least, that is what Max thinks it feels like.

James gladly hands the money over to Max. "How long do you think that it will be before I can pick up the piece?"

Hoping that he doesn't offend James, Max replies, "Oh, perhaps 2-3 weeks?"

James' face lights up. He exhales in relief, bending over and smiling like he has just been given a clean bill of health from his doctor. "Wonderful! Wonderful!"

Max is relieved. *This is too good to be true*, he thinks, *lots of money and extra time!*

"Great. Here, write down all of your contact information. Let me type up a contract, and I will call you as soon as I am done. I will give you top priority!"

* * *

Max closed early to go home and celebrate. He could hardly believe his luck. In fact, he made a stop at the bank to deposit the cash. He just had to make sure that the money was real. The teller marked every bill as she counted it, and handed him a receipt. His account just exploded.

Max stopped by his favorite Thai restaurant, and orders the biggest bowl of Tom Ka he can, with a side of salad rolls.

His apartment at Lovejoy Fountain looks like a larger version of his shop. It would put Ripley's Believe it or Not to shame. A large, round U.F.O hangs from the corner of the ceiling, next to a life-size hard wax alien.

He collected numerous human and animal skulls. One set started with a small monkey skull, a Rhesus Macaque. The next 7 skulls are various primates leading to a large silverback mountain gorilla skull, completing the flow of evolution to a perfect human skull, one of Max's best. Fully complete, that one put Max back $2,000.

Max sets the curious case on a coffee table. Despite the clutter, his apartment is well kept.

He clicks the gold locks. They snap open and the case opens easily. It is solidly built, with a fine leather casing. The case smells traveled, yet it is in perfect condition. Inside, the trays are cut to fit. The wrapped pieces of skull are neat and orderly. Itemized.

Max notices a file underneath the lid. There is an old picture of the skull. A side shot. Max doesn't need it to re-assemble the skull.

Max notices something different in the air. His nostrils are filled with lavender and fine tobacco. He curls his eyebrows and grabs a large bag with a piece of skull. He holds it close to his face, inhaling deeply. He is intoxicated.

He's fairly certain that the peculiar man is probably the owner of the fragrance and doesn't want to imagine the perversions behind its use.

Max sets all of the pieces in the bags out. He knows enough anatomy to know which bones are which. He visualizes the structure: how the bones will sit out, and the length of wire he needs. He will start in the morning. The shop is closed tomorrow.

* * *

Max slept heavily that night. Dreamless. He awoke refreshed and full of spunk. He was so happy about his bank account, but first things first. He paid his rent. Got coffee. Stopped by a hardware store. Then he went straight to his apartment. Lining all of the bone fragments in order to how they would be attached to the frame of the display.

He looked at the bones spread out before him. He felt warm and alive. Sometimes he would wonder about the lives of the people behind the skull, though he knew better. Sometime the skulls were collected from grave robbers, murders, and executions.

It usually took him several hours to really plan out the mapping of the skull, yet like a man possessed, he worked with frenzy and only realized how many meals he'd skipped after the second lunchtime had come and gone.

A job that would normally take him at least a week was completed in 37 hours. He crashed on his couch, sleeping deep and heavy.

He awoke at 3 AM, wide awake, his eyes pulled back by an invisible force. Lavender filled the room. Smoke from expensive tobacco mixed in exquisite perfection. He wasn't sure if he was dreaming. He thought he'd just stayed up way too late.

The perfect Beauchene skull was set in front of him in a better display than he had ever made. Usually the wires that assemble and move the pieces don't stay perfectly straight; sometimes you had to tweak the wire to get the pieces to line up when you push them together.

Max reaches over and loosens a knob that is part of a special add-on that he adds to his work, allowing the skull to tip backwards for better view. He inspects every aspect, pleased with his work.

Finally, he makes the final test, pushing all of the pieces together for the complete assembly. The pieces slide effortlessly, lining up with perfection. His heart flutters. His eyes widen. His road map of veins flood with life.

He can't believe the perfect form. The precise fit of the bone. Never has he seen or built anything with such perfection.

Max jumps up and grabs his camera on an end table near the front door. He holds the power button and sets the flash for a soft lighting, framing the future photo like an eerie museum portrait.

He holds the camera up to the skull. The image is blurred by a bright light. Confused, he looks back at the skull. It looks nothing like the screen. He holds his camera back up to the table, starting low at the base of the table, then moving upwards. Perhaps there was a light anomaly that confused the lens.

The table appears in the screen, looking normal. In fact, he can see a corner of the jaw. He raises the lens and fills the frame with his piece. The screen whites out. He might as well be taking a picture of the sun.

"Fuck. What the hell?"

Max looks up from the screen. The skull is suddenly glowing, brighter and brighter. His eyes close in pain. He winces, covering his face with his arm. His apartment lights up brighter than any time during the day, like a massive floodlight in the center of his room.

It's blinding. He feels a little queasy. His head pounds. There is a cool rush of a breeze. The lavender and tobacco become stronger.

The lights dim. She is there. Her red hair shines bright and sleek, pulled into a wave behind her head. Her skin is warm. He tastes the tobacco on her tongue.

They kiss passionately for several seconds. He isn't scared, or even curious about the beautiful woman who suddenly appeared. She pulls him closer to her. He melts in her arms.

They part from their embrace. Her face is angelic, soft. Her green eyes pierce into him. She brushes her hand along his face, and his mind is flooded with images of their bodies, sweating and entwined, rolling on fine silk sheets in a large room with candles lit.

He doesn't ask anything. He knows everything in a glance.

"Madeline," he whispers breathlessly. "Sweet Madeline." He isn't sure how he knows her name, nor how the images of them appear so clear in his mind. He doesn't care.

"Baby, I've missed you." Madeline grabs his hands, pulling them close to her chest. His face blushes as they brush against her vanilla breasts.

She brushes his hands against her face. More images: Passionate nights. Her being pulled away from him by soldiers dressed in Nazi clothing. Another solider bashing the butt of his rifle against Max's face.

He suddenly wells up with tears. He feels her pain, and his sadness. The love of his life was taken from him.

Another image flashes: She is strapped to a table. The images flash faster and faster. He can hardly keep up with them. Her life passes. Bogus doctors hack away at her, looking for something.

He is intoxicated by her beauty. The images fade. He looks deep into her eyes. She pulls him close, and kisses him again. Then she pulls away slowly, moving her hands behind her back. Her dress drops. She takes his hand, and pulls him to his bed. They entwine with passion.

* * *

Later in the evening, he dreams. He sees her life. As a child, she could predict things. Obscure events. She could also find things. Lost wallets, toys, and jewelry. Her parents hid her, yet her beauty made her stand out.

The war breaks into Poland. Hitler's crazed fascination with the occult leads his henchman to whispers and rumors of a beautiful witch. He wants her for his needs. His desire for the occult and mystic power leads some of his most twisted doctors and scientists to her.

Not to mention the power for psychic ability–imagine the entire SS with clairvoyant ability. Kill the enemy before they even know there will be a battle.

She was easy to find. Anyone can be bought for the price of life.

She is locked in to a room. Various crystals and rare wood pieces line the walls along with statues and macabre paintings. She is supposed to be reading the future and psychically finding prized possessions for the Nazi Party. Anything that will help the Third Reich win the battle against the world.

She refuses to eat. She tried multiple times to commit suicide, failing due to constant supervision. She cries for her release; they threaten to kill her family and her lover. She doesn't want to use her gift for evil. She died slowly of dehydration and malnourishment.

The crazed doctors felt that the key to her power was in her head. They carefully and precisely dissected her skull and brain, breaking apart her skull into 29 individual pieces. Only to find nothing. The mad Doctor Shanz pulled the brain apart piece by piece, thinking for sure the key to psychic ability was there.

In his rage the mad doctor ordered the execution of the commanders the task force that found her.

* * *

Max awakes to more tender kissing. He can't refuse her touch. No words are exchanged the whole day.

More and more visions are passed. A crazed doctor obsessed with her beauty keeps her skull. She appears to him at night. He keeps her in silence.

She amuses him sexually. Her energy is pulled from the physical contact. She discovers she can lure other men.

Her skull is stolen, and sold time and time again, finally ending with the strange man that entered his shop a couple of days ago. He is much younger. He has heard the rumors. A widow had found the skull in her late husband's closet. She doesn't know anything about it. James through research tracks down the skull. He paid $500,000.00 for it more than 30 years ago.

He uses séances and magic spells that he believes will bring the sultry spirit to him. He finally gets her to appear by crudely taping the skull together and using wire to hold it.

James' every fantasy is fulfilled with Madeline. She grows stronger and stronger with every bit of physical contact. She knows that with enough power, she will be set free of her physical prison. She makes sure not to show this to Max.

She shows Max how she has been abused and tortured. James was no better than the crazed German scientists. Nor the demon-seeking man whose wife sold James the skull.

Max knows what he needs to do. He needs to lure James to his apartment. He needs to have Madeline for himself.

"I can be your woman. I love you. I only want to be with you," she coos, kneeling down and crawling over to him. Her cleavage pours out of her dress.

Max is flushed. His desire for her overwhelms all sense of reason.

"Tell me what to do! I will do whatever it takes!" Max pleads, as she unzips his pants.

Visions return to him. He is calling James. James comes over. She appears. Then everything goes dark. The fuzz clears up, and he sees their bodies entwined, sweat beading.

He dials the number written down on the plain white card. James picks up the line on the other end.

"I have been expecting you, though not so soon!!! Is it complete? May I see it?" James answers excitedly. Not even waiting for a response from Max.

"Yes. Come to the Fountains. Apartment #320." Max answers. "It is ready for you. "

"I will be there in a half hour."

"That will be fine. I will be here."

Madeline floods Max with affection. He hardly has time to pull clothes on when his buzzer goes off.

"Hello?" Max calls.

"This is James; I am ready to come up."

"Let me buzz you in."

The buzzer rings and the doors clicks open. James walks to the elevator. His heart is racing. He is aroused. He can't wait to get his sweet Madeline back to his house. It has been too long.

Max is waiting by an open door. James walks faster. Today, he is dressed in fine suit. No cape. He walks briskly, a wide smile across his face. He extends his hand.

"Wonderful young man, you have made my day. I have a little extra for you because of the quickness of the job."

Max puts on the perfect façade. "Thank you so much! Are you sure?"

James reaches into his jacket and pulls out another large wad of bills, handing it over without hesitation.

"Here is another $5,000. Well earned."

James' smile drops like a landslide. His nostrils are hit with lavender and expensive tobacco. He grows pale. Max closes the door and stands in front of it, locking it.

James turns around slowly, shaking now.

Madeline glides into the living room. Her perfect form is exquisite in that dress. James is breathless.

"Madeline… I did this for you," James says shakily.

"Hi, baby." Madeline walks close to him. Her warm eyes lock into his. "I have been waiting for you."

Max waits by the front door. He makes no movements, and says nothing.

"I always knew my time would come. I only hoped to be with you longer." James starts to tear up. His voice is becoming more and more weak.

"I'm sorry, baby. It's not meant to be." She reaches to him and touches her hand against his cheek.

James melts under her touch, filled with ecstasy. He desperately wants to be alone with her, to relive the moments of passion that he has been waiting for. He would have never have given her up. She was stolen by another collector.

He accepts his fate, and her kiss. Max watches as a glowing light grows brighter and brighter in the room. He is blinded by it.

Moments later, there is a thud. James' lifeless body is shriveled, drained of all liquid and tissue. He appears to be mummified, flopped in the middle of the living room. Max quickly closes the front door.

She strips off his fine suit. His skin is dark brown. It looks like leather. Effortlessly, she picks up the body. It is stiff, like it's been that way for hundreds of years. Perfectly mummified.

She sets it in the corner, with some other random bones and stuffed creatures. Oddly, it looks like it should be a part of the collection. Before Max can process all of the information, before he can realize the horror, Madeline is in front of him.

Her dress drops, her perfect body alabaster and soft. She grabs his hand, and places his palm on her breast, pushing his hand against it, then slowly drags his hand down. She bites her lip and smiles. She kisses him.

He has a moment of clarity. He knows that someday he will share James' demise. In that moment, he accepts his fate.

"Baby, I love you. We will be together forever," she coos.

Max is breathless. "Sweet Madeline."

Coffee Mate

BY KEN GOLDMAN

"Well, isn't this a hoot?" Audrey said to no one in particular among the secretarial pool. "It was here the whole time, and there's still some coffee in it. I thought something in this desk smelled a little ripe."

She pulled out the massive desk drawer where the familiar yellow ceramic coffee mug had been tucked away and forgotten in a hidden far corner for the better part of the last month. Reaching deep inside the drawer she held up the lopsided cup to show Roberta, who sat at the desk alongside hers. Its handle had been placed way too high and the rim was more oval than round, but Audrey pressed the ugly little hand-made ceramic close to her as if she were holding the Holy Grail.

"I must've stashed this in the back of the drawer when old man Coughlin made that surprise visit to the fifteenth floor. After that lecture the old fart gave last Christmas about coffee breaks on company time, I remember thinking maybe I'd better also ditch the diet creamers I keep in my purse when–"

"That's real good, Audrey, real good. I'm happy for you," Roberta interrupted without looking up from her keyboard and without missing one chomp on her Chicklet. A single well-timed snap of her gum conveyed the immediate impression that somehow her world had continued along nicely despite the disappearance of Audrey's coffee mug.

"My kid made this in school, back when she was in first grade. This mug's the first thing she ever made herself. Must be over five years ago, now," Audrey continued, not particularly concerned that her expressions of maternal pride did not have the most attentive audience in Roberta. She seemed to be speaking more to herself anyway. "Guess you can't stop kids from growing up, but there's something so damned sad about it. Right here, it says 'I

Love My Mom, From Barbra'. She's at that age where she'd be too embarrassed to say that to me now, especially when she's been living with Frank since the divorce. I was so afraid I'd lost this, 'cause the kid worked so hard on–"

Inside the cup something went splunk!

Audrey gasped.

For only a moment she saw a ripple in the dark sludge that had congealed on the bottom of the cup. The murky liquid heaved and swelled like a tiny breaker, then settled back into an inert brownish puddle of glop. Maybe some kind of vermin was in there, and Audrey hated those leggy suckers with all the passion of a woman without a man around the house to squash them.

But unless the little cootie in the cup had brought his snorkel, how could any bug have survived after doing the backstroke for days in a pool of thick congealed java? Still, Audrey could have sworn that she had seen something slogging around in there under that dark gunk that no longer could properly be called coffee.

Audrey slid the mug away from her, then looked over her shoulder to see if she had attracted an audience. This kind of fear was not very fashionable among working women of the New Millennium.

Like most of the secretarial pool, Audrey knew that going eyeball to eyeball with a computer monitor all afternoon could do some pretty bizarro things to one's visual perceptions. A moment later when she looked again at the liquid the sticky goop had gone to ebb tide. She picked up the mug and placed it carefully on the desk blotter of the desktop next to hers, keeping her eyes fixed on it as she spoke.

"'Berta, would you take a look at this for a minute?"

"No, thanks," the woman answered still typing. "Got my own coffee right here, the brand that's supposed to make me remember getting laid in Paris."

"'Berta, please ..."

Roberta looked up from her keyboard and managed a weak smile of resignation. "Fine. Sure. What else have I got to do but these three weeks' worth of pay schedules?" She picked up the mug and perused it top to bottom as if for a full ten seconds she were poring over the last remaining copy of the Dead Sea Scrolls.

Her deep concentration on the mug shorted out as quickly as if someone had clicked a cut-off switch.

"Yeah, that's real cute the way your kid spells her name like Streisand, Audrey. But now if you'll excuse me, I've got–"

"No, Roberta. I mean look inside the cup. Tell me what you see on the bottom, there in the coffee. I have this thing about bugs, and–"

"Right," the woman replied, as if she knew that any questions she might ask at this point would only take up more time. Roberta pulled out her tinted glasses from her drawer, and holding them to her nose still folded she dutifully studied the cup's insides. She tipped the mug to the right and to the left close to her eyes, allowing the dark gunk inside to swish lazily around. Holding it to the light she looked at the mug's underside. She hesitated a moment before she spoke as if going for some sort of dramatic effect.

"Audrey, all I see in here is a picture of Pebbles Flintstone. Of course I'm only guessing, but I don't think this is as important a discovery as digging up a ceramic Virgin Mary that both bleeds and pees. But I'll put in a call to People Magazine later just in case."

She returned the mug to Audrey's desk. "Look, hon, I'm really sorry to put it to you like this, but I'm too busy to admire your daughter's artwork right now, and I'd like to make it out of here by five. I've got kids at home too, y'know? You might want to wash that thing out, though. Smells kind of gamey with all that sour milk in it, don't you think? Unless, of course, you take your coffee with cream and maggots."

Roberta's tone suggested that maybe she should consider taking up smoking again. The woman had twin teenaged sons who were currently being bulldozed by their raging hormones, so that could explain her recent temperamental meltdowns.

Audrey managed a weak smile, but it was even less convincing than Roberta's and vanished faster. Nothing inside her daughter's mug was going to capture an audience around here. The roach patrol responsibilities fell clearly on her shoulders.

There probably wasn't anything with legs inside that cup, Audrey told herself. Most likely all she had seen was a little coffee with some congealed cream pushing itself to the surface, some of which had gone to mold after being hidden in her desk drawer for over a month. Her imagination had just provided her with a quick mind video, like the floaters she sometimes saw after staring into her IBM monitor for several hours. Or maybe her eyes were simply adjusting to her new contacts. It didn't really matter, because there was nothing inside that cup that she could not rinse out right now in the ladies room with some hot running water. And if her eyes were getting a little fuzzy on her, there was not a secretary on the planet who did not know how to fix that problem.

All she really needed was a nice hot cup of coffee in her favorite mug.

* * *

Audrey turned the hot sink water on full force, and most of what liquid sludge remained inside the mug washed down the drain. She had not discovered any quadrupeds doing their laps, and that much was a relief. But a stubborn wad of green mold had remained on the bottom of the cup, and the mushy stuff had not budged despite the force of the water she had aimed at it.

The hot water had released an odd stench from the cup more noticeable than before, and not even the lye inside the near-by toilet bowls was a match for it. The rancid pungency made Audrey wince. It reminded her of warmed over after-birth, and that was not a bouquet likely to go over big with the gang doing the paperwork of Coughlin Industries, Inc.

Maybe the mug would have to be retired, but Audrey had no intention of tossing it into the company dumpster. She pulled out a small bottle of Obsession from her purse and sprayed it into the cup. The result was not exactly a fragrance that would have made Calvin Klein proud, but it seemed to work.

Again she tried scooping into the gelatinous matter with her coffee spoon, but the residue had practically embedded itself into the ceramic. The mucous-like substance clung to the bottom of the mug gathered in a lumpy pile maybe half an inch thick. Although soft and malleable, the stuff was as rigid as if it were glued there, clinging to the cup like some sort of sea muscle. After another five minutes spent poking and scooping at it with the spoon Audrey considered just giving up and spending the next few months watching the mold grow inside her kid's mug like a Chia pet, but the idea of keeping a fungus terrarium inside her desk did not sit well with her. If only she could just loosen up the stuff a little ...

Reaching into her purse Audrey found a book of matches, struck one, and dropped it into the mug. For a moment the mold ignited with a sudden *Poof!* and she backed off.

"I'm switching to tea," she muttered, running her fingers through her hair.

When she again looked inside the cup her eyes went wide. The pile of green stuff shifted suddenly to the opposite side. The wad of fungus seemed to contain something within it that punched and beat against the gummy surface once the lit match had scorched it. Moving like a body in a burlap bag the small lumpy sac of mucous bounced off the sides of the mug, spewing coffee-colored liquid as if an artery had been severed. The match fizzed out. A moment later the sticky pouch bubbled as if percolating in the murky liquid inside the cup.

The mold's soft pulpy surface puffed in and out, perhaps kicked and pummeled from within it. Something inside that teaspoonful of larva-like goo was trying to tear its way out.

Audrey's first impulse was to shag ass, leaving her body's fleeing imprint splintered through the rest room door like a character in one of those Daffy Duck cartoons. But a stronger force worked on her, something almost primitive that was more than curiosity and twice as powerful.

Through the energy of whatever chromosome conspired to create her as a woman, Audrey watched the coffee cup drama unfold, drawn to it by a power that was so much a part of her that she did not question it. Only once had she seen anything even remotely similar to this curious event, but one time was enough to know.

"Isn't that a hoot?" she whispered to herself. The words felt ludicrously inadequate.

The strange living thing inside the sac shrieked in the painful throes of the agony of its own birth. With complete understanding of what she was witnessing Audrey could not tear her eyes from watching its life begin.

The decaying glob of mucous separated as if pushed apart from within, and a tiny figure no larger than a kid's pinkie finger emerged from the ooze collected on the bottom. The hatchling looked like a skinny miniature gingerbread man dipped in pink icing, a bizarre crossbreed between a finger puppet and Gumby.

Frightened, it cringed in the corner of the mug with eyes that seemed sewn shut, turning its head about and flailing reed-thin arms blindly, trying to explore its new world. The tiny hands of the pink thing rubbed eyes that had not yet seen light. Unaware of Audrey, yet completely aware of its own solitude, it cowered in the sludge collected at the bottom of the coffee mug, squeaking cries so high-pitched that they were practically inaudible.

Audrey placed her ear against the rim of the mug to make the sounds out. The faint shrieks cut off and began anew every few seconds, But there was no mistaking the sounds it made. The thing inside the mug was crying for a mother it did not have.

When Audrey finally spoke, the words surprised her as if someone else had spoken them.

"Don't be afraid," she said, and the words seemed to come from some place independent of her brain. Having said them she felt uncertain whether she were addressing the thing inside the coffee mug or herself, but it was difficult to feel terror toward a creature that was so small and so terrified itself.

Inside the cup the small fleshy thing froze. Sensing that it was not alone it awkwardly tried to shimmy up the side of the mug. But the sides were too high and slippery, and the creature fell painfully to the bottom, splashing in the brown liquid and shrieking like a captured bird.

Its wails sent shock waves of memory through Audrey's brain. She had almost forgotten the intensity of the feelings that had once felt so familiar...

Barbra had once cried like that! On the day her daughter was born, Audrey had been handed the infant wrapped in a soft pink blanket. Frank had said simply, "this is your daughter, sweetheart," but his words were unnecessary for both mother and child. When Audrey held the infant girl close to her heart for the first time she had whispered to her "Don't cry, baby," and the child's shrieks stopped cold. The little girl somehow knew in whose arms she belonged.

But this creature, this tiny slab of pink flesh whose life began inside her daughter's coffee mug, this inexplicable violation of nature, was an orphan. Audrey rummaged through her purse for the small creamer pack and punched a tiny hole through the bottom with a safety pin, squeezing the plastic until a tiny bubble of thick creamer squirted through the puncture. She held it pinched between her thumb and forefinger just above the head of the quivering thing inside the cup.

For an instant the small creature stopped shaking, as if instinctively recognizing the milk that had given it life. Two tiny hands reached up for the container, and the little pink mouth hungrily sought the small pinprick hole.

This was shaping up to be one hell of an off-the-wall coffee break. Audrey could not help but smile as she watched the little creature drink. Something warm filled her insides, and it felt good. The tiny hands struggled to reach hers, as if seeking warmth from her as it drank. Its touch felt as soft as the petal of a small flower, and Audrey did not pull her hand away. Instead, she leaned forward and whispered into the ugly little coffee mug.

"Don't cry, baby," she said.

Audrey gently picked up the mug and pressed it close to her heart.

The crying stopped. It was 2:43 p.m.

At 2:46 p.m. in the accounting department on the 5th floor Cheryl Canfield set down her cup of Jamaican pure-blend mocha flavored coffee alongside the IBM keyboard and spent the next three minutes staring at the dark liquid inside the cup.

She could have sworn that she saw something move in it...

Moment

BY NICHOLAS CONLEY

Chase Bochner sped down the empty miles of the New Mexico desert in his SUV. Wind raced in from the open windows, throwing his long black hair behind his large, bulbous head. He was a man on a mission. Trying to reach Area 51 was a fool's errand, but he felt like it was his destiny.

The Day I Tried to Live blared from the radio. Chase started mouthing out the words in recognition but stopped himself; he needed to concentrate on the task at hand. He was a man so obsessed with conspiracy theories that even other fringe theorists like Jackson Ubel, his rival at the local bar, would sometimes shake their heads in disbelief. Chase was certain that if he could make it to Area 51, he'd be a legend.

The SUV started rattling around a bit as it reached 70 miles per hour. 85. 95. Road signs disappeared behind him.

"One more time again…" Chase sung along.

The road continued and Chase began to feel like a man searching for water in the Sahara Desert. Weariness was setting in. He turned up the music as far as it could go. It still wasn't loud enough; he carefully reached past his obese stomach to fiddle with the bass.

As all of this went down, a long shadow stretched across the road. Chase looked up only at the last second. Suddenly, all thoughts of conspiracies, aliens, Area 51 or the radio disappeared instantly.

A tall, thin man stood directly on the road ahead of him.

Chase slammed on his brakes only to realize that they had gone out; his mind swam in horrified memories of his mechanic telling him that "Your brakes is wooooorn out, boy, get them things fixed, fast," and he mentally negotiated the many ways that he could have prevented this scenario. For the first time in his 26 years of existence, Chase Bochner was living out the worst nightmare of all drivers: losing complete control of the car.

Chase jerked the steering wheel all the way to the left. The SUV swerved…but not enough. It was going to hit him.

Then, the figure lifted up a hand and with that motion, it was as if time froze at his command.

It was as if all of space and existence itself bended to the authority of the hand. The SUV's tires screeched off the road and it was flung into the air like it was on a wave.

Time suddenly sped up again. The SUV smashed into the ground. Its metal body crunched together like a balled up piece of tinfoil. Since he was a kid, Chase hadn't so much neglected to wear a seatbelt as he had refused to wear one out of sheer stubbornness; as he was thrown through the front windshield, shattering it to pieces, this was another decision he regretted.

His round body crashed onto the distinctive red dirt of the southwestern desert. He was covered in blood and his bones were shattered, but he was still conscious. With a strain, he turned to look at the person in the road who he deemed partly responsible for this wreck.

Then, he realized that the person wasn't human. It was… no, it couldn't be–could it?

Standing in the road was a naked creature that could only be described as some kind of hybrid between man and reptile. Its scaly skin was greenish-white, as if it had been dipped in powder. Its long arms, which had a row of spines spread down each, stretched out to below its knees and ended in sharp white claws. It eerily turned its round head to look back at Chase, revealing a bizarrely elongated face and golden, snake-like eyes that caused Chase's cut-up fingers to twitch in discomfort.

It was the very image of what famous conspiracy theorist David Icke would've described as a "reptilian," or a "reptoid." Reptilians were Icke's brainchild and a symbol to conspiracy theorists everywhere. Many theorized that the reptilians were our overlords from the fourth dimension, the ones who secretly control the direction of the human race through their mastery of time-travel. Chase's heart was beating like a hummingbird, but he tried to calm himself down. Maybe it was a reptilian, but maybe he was jumping to conclusions.

"You are correct," a slimy, foreign voice said in the back of his mind, "But do not believe everything that you've heard about us."

Chase stirred. Was he hallucinating? The dirt underneath his body was moving. It was carrying him.

"W-what?" he groaned.

"You are not imagining this, Chase Bochner. This is reality," the same voice echoed.

The reptilian's golden eyes were now glimmering. The red dirt spiraled into the air. Chase, who'd been chain smoking in the last year since his life had fallen apart, coughed ferociously as the dirt flew down his throat, up his nostrils and into his eyes. The spinning dirt obscured the world around him and pulled him in.

It was a vortex.

"Welcome to the fourth dimension," the reptilian whispered.

Chase shook his head in disbelief. He suddenly realized that he was standing in a black room, with various purple orbs floating around like bubbles. His injuries were fully healed, as if they'd never existed. If he hadn't just been in a car wreck, seen a reptilian and been thrown into a dirt vortex, this would've disoriented him.

Well, okay, maybe it still disoriented him a little bit.

He took a deep breath. His lungs felt crisp, like they were covered in frosty crystals. He tried to touch one of the purple orbs but it darted away from him. Chase jumped back, losing his balance in the process and collapsing onto the ground.

He cursed his own weight as he struggled to pick himself up. Only a year ago it hadn't been like this; he would've been lucky to have pushed 140 back then.

Once he finally got back on his feet, he was greeted by an ominous presence. A group of reptilians had circled around him.

"You are among us now," all of the identical creatures spoke in unison, "Why are you among us?"

"Why? Well, I… I don't know why, I guess I… I… I–"

"He stutters," one reptilian spoke separately, causing its eyes to flicker black. It held its tongue on the letter 's,' producing a slithering sound.

"Yes, he appears to be very uncomfortable," all of them spoke together again.

"Of course I am!" Chase replied, "You things are… you're reptilians! Or reptoids, or whatever you call yourselves, from the fourth dimension!"

"I suppose they might phrase it that way," one reptilian mused. Another stepped forward.

"How do you know who we are, Chase Bochner? What do you know of us?"

"Heh, well, I'm a conspiracy theorist," Chase replied, "You things use the fourth dimension to travel through time, to control and monitor every point in history, right? Right?"

There was no immediate response. The reptilians gazed at him with their unblinking eyes. The purple orbs weaved between them. Finally, they spoke simultaneously again.

"What exactly is this 'time,' this 'history' that you speak of?"

"It's, well…" Chase said hesitantly, "it's the way that things move forward. How one moment leads to the next, how for us humans we can never go back or stay static. We're always moving forward, flowing to the next moment."

"Is that so? How could it be so? You do not exist in this moment. You exist in others, now and then."

"No, no, see, I existed in others before but–"

Chase felt a lump rise in his throat and was unable to speak. He began to gag and black out. The red dirt spiraled around him again.

The dark room with the reptilians was gone, but its replacement was even more bizarre. Chase almost fainted in shock as the familiar smell of his mother's fresh doughnuts greeted his nostrils.

He was sitting in her kitchen, in the same house he'd grown up in. He was six years old again.

His brain felt as if it'd been stretched beyond its limits. Chase leapt off the chair and was surprised to discover that the table was taller than he was. He turned back around. His six-year-old self was still sitting in place, holding a scrunched up napkin. His mother walked over with a big grin and set down a tray of fresh doughnuts.

Chase looked down at his body to make sure he was still there. He was. A cluster of those eerie purple orbs started to float around him.

"So this is what you call the *past*, correct?" the reptilians asked.

Chase turned around to face them.

"Yeah, exactly like this. At one point I was here, but not anymore. I moved on. Time moves in one direction for us, a straight, linear progression. It never stops, never goes back. It's just that you guys can go to any point along that progression."

"You are very convinced of this," the reptilians said, more as a statement than a question.

The childhood scene faded away. Chase and the reptilians returned to the dark, empty room. Again, Chase was an overweight, 26-year-old man.

"Yes, because that's how it works!" he said.

Chase's throat swelled up again and he was teleported back to the driver's seat of his SUV, through the New Mexico desert as he had been an hour ago. *The Day I Tried to Live* blasted from the radio. This time, one of the reptilians was riding shotgun, staring at him intensely. No matter how many times he looked into those golden eyes, they never ceased to make him uneasy. There was nothing human about them.

"So, you were here," the reptilian stated.

"Yep. Just an hour ago I was right here, driving through New Mexico until I almost wrecked into one of you guys. You see what I mean, now?"

"No," the reptilian answered, "You are incorrect. Time is not linear. Not for us, not for you."

"How do you not understand this?" Chase asked, noticing that the purple orbs were now splashing against the windshield like giant drops of rain, "I was here, then. I was a kid before. Now I'm here with you guys, jumping through time."

"When you were here, you were not here. You were somewhere else. You existed here only in the simplest of ways."

"What?"

Chase's throat felt as if it was about to burst and he closed his eyes in an uneasy mixture of anticipation and dread. The scene around him changed again.

"Chase, it's just that… it's not you, don't ever believe it's you, it's nothing you did wrong," Hannah's voice said quietly, "This relationship… it isn't working…"

Chase felt as if he'd been hit across the face with a brick. He hesitated before opening his eyes. He had returned to the one scene he dreaded seeing the most.

Chase was lying in Hannah's bedroom, cradled in her arms, one year ago. They were wrapped around each other. Her eyes were flooded with tears, staring at him mournfully. Her mouth twitched, hesitating to speak the words that she felt she had to say.

"Chase, can you please understand? I loved you, I loved you so much but I don't… I don't…"

"No!" he cried out, rising from the bed, "No, no, no! Get me out of here!"

A reptilian cocked its head to the left, watching the scene with a studious expression.

"Why? You are here now," it slithered.

Chase looked back to see himself and Hannah lying on the bed together, seconds before the breakup. Back then he had been skinny. His hair was long, but not greasy as it was now. It was like looking at a different person. He shook his head and turned away.

He teleported back to the black room. Chase wiped the sweat from his brow. The circle of reptilians around him were closer than before.

"You were there then," they slithered, "You are here now. That is what you are trying to suggest. But it seems that then, while you were there, you were also here in this scene…"

"Wha–," Chase stopped, as his throat closed up again.

He was in a field, on a rainy afternoon. He and Hannah were embraced in a passionate kiss, rolling around in the mud together laughing. Her hands grasped onto his back tightly, taking hold of the moment and making it theirs.

"I love you!" she cried out with a giant grin, "That's right, world, I love this man! I love Chase Bochner!"

"Shh," his past self whispered into her ear, "It's a secret–but I love you too."

The touch of her lips was everything he had wanted in the last year, but at the same time, too much to handle. He pulled away. It was easier to watch his younger self roll around in the rain with the love of his life than it was to relive it, knowing what the future held in store for them.

"I would've given anything to stay in that moment forever," he sighed.

"But you didn't. You progressed from it."

"Yes," Chase said, his eyes brightening, "You get it now! Time moves in a linear–"

"No. You progressed, but in that previous moment you existed in this one as well. Then, at *this* moment…"

"What?"

They were back in her bedroom, back to the scene of the breakup. He turned away. He couldn't stand to even look at it.

"It's not you, don't ever believe it's you," Hannah said.

Chase put his head down; "But…"

"You existed at this moment and that moment, while this one went on," the reptilians said, "Then, when you were here…"

Chase's throat only felt a mild twinge this time. Now, he was sitting at his computer, typing an editorial about Area 51. It was six months ago. His hands reached out next to the computer, to grasp onto a dusty photo of him and Hannah at the park.

"Here," a reptilian said, snaking up from behind the computer chair, "You existed here, at this time, while at the same time you also existed in the previous scene, the 'breakup,' as you call it. Simultaneous, mutual, symbiotic…"

"No, it's linear. In the past times we've gone to, the oldest memory was the one of me as a kid. After that, there was the time me and Hannah were rolling around in the rain. Then, the breakup. Later on, this here, of me on the computer. Finally, there was me driving the SUV in New Mexico. In that order. How does this not make sense?"

The reptilians were silent for a moment. Their golden eyes were piercing, thoughtful.

"What?" he asked.

"During 'the breakup,' you also were on the field. You also were in the oldest memory of your childhood. However, during both of those last two points in time, you were concurrently experiencing the breakup."

The time shift happened again, this time to a memory of him lying in bed, shaking. This had only been a few months ago. He was big, greasy, twitching: a broken man who was struggling to find a purpose. He remembered it all too well.

They continued their hissing monologue; "You were here, just as you were there."

"Yes, in a memory, but…"

Chase was transported back to the breakup scene before he could finish. He and Hannah were in bed, holding each other for the last time. Now, she was finally letting go of him. He rose from the bed solemnly.

"Time is not linear," said the reptilians, "You are pulled forward, to continue in one direction but you, Chase Bochner, go against that. No matter how much time changes, this moment is frozen. You exist in this moment, at all times."

"Yes," Chase sighed.

He put his head down, crumpled up in a ball and watched his old self walk out Hannah's door forever. In reality, he had never turned back to look at her. This time, though, he had the chance to do just that. As it turned out, her features were painted with a look of regret. She almost called out his name…then stopped.

A tear slid down his face. The realization of it all had finally come to him.

"I exist in that single moment," he stated.

"Yes."

Hannah's bedroom melted away and Chase was brought back to the black room. Every pound of his body felt a thousand times heavier than it had before. His eyes followed the purple orbs.

"So how is time linear, then?" the reptilians asked mockingly.

"It… it isn't."

He sat down on the floor, head buried in his hands. His palms became flooded with tears. He breathed deeply, in and out, until his chest relaxed.

Then, Chase stood up.

He reached out, grabbed one of the orbs and squeezed it. He walked up to one of the reptilians and stared straight into its menacing golden eyes.

"It isn't, for me, because I've chosen to exist in a single moment. I've chosen to dwell on it, to let it control me. I've let it turn me into the overweight, depressed guy I am today, just to get away from that moment. But time is linear. Time *will* be linear if I allow it to be."

"So," a reptilian said, "you are going to change the flow of time. You're going to control it, as we do."

"Yes, to the best of my ability. I'm going to control it for myself. I'm going to make it flow in the right direction. That moment's in the past and I'm… I'm going to leave it there."

The purple orb vanished from his hand and all the others followed suit. The reptilians all stepped into the dark. They were fading away.

"We will always be there, even if you don't see us," they whispered from the darkness.

As the reptilians faded, so did the scene they had created. The aroma of the desert eased its way back into his nose. He slowly fell onto the ground.

"I'll remember that," Chase answered.

His throat filled up again. This time, it was with a mixture of blood, dirt and phlegm. Chase coughed it out and realized that he was once again sprawled out on the side of the emptiest stretch of road in New Mexico. His bones were broken, his muscles torn and his SUV lay several yards away from him, crumpled up like a crushed tin can.

But as luck would have it, he could hear an emergency vehicle in the distance. Things were going to be okay. Soon, very soon, that vehicle would arrive and would drive Chase to the hospital. It would only be a few minutes now.

With that thought in mind, Chase Bochner finally moved forward in time, ready to see what the future had to offer.

Contents of a Canvas Bag

BY ROBERT ESSIG

It was behind the thrift store that I found the bag of goodies, old things from the life of an old person, probably someone who recently passed on, their life rifled through by their kin and left in boxes outside the thrift store. What would this person think about a complete stranger rummaging through their possessions? They probably wouldn't like it very much–especially the contents of the canvas bag, the one I took home with me.

Why not? I said to myself–the contents would have either been taken by some other passerby or picked up in the morning by the thrift store workers and sold.

I decided then and there, standing in the dark alley amazed at the treasure I had found, that the possessions were no longer personal.

I took the bag under that conviction.

* * *

As I sat under the looming glow of the lamp above my pool table, gleefully arranging the bag's contents over the green felt, I began to understand just how important my find really was, just how irreplaceable the items were.

Had I not been driving through the alley after a fine Mexican meal, I would have never known the opportunity I would have lost, and I am certain that the antiques would have never seen the florescent lighting of the store's interior, but would no doubt have been stolen by the employees.

I hadn't wanted Mexican food initially. I was more in the mood for a hamburger and fries, but for want of atmosphere I went to the Hacienda. Now I think it was fate.

As I drove down the alley, I caught a glimpse of something shining from amid a litter of black bags and clothes. I thought it was a street person's makeshift shelter at first, but the distracting glare of the shining object nearly caused me to run my car into a dumpster.

I stopped, I looked–it gleamed.

It called.

Of all the bags, it was the only one made of canvas, the only one with antiques, and the only one I brought home with me. Not wanting to be seen looking like a dumpster-diver, I took a brief look in the bag–unsure of what it was that caught my attention–put it in the seat next to me, and drove home.

I thought about the sequence of events as I hovered over the bag's entrails on the pool table. I thought about the Mexican food (I could still taste it on my lips), and the alley, and fate. I also thought about the great gleaming that lured me to the canvas bag.

I looked over everything and, curiously, I could find no object that had the least bit of luster. There was a brass figure that was tarnished beyond any possibility of a shine and some ancient looking silver that was in much the same condition. Nothing else in the lot could ever have shone.

I decided that it didn't matter. I now realize that gleaming light was a pawn in fate's lurid game and, as in chess, I would find out that there are players beyond the wall of pawns–stronger players that could do amounts of damage pawns could only dream of. The pawns were merely the messengers. Perhaps that gleaming messenger fell out of the canvas bag as I loaded it into my car.

It was a strange lot, there was no doubt about that. There were woodcarvings that looked like absurd totem poles: skull carved atop demon, carved atop monster. There was a series of odd masks–one I thought may have really been fashioned from a human skull. And then there was something of a deep personal intoxicant, a leather satchel that contained four 78-rpm records. As a collector of old records, I found this to be the highlight of the treasure. There were other items, knives carved of wood and stone and even ancient coins, but the records drew my attention away from everything else.

The records were black and without labels. I was hoping that they might have been of Thomas Edison's first recordings, as far-fetched as that would be, but my assumption is that those records are in a museum somewhere. Each side of each record was marked near the center with a scratched roman numeral, I - VIII, which distressed me some.

I pondered this. Even a date would be something to work with. I decided that there was no better way to understand the records than to play them. That is when things became quite strange.

* * *

I placed the record with the Roman numeral I on the turntable and flicked the RPM switch to 78. The record lay there waiting to be played, the scratches calling to me like open wounds, all with a tale to tell. I wondered how many people had played the record, or was it always in hiding, becoming scratched from people moving it rather than listening to it?

Who could tell? The scratches perhaps.

I lifted the needle and gently rested it on the outer lip of the record, and as I pulled my hand away the needle was rejected. It fell from the edge of the record, making an awful scratching *plop*. I lifted it and tried again as before with the same result, and then again with the same result, cursing the record for wanting to break the needle.

I decided to place the needle carefully in the middle of the record.

It played, but something was wrong. As it played a strange cacophony the needle was gliding outward instead of toward the center. I have never seen such a thing. I thought it was impossible, but the groves in the wax were backwards and that was why the needle kept falling off the edge of the record.

I wasn't impressed with what I heard: time and wear might have done their damage to the antique. I decided to place the needle in the center and start from the beginning.

There was a thumping, like a drum pounding in a heartbeat rhythm, and a swishing fluid sound like water in pipes. The beating became louder and more intense, increasingly like a human heart.

I noticed that my own heart was beating in unison with the record, and my body began to feel a rush of adrenalin as my breathing became heavy. It felt as though my heart was trying to jump out of my rib cage, as if it wanted very much to escape me and frolic with the nonsensical sounds of the recording.

Both the recording and my own heartbeat throbbed in my head, eliminating everything around me. I could hear nothing but a primal beating and the swishing of liquid, thicker than water: perhaps the blood rushing through my veins. The adrenalin was shaking my nerves and quivering my body like a narcotic.

The sounds were louder than anything I have ever heard, causing a feeling of drowning in a mental sea of noise. Realizing I was holding my eyes closed hard enough to cause a headache, I opened them.

There was nothing... and everything.

The strange sounds were more tolerable now, and all consuming. The beating in synch with my heart's beating felt like heaven–or what one would imagine heaven to feel like. I floated in this amniotic state and felt warmth I never knew existed. I have never been in a sauna, but I have to assume that's what it feels like.

My eyes were closed again. I opened them, finding myself in a dark chamber, the hues red and orange with deep shadows. I felt a spasm of fear, replaced with the soft vibrations of a violin calming me, sedating me.

I realized then that the music was absolutely amazing. Where I was I did not know, and I did not care. I felt something that could never be replicated, something I know now was never *intended* to be replicated.

How long I floated there in that chamber of darkness, like an astronaut in deep space, I do not know. I kept my eyes closed. Opening them seemed to trigger slight panic, slight claustrophobia. I listened to the violins and the deep bass of the violas, replaced mysteriously with what sounded like flutes and recorders.

I tried to imagine who could have written such beautiful music, but was too distracted to concentrate. It was as if I wasn't allowed to concentrate.

Then there was a pregnant pause. Then the beating, parallel with my pulse, then pain.

* * *

Pain. I now know what the pain was. At the time, I thought I was dying. That thought is laughable now.

That was the end of the first side of the first record, Roman numeral I.

* * *

I flipped the record. After such an excruciating experience, one I can only attempt to explain in these pages, I flipped it and placed the needle in the center. I didn't think twice about it.

The needle hit the record with such a loud *pop* that I felt it in my heart. I was taken away abruptly–where I don't know; probably some lost corner of my subconscious. Even now I'm uncertain where the records were taking me, which makes this writing all the more difficult.

It was an orchard of apples, an orange grove, a field of cherry trees, rows of tomato plants and strawberries and gentle harmonies. The grass was soft and dewy under my bare feet. Though the trees and plants changed all around me, they had one thing in common: they were all in bloom bearing a hearty bounty of fruits and vegetables.

I grabbed a handful of cherries before they transformed into an orange tree. I ate. It seemed so real: the sweetness of the fruit, the pit I bit on, chipping my tooth. (I sit here staring at the record player and feel the crooked landscape of my teeth with my tongue, and indeed there is a rough edge that I chipped on that imagined cherry. That chipped tooth alone may be the reason for writing this.)

I ate. I laughed at nothing and listened to the delicate notes emanating from a record player I could no longer see, a record player that was in a place where I was no longer mentally present.

The imagery was perfect; it was beautiful. The fruit made me feel strong and youthful. How long I was in this state I cannot say, but eventually the music stopped and I was once again a man standing in his billiards room, staring at a silent record player, feeling the pains life had left him with.

It was after the first half of record two that I began to realize what the records meant. Why I was being transgressed into some otherworldly state, I cannot say–I assume I will never know–but

I was beginning to ascertain just what those transgressions symbolized.

As the second record took me to a beautiful beach in the sun of a paradise, the music not so delicate. I swam in the cool waters, I felt good, great, and I couldn't wait for the next record–that is, I couldn't wait to see if what I was pondering about these mystical records was so.

The second side of the second record, Roman numeral IV, seemed to come and go like a feather in a dust storm. It was wholly relaxing as I lay in the sun, listening to the music mingle with the sounds of gulls and waves crashing on the beach.

As I look at my flesh now, it is tanned. That's one for the record books: a man who actually got a tan in his billiards room. It is true, and once again I have no explanation–at least nothing based upon facts.

* * *

I understood only seconds after placing the needle on the first side of record three. I understood that fall always follows summer, as summer follows spring, and though the music was certainly not Vivaldi, I was listening to and experiencing the four seasons.

As I listened to the music, not quite as intense or as happy as the last record of summer, I watched as the beaches became chill as the leaves of the apple, cherry, and orange trees withered and fell to the ground.

The sky churned angrily, storms wanting to break through the grim darkness, thunder rumbling in the distance and...

...and my bones were beginning to ache.

The quality of the experience was no different from the other records, only I wasn't finding is as pleasurable. Whereas I had previously felt ten or fifteen years younger, I began to feel like myself–and worse. My arthritis was tenfold and I felt generally miserable.

That's when everything became clear to me. How many years have these records been in existence, traveling people through a lifetime in mere hours? How many people have listened?–for I believe that if one listened to the first record they would find it impossible to stop. After that first experience there is no turning back–at least that is my understanding.

How many people?

* * *

As I write this recount of my experience with these strange, mystical records I have but one side left to listen to: Roman numeral VIII, the second half of winter.

The first half was cold and miserable. I felt sick and weak. Why the pull for me to play the last piece to this musical puzzle is so strong, I do not know. If it is what I think it is, then I should do everything in my power to be rid of the records, to destroy them so no one else has to go through what I am going through, experiencing a lifetime in mere hours.

As I wrote about the first record I said that it felt like dying; only now do I realize it was the polar opposite. That first record was spring, and such as spring I experienced being birthed. It was my already-developed brain that thought of the experience as painful and death-like.

The seasons represent the tribulations of life from beginning to end: summer being the healthy peak, only to begin the slow decline with fall, and now... winter, cold and unforgiving.

I have to listen to the final record, I absolutely have to. I cannot explain why, therefore I will conclude this writing. You will find it sitting here on top of the other three records; the last will be on the turntable. As for myself, I may not be here at all, and if I am, no one will have ever seen these writings and I will destroy the records.

I know I will not be here though. As life begins after birth, it always ends in death. This isn't a suicide, nor is this a suicide note, I am merely doing what I have to. At this point it is out of my hands, but whoever you are that finds this writing and these records, I ask you to destroy them. They have a power close to that of God in them, and I think in the wrong hands they could become very dangerous.

This is my farewell as I visit frigid winter.

Daniel Roget
2010

His Blueness

BY BARRY ROSENBERG

Zac was a sculptor. He could have been an engineer and made money. He could have been an architect and made boxes. Instead he was a sculptor and made coffee. He did lunchtimes: eleven till two at *The CaffeInne*. Sometimes, he taught. And sometimes – though that was rare – he sold a sculpture. In other words, he survived. Sometimes he even had a girlfriend. Not many girlfriends, though; few survived just being able to survive.

It was eleven at night and Zac was flossing his teeth. He looked at his reflection and pulled a face. He didn't normally reminisce while cleaning his teeth. So why tonight? Why? Why was this night different from all other nights? Why? Well, that was easy: because tonight, he was turning thirty.

Zac went to bed and drifted into an uneasy sleep. Right on midnight, however, he suddenly awoke. He saw the digits *3-0, 3-0* flash in vivid red before his closed eyes. He heard *thirty, thirty* in his mind's ear. He breathed the numbers in and out, in and out. His mind had gone manic. *You've turned thirty and what have you achieved? Nothing! Niente! Nada!*

Achieved? he argued with himself. *What was that supposed to mean? Achieve what, exactly?*

After a broken night, Zac rose early. It wasn't fair. This was his birthday and his head hurt. He munched morosely on muesli and meditated on what to do. Go to his studio? No, not yet. What then? Well, his sculpture required found objects. Right, so he'd go to the beach and find some.

Zac locked his granny flat and slid into his old Corolla. It wheezed to life and, more on prayer than on petrol, lurched from Nambour to Maroochydore. Under the dawn sky, the sea was slate gray. Only two fishermen were on the sand, seagulls swirling around them. Zac trudged towards the water, his steps squelching out: *thirty, thirty*. Head down, he pretended not to hear.

With a few shells in his hand, Zac clambered onto the rocks and scanned the crevices. A bright glint caught his eye. He squinted. There! There was an object. He held it up. A teapot? Zac turned it over. It looked more like a lamp than a pot. Great! A lamp would fit his sculpture. He'd take it home and clean it. At that thought, the sky seemed to darken. With a shiver, Zac looked upwards. The sky, however, was clear again.

Back home, Zac carefully chiseled off one bit of gunk and then another. After twenty minutes, he had sliced off enough to expose the metal beneath. It was a curious red-blue. When clean, Zac gazed at the pot with excitement. It was a lamp, a true Aladdin's lamp, mostly bronze but with blue streaks. Excited, he felt as light-headed as Superman faced with a load of kryptonite.

Zac chuckled. *May as well have a wish*, he thought, *now I'm thirty*. His began to rub the lamp. The hairs on the back of his neck rose. *Silly*, he snorted. Then he thought, *If not now, when?* He started again. His fingers grew warm. He paused. Or was that the lamp? He rubbed and rubbed. The room grew darker. His ears buzzed. The hairs on his arms stood up.

His ears popped. The room popped. A strange figure appeared!

Zac jumped. "Who… who are you? Where did you come from?"

"Sire," the figure, a man, bowed. "You called and I did but answer. That is the way of the lamp."

"Nah." Zac backed away. "You're… You're having me on. You… you're a sing-a-gram or something."

"Indeed, sire, I sing. But not for a gram. Perhaps forsooth for a ducat."

"What about your funny clothes?"

The man looked down. "But doublet and hose were quite the fashion in my time."

"What time?" Zac snorted. "Look, who the heck are you?"

"Sire, my time was sixteen-sixteen. And as to who I be." The man bowed deeply. "Shakespeare at your service." He slyly glanced upwards. "You have, I doth hope, heard of me."

"Oh, yeah, sure. Shakespeare. Everyone's heard of him." Zac took a good squizzy. This bloke certainly looked the part. "You're… I mean he. He was the most famous writer that ever lived."

The bard stroked his small beard. "That was the arrangement."

"Arrangement?"

"One is granted three wishes, young sire. Though I had no ability to write, I did desire to be famed. I am pleased to see that my genie was successful."

"Your genie?" Zac thought *Walt Disney*. "Big blue smoke of a bloke in a turban?"

"Once, young master, mayhap. But the genie changes when the three wishes are done."

"Oh?" Zac detected a hint of menace in the man's tone. "Why?"

"The wisher goes into the lamp." Shakespeare smiled sadly.

Teetering on belief, Zac asked, "But what if the wisher, that's me, doesn't want to wish?"

"Everyone wishes." Shakespeare again looked sly. "Just to call me is to wish."

"Jeez!" Zac was shaken. "I'll have to think about that."

Shakespeare bowed. "You have till midnight." His face lit up. "But till then, while the magic doth abound/I will give this modern world a round." And the playwright faded.

Zac groaned. The fade-out was pretty convincing, which meant that he was trapped by a genie! Trapped! What could he do? He knew nothing about genies. Nothing. Only what Walt Disney had told him. Hands shaking, he turned to the Internet. Yet hours later, when he began work at the *Caffelnne*, he was hardly any wiser. Zac was now seriously worried. Sure, he wanted three wishes. But to end up in the lamp? No way! He'd have to trick the genie. Lost in thought, he totally forgot that he was thirty. Yet when he arrived home, birthday cards popped out of his letterbox. Tonight was party night.

Tracey, owner of the *Caffelnne*, arrived first with a huge cheesecake.

"Good, excellent," Zac said hollowly.

She also handed him a book of raffle tickets. "Your chance to win a night out with April Summers."

"April Summers?" That got his attention. "Wow! That's fantastic!"

For the moment, Zac's problems fell away. Instead, his mind dwelt on happy thoughts of the beautiful April Summers, the finding of true love, and the haring of hot kisses of wild passion. He was lost in this daydream when the bell rang. It was Shakespeare.

But what a change! Jeans had replaced his tight hose, a white shirt his long tunic, and a leather jacket his cloak.

"G'day, mate," he cried and opened his arms to display his new gear.

Zac backed away. "But I've still got a few hours," he said.

"Of course, of course." Shakespeare tiptoed up to Tracey. "And this lovely lady is?"

Zac waved a hand. "Tracey meet, er, Shakespeare."

"No, no!" The playwright shook his head. "Will, please call me Will."

"Will do." Tracey laughed. "You're not related to the great Shakespeare, are you?"

"Well yes, actually." The bard extended his arm and led her into a corner.

While Shakespeare spun a yarn, and he was probably pretty good at it, Zac's thoughts returned to the raffle. *If I were to win it*, he thought. *If only I were to win it*. Catching Shakespeare's eye, he nodded. The bard winked. Zac caught his breath. It was true! A nod was as good as a wink.

Two weeks later, Zac won the raffle!

A week after that, a limo came to take a very nervous sculptor to *The Top Notch* in Noosa. A gorgeous April Summers waited to greet him. Besides her were… The cameras! Cameras? Yes. Cameras that tracked their every movement! Zac was reduced to a babbling wreck. Did he make jokes? April definitely laughed though that might have been because he put his elbow in the soup. Did he wax philosophical? She certainly looked serious though that might have been because he could only whisper. At the end of the most fantastic meal that Zac had *never* tasted, April pecked him on the cheek. She then waved ever so merrily as the cameras tracked him back to the limo. The whole event was a blur. He arrived home with neither a phone number nor an email. He had achieved nothing. Nothing!

Outraged, Zac picked up the lamp. "I didn't want to just meet her," he shouted. "I wanted to get to know her." He almost rubbed the lamp but didn't. One thing he did remember from the Internet: never trust a genie.

All the same, Zac burned to get even. With the genie. With April. With being thirty. That night, he tossed and turned. Suddenly, an idea came to him. Having tossed and turned his body, he tossed and turned the idea. Yes, it could work. It could. It would. Satisfied, he fell into a deep sleep. In the morning, he sprang out of bed, raced through breakfast and cycled down to his studio. Speedily, he prepared his clay. When ready, he began to build. *April Summers, here I come.* But his sculpture would be more even beauteous. The legs would be longer, the breasts higher, the waist narrower. And her complexion? April Summers, huh! No hairs, however fine, on his great beauty. And he'd put it in a competition. The *Artibalds*, perhaps. Call it: *Hotter than Summer.* She'd know. And she'd be jealous, oh so jealous.

In six days, Zac created woman. And on the seventh day, he didn't rest; now he had to deal with the genie. He wrote and rewrote list after list. He wasn't going to be cheated, not a second time. When satisfied, Zac brought out the lamp. He contemplated his list until he was certain. Then he rubbed. The room darkened. His ears popped. A shape shot out of the spout.

"My troth," Shakespeare began. He corrected himself. "G'day, mate, it's been a while."

"Sit," Zac said, "and listen. I don't want you to cheat me again."

The bard frowned. "It's not me exactly."

"Who is it then?"

Shakespeare made an I-don't-really-know gesture. "His Blueness."

Zac grunted. That answer was as good as nothing. He turned to the matter at hand, his list. "I want to meet a real flesh and blood woman, as beautiful as my April Summers sculpture. And not for just one night. We are totally compatible and live happily together for at least forty years."

"A rare marriage," Shakespeare said dryly. "But it will be done." The bard looked at the clock. "Well, mate, I've got till midnight. So now I shall leave and down some strong ales/To rub my shoulders with the Rude Mechanicals."

"Rude Mechanicals?"

"You'll find them in *Midsummer Night's Dream.*"

"Oh."

With a merry laugh, the bard walked outside. He seemed so normal that Zac almost forgot that this was a blue be-jeaned genie.

Yet when a brand new Harley-Davidson appeared, belief came flooding back. Even so, Zac didn't expect his wish to be fulfilled before midnight. Nor was it. The next afternoon, though, he went to the beach. Here, if anywhere, he expected to meet a bikini-clad beauty. But he didn't. He only managed a sunburn.

Disappointed, Zac drove to *KilnWorks*. As he placed his order for clay, another person entered. Zac turned. And gasped. He turned and gasped. Here was a young woman of stunning beauty, of long legs and high breasts. She was his sculpture made real. Their eyes met. Unable to stop himself, Zac stuck out his hand.

"I'm Zac." He bowed. "Sculptor extraordinaire at your service."

"I'm June." Their fingers met in a burst of electricity. "June Springsong, painter."

"June Springsong. What a fantastic name." Zac was ecstatic. "Are you free? Would you like a coffee?"

"I'm free and coffee would be terrific."

Hands bumping, they began to walk out. "Hey!" Behind them, a bag hit the counter. "Hey, Zac, don't forget your clay."

But they didn't hear. They ordered coffee but scarcely noticed it. The other was all. Eventually, Zac jumped up. "I've got to show you something. Follow in your car."

Zac drove to his studio. There, with a flourish, he presented his sculpture.

June gasped. "It's me! It looks just like me."

"Better than April Summers," Zac said with satisfaction.

"A premonition." June squeezed his hand. Then her eyes widened. "April Summers? How do you know April Summers? She's such a celebrity."

"How?" Zac looked uncertain. "I won a raffle."

He lightly touched the sculpture, wondering if he should mention the genie. But that sounded so crazy that he didn't. Madly in love, he put the threat aside. So it was not long before June, ceramic painter and waitress, moved in with Zac, sculptor and coffee maker. They were poor but happy. Deliriously happy, the kind of happiness that quickly bore fruit. One afternoon, June returned home and did a merry little dance.

"I'm pregnant," she announced.

"Preggas!" Zac joyfully embraced her. Their happiness was supreme.

That night, they broke the bank and went to *The Top Notch*. On the second course, Zac snapped his fingers. "This is where I met April Summers."

"By accident?"

"No, I came to meet her." Zac pulled at his collar. He was going to risk telling. "A genie made it happen."

"Zac, a genie?"

"Yes, Shakespeare."

"Shakespeare?" June laughed. "C'mon Zac, pull the other one."

Given her reaction, Zac thought it best not to go on and so just forced a laugh. Even to him, it seemed unreal and so for the next few days, they both wafted on clouds of joy. After a while, though, Zac had a realization. As June became bigger, their flat became smaller. He began to think, *If this is what it's like with two, what will it be like with three?* They needed more room. But how could they afford it, especially if June wasn't working? They needed more money - but how to get it? How? Zac racked his brains. He wrecked his brains. When the answer came, it was obvious. The lamp, of course. That was the only way. But did he want to use it? The implications were terrible. But it worried at him, day and night, night and day. He even worried if the idea was his or came from the lamp itself?

June, of course, couldn't help but notice his worry. "Zac," she asked, "why so blue?"

He kissed her. "I'm not blue. Just thinking, that's all."

"About?"

"Well, we really need more room."

June's face grew wistful. "That would be nice, so nice."

Zac's lips became dry. "I told you about the genie."

"The Shakespeare thing? That was a joke, wasn't it?"

"No, I was serious. Look, I'm thinking maybe if I made half a wish. Like, instead of asking for millions, I just ask that we sell more."

"Is this genie an Auntie Jeanie?" June laughed.

"No." Zac sighed.

Though he said no more, the idea of a half wish gripped him. Surely the genie would agree. *Half a wish, half a wish.* It went round and round in his head. He so much wanted to please June that he brought out the hidden lamp. He held it in his palm. *To rub or not to rub?* At that very moment, June entered the flat. She looked so radiant that Zac felt wretched. He indicated the lack of space.

"You deserve a palace," he groaned and impulsively rubbed the lamp.

The light dimmed. The room popped. The genie popped. June screamed.

Shakespeare patted the air down with his hands. "Sorry, sweetie," he said, "my bad." To Zac, he snarled, "Good thing I wasn't holding my breath. About time you called. A palace, was it?"

"No, no, not a palace. Not a big wish. A little wish. A half wish."

"A wish is a wish..."

"But just a half wish."

"… is a wish."

Zac collapsed into a chair. "You mean…?"

"Yes."

"I go into the lamp?"

"Yes."

Zac groaned. "But I specified that we were to spend a long time together."

"You will." A reluctant slyness crossed Shakespeare's face. "You inside, she outside."

"No!" Zac cried.

"No!" June moaned.

"Yes," Shakespeare said.

There was a long heavy silence. Zac broke it. "Well, if a wish is a wish…?"

"Yes?"

"I may as well go for zillions."

"No," June said. "Let's just keep it that our artwork sells."

"Okay." Zac sighed. "My third wish is that we always sell enough to live decently." He blinked. "Oh yes, and that includes petrol." Suddenly though, Zac punched his palm. "Bloody hell, there must be something we can do! Something to beat this! Listen, Shakespeare… William… Will, you've got to help us."

"I've not got to anything."

"Please," June implored.

175

"Ah *please*. Well, that's different."

"Right. So we've got till midnight." Zac touched the lamp. "What's it like in there?"

"Strewth." The bard looked puzzled. "I don't really think about it. But now you ask: it's blue, yes, definitely blue."

"Blue? That's what you said before. Is that all, blue?"

Shakespeare stroked his beard. "Listen, mate, once you're inside, you don't want to be too conscious. Being blue is okay. Right, it's a *light* blue. Better?"

"Right, right, I'm sorry." Zac did some heavy-duty thinking. "Is anyone else in there?"

The bard's gaze turned inwards. "The blue, I guess. You understand the power of the lamp doesn't come from me. It comes from the lamp. From His Blueness, I suppose."

June was looking from one to the other. Her shock had passed. She was a believer. "You were in the sea for a long time. Fishes or seagulls must've rubbed against the lamp. Why didn't you come out?"

"Wow, lady," Shakespeare peered into the spout, "you ask a difficult question." He squinted with one eye. "His Blueness must distinguish somehow. Don't know how."

"Octopuses are pretty intelligent," Zac said. "So it's probably not on intelligence."

"I don't think His Blueness is very intelligent. Once, maybe, not now."

Zac scratched at his hair. "It must be shape, then! That's how people recognize people - through shape." He began to pace, his mind working. "Will, I'm gonna need a bit of muscle. Can you help?"

"Mind my hernia."

Zac ignored him. "I've got a plan. We might just be able to beat His Blueness."

"Oh?" Shakespeare balanced his chin on a finger. "Tell me. Yes… Yes… Yes… That could just about work." He nodded. "It just could."

"It has to" Zac put his palms together in prayer mode. "We've got to beat His Blueness."

"My troth, we do. So let's get to it."

They piled into Zac's Corolla. To his surprise, it started smoothly. He glanced into the rearview mirror. Shakespeare was looking smug. In a few minutes, they arrived at the studio. The bard looked at the sculpture and whistled.

"Kiddo," he declared, "you've got a bit of the magic yourself."

June stared at it. "I'd forgotten how lifelike it is."

Zac tested the statue. "It's heavy. Can you magic it?"

"Of course." Shakespeare concentrated but nothing happened. "No," he gasped. "Now I'm on the outside, my magic has faded. I used my last bit on starting the car."

"Never mind." Zac patted the sculpture. "The three of us can lift her."

First, though, he layered a trailer with blankets. Then they carefully loaded the sculpture into it. Zac slowly drove back to the flat, where they again unloaded.

Zac held up the lamp. "Do we need to rub it?"

Shakespeare put out a restraining hand. "No, don't. His Blueness is a being of little wit. Best not to try."

June selected an ordinary teapot. "This is the right size. Use that."

Zac took the pot and began to experiment. The sculpture, however, proved obstinate. "It needs to rock," he said.

"I could go down to the pub," Shakespeare suggested. "The Rude Mechanicals rock."

"You and your Rude Mechanicals." Zac tapped a finger. "A thin doweling would do it."

"There is a buxom darling among The Rude Mechanicals."

"Dow-el-ing," Zac almost smiled, "is a thin wooden rod." He fetched a segment from the garage and used superglue to attach it to the base of the sculpture.

"Well done," June said. "That works. Now, we're rocking n rolling."

Shakespeare eyed their construction. "You've got till midnight. Till then, my thin doweling/I shall seek out my buxom darling."

He roared away on his Harley. Zac cuddled up with June. The remaining hours passed too quickly. Just before the digital clock struck midnight, Shakespeare reappeared. A little later, a powerful vacuum gripped Zac and his feet were pulled towards the lamp.

For one moment, he was horizontal and June tried to hold him. Yet, with a wail, he was yanked away from her, transformed into a mist and sucked into the spout. Gazing at the lamp with horror, June burst into tears. Shakespeare enfolded her and she cried and cried. Eventually, he handed her a hanky.

"Honk, my lady," he said. "Clear out the sad moistures."

She smiled sadly. "Should we rub the lamp yet?"

The bard patted her hand. "Wait a day. We don't want to confuse the small wits of His Blueness."

June sighed. It would be so hard to wait.

For Zac, though, time was in abeyance. He was more asleep than awake. Images drifted by, too light to be captured. Mostly, he just felt blue, the endless blue of the sky. Zac sank comfortably into the blue, comfortable except for a faint background hint of malice, the faint hint of a weak and frustrated intelligence.

It ended with a whoosh. From zero to a hundred in nothing. Zac gazed at June. June gazed at Zac. Spontaneously, they flung their arms around each other. Shakespeare bustled around like a maiden aunt. The two separated.

"It worked!" Zac cried.

"It worked!" June sobbed.

"Thank god!" Zac kissed her hand. "It really is blue in there. Like being on the beach and gazing into the blue sky."

"Just blue?" Shakespeare grinned.

"Light blue. Okay?" They laughed. Zac became thoughtful. "I have to give a wish." He held out his hand and a pearl necklace appeared. Placing it over the sculpture, he put an arm around June.

Shakespeare backed away. "Just going. See you later."

They waved. So little time and so much to do.

At the digital stroke of midnight, Zac waiting, was again vacuumed into the lamp. June played safe and delayed two more days before again rubbing. This time, Zac put a diamond bracelet on the sculpture's wrist. Two days later and he added gold anklets.

"That's three wishes," June said.

"Three," Zac agreed. "Now we wait."

"See you, kiddos." Shakespeare headed for the door. "I'll be back at midnight."

"Wait." Zac bit his lip. "Come back a bit earlier. Just in case."

The bard nodded. "I'll be here - just in case."

So little time and so little to do. Anxiety prevented activity. The hours were millstones. Finally, however, eleven arrived. Shortly afterward, Shakespeare returned.

"How's it going, kiddos?" he asked.

"Not good," Zac replied. "Waiting."

"How about a pizza, then?"

"I'll ring," June offered.

"How about a pizza, magic style?"

"What?" Zac muttered. "Okay, yeah."

He held out his hand. There was a fizzle, more a fart than a pop, and just one cold slice appeared. Zac gazed glumly. But Shakespeare thumped him on the shoulder. "See, your magic's fading!"

"Fading?" Zac's eyes widened. "You're right. This really might work."

June did the ghost of a dance.

All the same, at midnight, they scarcely dared to breathe. They looked between the sculpture and the lamp. The statue was balanced on top of the doweling so that June could easily rock it. As it rocked, the outstretched clay hand rubbed against the lamp on the pedestal. The sculpture evoked the genie. Maybe.

Suddenly, the lifelike figure shot off the floor and rammed into the lamp's spout.

"Yes!" Zac punched air. "His Blueness accepts the shape as a person."

Ram! Ram! Ram! But whatever the lamp could do to living beings, it could not do it to clay. The figure was not vacuumed down. Briefly, ceramic and metal battled. Unresolved, the statue was set down. A blue haze, faintly menacing, poured out of the lamp. It flowed over the figure. If the statue wasn't going into His Blueness, then His Blueness was going to go into the statue. But it couldn't. Blue sparks flew off, gradually growing more and more feeble. There was a final flash. The Blue disintegrated and the sense of menace faded.

They used the sculpture to again rub the lamp. Nothing happened.

"We've done it! We've done it!" June shouted. "It's gone. It's gone!" But almost immediately, her face fell. "We've killed it," she groaned. "Killed it."

Zac, however, shook his head. "I was inside. We haven't killed it. We've freed it."

Shakespeare nodded. "It's free. It's, how do you say, free to move on."

June looked from one to the other. Her face brightened.

"And I'm free, too!" Zac shouted. "Free!" Joyously, he ran into the garden and along the street. "Free! Free!"

June danced alongside of him. He was roaring with laughter, when a glint caught his eye. "What's that?" he said. "Oh, a ring."

Still laughing, he put the ring on June.

"Don't!" Shakespeare shouted.

But it was too late. A big blue bloke was billowing behind them.

The Anonymous Portrait

BY ALEX AZAR

"Mr. Riley, sir, what a pleasant surprise. Thank you for gracing my humble establishment." Luis Feldman, proprietor of Feldman's Antiques is unaware that Malcolm Riley is there by chance. His automobile broke down just outside and Riley entered in an attempt to escape the heat.

"Stop your cobbling, man. Money and a title doesn't make me a better person, nor is this a humble shop if it provides for you and yours." Riley stands at an impressive 6'2" with a good 300 pounds of supporting girth. "Now, why don't you show me around your fine establishment, while I wait for my automobile to be repaired."

Luis didn't need any more of an invitation; he takes Riley directly to his backroom of fine antiques that the average customer couldn't afford. Hoping to make his first sale in a fortnight, he begins rattling off the history of each item Riley even momentarily pauses on. "Ah, that chest migrated to Baltimore by way of Rio Jaina, originally brought across the ocean during Columbus' fourth and final voyage.

Riley replies more flippantly than Luis would have preferred. "Hmm, interesting."

"If that doesn't suit your tastes, perhaps this credenza salvaged from the original White House when most of the interior was burnt beyond repair in 1814."

As it appears that Sir Riley's interest is piqued by the credenza, his attention is pulled through a doorway into what appears to be a closet. "What's in there? I'd very much like to explore that room if you don't mind."

Not wanting to outright refuse a man of stature like Malcolm Riley, Luis explains, "Ah, that is just a storage room for items labeled 'undesirables,' nothing that would be of interest to a man of your wealth."

"Tsk, tsk. I didn't become a rich man by passing up a good deal. Consider this: if I don't find something of interest in there, I'll purchase the chest."

Unable to reject such an offer, Luis leads the gentleman through the clutter of coverless books, broken mirrors, scratched furniture, and....

"Who is that in this portrait?"

"Apologies, sir, this is an unidentified portrait by an unrecognizable artist. That is the reason it is among the undesirables. However, in *this* portfolio there's a rare sketch by author H.P. Lovecraft."

Unable to pry his eyes from the painting, Sir Riley says, "no, you must tell me about this painting; I know this man. I cannot place his face but I undoubtedly know this man."

"I'm sorry, sir, I've done all the research I can but the subject and artist remain a mystery. If you know this man, I dare say you may be the only person who does."

"Nonsense, why would you purchase a painting you knowingly couldn't sell?"

"Again, sir, I must apologize: the painting was amidst a crate of paintings from a private collection. The bank auctioned off the entirety of the collection when Lord and Lady Williamson were found dead with no heirs."

"How did they die?"

"It appears each of your inquiries leads to another mystery to which I do not know the answer."

Before Riley can ask another unanswerable question, they are interrupted by his driver. "Sir, the automobile is operational. It needs extensive repairs; however, it will return you home."

"Very good. Load this painting as well." Shaking Luis' hand, he adds, "thank you for indulging my elderly curiosity, Mr. Feldman. Please send me a voucher for three times your asking price–and not a penny less."

* * *

The painting now hangs opposite Riley's desk in his private study where it has hung for the past five years. For those years and many more before, Riley spent the majority of his days managing his shipping company; however, on this day his thoughts are elsewhere. "Thank you for seeing me on such short notice, Mr. Quinn. I trust the travel accommodations met your expectations."

Used to the traditional horse and buggy, the New Jersey native, Peter Quinn, is still unaware of the reason for the meeting. "Yes, sir, of course, but please call me Peter."

"Only if you grant me the same courtesy. I am sure the secret nature of my request for your presence has piqued your curiosity; however, the time of the cloak and dagger is over. Peter, I would like to hire you to discover the origins of that painting."

Following Malcolm's finger, Peter's gaze falls upon the unidentifiable portrait. After a moment he returns his attention to Malcolm. "I'm sorry, sir–Mr. Ri... Malcolm. I believe there's been a misunderstanding."

Knowing where this is leading, "I assure you, there is no misunderstanding, Peter. I am aware that you are a curator for an exclusive gallery. I am also aware that you are you have no detective or investigative background, but your knowledge and passion for art is unparalleled. Your eye for art should provide unique insight that a detective would lack."

Malcolm asks Peter to retrieve the painting. Still confused, Peter examines the painting. "The brush work is amazing. I can honestly say I've never seen such quality. Who did this?"

"That's one of the two things you're to find out, if you agree to this job. The other is to discover who the subject is."

"I'm sorry, but I have to ask: if you don't know the subject or artist of the piece, why is it of such importance to you?"

"Yes, I suppose a little back-story is required. Did you know I was the first automobile owner in Baltimore? More trouble than it was worth. Five years ago, on a disturbingly hot day in July, the nightmare broke down outside an antique store. The shopkeep was a humble man who has since passed; he initially refused to sell the piece to me. He received it as a part of a bulk item at a bank auction, and he was himself unaware of who the subject or artist were. From the moment I saw it I was captivated. To this day I will swear that I know the subject, but from a memory beyond recollection."

Malcolm allows the image to settle in Peter's mind as he packs his pipe, asking if Peter minds. "Not at all, sir. I believe a man should have the freedom to do as he pleases in his home, despite company–perhaps even in spite of some guests."

After a short chuckle from both of them, Malcolm removes the pipe from his mouth, and examines it before continuing. "Everyone tells me it's an unhealthy habit, but I always believed habits were meant to be unhealthy. Besides, at my age death is the next logical step–and that painting will be the cause of it, nothing else.

"It was immediately following the purchase that my life began unraveling. Upon returning from the antique store, I had a servant hang the portrait, and there it hung until you just removed it. The day after I brought it home my wife became ill. Six weeks later she died of unknown causes. The same has happened to my two sons, daughter, brother and even a cousin out in California."

Malcolm takes a few drags from the pipe. "That painting, or more accurately the man in the portrait, has taken everything from me." Putting the pipe down, he begins pacing the office, using the signature cane that has worked its way into all of his recent pictures, talking to Peter without looking at him. "Even my business is failing. Some ships were lost at sea, investors have pulled out–these five years have been the worst stretch my business has seen since it was established."

Feeling his presence in the room has been forgotten, Peter chimes in, "I've read about your recent financial troubles."

Startled, as though just awoken from a dream, Malcolm comments, "have you now? It's unfortunate that my failings have become national news."

"It's not just your failings, sir. I grew up reading about Malcolm Riley and Longbody Shipping."

"Is that so? Would you mind informing me what you've read about my company and me?" Seeing the reluctance on Peter's face, Malcolm continues after flashes a smile so filled with charm it's credited with the success of his company. Peter didn't stand a chance. "Indulge an old man if you will."

"Well, I know you were able to get the company off the ground after you discovered a genuine treasure chest sunk in the harbor with a friend." Pausing, Peter is unsure how to proceed due to the nature of the following detail.

Sensing Peter's trepidation, Malcom says, "please continue; I survived what happened next, surely I can handle you recounting the events."

"If you insist. I've read that as you and your friend were salvaging the chest... there was an accident that cost your friend his life, and in honor of him you named the company after him, Jackson Longbody."

"I'm somewhat surprised our tale has spread so far, but I am glad Jackson hasn't been lost in the story. In his short time with us, he lived a more fulfilling life than most people my age. It wasn't just the fortune his sacrifice provided, also his example. Without his guidance the treasure would have been wasted on me." Catching himself in his own musing, Malcolm once again returns his attention to Peter. "But we digress… are we understood then? I want you to discover who painted this, but more importantly I need you to find out the subject of the portrait. My grandson has been ill for a week. That gives you five weeks to complete these tasks. Upon completion I'll pay you a year's worth of your current salary."

Almost too enticed to ask the logical questions that one in Peter's situation ought to remember, he stammers out, "what if it takes more than five weeks, or if I can't do it at all?"

"I have full faith in your abilities and trust that you will succeed. However, if the unfortunate occurs, I'll pay you your standard five week rate, and you may return to New Jersey." Malcolm picks his pipe back up, reigniting it as he looks out the window overlooking his circular driveway. "Now, if you don't mind, my assistant will fill you in on the few remaining details. I think I will tend to my grandson."

Malcolm leaves Peter alone in the study to be replaced shortly after by Nancy Allegra, Malcolm's assistant for the better part of the past 25 years. "I'll assume your presence means you accept the conditions? Good. In this file you'll find the receipt from the antique owner's original purchase log, as well as all known information on the previous owners. Mr. Riley's driver will be available to you at all times, and should the need arise to travel beyond the Baltimore area, all expenses will be paid. I ask that you retain all vouchers. One of the guest rooms has been prepared, and if there are no further questions I'll show you there now."

Unable to recall ever agreeing to the mission, Peter confusingly follows the automaton-like woman before him.

* * *

The following day, after a hearty breakfast, Peter begins by carefully examining every stroke of the portrait, as well as removing the frame and inspecting the reverse of the canvas. He didn't expect to find a signature, but still thinks it odd that an artist of this caliber wouldn't claim his work.

Peter decides to concentrate on everything in the image other than the actual subject, taking careful notes on everything, even the most seemingly insignificant details: behind the subject's left shoulder is a lighthouse overlooking a rocky shore with five evergreen trees of varying heights above his head. In his right hand he holds a nautical compass with the needle pointing west. Over the right shoulder is an empty brown clay flowerpot with a 'v' shaped wedge missing from the rim and a crack trailing the point to the bottom of the pot. All in front of a dark green wall.

Emerging from his room for the first time since he began his research five hours earlier, Peter finds Mrs. Allegra "Please notify the driver I'd like to visit the bank that acquired Lord Williamson's paperwork."

* * *

"Thank you for indulging Mr. Riley, Mr. Quinn," the driver says without looking back, while continuing their bumpy journey. "The master has been obsessed with that painting the moment he saw it. He claims it has otherworldly qualities causing all his miseries."

"Yes, I've noticed that, although he never actually claimed it was cursed."

"Oh no, sir. If you ask him he'll say it's haunted, not cursed."

Shortly after, Peter is in a private chamber of the bank, reviewing all paperwork the bank has but instead concentrating on the lord's receipts. Near the end of the business day, the bank manager, having already heard from Riley, advises Peter to sign for all the paperwork he believes he'll need and to return them after his investigation is over.

As Peter and the driver are loading boxes of vouchers and property claims, the bank manager pulls Peter to the side. "Sir Riley has asked me not to mention this to you, however… he's hired private investigators in the past. They each became stuck at the next step in their investigations. Pointing to a box currently waiting to be placed in the automobile, "You'll find in that box a receipt for an anonymous painting." Seeing the excitement in Peter's face he cuts him off before Peter can jump to conclusions. "The seller passed away long before Mr. Riley purchased the painting. The seller was not an artist and there are no records of how he procured this portrait. I fear that if this mystery has a solution, it won't be found through paperwork."

Back in the automobile, the driver resumes the conversation from earlier, "Even if you can find something on this artist that's not going to satisfy Mr. Riley. Unless you figure out who is in that portrait and can prove it has something to do with what happened to his family, he won't be happy."

"What if I can prove there is nothing special about the painting?" Peter asks while riffling through the box the bank manager pointed out earlier. "Look at this: a voucher for an anonymous portrait. Might be worth checking out."

"Oh, sure thing, Mr. Quinn. Let me see the address." After barely glancing at the sheet of paper Peter handed the driver he replies, "I know where this is, we could head there right now if you'd like."

Curious that the driver will continue the facade Sir Riley created, Peter wonders, "If this has consumed Sir Riley so thoroughly for the past five years, why has he waited so long to hire someone to investigate?"

Anger seething in the driver's voice. "Did that bank manager open his mouth?"

"What? No. But… are you saying there were earlier investigations? Why wasn't I made aware of this?"

* * *

It is only back at the Riley estate that Nancy Allegra answers his question. "Mr. Riley was hoping your methods would differ from theirs, producing a unique result; he didn't want the work of previous investigations clouding your own. In the past, he's hired private detectives from across the country, even an inspector from London. Unfortunately, all have been thwarted at the residence listed on the voucher, which you are about to enter. There are no tenants there who know of the seller, only that there are some remaining paintings from varying artists. Perhaps..."

"Perhaps I can see something an untrained eye would have overlooked." Peter cuts her off, still upset at the deception. "However, if this arrangement is going to work, I'll need full disclosure from the both of you. I can forgive the old man for his eccentricities, but you must be forthcoming with me."

"Very well, Mr. Quinn; however, I must stress that you not think of Mr. Riley as a senile old man. He is very much in control of his faculties. Meanwhile, your visit to the residence can wait until tomorrow. Tonight Mr. Riley would like you to join him for dinner. I will notify him that you are aware of the previous investigations."

Sitting across from one another, Malcolm and Peter eat in silence for longer than either is comfortable with. Once it becomes too much for Peter, he says, "I understand why you didn't tell me that I wasn't the first you asked to do this."

"I'm glad, and I would like to assure you that you are the first curator I hired. I do respect your abilities as much as I have said in the past, and appreciate you doing this." The remainder of the evening is spent in a pleasant discussion about Malcolm's grandson, Jackson.

* * *

Once again, following a heartier breakfast than Peter is used to, he and the driver are on their way to the seller's address. "You know Mr. Quinn, I've never told this to anyone before, but sometimes I could swear the man in the painting has aged. Now, before you think I'm crazy, I know he was already old when Mr. Riley first bought it, but I think the old man's hair has gotten more grey. I don't see it everyday like Mr. Riley and maybe that's why he never noticed–or maybe Mr. Riley's crazy is just rubbing off on me."

Not exactly sure how to process this last bit of information, Peter is glad to discover they have arrived at their destination.

"If it's alright with you, Mr. Quinn, I'd appreciate you not telling anyone what I just said." After a silent nod from Peter, the driver continues ashamed, "I think I might just stay here, I've seen what's inside before."

No more words were exchanged between the two as Peter left the automobile and was escorted to the residence. After a brief introduction that the various occupants of the communal home were both expecting and have grown accustomed to, Peter is left to himself in a large room of "the seller's" belongings, from a time prior to any of the current residents' recollections. Among a cluster of ambiguous impersonal affects was a spattering of paintings from various artists. Peter quickly sets himself to the task of examining the work.

* * *

Early in the afternoon Riley asks Jackson's attendant to give them a moment of privacy, the first that he's had with his grandson since he became ill. "Jackson, I'm going to tell you something I've kept a secret for over sixty years: this is entirely my fault. I don't know how, but your namesake is seeking revenge upon me from beyond the grave."

Shaking his head while placing a hand to his forehead, "I know it sounds absurd, crazy even, all more so after saying it aloud; however, my secret is that Jackson Longbody didn't simply die that day we discovered the treasure. Seeing the vast fortune within, I was consumed with an overwhelming sense of greed and desperation to be the sole owner of the treasure. To this day I am positive that he would have done the same given the chance– just as much as someone haunts the painting, that treasure was cursed. After Jackson dragged the chest to shore, and as he lay exhausted in the sand, I hammered him in the head with a fallen branch."

Patting his hand with his cane, "In fact, it was from that very branch I had my cane fashioned. I know now that it was my guilt plaguing my mind that drove me to keep Jackson close to me–why I named your father, you, and my company after him, and why I keep this damned cane with me. But mostly it is why I know that the painting is responsible for your condition. The subject is obviously much too old to be Jackson, but I know in these old bones that he's responsible somehow.

"Thank you for not judging me too harshly; I only hope expressing all this will give me a good night's sleep tonight." Sir Riley rises from his chair, patting his comatose grandson on the head before departing teary-eyed.

More time has passed confessing his sins than Sir Riley imagined, for Peter has returned from the seller's former residence. "I've been able to discover the artist of the portrait, an American artist out of Washington D.C., Clay West, and although he passed several decades ago, I've also been able to identify the two subjects represented."

Excited, afraid and confused Malcolm asks the obvious question, "What two subjects? There's only one."

"That is what I believed, a belief that I feel is what hindered the previous investigations." Producing the portrait from its protective sheath Peter points out, "See these five trees above the subject's head–do you notice how they vaguely resemble a hand? Now look at the window placement on the lighthouse: they appear in the pattern of a face. The brushwork matches exactly one other painting: a portrait by Clay West of two gentlemen, dated to roughly sixty years ago."

"What are you saying, Peter?"

Noticing that Nancy Allegra and the driver have come within ear shot, Peter asks, "are you sure you're ready for this?"

"If I'm to believe your story, I've been waiting sixty years for this."

"I would have overlooked this like the detectives prior, however the exceptionally clean brush strokes made me look twice. You were right in having hired a curator; however I don't know think you'll be happy with my findings." Peter displays the second painting carried within the case.

"I haven't seen a picture of you from your youth–presumably neither have any of the detectives–but this is you standing behind your friend Jackson Longbody, correct?

"I take your silence as a 'yes.' Do you notice your positioning that your positioning in this portrait is the same as the lighthouse and trees stand-in? The hand above Jackson's head symbolizes death–more to the point, murder. The only question I have is why you would commission such a painting, only to investigate it later."

Somewhat recomposing himself after the recent revelations, Sir Riley say, "there is one detail you're mistaken on: I did not know of this second painting until this very moment. Nor does any of this clarify the portrait that has hung in my study for the past five years."

Holding the painting of Jackson and Malcolm, Peter explains bewildered, "This painting was done five years after Jackson's death. If you didn't do this, who did?"

Seeing a shimmer in the eyes of the aged Jackson in his portrait, Malcolm asks, "isn't it obvious?"

* * *

That night Malcolm Riley sends everyone home, including Peter Quinn and Jackson's aide. Alone in his study, Malcolm sits in his favorite chair opposite the two paintings propped on a couch, "Jackson, old fellow, leave the boy be. Take me. It was always about me. Spare him and I will submit myself to you."

There is no reaction from the paintings. Enraged, Malcolm grabs his cane and bashes both portraits: tearing the canvas, and breaking the frames. Stopping to catch his breath, he looks at the cane and laughs at the cycle of things.

Thinking he's figured a way to stop Jackson Longbody once and for all, Malcolm takes the broken masses that were once the portraits and throws them in the fireplace. For good measure he adds the cane to the fire.

Grabbing a bottle of whisky from a drawer in his desk, Malcolm makes his way to his private chamber to properly celebrate. Finally, in the early hours of the morning, Malcolm is drunk asleep in his bed, but with a smile on face.

Mere hours later, Jackson Riley's attendant finds the boy awake, in good spirits and full of energy, while simultaneously Nancy Allegra finds Sir Malcolm Riley in his bed, with his head bashed in by his own cane. On the wall behind the bed hang the two portraits smiling down on his lifeless body.

The Lens of the Innocent

SUZANNE ROBB

Scott Winder searched everywhere. The dresser too obvious, as was the lingerie drawer. He tossed the bed, searched the kitchen, laundry room, and bathroom. At a total loss as to where else it could be. His wife, Heather, was a master when it came to hiding things; he on the other hand was a novice at finding them.

"Scott, honey, you aren't going to find it so you'll just have to wait until your birthday."

Scott leaned against the wall and let himself slide down the wall to the floor. How did she know? It was like living with God. He kicked out his foot, letting his inner three-year-old exert himself. After a few moments, he decided to be an adult and stood up. About to go downstairs, when he thought *sewing kit!*

* * *

Heather watched her husband come down the stairs, a pout hung on his face. She absolutely loved to torture him with stuff like this; he was such a kid sometimes. Of course, this was why the gift fit him so perfectly. She picked it up at an antique store off the beaten path. The minute she saw it, she knew it was meant for Scott.

The owner of the store told her the item she purchased was special, but she didn't pay much attention, too busy wondering where to hide it so Scott wouldn't find it. Her husband, God love him, was a snoop, literally. He worked as a private detective, but for whatever reason he could never detect what she did. She laughed about it, he got annoyed.

"Didn't find it, huh babe?" Heather tried to look empathetic.

"No. Why do you have to be so good at hiding things? You make me feel inept."

"You know the whole inept routine isn't going to work."

"Foot massage, body rub, bubble bath, dishes for a week…" Scott looked at her with such a hopeful expression.

"Nope, not going to work. You have three more days until your birthday, buddy." Scott stood up and looked at his wife with a serious expression.

Heather just laughed and let him do his thing. There was no way he was going to find it, so she sat back and read her book.

"I'll take that as a challenge. I'm off to find treasure." Scott left the room and began shaking books on the shelves, magazines on the table, and looking under couch cushions.

Hours later Scott returned to the room. Heather fell asleep on the couch reading. Scott walked over to the couch and sat beside her. He poked her with a finger until she woke up.

* * *

Heather looked over the top of the book to see a scowl being thrown her way. She decided to try and make nice.

"What do you want for dinner?"

"My present."

"I'll order pizza then?"

"Ha ha, I'll get the phone." Scott stood up with a dramatic sigh and walked to the kitchen.

Heather stayed on the couch and watched Scott go get the phone. How she loved this time of year. She smiled to herself, knowing he secretly loved it too.

* * *

The next morning when Heather left for work Scott sprang into action. He knew the gift had to be in the house. No one could outsmart him ten years in a row–it was maddening. He put on his investigative cap and decided to approach this like a case.

Known information: Heather returned home from a trip to the mall five days ago. Scott was out at the time on assignment, making it the only time he was not around. This meant she would have had to have hidden the gift at this point in time in order to not risk being discovered.

Scott went out into the driveway pretending he was Heather. He mimed getting out of the car. A few neighbours watched him, but not in an odd way. They had seen him do stranger things. Scott looked around at possible hiding spots; a birdhouse hanging off the front tree caught his eye. Aha! That had to be it; he would never think to bother a bird.

Scott ran to the birdhouse and looked inside: empty. He looked around again. A trash can, recycle bin, and bicycle,–no prospects there. He lifted the door to the garage and thought, no chance. As he shut the door he stopped. This would actually be the perfect place. Scott was like every other man when it came to tools: he bought them, but never used them. He spent the next hour going through his tool collection.

He discovered he had three cordless drills missing the batteries, two handsaws, six hammers, no nails, one box of screws, but no screwdrivers. He made a mental note to go buy a drill with a cord, preferably something cool and powerful. Then he put all the tools back and closed the door with a sigh. He had come up empty.

Heading back into the house he started at square one. He knew the backyard was safe because their dog, Watson, would have dug up anything Heather hid. In the front hall Watson, a ten year old French bulldog, looked up at Scott. He shook his jowls and went back to sleep.

"You know a little help would be nice, buddy."

A loud snore his only response. Scott knelt next to the dog and spent a few minutes petting him, and also looking under the mattress of his bed. Again, he found nothing. Standing up, he was more determined than ever. Trying to think like his wife, he knew the best hiding places were in plain sight or somewhere so obvious no one would think to look there.

Going from room to room he glanced around and saw nothing out of the ordinary. That left the obvious places. He began with drawers, cabinets, jars, and mugs, anything he could think of. Just as he was about to go into the laundry room, one of the light bulbs burnt out.

He had a decision to make here–it was one of those good husband things. If he changed a light bulb and Heather didn't see it, did he really change it? He could wait for her to get home so she would have visual confirmation he did in fact do it. He stood there for several moments deciding what to do.

Finally, he decided to change it, for two reasons. One, he could place the burnt bulb on the counter where Heather would see it, then claim he meant to take it out to the recycling bin but forgot. Secondly, he really wanted to search the laundry room, usually Heather's area since he made everything green that one time; he had been banned since then.

He went to the storage closet and looked around for a light bulb. Paper towels, toilet paper, tissue boxes, tampons, toothpaste, canned corn, soap–ahh, there it was: light bulbs. He grabbed one and shut the door. He took three steps before he recalled the canned corn. What the hell was that doing in there?

He had done it, he had found the present! He backed up three steps and opened the door with a shaking hand. He put the light bulb back and stared at the can. It looked so innocent, and in such an obvious location–not to mention he never grabbed anything when it needed restocking. She was good, but this year he got her.

He reached in and picked up the can: it was light. His hand shook. He nervously took it into the kitchen. Carefully placing it on the counter, he just stared at it. Did he want to ruin the surprise? Did he want Heather to be mad at him?

Yes, he wanted to know what it was. No, he didn't want to Heather to be mad at him. Then again, she was always mad at him for something. He reached out to the can and pulled at the top; it came off and he peered inside. A small piece of paper and little brown leather bag filled the can.

He pulled out the paper and set in on the counter. Then he reached in and wrapped his hand around the little leather bag. He felt good about having found it, but so guilty too. Still time for him to put it back, he debated; then again, she would know. She would find out and accuse him of looking even if he didn't. At this point he had to look, there was no going back.

He opened the small bag and dumped its content carefully onto the counter. He stood in awe of what lay before him: an antique magnifying glass, at least 100 years old. He could only imagine the stories it had to tell, the mysteries it had unravelled, the bad guys it had helped apprehend. He picked it up and looked through it. His eye popped wide open in surprise at what he saw.

He should have seen the kitchen sink; instead, he saw a smoky room and a man drinking a beer, a magazine half open on the dirty floor, and a baseball game on the TV in the background. He knew the game, he had watched it two weeks ago. He looked around the room for more clues and saw a paper dated over a week ago.

Looking around the room for more information, he saw the front door of the smoky apartment open. A man entered and started talking to the grubby looking man in the chair. The one who broke in pulled out a gun and fired.

Scott pulled the magnifying glass away from his eyes suddenly. He had to be hallucinating. No way had he seen what he just did. He put it on the counter and took a step back. As he did this, he noticed the piece of paper he had removed from the can off to the side of the counter.

He picked the paper up and unfolded it carefully, it was aged and for some reason he felt what it said would be important. The words were going to change his life.

The item you now possess is going to be a blessing and a curse. Each generation it finds the one who is meant to hold it. This person will solve great crimes and bring justice to those who would otherwise go unnoticed. This person will also pay a great price. The Lens of the Innocent, on occasion will show a crime which has not happened. Many men have gone insane with guilt at not being able to prevent it. Accept this gift with grace as you have been chosen to help those in need.

Scott refolded the note and placed it gently back on the counter, at a loss as to what he should do. Did Heather know what she bought? Was this even her gift to him? It did say that it would find the right person in each generation. Perhaps it was meant for the next owners, or the prior owners left it here. He tried to convince himself of any scenario in which it didn't belong to him.

"Scott, can you help with these please?" Scott jumped in surprise.

He hadn't even heard Heather come into the house. He kept his back to the counter and shoved the items away.

"Uh….yeah sure, I'll follow you out to the car to get the rest."

Heather just looked at him oddly and went about her tasks.

* * *

She pulled items out of the grocery bags, all the while watching Scott act nervous.

"Okay, spill: what did you do?"

"I found the present. I didn't mean to I swear." Scott let it burst out of him like a five year old admitting to taking a cookie.

"How did you find it?"

"Light bulb…"

"No seriously, how did you find it?"

"Heather, light bulb, and please tell me, did you know what this was when you bought it?" Heather noticed Scott had paled and was looking at her with an intensity she had never seen in him. She stopped giving him a hard time and answered him.

"Yes, I knew what it was, Scott. The guy at the antique store told me it was very old and special. I just saw it and knew it was for you."

"The owner knew about it?"

"Yeah, he did. Why, what's wrong? Don't you like it? I thought it would be perfect for you."

"Honey, it's perfect, I love it, but the guy was serious–it is magical." Heather just looked at him waiting for an explanation.

"I looked through it and saw the past–more specifically, a past crime."

"Scott, I love you, but that's impossible."

"Here, you look through it. Tell me what you see."

Heather picked up the magnifying glass and looked at Scott through it.

"The only thing from the past I see is a bit of breakfast in your stubble, but what does this magnifying glass have to do with your present?"

"Okay, read the note then." Scott reached for the note, but it was gone.

"Honey, are you okay? I know that last case was really stressful on you. Maybe you need a vacation."

"I don't need a vacation. I'm not going crazy. I looked through the lens and saw some guy watching TV. Then some guy came in and shot him. The papers in the room were a week old."

"You know what, easy to figure this out. You're a private detective. Call one of your police contacts and ask about a case resembling what you saw."

"Sure, if I want to become a suspect."

"Then look up shootings in the news archives."

"What did you mean, what does this have to do with my present?"

"Well, you told me you found it, but I don't see it anywhere. All you keep talking about is this magnifying glass."

"But that's the present, isn't it? I mean, it was in the storage closet in a can of corn."

"I love you very much, but I promise that is not what I bought you."

"Then how did it get there?"

"I have no idea, maybe it's someone's idea of a joke?"

"I don't think so."

* * *

Scott went to his computer and started searching online for any information on the crime he had seen. Less than an hour later, he knew who the victim was and when the crime occurred. The victim, John Dunhill, had lived about five miles from them. He was found a few days ago, but had been killed earlier. Neighbors called the police when the smell of decomposition began to waft into their vents.

Now that Scott knew the who and the when, he had no idea what was next. Through the lens he had a perfect view of the shooter. According to the police they were no witnesses, no leads, therefore no case. If Scott came forward they would suspect him, he had no reason for being in the area.

He went downstairs and explained the situation to Heather.

"Well, you tried, honey. Now, let's talk about this whole finding the present thing."

"Light bulb burned out in the laundry room, so I went to get a new one. I saw the can of corn in there and knew it didn't belong."

"Well done, I'll have to do better next year. I was banking on the whole 'if a husband fixes or restocks something did it really happen if the wife didn't see it'."

"Ha! I knew it. I even had a plan for that. I was going to leave the burnt bulb on the counter for recycling."

Heather gave Scott a kiss on the cheek and went to the fridge. She grabbed two bottles of beer. Opening both of them and then handing one to Scott, she leaned against the counter with her hip. She had an odd smile on her face.

"You know I have to try and help this guy, right?"

"Yep, so what's the plan?"

"Tomorrow I go to his apartment with the magnifying glass and see if it shows me anything the police might have missed."

"You know, I would like to point out here that I deserve some good wife points for supporting you and your magical magnifying glass-to-the-past thing you got going on."

"Twenty points and I'll throw out the take-out dishes–Chinese sound good?" Heather nodded as Scott went over to the phone.

* * *

Scott stood in front of the door to John Dunhill's apartment. He was nervous about going in. What if he was wrong? What if it was all some big joke? He decided to knock first. He waited five minutes to see if someone would answer the door, though the crime scene tape indicated he had the right place. A woman came out into the hallway and looked at Scott.

"You don't know about your friend?"

"Um no, I was out of town. Did something happen?"

"He got killed last week."

"Oh…"

The woman walked on as if she hadn't delivered tragic news. In these parts though, it really wasn't uncommon. Scott waited for her to round the corner and then tried the doorknob: locked. He had to use his set of lock picks to get in. Thankfully, pretty good at it; he had the door open in less than thirty seconds.

Scott gripped the handle of the door and slowly opened the door. He ducked underneath the tape and shut the door behind him. The smell of the small apartment overwhelmed him at first and he took a moment to adjust, as his eyes watered and his stomach protested.

The chair John had been shot in had been removed, but a large stain on the floor told enough of the story. John took out the lens and looked around the room. He was still in the present, but certain parts of the room stood out in contrast to others.

A set of fingerprints turned purple, a footprint neon green, and a small piece of fabric bright red. Scott looked at all these things and knew he had to call his police buddy, Kyle Chandler. He and Kyle had gone to the academy together, and had been close friends ever since. If there was one man he could trust, it was him.

Five minutes later, Kyle was on his way over to the crime scene with a forensics unit. Scott made sure to be exact about the location of what to look for. Kyle was leery at first, but Scott kept pressing him until he agreed to check it out.

On the drive home, Scott felt pretty good about himself. He had helped catch a killer and found his present. Wait a minute–he didn't find his present! In all the commotion he had forgotten Heather never said she had bought the magnifying glass. Plus, she had not been nearly upset enough.

Damn it, that meant that he had less than a day to find it. He smiled to himself, thinking how easy it would be with his new little toy. This thing was going to make his life so easy. Not only would it help him get more clients because of an amazing ability to ferret out the truth, but it was going to help him find that present.

Scott pulled into the driveway and stepped out of the car. He whipped out the lens and started searching. There was nothing strange or odd, no weird colors. Obviously, he had to move into the house to find the elusive present. Entering the house he looked around with the lens again. Nothing, nada, zero showed up.

He sat on the couch and sighed. Apparently, his toy only worked when it wanted to. He brought it up to his eye one more time just to make sure he wasn't missing anything. A shadow crossed in front of him; it could have been Heather, or it could have been the lens showing him something.

He was still in his living room, but the light seemed wrong: too dark. He looked to where Watson should be snoring away and saw an empty bed. Standing up slowly, he started towards the front door, broken glass littered the floor. Scott pulled the lens away and saw everything was fine.

He locked the door and stooped to check on the dog. He put the lens to his eye once again and saw things had changed in the house. Dark again, there was another shadow, this time heading up the stairs. Scott followed it and saw the shadow enter the main bedroom.

As Scott entered the room he saw Heather dead, two bullet holes in her chest. Next to her lay his blood-covered body, one shot to the head. The shadow turned and he saw the man who shot John Dunhill. Scott's blood ran cold. He tore the lens away from his eye and stared at the bed. Then he went to it and ripped it apart making sure Heather was not in there bleeding to death.

* * *

When Heather got home, she was surprised to see that every light in the house was on, as well as every light outside of the house. She was also greeted by loud barking which was new. Shoving her way into the house she saw Scott trying to hold onto the collar of a very large German Shepherd.

"Come on, be a good boy. Down, Sargent! That's Heather, your Mom." This had no effect on the dog.

"Heather put her purse down and walked up to Scott and the dog. She got down on her knees to look into Sargent's eyes.

"Knock it off, dog. I'm not the enemy." When the dog stopped barking, she reached out and scratched under its collar, the magic place that made any dog your friend.

"Hey, honey, guess what?" Scott wore a guilty expression.

"Wait, I got this one. You bought a dog."

"Yep, Watson is great and all, but not exactly a guard dog."

"And we need a guard dog why?"

"Just to be safe."

Heather looked at him warily. She knew when he was lying, and right now he was holding back big time. Something in his eyes told her he was doing it for a very good reason. She decided to let it drop for now.

"So, what have you been up to today?"

"Nothing too exciting; looked for my present. I realized you weren't nearly mad enough at me for finding the lens, it had to be a decoy."

Heather turned and looked at Scott, he sounded scared. "Yep, you know me, all about the decoys."

"I know, keeps me on my toes." Scott looked around nervously and Heather wondered what was wrong with him.

"Good, makes me happy to know I can still surprise you sometimes. I'm going to go and make us an actual dinner for tonight, so why don't you go and relax with your new best friend."

* * *

Scott smiled while Heather walked into the kitchen. As soon as she was out of sight, he leapt over Sargent, nearly knocking himself out, and locked the front door. Earlier he installed two extra deadbolts and a chain Heather either didn't notice or didn't comment on. His pocket started buzzing, scaring the crap out of him until he realized it was his cell.

"Winder."

"Hey, buddy, just wanted you to know that with your help we got the footprint, fabric, and fingerprint."

"Fantastic, when are you going to go and arrest the guy?"

"Well, we still need to run the print to get an ID on it. My guess is a few days. I'll let you know. Thanks again."

Silence on the other end signalled Kyle hung up. Scott was not happy about this. He had to endure three days of wondering when the psycho was going to come crashing into their bedroom and kill them? There was no way he could pull it off. Perhaps he could convince Heather to take a few days off for a surprise getaway. If that didn't work, he would suggest repainting the house and staying in a hotel for a bit.

Scott entered the kitchen, deciding he would go with the weekend away bit first. Offering to paint the bedroom would be a dead giveaway something was wrong, as he never volunteered to do things like that.

"Hey, honey, I was thinking we could go away this weekend, what do you think?"

"Can't this weekend, too much work to do." Heather continued chopping something on the counter.

"Okay, how about repainting the bedroom, that color in there is making me insane. We can stay at a hotel, paint fumes and all."

"Scott, we just had it painted a year ago, and you picked the color."

"Well, I don't like it now."

Heather turned around from the counter. She had a knife in her hand from cutting vegetables. The look on her face was one he knew. The interrogation was coming.

"What's going on with you? You've been acting weird ever since you got that stupid magnifying glass."

Scott just stared at her and smiled.

"Now you go and get a guard dog, every light in the house is on, we have more locks on our door than Alcatraz, and you want to go away for the weekend. You don't even seem to care about your birthday present, which is so not you."

"Okay, you're right. I'm dying and wanted to spend my last days with you." Heather just raised an eyebrow.

"You're dying and wanted to spend your last days with your loving wife?" Heather turned around and started chopping again.

"You won't believe the truth."

"Try me."

"I looked through the lens and I saw you and me get shot to death in bed while we were sleeping. It was the same guy I saw shoot John Dunhill." Heather slowly turned around.

"Scott, you know I love you, right?"

"Yes, but can you just put the knife on the counter." Heather smiled and placed the knife on the counter.

"So, this lens of yours foretold our deaths. You're obviously trying to prevent them with dogs and locks. I understand you're scared, but it's just a possibility. I bet since every light is on and we have the loudest dog on Earth, you have already changed our fate somehow."

"You don't know that. I need to be sure you're safe."

"Scott honey, nothing in life is certain, you know that."

"This I can be sure about. I can keep my wife safe."

"Let's have dinner and talk about this tomorrow. I don't think anything is going to happen tonight."

"Fine, but we're talking about it, Heather."

"Yes, dear. Now, will you please clean up after your dog." Scott looked down to see Sargent had just taken a huge dump at his feet.

* * *

Scott laid in bed listening to the sounds of the house. Everything seemed normal, but his sanity balanced on a sharp edge. The fact that every time he looked over at his sleeping wife he saw two holes in her chest didn't help. Watson and Sargent slept on the floor when all of a sudden both of them perked up their ears. Sargent started to growl and went to the door.

"Heather, wake up…wake up…" Scott shook her awake. As she slowly came to, he made the quiet motion by holding his finger up to his lips.

Heather noticed Sargent growling and pacing at the door. That was when they heard the glass shatter on the back door. Scoot cursed himself. He had been so preoccupied with what he had seen, he didn't think what might have changed. He slowly got out of bed.

"Call nine-one-one, then go out the window and hide."

Scott figured the guy wouldn't follow Heather onto the roof for a gun battle. Heather tried to stop him, but he was on a mission. He opened the door and Sargent charged out after the noise. Scott crept down the hallway and looked down the staircase. He could hear the grunting of a man, and the growling of a dog with a bone.

Scott took advantage of the distraction and went down the stairs slowly. He opened the closet door and reached inside for his baseball bat. He watched as the man struggled with Sargent, trying every which way to get loose of him. Creeping up behind him Scott hefted the bat and brought it down as fast and hard as he could.

A thump was all he heard as the killer hit the ground. Heather flipped on the lights at the top of the stairs and came running down. Lights outside indicated the police had arrived, and Sargent sat guard on top of the man.

"Hey, you found it."

Scott just looked at Heather.

"Your birthday present. The bat, it's autographed... look."

Scott looked down at the bat that had a patch of blood on it. He could barely make out the letters, but pretended to know who it was.

"Honey, it's perfect thanks. Now I can put it with that glove and ball you got me. Oh yeah, and those cards." One of these days he was really going to have to talk to her about the fact the he didn't like baseball. On their first date he had wanted to impress her so much he agreed with everything she said. Over the last ten years, he learned one of the things he agreed with was that baseball was like a religion.

They watched all the games together, got season passes, jerseys, and hats. He hated every moment of it, but loved every moment with Heather. He figured it was a fair trade.

"By the way if you ever pull that hero crap again, I'll kill you myself."

Scott simply held his arms open and let Heather walk into them. They stood like that until the police started knocking and Sargent looked like he was going to eat the intruder. Watson stood guard at the top of the stairs snoring softly.

The police came in and lots of questions and much paper work later, things were cleared up. Scott was defending his home, and it was just a creepy coincidence this guy was the same one who shot John Dunhill.

That night when he climbed back into bed Scott thought about the magnifying glass. It had saved his life, but if he never had it in the first place would his life ever have been in danger? He thought about that a lot the next few days. He finally decided he would only use it on hard cases, or when there was something in the news he felt The Lens of the Innocent might be interested in.

Fate could not be changed, but he could help people who went by unnoticed and unsolved.

Under White Sheets

BY RICK MCQUISTON

"The old place has been deserted for years," Rob said with a glint in his eye. "Nobody has gone inside since that crazy old guy, Paater, went and died. He croaked right after the *Big Freeze* hit town." He paused for a moment, just to gauge the reaction of the new kid. "Yeah, he was a real weird one too–had more money than God."

Timothy remembered hearing about the *Big Freeze* from his parents. It covered half the state of Ohio. The temperature had suddenly dropped like sixty or seventy degrees. People froze to death, businesses shut down, and power lines cracked.

"So what's the deal with the house?" he asked. Being the new kid in town and trying to get into the club, he didn't want to seem too pushy, but he felt like he had a right to know, especially since he was going to be the one going into the place.

Rob looked back at Nate, who in turn glanced over at Jack.

"Well, the story is," he said slyly, the yellow glow of the flashlight illuminating his eyes, "that when Paater died he left no heirs. He stipulated in his will that all his possessions, including the house, were to be locked up tight as a drum. Sealed for all eternity."

Timothy was dumbfounded. "How could he do that? I mean, you'd think that somebody would have been able to get their hands on the place."

Rob grinned as Jack and Nate leaned back. They all loved it.

"Paater knew that others would try and get his stuff so he made it crystal-clear that the house and all it contained were never to be touched. And to this very day, nobody has set foot inside that place, although some have tried. Paater left enough money to pay the taxes and saw to it that the only thing to ever get the house would be time and the elements."

"And that's where you come in," Nate added, his bony finger pointing at Timothy.

"Yeah," Jack said. "If you wanna join our club you have to go into the house tonight and bring something back to us."

Timothy was starting to feel scared. "What do I have to get?"

Rob leaned in close, so close his thick black hair practically tickled Timothy's nose.

"Three things actually. My dad used to work as a paralegal in the office that handled Paater's will. He told me that he saw an itemized list of some of the stuff in the house. He said that besides the usual collection of antiques and old books and stuff there were these three vases…"

"Urns," Jack corrected.

Rob looked annoyed at the interruption. "Yeah, urns that held the ashes of Paater's favorite pets. My dad said that the urns were priceless, laden with gold and precious gems. The old guy kept them in his basement, hidden under white sheets."

Nate smiled as wide as Rob. "And all you have to do is bring them back to us and you're in."

"Why do you guys want those?" Timothy asked. "They're just ashes."

"Duh," Rob snapped. "Gold, jewels. Do the math."

Timothy felt a wave of courage come over him; he'd do it. He'd go into the house, find the urns, and bring them back. He was a little frightened of the task before him but it would make a man out of him.

"I'll do it," he announced. "Tonight, eleven o'clock. I'll sneak out and be home by midnight. I'll have the urns for you guys first thing in the morning."

"Good," Rob said while patting Timothy on the back. "Just don't be late. Meet us here at ten."

* * *

The house loomed in front of Timothy like some huge, squatting beast. It sat in relative darkness, lit only by thin streams of pale moonlight dotting the ground and two small lampposts on either side towards the rear. The ghostly light gave the house an aura of malevolence, adding to its creepy disposition.

Timothy held his flashlight out in front of him as if it were a weapon. He slowly but steadily trod his way up the cracked, weed-strewn driveway until he came to a tall, wrought-iron fence. The enclosure wound its way through dead or dying bushes and several gnarled trees, effectively sealing off the time-weakened building from any potential intruders.

But Timothy was young and agile and he had a purpose, a mission to fulfill. He'd climbed many a tree in his short life and a simple iron fence was not going to deter him. So with one swift effort he scaled the rusty bars of the fence and gained access to the front entranceway of the house.

Excited and determined thoughts flitted through Timothy's mind. He was a stubborn kid, perhaps to a fault, but he had learned how to use it to his advantage. If one tried long enough they'd eventually succeed.

The front door loomed before him like a present on Christmas Eve, inviting and yet unattainable. He stepped up to the door and reached for the handle. It felt cold and neglected. Speckles of rust dotted its surface. He spit into his hands and gripped it tightly, and with all his strength, twisted.

It only took a few seconds for him to realize the futility of attempting to access the house through the front door. And so his attention focused on a small window to the left of the porch. It was partially hidden by vine creepers which snaked up the side of the house like arteries. Over the years they had grown right over the windowpane.

Timothy inched his way along the brick until he was right in front of the window. It was small but still accessible. With determined hands he reached for the frame and gave it a sharp nudge.

And to his surprise it lifted up!

His inner voice immediately warned him of the possibility that the window had been left open on purpose, but he dismissed the notion. There simply would not have been any reason for it.

With determined effort he pulled himself up into the opening and into the house. The flashlight's yellow beam roamed around Timothy's surroundings. The room was bare, basically void of furnishings one would expect a wealthy person such as Mr. Paater to have.

Feeling nervous, Timothy swung his flashlight around and checked the window. To his relief, his earlier worries about it being left open were unfounded. It was the latch mechanism which had simply rusted to the point that only a slight jarring shook it apart. The remains of it lay on the floor below the window. Satisfied, he turned his attention back to his task. Time wouldn't wait for him; he needed to find the urns and get out of the house quickly, before anyone became suspicious. Trespassing was a serious offence. Stealing was worse.

The room was fairly small despite an unusually high ceiling. Cobwebs hung from every wall and every corner, effectively adding to the already dismal atmosphere. A dusty chandelier dangled in the center of the room, reflecting sparse glints of moonlight. Timothy thought how grand it must have looked when it was fully operational. Several paintings of gloomy looking old men and women stared down from their perches on the walls, past trials and tribulations staining their weathered features.

Timothy assumed one must be of Paater himself. It was larger than the others and had an ornate frame that alone must have been worth a fortune. The man in the painting appeared troubled and was looking off into the distance, as if he were unaware that he was being painted.

The need to find the basement snapped Timothy out of his thoughts. His time was limited and he knew it; he couldn't afford to sightsee. Without wasting another minute, he briskly walked out of the room.

The corridors of the house wound through the gloom like blind snakes, twisting in every direction. With only the thin beam of light from his flashlight, Timothy worked his way through the darkness. He wished he had brought along some type of schematic of the place, then he'd at least have an idea of where he was going, but he foolishly had thought that despite it being a mansion he'd have little trouble locating the basement. After all, how many basements could one house have?

A damp, moldy smell wafted up from the floorboards. The odor clung to the dark-paneled walls, coating the empty rooms with its stench, sucking up whatever traces of fresh air still lingered. Timothy covered his face with his arm, trying not to breathe too deeply. Up ahead he noticed that the hallway opened into a large, furniture-laden room. He could see long-discarded chairs and tables stacked one next to the other. He picked up his pace and moved towards the room.

Swinging the flashlight beam in front of him, Timothy gazed at the ghostly shapes beneath the dust-coated sheets in the room. There were so many pieces of furniture that he would have a difficult time, to say the least, just getting past them. Valuable time would be wasted, but he also couldn't afford to turn back. He suspected that the open door on the far side of the room might lead to some type of basement. He directed his flashlight at the black rectangle in the doorway and, sure enough, he saw a flight of wooden stairs descending down into the darkness. Taking a deep breath, Timothy squeezed through the furniture in the room until eventually he reached the basement doorway.

And then he hesitated. Was joining the club really worth it? What would it prove if he got caught or, worse, if he was hurt? What if he fell and broke his ankle? One of the steps might be rotted and could completely break under him, sending him crashing down into the basement. But it wasn't in his nature to quit. Giving up wasn't in his vocabulary. Turning back simply wasn't an option. He was determined to see the challenge through to the end; he'd already come so far.

The first step felt soft as it yielded to his weight of his body. He crept forward slowly. Time had obviously weakened the structure of the house and everything in it, so he had to balance safety with his desire to hurry.

Timothy was on the fifth step when his flashlight began to flicker. He cursed himself for not replacing the batteries before he left his house; it was just one of those small details that are so easily forgotten.

The staircase seemed to twist and turn forever. With every step Timothy took five or six more appeared in front of him. The air was growing colder as well. It had a dry quality to it, making it hard to inhale and causing his allergies to threaten.

Timothy slipped into darkness at that moment, as his flashlight faded out completely. He stood there, alone with his fears, struggling to maintain his resolve. He frantically shook the flashlight in a desperate attempt to get it to work but it wouldn't.

The silence was deafening, and despite knowing he was the only one in the house he still found himself almost wishing for some sort of noise.

Almost.

Eventually the flashlight popped on again and Timothy almost fainted in relief. But now the urgency to move quickly was even greater: the thought of being stranded again in total darkness was simply not an option he wanted to contemplate.

The basement was nothing more than a damp cellar, complete with stained cinder-block walls and a dirt floor. Thin strands of cobwebs dangled from every corner, every scrap of rubbish. The light from the flashlight was the only illumination. It was a fairly narrow space, no more than ten feet wide with a low ceiling of crumbling stone supported by thin, warped wooden beams. The dirt floor was cold and layered with mold. Small stones littered its surface.

Timothy had to step around the debris and stifle his breaths. He moved carefully and quickly. His stomach grumbled with every step he took, but he managed to ignore it. He had more pressing things on his mind, such as finding the urns and getting out of the house. Up ahead, a small, misshapen archway appeared in the flashlight's beam. A dense blackness filled the opening, revealing nothing about what lay beyond it. It was inviting and yet ominous. A chilled breeze lazily drifted out from it.

Timothy pressed forward despite his desire to turn back. He was so close he couldn't leave, not when the goal of his mission was so tantalizingly close. Joining the club was secondary to him by then, as was showing Rob, Nate and Jack he was brave enough to do as they asked. What really mattered to him was proving to himself he was capable of the task.

Swinging the flashlight in front of him Timothy entered the opening. Three objects were in a corner of the otherwise empty room. Each was covered in a dingy white sheet and perched on a three-foot high rectangular stone. There were strange circular carvings on the rocks, similar to Egyptian hieroglyphics.

The flashlight began to flicker yet again, testing Timothy's patience. He had to move quickly. He'd just grab the urns, shove them in his bag, and leave the house. He could keep them in his garage overnight, and in the morning he'd head over to Rob's place. Then he could…

Darkness covered him as the flashlight sputtered out.

Then, just as quickly, it came back on, although it briefly flickered again as if to remind its owner to hurry up. Timothy wasted no time. He sprinted over to the urns and in a one swift motion yanked the sheets off all three.

They weren't what he expected.

Each was nothing more than a plain metal box, studded with broken stones and capped by a weathered lid that was clipped into place by a thin latch. All in all, something barely worthy of a garage sale. Could Rob's dad have been wrong? Or maybe Paater had switched them out before he died. Or perhaps…

Darkness once again interrupted Timothy's thoughts as his flashlight faded. He stood there, alone in the dark, unsure what to do. His head ached and the smell of the cellar was starting to get to him, but it was too late to turn back, so he quickly pulled the bag from his back pocket, unfolded it, and stuffed the urns into it. The containers clanked together, echoing in the dank room.

The darkness was sapping his strength, draining his desire to escape. He whirled around and attempted to find his way back the way he came. The flashlight started to flicker on and off so he tapped it a few times against his leg.

The stairs seemed made of mud as he climbed them. They groaned in protest as the weight of his body pressed down on each one. With every movement he felt as if he were going to crash down through the steps and wind up back in the cellar. It was a thought so horrible, he couldn't get it out of his mind. Timothy had never been especially afraid of the dark or anything that it contained. He had a vivid imagination, but a firm grip on its boundaries; common sense usually won out with him. But when he finally reached the top of the stairs and stepped back into the large, furniture-laden room his irrational fears spun out of control.

The place was different than it was before. Dozens of pieces of furniture, all hidden under dingy white sheets, were arranged in tight rows from wall to wall like soldiers lined up in formation. With the bag draped over his shoulder Timothy started to make his way through the room. The obstacles slowed him down (he was forced to navigate around them, occasionally squeezing through pieces so close they were nearly touching), and it seemed like it took days just to reach the far side of the room.

And then he made the mistake of turning around and shining his flashlight back into the room.

All his life Timothy had rationalized everything. Nothing happened without a plausible explanation, without a reason. But what he saw then defied any reason or explanation. It was impossible and yet it was right there in front of him.

The objects under the white sheets were shifting, trembling beneath their dusty covers as if trying to escape. What appeared to have the shape of a high-back chair suddenly distended outward, twisting like a newborn chick breaking out of its shell. A supposed coffee table arched upward, forming an entirely new shape altogether. A small love seat shortened, curving in on itself like a massive worm that had been cut in half. It appeared to be in pain.

The furniture, or whatever it was, then formed a symmetrical formation. There were dozens of them: all lined up, squirming beneath their respective white sheets. They filled the room completely. Timothy nearly tripped over his own feet as he stumbled backward. The thick air clogged his senses, disorienting him to the point of passing out. He knew his flashlight, and his time, was running out.

But his situation grew worse. Much, much worse.

The things started to thread their way towards him. He stared in disbelief as the white shapes shimmied back and forth. They no longer resembled furniture. Now they were wholly and utterly alien, twisting contours of multi-limbed abominations writhing in pained movements.

At that moment the flashlight sputtered a few last times and then plunged the room into darkness. Timothy took a cautious step back, and then another. His heart thumped wildly in his chest, beating so hard it hurt. It was the only sound he heard, and it was deafening.

Part of him wanted to simply drop the bag and run out of the house as quickly as he could, but his inner voice reasoned against it. He'd come so far, facing impossible and frightening scenarios, and he'd survived. That alone said a lot about his character, and would prove to Rob, Nate and Jack that he was more than worthy of their club. He stood his ground.

Directly in front of Timothy, cloaked in darkness, he could hear the things moving towards him. The flashlight was useless, the batteries completely dead, and all he had were his wits. The sounds were drawing closer and closer to where he stood, the darkness punctuated by unnatural grunts and growls. It sounded as if there were hundreds of the things, thousands, all struggling to get at him. Timothy backed up, while smacking the flashlight on his leg. If only he could get it to work again he'd have a chance. He'd at least have a fighting chance. The flashlight then suddenly kicked back on and immediately shone on what was approaching him.

The creatures resembled distorted dogs. Mangy fur covered their grotesque bodies. Sporadic spots of infected skin poked through where the fur was thin. Their legs barely supported the swollen mass of their bodies, and their hanging jaws were so full of jagged teeth it looked as if they couldn't close them if they wanted to. And the eyes: a myriad of dripping red orbs reflecting a ruined perception of good and evil.

At that moment all notions Timothy had of becoming a man fell away. The instinct to survive kicked in, overriding anything else. His desire to see another sunrise, to feel another warm summer breeze in his hair, to see another smile on his mother's face, became paramount. He wanted to live, and he intended to.

He turned around and ran.

It was difficult to locate a way out of the house in the dark. Things became distorted, his sense of perception changed: a light switch suddenly higher up on

a wall; a chandelier hanging lower than it did before; a hallway seeming narrower than it actually is.

The faint glow from a full moon streamed into the house through a small rectangular window. It guided Timothy somewhat, and he wasted little time stumbling towards it. His flashlight fell from his hands and the impact caused it to click on one last time before failing completely. Once again darkness reigned. Timothy turned and glanced at it just as the light went off.

The dog things were stacked two or three high, their twisted bodies lying atop one another. The ones below were jiggling as they strained to support the weight of their brethren. The tattered remains of the white sheets that had covered them lay draped across their broad shoulders, necks, and feet.

And they were all glaring at Timothy.

In one swift motion Timothy bounded for the solitary window, flung the bag of urns through the glass, and leapt out into the front yard of the house. And as he jumped to his feet he noticed that the window was empty.

Confusion swirled in his mind. He half expected to see multiple sets of red eyes trained on him, but much to his relief there were none.

Timothy never looked back as he ran straight for his house.

* * *

When he rolled over in bed Timothy looked at the alarm clock and a jolt of panic struck him.

He'd overslept! It was nearly 11:30!

Sitting up in bed, Timothy felt the previous night's memories rush into his aching head all at once: the deserted mansion; the changing parts of the house; his flashlight dying; and most of all the things under the white sheets. He would have gladly chalked it all up to having a bad dream, but the vividness if the recollections was startling to say the least.

That and the bag of urns was lying in the corner of his bedroom.

Within five minutes, Timothy was dressed and shooting out the front door of his house. He headed straight for Rob's house, hoping that the guys wouldn't be too mad at him for being so late.

Overhead, the morning was gradually sliding into afternoon as clouds began to gather. A stiff breeze crept in from the west, further dulling the day's attempt at nice weather, and the temperature was rapidly dwindling, hovering precariously closer and closer to fifty degrees, far below normal for that time of year.

Timothy hardly noticed. All that mattered to him was reaching the clubhouse with the urns. He'd accomplished his mission. He was a man. The things in the house were probably just his imagination, his mind fabricating things to challenge his resolve, to put him to the test so to speak.

"You made it!" Rob cried, an enormous grin plastered across his face. "You're late, but you made it!"

Timothy walked up to him and dropped the bag at his feet.

"I told you I would," he said confidently. He gestured to the bag. "And they're in there. Three urns. They were in Paater's basement just like you said."

Rob grinned even wider. "Good. Hey guys, come here."

Nate and Jack stepped out from behind a row of trees. Each wore an expression of dulled surprise. It was as if they expected Timothy to return empty-handed.

"He made it back," they said in unison.

Timothy felt an uneasy feeling settling over him. He sensed something was wrong, very wrong. The fact that he didn't really know Rob or Nate or Jack very well suddenly struck him. Rob continued smiling as he bent down and picked up the bag at his feet. He reached into it and slid out one of the urns. His eyes lit up as he held the object up for all to see.

"I'm home," he announced. Nate and Jack strolled over to him, excitement on their faces.

"As we all are," Jack replied. "As we all are finally."

Timothy took a step back. He knew he'd made a terrible mistake, and now all he wanted to do was get away.

"You may as well just stop right there," Rob said sternly. The warning in his tone was clearly evident. "There's nowhere for you to hide…or anyone else on this miserable planet for that matter."

"Hey Rob," Nate snorted. "Give me my ashes now. I'm sick of this shell."

Rob laughed. "Here ya go, buddy, catch." He tossed one of the urns to his friend. "Don't let me hold ya up."

"Hey, give me mine too," Jack added.

Rob shook his head like a parent disciplining a toddler. "Patience, my friend, patience." He then handed the third urn to him.

Timothy stood frozen as he watched the three of them holding their urns up to their faces. Each then popped the lid and inhaled deeply. A faint grunting noise echoed into the containers as they were emptied of their contents.

Rob lifted his head up out of the urn he was holding. Black soot smudged his nose and mouth.

"You see Timothy, we crash landed on this foul planet decades ago. That old fool Paater captured us one night while he was practicing his magic in the woods behind his house. Before we knew it, we were reduced to ashes and imprisoned in these containers." He held up his urn. "The sheets were applied to restrain our essence, our will to be free so to speak. They held our remains in check, prohibiting our escape."

Timothy was at a loss for words. His head ached, his legs felt weak, and his stomach felt sour, but most of all he felt cold. The temperature was falling steadily, and his heart skipped a beat when he saw the white mist of his breath before his face.

"That's right," Rob said as if he could read Timothy's mind. "It is growing colder. I suppose it's a byproduct of our biology. We somehow affect the surrounding landscape. When we first came here the result was called the *Big Freeze*. It's been talked about ever since."

Timothy felt his head grow light. "What are you?"

Rob smiled, the corners of his mouth curling up towards his ears, stretching further and further until it was so impossibly wide it almost looked comical.

Almost.

"I think we'll like it here," he mused as he looked around. "The heat will sustain us, it will help us thrive. You see Timothy, we're the last of our kind. When we're gone, our race will be no more." His expression grew dark. "But we won't let that happen."

"But what about the things in the house?"

Rob raised his hand up to his face. "Those filthy things were created to guard us. Paater used his magic to make them." He pulled back a sheath of flesh from one of his fingers. A razor-sharp talon sprung out. "But he had to restrain them as well, thus, the sheets."

Nate and Jack casually strolled up behind Rob. Each cradled their urns in their arms. Their eyes burned with feral hatred.

"But how did you…"

"These bodies?" Rob interrupted. "Merely temporary vehicles, so to speak, that we borrowed from the unwilling former owners. And now that the remains of our true bodies are within living organic tissue we can regenerate."

Timothy stood there, mouth agape as the flesh from Rob, Nate and Jack simultaneously split open. Stubby black fingers pried open the slits further, followed by thick masses of writhing tendrils. They blindly grasped the air as a newborn baby would struggle for its first breath. And it all happened so quickly Timothy hardly had time to react.

The ethereal figure descended down from the sky, and planted itself firmly in front of the thing that had been Rob. It was semi-transparent and yet quite dense, gaseous and yet solid. A warm, gentle breeze accompanied it. The flowing garb it was wearing billowed out behind it. It seemed to have a will of its own as it silently drifted in and out of view.

Timothy stared at the apparition. He recognized it. He'd seen the face before, in the mansion, on the wall. The portrait of Paater. It was him! It was the ghost of William Paater! He was sure of it.

The flowing garb he was wearing billowed out behind him. It seemed to have a will of its own as it silently drifted in and out of view.

"You!" Rob snarled, a fierce expression of recognition on his ruined face. "You came back to stop us, but you won't succeed you old fool. It's too late. We are reborn."

A squirming mass of black tentacles shot out of Rob's chest and viciously speared the ghost's body, but it was like trying to catch air. The appendages simply fell to the ground.

"No! Nooo!"

The flowing material that was draped over the ghost's form then rose up behind it. With lightning speed it expanded outwards, and up and over the three things that used to be Rob, Nate and Jack, and with quick efficiency molded over the creatures like hot wax, contouring every angle, every bump, every feature exactly. Cries of rage quickly dissolved into guttural moans, and then silence. Gradually, the ghost's robes drew back. Only the three urns remained, clamped tightly closed, looking just as they did when Timothy had first found them.

The ghost swung its tired gaze over at Timothy, a faint trace of a smile on its face as it nodded its head gently. And then it dissipated into thin air.

Slumping to the ground, Timothy couldn't help but wonder what the things masquerading as humans really were.

Aliens? Probably, but from where? And why were they so hostile?

Eventually he decided that it didn't really matter. After all, nobody would believe him anyway. There was virtually nothing left of Rob or Nate or Jack (just a faint residue of blackened dust) or the ghost of Paater. And so, after mustering up enough courage, he returned the urns to the mansion, being careful to put them back exactly as he had found them. Much to his relief the guard things were merely pieces of furniture again with dusty white sheets covering them.

He collapsed into his bed, aged prematurely for his foolish efforts, and harboring an altered perception of life. But through it all he had proven, to himself if nothing else, that he was a man.

* * *

Jenny set down the spoon she'd been using to stir the homemade vegetable soup she was making. She felt the urge to pour herself another cup of coffee but decided against it. She'd already had three cups that day.

In the corner of the kitchen, perched above an over-sized toaster oven, was a small television. She'd grown accustomed to having the news channel on while she made lunch or dinner, it kept her up to date on the world's events. On the screen a pretty, dark-haired newswoman spewed out the top story of the day.

"Good afternoon. A strange fluctuation in the weather in Southeastern Michigan was reported over the weekend. Four people died as a result of the temperature, which plummeted from seventy-five degrees Fahrenheit to just below zero in a matter of minutes. The lowest recorded temperature was three below. All of the victims were homeless people unable to find sufficient shelter in time. Oddly enough, the temperature then rose back up to seventy-one degrees Fahrenheit within a few hours.

"Officials are at a loss to explain the anomaly, and can only cite a similar occurrence in the state of Ohio several years ago, known as the *Big Freeze,* as precedence. Whether or not these two unique situations are connected in any way is only a matter of speculation."

The Thing Behind the Wall

BY A.J. FRENCH

The ad in the paper said *One million dollars offered for city's largest cockroach!* The money was being put up by a local pest control company called *Rent-A-Kill.*

He read the ad again, sure he'd missed something, some crucial bit of information that would proclaim the whole thing a joke.

Summer been hot enough for yah? the ad began. *We thought so. Well, kiddies, your pals at Rent-A-Kill are here with a cool refreshing treat. Cool hard cash, that is.*

With temperatures soaring into triple digits this summer, the city has run amok with cockroaches. That may sound like horrible news to some of you New Yorkers out there, but here at Rent-A-Kill it's the best news we've had in our thirty years of operation. The calls have been rolling in, so many that we can hardly keep up with the demand, and with extra business comes extra cash. We're ready to give back to the community. We thought, "Eh, if we can have such a lucrative summer, why not give some other lucky New Yorker a break?"

Or should we say "unlucky" New Yorker? Here's the scoop: One million dollars offered for city's largest cockroach! That's right. Send us a picture of your largest, hairiest, slimiest cockroach, and on September 1st we'll sort through 'em and determine which one is the biggest. The winner (provided they can prove the photo ain't a fake) will receive 1 million dollars in cold hard cash, compliments of Rent-A-Kill Pest Control. That's it! Good luck to you all, and happy hunting!

Dave searched meticulously for a binding legal clause, some fine print, a *This isn't a real contest* warning, but found nothing. The only item accompanying the ad was a crude cartoon of a cockroach having its picture taken by a middle-aged person.

Dave put the newspaper down on the kitchen counter. *It's got to be for real*, he thought, *or else they'd include a disclaimer of some kind to avoid being sued.*

His excitement grew. He looked around his studio apartment, with its crummy wallpaper, dirty floor, smudged countertops, the nest of blankets that he called his bed; the volcano of dirty laundry in the corner, the numerous pizza boxes and fast food containers all stained with grease, the empty coffee mugs, the stacks of porno mags, the sprawling compact discs.

He shook his head. Christ, what a pigsty. No wonder he had such a roach problem. This summer had been the worst. He'd even called Rent-A-Kill, had them come out and spray. That'd kept the roaches away for a while, but eventually they came back.

They always came back.

His apartment was on the ground floor of a building that was built in the late forties. The sewer pipes were so old that they were the size of hallways and they reached down under the city like tree roots. He imagined a tumultuous hive down there, thriving below his hardwood floor, billions of roaches all jumbled together: countless antennae, countless eyes, countless brown bodies–a sea of shit-colored water and a sound like crumbling leaves.

He shivered. Not because he feared roaches or even detested them, but because he feared the vision wasn't far from the truth.

He'd gone to great lengths to seal up his apartment. He covered every drain when he was done using it; he kept his windows and doors closed; he even weather-stripped the few cracks in the floorboards.

But that didn't keep them out.

There was one place in particular, one terrible black place, where they were getting in at. Down below the kitchen sink, in the space behind the cupboard, where a section of the wall was missing. He didn't know how it got there; he'd never bothered to ask. He'd covered it with a loose board he found in the closet. Still, the board never held. No matter what he tried—nails, wood glue, duct tape—it always came loose. He knew the distinct noise it made when it came undone; he'd heard it countless times.

Sometimes when he was lying in bed at night, stoned, trying to fall asleep, he would hear it come undone and hit the floor with a *thwap*. An unsettling sound. He knew the roaches got in there; he'd even seen them crawling out from under the cupboard doors.

He had yet to summon the courage to reach into the missing section of the wall, but right now he was thinking about doing it. Because of the damn ad in the paper. He imagined reaching in there and pulling out some god-awful mutha of a cockroach, just like a magician pulls a rabbit out of a hat.

He fetched his digital camera then went back into the kitchen. Opened the cupboard doors beneath the sink. Instantly a dark-brown cockroach plopped onto the tile and skittered across the floor.

"Sonofabitch," he said, drawing a can of Raid from among the chemicals under the sink. He sprayed the roach and it flopped over onto its back, tiny, spindly legs wiggling. He crushed the bastard with the bottom of the can. A spray of guts like bird shit splattered across the tile. *Teach you to trespass on my land, pilgrim,* he thought smugly, hearing John Wayne's old drawl in his head.

He crawled back under the sink, moving the unused cleaning supplies aside to get at the missing wall section. Sure enough, his last fix-it job was just wearing off. It hung on by a single nail, dangling askew in front of a large patch of darkness.

Another roach clambered over the ledge into the crawl space. Puny fellow, no more than an inch. When it reached the inside of the cupboard, it made a beeline down the wall, leaving a faint trail of slime in its wake.

"*Sonofabitch,*" Dave said again, this time more vehemently. He used the Raid can to get rid of it in the same way he'd gotten rid of the first one. It lay there twitching for a moment, then went still.

More roaches slipped through the missing wall section. Dave disposed of them swiftly and dispassionately. For the next five minutes a steady stream poured in. Dave continued killing them until a nice pile had formed around his knees.

He had to remind his lungs to work again. *If those bastards all hang out in the same spot,* he thought, *then there's got to be a leader, a big one, a hive mother, a whatever.*

A mutha that's gonna make me rich.

He inched toward the wall, knees swishing across the floor. Almost on instinct, he got his camera ready, utilizing its blue light to see into the dark. The loose board dislodged easily, and Dave set it aside before peering into the opening. Blue light streamed into the darkness, cutting a swath like a spotlight, its eerie glow penetrating deep into a vast open space.

At first Dave saw nothing but unending black, but then something moved. It was subtle to begin with, almost dreamlike, as if he were standing on a steep cliff while the ground below rose up to meet him, or like he was peering through a porthole on a submarine, seeing a mammoth whale swim by.

He gasped audibly and shrank away from the opening. What he saw turning way down there in the darkness was enough to make his skin crawl, enough to suddenly alter his foundational concept of reality: how he viewed it; what was possible *in it*.

More of a reaction to fear than a conscious choice to take a photograph, his finger started clicking the button. Lemon-green flashes lit the darkness in a variety of dazzling ways. And they illuminated, albeit briefly, the horror lurking in the dank cold fathomless darkness, a creature that was larger than any human eye could register, so large only a portion of its brown scaly backside was visible.

It was more like the rolling surface of a planet as viewed by some unmanned spacecraft landing in the far reaches of space. A trundling insectile planet made of goo and slime and muck, and a hard carapace-like shell with a web of antennae stretching off into the benighted distance.

Dave saw all this while his finger kept snapping photos. His knees drove him backwards onto his ass. With the vision of that horrid beast burned into his retinas, he scrambled away from the opening, out from beneath the sink and back onto his feet. He now felt like a bug himself, having been spotted by something much larger and nastier, which was going to smash him underfoot.

He wanted to flee.

Instead he gathered his wits about him and went to work barricading the missing wall section. He used every piece of wood, every nail, every roll of duct tape in the apartment. When he was done, it looked like a mad scientist had been at work.

He checked his camera and, sure enough, he'd gotten the pictures. The next day he printed out a few sets and sent them off to the Rent-A-Kill Pest Control Company.

Then he waited, but never again did he venture into the crawl space beneath the kitchen sink. He slowly began packing his things. He started checking the classifieds for available rentals. Eventually, he moved into a new apartment.

Towards the end of August he got a phone call. It was from Rent-A-Kill Pest Control. He had won the contest, they were happy to inform him, and he'd be receiving the one million dollar prize.

The next week Dave's smiling face appeared in the newspaper, along with a short article describing his story. Accompanying the article was a single unspeakable photograph of the thing behind the wall. A quote from Dave ran under the photograph, and said simply, "I just happened to look under the sink one day, and there she was.

A Unicorn in the Heart of the City

BY JOSHUA RAMEY-RENK

I watched a unicorn die today.

Which was somewhat less astonishing than where I saw it happen.

I was walking back to my car from a late meeting. It had been one of those interminable sessions where the participants are really playing a game of whose dick is bigger. Even the women get into it and jockey for position under the guise of being "team players" and "supportive". They try to get every decision made at previous meetings re-examined and pushed in the direction they wanted it to go in the first place. The meeting had been scheduled for 45 minutes, but after three hours so much chaos had cropped up that I was seriously considering quitting my career and taking up personal fitness training as a new income choice. At least the girls would be breathing heavy.

When it finally ended I had dashed out of the meeting so fast that I ignored my need to pee, and was half-way to the parking garage before I realized that I wouldn't be able to make the 30-minute drive unless I got some relief.

There's a small urban park between my office and the parking garage. You know the kind of place: a few trees, some benches, grass. A place where secretaries take bag lunches on their breaks, getting a little sun on their thick legs while catching up on their bodice-ripper literature.

The park is surrounded by a low hedge and waist-high wrought iron fence. In the middle there's a fountain that runs intermittently depending on the city's budget and the current political climate regarding water shortages and environmental concerns. Tonight it was running and splashing quite loudly, making my bladder ache in sympathy. I looked around quickly to make sure that nobody was looking, and ducked into a small stand of trees and shrubs to relieve myself.

A snort and a rustle coming from deeper in the bushes startled me. In the middle of the city I wasn't too worried about some kind of wild animal, but plenty aware of the fact that the summer months had brought the homeless population out in force, and they were more dangerous when disturbed than most other wildlife I knew.

I quickly finished, zipped, and was about to step out of the bushes to make my escape, when a stray shaft of moonlight came through the clouds and pierced the darkness ahead of me.

A white horse lay on its side on the dirt in the bushes, flank heaving and blood running from, of all things, an arrow wound. The eye that I could see rolled wildly as the beast struggled to rise up, steam smoking in clouds from its labored breathing. The arrow sticking out of its side looked wicked, in the shadowy moonlight it appeared ragged and black. I could see that the shaft had several barbs along it, in addition to whatever was buried in the bleeding animal.

With a movement so sudden that I jumped back, the creature heaved itself to its feet, shuddered, and swung toward me. I stopped dead.

It had a horn! Also bloody, but as there were no injuries there, the blood must have come from something else, something that I realized must have been gored. The horn swung in my direction, the head dropped down, but the animal didn't charge. He - now that the animal was up, I could tell it was a male - stood on shaky legs in what I realized was a defensive posture.

A sound like a hummingbird sped past my ear, and another arrow flew into the little clearing and struck the ground in front of the unicorn. He screamed and reared, forelegs kicking wildly, head swinging back and forth to locate the origin of the attack. From behind me stepped a second other-worldly creature of the night. Tall and ethereal, my mind instantly named it "Elf" even as I was taking in the flowing tunic with folds that created deep shadows in the moonlight, the hunting horn slung at its side, the bow held in one hand and the small knife in the other.

"Do not move," said the…elf, I supposed, "You stand in the way of my prize." I heard a slight breathlessness in his voice, and realized that what I had taken for shadows was blood running from his side. The hand that held the dagger was also pressed against his side. Instantly I understood where the blood on the unicorn's horn had come from. That animal seemed to have regained some strength, at least momentarily. It no longer quivered or shook, but stood firm, horn raised high and always keeping the tall hunter in view.

The stallion snorted once, and lowered its head slightly, body tensing. This time there was no question-it was preparing to charge; at me or the hunter remained to be seen. The air was tinged with a metallic taste, like after a lightning strike, and electricity seemed to crackle between the hunter and his prey. Too quickly for me to react, the creature, horn lowered and nostrils flaring, charged past me and struck the hunter squarely. I saw the horn vanish into the depths of the elf's robes. He grunted, and the bow dropped from his hand.

But his knife was ready. Even as he buckled to his knees, he lashed out, a great gout of blood sprayed from the Unicorn's neck, and in what looked to me like a silent, slow-motion film, the two of them toppled in a deadly embrace, the Unicorn landing on top of the Hunter.

All was still for a heartbeat. In the silence, I saw the hunter struggle to bring the hunting horn to his lips, then he blew a single clear note, and turned to look at me. I stammered something, asking if he needed help, a pointless question as blood poured out of his mouth while he struggled to move beneath the unicorn. Finally, he gave up and in a whisper like the wind in oak trees said, "no matter, it is the way of the hunt." I watched as a final tremor went through him, and the knife and the hunting horn fell from his hands, the fey features going slack in death.

The Unicorn still moved, although a dark river ran from its flesh. I knelt down, tentatively reaching to touch the mysterious horn. It felt hot to the touch, and firm, more like flesh than bone or the horns of other animals I had touched. Like the hunter, a final tremble ran through the fallen animal, and I felt the heat drain out of the horn as it died.

A single note of music came through the air, an answering note to the hunter's last call. The sound of hooves and raised voices began to come closer, and I stepped deeper into the shadows. A troop of hunters rode into the clearing, bows at the ready, horses lathered and blowing as they were reigned in. The horses had oddly misshapen heads, thick knobs where the fallen Unicorn had a horn.

One of the newcomers dismounted, glided over to the scene of the carnage, knelt, and seemed to be murmuring a brief prayer. The rest of the troop was silent as the solitary mourner rose to his feet, holding the bow of the fallen hunter. He spoke clearly, but emotion was strong in his voice, "My son's hunt is finished-he will ride among the stars but no longer by our sides." Silently, he disentangled the limbs of the fallen animal and hunter, and the rest of the troop lifted the elven body up onto their shoulders. They turned away and began to file out of the clearing. As they did so, the mounts whose riders were now on foot silently followed; but before leaving the clearing, each animal slowly passed by the Unicorn, and dipped their heads to the body of the arrow pierced animal. Had they still been intact, their own horns would have gently touched the fallen creature.

A cloud drifted over the moon, deepening the shadows and obscuring my view. When it moved away, the clearing was empty, the only sign of the night's mystery was churned earth and broken branches from the surrounding trees.

I thought I heard a final distant note from a hunting horn, but as it grew louder I recognized it as the wail of an ambulance, growing louder and then fading into the night, a mystery of its own in the moonlight.

Because You Feel It

BEN NORTH

Human Keating placed the cardboard sign on the footpath outside the sixty level MLC building and sat down beside it. About twenty seconds later a man in a business suit stood above him crying and took out his wallet, removing a wad of bills, and placing them on the sign, then he turned and walked into traffic. A taxi hit him and he tumbled over the roof and landed at an odd angle with his head split open on the street. A crowd gathered around the man and nobody noticed when a pretty businesswoman threw a handful of bills at the sign and pulled her hair free from her ponytail and punched herself in the face twice. As Human gathered the money and put it in his jean's pocket an Asian man in a courier uniform threw an envelope onto the sign and took two steps back, pulled out a gun from a back pack and shot himself in the head. Blood flew up like a sprinkler and covered Human and the crowd screamed and scattered. Human picked up the sign and envelope and got to his feet and began walking towards Central Station. He assumed the pace of the street and a block later he had blended in. His face, T shirt and jeans were covered in blood and he attracted looks as he waited for the lights to change at Town Hall. He didn't feel bothered by them, and as he wiped some blood from his face with his shirt, he smiled at a little boy playing a Nintendo DS.

Just as the lights changed a Policeman came up behind Human and called out. People started to cross the street and Human held up the sign to the cop, who looked terrified and took a step back. Human flipped the sign over and the cop took two more steps away. Human turned and ran across the street, leaving the cop standing as the lights changed and the traffic started.

Human didn't know it but the cop, who had a pathological fear of HIV, had seen 'I have AIDS.' when he looked at the sign. When Human looked at the sign now he saw nothing, just blank cardboard. The sign had only ever had a message for him once;

when he first saw it and took it from his previous owner three years ago. Since then he had flashed it to others thousands of times. He never knew what they saw. Only that the sign worked for him. It got him what he wanted. The price was having seen the sign's message for him.

Whatever you do with your life enjoy it because you are going to die on the 10 /10/ 10.

Today.

Human wiped himself clean with his shirt which he discarded in a bin, and then walked shirtless into a Gowings store on George Street and purchased a beige button up shirt, grey pressed pants and some deck loafers which he changed into immediately, pulling off the tags and handing them to the sales assistant to scan at the counter. He stopped in a Hungry Jack's for ten minutes, sat down and ate a Chicken Burger and fries with a large Coke and then walked the three blocks to the Armani store on George St. The doors were thick glass with a stainless steel strap diagonally across them. Human walked inside and surveyed the store. Two years ago when he was blind drunk and crying he promised himself that when this day came he would be wearing an Armani suit. A salesman in a blue pinstripe suit approached Human.

"Can I help you sir?"

Human held up the sign and smiled. "You bet your ass."

* * *

Match looked on Sarah's Facebook profile. '*Sarah Foster: wants to watch a happy upbeat movie, any recommendations?*'

Match looked over the responses, *Pineapple Express, Step Brothers, Zoolander* and *House Bunny* and typed in his own suggestions: *Schindler's List, Doubt, Philadelphia, The Elephant Man, Million Dollar Baby, The Passion of the Christ,* then a minute later *Mystic River,* then *Open Water,* all of which he deleted and then posted as *Open Water!*

Match logged off and walked into the bathroom. On the floor wrapped in a towel with only its head showing was the mauled possum his cat had brought home. He squatted down and looked at its eyes. They were closed shut and the twitching of its whiskers that had been going on when he first brought it inside an hour ago had stopped. He leant in even closer, scanning for signs of life, looking at the dirt in its nostrils. From a certain angle it appeared to be smiling. Match considered the possibility that the possum was 'playing possum', and might come back to life.

That's not going to happen.

He picked up the bundled towel and walked with it to the bin at the front of his house. As he held the possum above the open bin he looked down into its eyes, shut tight and wet, and its mouth–cute, not vermin like at all–and willed it to show some sign of life, a noise, a motion, something; but it just lay there wrapped up with its tail hanging out in a spiral. Match let the possum go and it dropped onto an old lettuce leaf and an empty box of chocolate chip cookies.

He walked back inside and stood over the computer for a moment before beginning the shutdown process. As the icons vanished all that was left on the screen was a black and white picture of him and a girl, their cheeks, eyes and hair colored in by hand. His hand around her waist, looking away to the left; while she stared straight into the lens, smiling. The picture flashed, and then disappeared. The computer's fan stopped turning.

Match walked into the kitchen and grabbed a glass jar from the shelf. There were three chocolate chip cookies inside. He opened the lid, took out two, and then looked at the last cookie, thought *who am I kidding?* and took the third cookie and walked into the living room. From through the open window he heard gravel crunching outside and saw his mother's Black Toyota Prado pulling up in front of the farmhouse. The Prado's horned honked twice. He walked into his bedroom and took a black zip up hoodie from his closet and put it over his T shirt unzipped. His mother kept the engine idling and waited behind the Prado's tinted windows at the front of the farmhouse.

Match got in the back seat and didn't speak a single word the entire two hour trip to the child psychiatrist in Sydney.

The psychiatrist's office was outfitted with recessed lighting, rows of leather-bound books and a weathered brown leather couch for Match to lie on. Doctor Prock was in his forties, balding with a grey specked beard. He flicked his pen back and forth in his fingers and looked down when he spoke.

"I'm going to ask you about the accident, only because this is the first time I've seen you and I only know what's in the notes. I'd rather hear it from you."

Match put on his sunglasses. Doctor Prock couldn't tell if Match was looking at him from behind the dark lenses. He was. Match sat forward on the chair and took off his hoodie to show his T shirt with 'I only slept with her because I'm in love with you' printed on it.

Match lay back on the lounge and pulled out a packet of cigarettes from the pocket of his hoodie. "We wanted to see it so we had to go fast. Over two hundred kilometers an hour."

"You can't smoke in here." said the psychiatrist, standing up. Match inhaled and blew out smoke from a laying position. "If I'm going to tell you the story I'm going to need a smoke. Open the window."

Doctor Prock paused for a moment and looked down at Match smoking from behind dark glasses and walked over to the window and opened it. A cool breeze and the noise of the traffic seven stories below rolled in. The air in the room became an odd smelling mixture of old books, leather, nicotine and city air. The psychiatrist sat back down and waved a curling puff of smoke away from his face.

Match drew on his cigarette and exhaled as he spoke.

"We only had one week left. She was only going to be sixteen for another week. It doesn't work unless you are both sixteen."

* * *

Mercy kicked a stone over the edge of the cliff and watched it tumble onto the rocks below and wondered if there was any chance that she might survive the fall. Suicide was a sin. But so was sex out of a union sanctified by God.

She looked up. The sky was a film of grey haze and it started to spit on her. She thought back to her trip to England. Gavin from her Church group. The implied promises. The morning after and his disinterest. The unanswered calls to his mobile. The trip home and the stories she told to try and bury the whole thing, let it go cold.

When she told Father Hill about the situation, being careful to phrase it hypothetically, he had just smiled at her, pointed up to the sky and said "God has a plan for you. It's your job to be listening when He tells you what it is."

The rain started coming down heavier and the wind picked it up and blew it into her face. A gust caught her back like a sail and nudged her towards the edge. She pulled her iPhone from her jacket pocket and looked at the screen. It showed a picture her and Gavin together with a large church outing, posed in front of Westminster Abbey, everyone smiling and goofing around for the camera. Rain drops began to land on the screen. She looked at it for a few seconds and then motioned to put it in her pocket. It slipped from her hand and landed at the edge of the cliff. She leant down to pick it up and the wind gusted. She stood up and swayed before losing her balance and falling over the edge, flaying her arms and grabbing handfuls of air. She fell backwards and saw the lighting cut across the sky. Her heart pounded in her chest and she closed her eyes. Time seemed to slow and her thoughts relaxed; unlocked. A voice drifted through her mind, soothing her.

Deny ten men unto my name and it shall be yours again.

A feeling of peace overcame her and she opened her eyes and saw the cliff tops falling away up towards the sky before she landed on the rocks.

* * *

Janet gripped the steering wheel and willed the red light to change.

If he says, "it hurts," again I'm going to scream.

"It hurts, mommy." Ryan said.

She unfurled her fingers from around the steering wheel and pulled her nails into her palms as hard as she could while Ryan held his hands around his stomach and let his head hang forward over the seatbelt.

O God, please let him be okay.

"I know, baby. Mommy's taking you to some special people who can help. Just…just hang on a little longer, okay?"

The light turned green and she put her hands back on the steering wheel and continued straight ahead. When she looked back at Ryan his head was rolling back and his eyelids were fluttering.

"Ryan? Ryan, wake up!"

His head fell forward and the jolt roused him. He lifted his head and looked over at Janet. Perspiration condensed and dripped off his forehead. He leant forward again and raised his knees up to his chest and held himself around the stomach. His eyes were closed and he began making a low whining noise.

"It hurts."

Janet saw the sign, behind a billboard advertising America's Best Dance Crew 2011 and The Natural Energetic Healing and Aura Balancing Centre.

"We're almost there now sweetie. You've been so brave. Mommy's really proud of you. When you're all better mommy is going to buy you a Star Wars™ LEGO® toy."

If Ryan heard he gave no sign.

* * *

After Human flashed the sign whatever the Armani assistant saw made him very agitated. He seated Human and proceeded to measure him from ankle to ears, then brought out a pair of three-quarter length riding pants with red braces and a floppy cap. Human raised the sign again and said "I don't like it." and the Armani assistant convulsed. Human couldn't believe it. He had shown the sign and made people jump into lion enclosures, made people set themselves on fire, nobody had ever fought the sign's message, and now this guy was resisting; resisting over the selection of an outfit?

He lifted up the sign and said "Black suit."

The assistant ran his fingers through his sweaty hair. He packed up the riding outfit and walked back out to the stock area. He returned a minute later with seven boxes and started to unpack them. Human put on the black suit and white shirt. The assistant went white when he picked out a soft pink tie.

Human paid cash for the suit and walked towards Circular Quay with the sign tucked under his left arm. The Armani shoes were tight and bunched his toes painfully. As he stepped up a gutter he heard a screech and someone call out and then he was weightless. The Toyota Prado sent him flying and the world spun over and Human had time for one thought, *I'm dead*, before the back of his skull hit the edge of the gutter and burst.

* * *

Doctor Prock looked over at Match. "What do you mean? What only works if you are both sixteen?"

Match took the final drag on his cigarette and looked around for a place to stub it out. He put it out in a glass of water on the table next to him and lit another cigarette.

"If you wanted to see the ghost then you had to follow the rules."

"The rules?"

Match blew smoke directly at the psychiatrist. "Rule number one, you had to drive out on Line Road at over two hundred kilometers an hour. Rule number two, it had to be after midnight. Rule number three, you both had to be sixteen. And rule number four? You had to both be in love. We went out there on the Friday night, the same day the sergeant had come and given a talk to the school, saying that it was just a myth, and the only ghosts on that road are the ones that were going to be created from the dangerous driving going on there."

Doctor Prock had stopped taking notes and was sitting forward in his chair. Smoke trailed around him and he ignored it.

"Justin and Courtney had done it last week and they said it was amazing. Courtney had bragged all over school about how they had seen it and now she knew that Justin truly loved her. That when they saw the ghost on the road ahead of them it felt incredible. Melissa asked me if I loved her. I told her I did. She asked me if I would go out onto the Line Road with her. I told her I would."

Match held the cigarette and lighter but didn't light it. He looked over at Doctor Prock.

"We joked about what the cop had said—about us becoming ghosts. I picked her up from her parents at seven. We told them we were going to the movies, that we would be back around ten-thirty. We figured we would just stay out past midnight and wear whatever trouble we got into."

Match lit the cigarette. The smoke seemed to seek out the psychiatrist and lurk around his face.

"We went to the movies and saw The Town. I had already seen it but I told her I hadn't. I don't know why I did that."

He looked out the window at the smoke streaming away and sat still for a minute.

* * *

Darkness. Gavin's voice. And laughter.

"She's wet. My fingers slip in and out of her easily. I turn her around and I'm inside her and she's saying 'not hard' over and over and at first I think she's saying 'don't fuck me hard' and then I realize she's saying that I'm not hard. I pull out and she's right. I'm softer than bubble bath and she's still saying those words, 'not hard, not hard', and I have never been less aroused in my life."

His words dropped away as the interior of the ambulance came into focus. Mercy tried to lift her arm but something was holding it down. Equipment dangled and swayed in time with the movement of the cabin. She could hear the sound of Velcro straps being undone. Beside her a paramedic was leaning over a machine which seemed to be the source of a beeping noise. She tried to turn her head to get a better look at him but her neck was secured in a brace. She could feel something was not right with her hips, not painful, just not exactly right, but her head was held tight so that she couldn't look down to see.

The paramedic noticed her movement. "She's awake."

He was in his late twenties with short cropped hair and muscular forearms. He leant down over her and smiled. "You are going to be alright."

With some effort she raised her hand and rested it on his inner thigh near his groin and smiled back. "I know."

* * *

Ryan fell forward over his seatbelt and a thick rope of drool hung from his bottom lip. Janet reached over and pulled his head back. His eyes were rolling in their sockets and the waist of his T-shirt was saturated in blood. Janet pulled up the shirt. The flesh around his tummy looked split, cracked, and was weeping blood. A fold of skin on his stomach opened and an eye appeared in the slit and looked over at her. A low moaning sound filled the inside of the car and it took Janet a second to realize it was coming from his armpit–a mouth in Ryan's armpit–and when her eyes fell back on the road and she saw the man in the black suit she knew it was too late to turn.

Janet pushed hard on the brakes and the Toyota skidded diagonally and smashed into the back of a parked Mazda Getz, smashing its rear and side windows. She looked in the rear view mirror at the figure in a black suit laying in the gutter twenty meters back, and then over at Ryan who was lying with his head dangling over the seatbelt. The low moaning from Ryan's armpit persisted and she lifted his limp hand up and peered into the space between his arm and T-shirt saw it, a tooth-filled gash of flesh in his armpit opening and closing, releasing a low *oooooooohhhhh* sound. She lowered his arm and felt a wave of unreality wash over her as she looked at the cardboard sign that was stuck on the windshield.

"Why did you have sex with a demon Janet? Why? Why? Why? Why?" was scribbled in magic marker across it. Janet opened her door and stepped out of the car, keeping her eyes locked on the sign. She reached forward to grab it and felt nothing as the passing truck's rear view mirror clipped her head and knocked her under the wheels.

* * *

Mercy lay back in bed and looked out at the rain on the windowpane as it gathered and streamed down. She was happy with her physical and spiritual recovery. In the sixteen weeks since she was admitted to St. Sebastian's Hospital she'd had the steel pins in her left shin removed, taken her first steps in the Physiotherapy gym with the assistance of two staff and a pick-up frame, and drawn in and then repelled nine men, four in the last week.

First the male night nurse on Monday , then the physiotherapy assistant Tuesday morning, then the guy who came to visit his mother with a broken hip, then the occupational therapist who leant in too close during their sessions. She was sure that when she had denied sex to ten men and her pilgrimage was completed her Lord would give her a clear sign, a blinding light, a feeling of wellbeing, a booming decree from above. Something distinct. Something unmistakable.

Something.

The old lady with the red rinse in the bed next to her was watching the LCD screen on the ceiling bracket at the end of her bed. She was poised with the remote hanging limp in her wrist, channel surfing. The sound from the television filled the room.

"The monkey bit the child's face and carried it out the window. The child died when the monkey dropped it from the roof, startled by the parent's cries."

Click.

"- an apparent Dungeons and Dragons phone sex line operator. What's unknown to authorities at this stage is –"

Click.

"- a real breakout role in the new film The Beverley Hills have Eyes."

Click.

"Miss Veitch then told the court that she was handed a plastic bag which was labeled 'Fecal Testing Kit.'"

It was the old woman's third lap and Mercy sighed and looked out the window. The blonde teenage girl in the bed across from her grabbed the bedrail and tried to roll herself onto her side, cried out in pain, and then lay flat on her back. A tall female nurse with shoulder length black hair walked in and stood by her bed. "You know the doctor wants you to remain flat on your back. Until we can be sure that you don't have any spinal injuries he wants you to maintain bilateral pressure on your back. If you lay on your side the pressure on your spine will be uneven and … "

"But I don't like lying on my back, ok? It's not comfortable and I can't sleep like this."

"I know, but it's only until we can X-Ray your back and confirm that you don't have any spinal injuries."

The girl opened her mouth to say something and then turned her head to the side, defeated.

A man in a white button up shirt with floppy brown hair and a clipboard under his arm came up behind the Nurse and pinched her waist with both hands and she yelped and turned around. He looked at Mercy and smiled and laughed at his own joke.

She smiled back.

Number ten.

* * *

Match was about to light his last cigarette when he heard the crashing noise from the street below. He looked over at the psychiatrist for a moment before they both got up and looked out of the open window and on to the street. A crowd was gathering around a Silver SUV that had smashed into the back of a parked car. Broken glass was scattered across the street and Match could make out what looked like a woman lying in a pool of blood on the road. He stepped away from the window and walked past Doctor Prock, who was still looking out the window, and out through the doors leading to the waiting room and past the secretary at her desk. He pushed open the door leading to the fire escape and walked down them three steps at a time. He reached the bottom and opened the door that led into an art deco lobby and then began to run, slipping past a group businessmen and women streaming out of an elevator. The motion sensor doors leading out to the street opened and he was running, moving as fast as he could towards the silver Toyota. Broken glass was strewn all over the street and it crunched under his sneakers as he slowed to a walk and saw a teenage Japanese girl in a Krispy Kreme uniform tending to a young, bloodied boy in the passenger seat. The woman on the street was face down and her head was a collapsed arrangement of hair and skull and brain, sitting in a pool of blood. It stank and as Match put his hand up to his mouth to hold back the vomit he saw the cardboard sign. Sitting on the windshield of the Toyota with the writing facing the interior of the cabin, he thought for a second he saw his name written on it. He stepped in closer to the sign and then he saw it:

You never loved her Match. Not really.

He kicked the dead women's leg as he stepped over her and pulled the sign from the windshield. He held onto it tightly with both hands and read it over and over, feeling woozy. He shook his head and tripped over the dead women as he stepped away, landing on his back. He lay on the concrete carpeted with broken glass and looked down at the piece of cardboard in his hands.

This sign isn't real. This sign can't be real.

The howl of an ambulance siren a few blocks away cut through the voices of the gathered bystanders and Match laid his head flat on the hard ground next to the dead woman, holding the sign close to his chest, not moving as the pool of her warm blood expanded and began to soak into his hoodie and jeans. A whooshing sound in time with his heartbeat ran through his head and the straight profiles of the buildings above him swayed as the world disappeared.

* * *

The wheelchair caught on the wall of as Mercy maneuvered out of the way of a Physiotherapist walking an elderly Middle-Eastern man with lateral scars running across each knee. Mercy knew that those scars meant a double knee replacement. She had learnt a lot of things in her four months at St. Sebastian's, such as where and when the kitchen staff liked to sneak a smoke (after the lunch rush between the palm tree and the skip), who would let your visitors stay past visiting hours (Nurse Sevagian, but only if Doctor Reznor wasn't on duty), and where the new admissions tended to spend their time (the garden area in front of the maintenance sheds with the views overlooking the harbor). She angled her chair perpendicular to the elevator, pushed the down button, and then wheeled herself away from the double stainless doors as the button illuminated. The weather was good and she wanted to get outside before the cool afternoon change. Her legs ached when they got cold.

The elevator doors opened. There was nobody inside and she wheeled herself in backwards and then pushed the ground button. As the cable and gears whirred above her she thought about

Doctor Deriagio's lecture this morning. About how it was normal for patients to develop feelings for their caretakers, that a rapport between them was inevitable and perhaps even preferable, and that a genuine concern could easily be mistaken for something else. But *acting* on these feelings was not in anybody's best interests. He had smiled and brushed a loose strand of hair from her eyes when he said that last part, and tilted his head downwards, looking over his glasses and down his nose at her, a look that she took to mean *I know what's going on and this is your first and last warning.*

The doors opened and a young kid with a fringe that looked like it weighed more than he did tried to push past her and into the elevator, only to be pulled back by a man that Mercy assumed was his father. The man shook his head in apology and stepped back. Mercy wheeled herself out of the elevator and down the hall past the vending machine and through the automatic double doors that led outside into the Garden area overlooking the harbor. A warm midday breeze washed over her as she rolled down the concrete path towards the picnic tables. A lone figure sat at the tables, laying back with his legs stretched out straight in front of him with ankles crossed and elbows resting on the tabletop. Smoke trailed away from him and as Mercy wheeled herself closer and angled herself to get a look at his face he dropped the butt to his feet and stepped it out with a twisting motion.

"That's going to end up in the ocean, y'know. Probably end up choking the last of some rare species of penguin." she said.

The boy pulled another cigarette from the packet on the table. "We can only hope."

Mercy looked the boy over. He looked about seventeen, with pale skin and messy brown hair, wearing a black zip up hoodie over a hospital gown. On the seat next to him she saw a piece of cardboard wrapped in a T-shirt. He noticed her interest and pulled the bundle closer to him.

"What's that?" she said.

"You don't want to know."

"Yeah? Well maybe I do."

He lit the cigarette and rested his hand on the bundle, looking away across the terracotta rooftops that sprawled all the way down to the harbor. He still hadn't looked her in the eye.

Mercy flinched. "Is that security? You better watch out. No smoking in hospital grounds, don't you know?"

The boy turned and Mercy leant forward in her wheelchair and snatched the bundle from the seat next to him. He spun back but it was too late, she had already pulled out the cardboard sign and was staring down at it.

Your relationship with God only exists in your mind Mercy.

Mercy felt sick. Her chest felt tight; it was like trying to breath in a room with no air. She looked back at the boy. He was looking into her eyes now.

"Give it back."

"What is this? Who wrote this? You?"

The boy looked at the ground and extended an open hand. "Give it back."

"Where did you get this?!"

"Look, I don't know what you are seeing right now, but no, I didn't write it. I can't even see it."

The boy stood up and took the sign from her hand and she sunk back into the wheelchair. He wrapped the sign back up in the T-shirt and sat back down.

The boy lit another cigarette. "I have a theory. It's kind of like psychic predictive text–but evil, very evil. Whatever you are feeling right now–it wants that."

Mercy looked at the boy. His eyes had seemed sad.

"It wants that." he repeated.

The Isolation Method

BY DALE ELSTER

The place was a dump.

There were two lamps on either side of the bed, but only one worked. The walls were nicotine-brown, matching the curtains. The room reeked of urine and God knows what else.

It was perfect.

No distractions.

Aside from the quality lighting and world-class housekeeping, the room featured a TV, bureau, and tiny circular table. That was the piece of furniture I was most interested in. I dropped my bags onto the bed. The one with my clothes I left alone. The other I quickly unpacked, using the items inside - notepad, pencils, and laptop – to create a workspace.

I made my living writing dime detective novels. The books were short on plot and long on violence, featuring a character named Rock McGraw. He was a cliché. A short-tempered, vengeance-driven private eye hammed together from every cheap gumshoe novel that came before him.

Rock McGraw was a joke.

I created him that way.

My name was Robert Decker. I refer to myself in past tense because the Robert Decker I had always known was long dead.

`It happened shortly after I wrote my first novel. Serious, literary work. The opposite of the detective books.

It was roundly rejected by every publishing house in the country. But it wasn't just rejected. It was ridiculed. One publisher said I should focus on less depressing work.

Like clubbing baby seal pups.

But I didn't give up. I made changes to the book. I packaged it up and sent it off to meet its fate. Again it got rejected, and again I sent it back out. By the time I realized I had spent more time hating that damn book than I had spent writing it, it was too late.

My wife hated the book more than I did. Who could blame her? That massive pile of paper had first become the other woman, and then an anchor that had sunk my hopes for a writing career, and a better life for us.

My dream was gone.

She was gone.

I became a drunk.

So much for the storybook ending.

The problem was I never knew when to quit.

When to quit writing.

When to quit drinking.

I could have given up, gone back to teaching. Tried to piece back my marriage, somehow.

Not me.

I wanted to write again. Man fiction was all the rage. Guns. Booze. Broads. Different books. Different writers. All the same crap. I wanted to stab the genre in the eye.

I wanted to turn man-fiction into a joke. If the publishers wanted to laugh at me I'd give them something to laugh about.

It was a stupid plan.

But I was just a drunk; what the hell did I know?

So I sat back down and wrote. Wrote about a world of corruption and retribution.

Rock McGraw's world.

The book was not just hack – it redefined the word.

But it sold.

Once again, the joke was on me.

There were more books. I couldn't stop them. Each book was worse than the one before, but it didn't seem to matter. They were popular. Websites were created. Movie rights were purchased. Book signings were major events.

All of it happened, yet none of it felt real.

Because I was dead.

Something else had taken over within me.

No.

Not something–someone.

Him.

Robert Decker, the other one.

In order to create Rock McGraw, I had to create another Robert Decker. A Robert Decker better suited for the world of pulp fiction than I was. By the time I figured all that out, it was too late. The other Robert Decker had taken over. All he wanted was the fast life. The books were just a vehicle to keep him supplied.

I was dead, which brought me back to my original problem.

I didn't know when to stop.

I didn't know how to stay dead.

One day I just woke up.

And I knew what I had to do.

I had to kill him.

I had to kill Rock McGraw.

The plan was to write another McGraw novel. The last McGraw novel. Just kill him off and be done with it.

Maybe he'd die too. The other one.

Then I could go back to being the Robert Decker I had always known. Back to being the good writer I knew I could be.

I sat there staring at nothing. I don't how long I had been sitting there staring at digital blank paper, but it felt like a long time. Hours, maybe.

He was still in control. And he'd turned off the tap.

Nothing new.

I'd suffered through writer's block before. There were methods for dealing with it.

My plan was to sit right there until the tap started flowing again.

Whatever happened, I was not leaving this room. Not until I took back what was mine.

Or until I was too crazy to care anymore.

My attention shifted from the computer to the door. It was a sudden and unexplained movement – I hadn't heard any noises. But I knew someone was there.

A moment later I noticed two dark shapes in the gap at the bottom of the door.

Shoes.

Then pounding.

The desk clerk, was my first thought. The desk clerk alerting me to something.

"Open up Decker! We've got business."

Not the desk clerk.

"Who's there?"

"Western Union. Who d'ya think?"

McGraw. Only Rock McGraw would say something like that. Impossible.

Several moments passed before I responded; my mind racing, calibrating my sanity. Waste of time. I was a drunk after all, and drunks can experience all sorts of craziness.

"If you're really him, you'd just kick the door down."

As I spoke, my hand curled around the object on my right, next to the bottle of water. It was a fail-safe. It was made of blue-gray steel and held six bullets. If the mystery man was real, if he kicked the door down, someone would hear the commotion and come. Even in this hole, someone would come. If whoever on the other side of that door was somehow other than real, then maybe it was time to rely on my friend to the right.

Because then I would know I had gone completely crazy.

Less than a second later, I had my answer.

The door burst open in a shower of splinters along the jamb.

It was him.

Trench coat. Fedora.

Rock McGraw.

The bad lighting cast him in a near perfect silhouette, but I didn't need to see his face clearly in order to recognize him. It was him, alright. His presence alone, palpable, breathing, told me he was real.

It told me something else, too.

I had finally lost my mind.

"This isn't real," I told myself, even though I could hear the words leave my lips in a confused blather of pathetic laughter and tears. "You aren't real."

I adjusted my grip on the gun. Fixed it properly in my hand. Raised it. The motions were not smooth. The half empty bottle it nearly knocked over on the way up dulled the coordination it took to make such a maneuver.

"You can't be real."

He stepped toward the pointed gun, enough to catch the nicotine-colored light, revealing the trademark features I once saw only in my mind.

The permanent stubble. The scar under the eye.

"Shoot," he said, pausing to light a smoke.

"Shoot and he wins," Rock continued. "Shoot me, and you're fresh outta friends in this world, mac."

He exhaled, refreshing the lingering odor in the room.

"So. What's it gonna be?"

The booze-fueled fog of confusion was beginning to break up. One problem solved. But there was another. The computer. The screen was blank. The keyboard was quiet.

"I'm not writing this," I whispered.

"I got news for you, kid. You won't be writing anything unless you come with me. Now."

Rock's massive fist swallowed up most of my shirt and yanked me out from behind the table and dragged me through the open door, across the narrow hallway and outside. Not into the parking lot of the motel, but out onto the streets of New York.

Rock McGraw's New York.

There was no sound as I passed through the doorway and into the street scene.

There was no sound because there was no movement. The traffic and the people were frozen in a state of suspended animation. As if some giant 'pause' button had been hit somewhere. Rock appeared to completely disregard the strange phenomena.

"We need to get to the library."

The detective turned and started walking. He was tall and covered a lot of real estate in a hurry. I had to jog to keep up with him. A hundred questions crammed my mind, but I couldn't ask a single one. No time.

A moment later we arrived. It appeared out of the darkness not as the marble and stone structure I was expecting, but a simple metal door centered on an unassuming brick wall. Not unlike the one I had just stepped through.

"This is the library?" The question, voiced as a whisper and intended only to be to myself, escaped my mouth and hung lifelessly in the surrounding darkness.

"This is your library, kid."

He opened the door and I followed him in. Suddenly the room went from pitch dark to dimly-lit. It looked like every library at closing time. We were staring end-on at rows of bookshelves. After my eyes adjusted, I noticed something odd about them.

`They weren't bookshelves at all.

They were people.

Hundreds of them. They stood frozen in neat rows in the same suspended animation as the street scene outside.

"What the hell is this place?"

"This is where it all comes from. All your ideas. All the characters you've created. All the books you've written."

"Books? My books? Can I see them?"

Rock shook his head, slowly.

"Not them, kid. One. One's all that's left. The one you were supposed to write all along. The one you gave me to protect."

"When did I -"

"When you created me."

Noticing the look on my face, the detective attempted to explain.

"I know. I don't understand it, either. Not all of it. I only know that that book was something to be protected. A job. My first job."

"Why is he taking the books? What's he doing with them?"

"Nothing good. You can bet on it."

Rock was scanning the large room as he spoke. Like a soldier establishing a vantage point.

Then he froze.

"Hear that?"

His usual commanding tone had reduced all the way down to a barely audible whisper.

I didn't reply, I just shook my head.

Then I heard it.

Noises above us.

Footsteps.

"Let's go."

Rock grabbed my sleeve and pulled me along toward the far wall of the room, ducking behind a row of still-life thugs I recognized from the first McGraw book.

He motioned me to stay down as he headed toward the footfalls. I could hear at least two of them up there somewhere, but probably more. Mixed in with the activity was another sound. Furniture being shoved around. Drawers being yanked open. Papers sent flying.

Then there was a clicking sound. A sound I had heard many times before, but until this moment, only in my mind.

Now it was real.

A metallic sound.

The sound of a mechanism being set in place.

The sound of a Tommy gun being cocked.

I froze.

The room exploded with gunfire. First the Tommy gun.

The spray of bullets tore through the wood floor at my feet then arced upward, striking the bodies in front of me with a dull ripping sound, like shooting sacks of wet laundry.

My heart pounded, nearly deafening me. I was only mutedly aware of Rock's return fire.

Two shots.

Barely a one second interval.

Unlike our mystery attacker, my detective had position on his target.

I was aware of something falling – something heavy – from the second floor onto the aisle ten paces forward and to the right of my position as the second shot fired.

A short scream as Rock's bullet found its second target and the dull thud of another body hitting the floor.

There were three more shots amid a flurry of commotion from somewhere further away upstairs, before the building went silent again.

I broke cover and rushed upstairs to Rock's position. The upper floor looked much the same as the lower floor, with rows and rows of bodies instead of books. Except for the office at the end of the hallway where we stood. An upstairs room in a library is not unusual. Not at all.

But a detective's office is.

As we approached it became clear. Everything was as I had written it. The name on the door in neatly painted black letters. Inside, the desk. The file cabinets.

Those were now tipped over, papers carpeting the floor all around them. One item in particular caught the detective's eye.

A floor safe. A file cabinet had been positioned over it to hide it. Its door was open, sticking up through the clutter.

Rock rushed to kneel beside it, as if it were a wounded friend.

"He's got it," he replied as he stood, the shape of his body expanding into a large silhouette against the city lights through the window behind him. "He's got the book."

I slumped onto the floor.

"So what do we do now?" I asked.

"We find him," the detective replied.

"And we take it back."

"How do we find him? You know where he is?"

"Yeah," Rock replied. "I gotta good idea." He stood, lifting me up with him. Then he clicked a fresh magazine into his gun.

"Let's go."

We exited the library the same way we'd entered the building.

Suddenly I had an inkling of what the plan was. But I had to be sure of something else first. The detective was several paces ahead of me, near the original door that brought me here.

"Rock, wait! What's the plan?"

He stopped and waited for me to catch up to him.

Then he said, "I walk through that door and put one right between his eyes! That's the plan."

Rock confirmed what I now realized I had I known all along.

That was the plan, alright.

But I was going to have to be the one to do it.

But that was only the half of it.

Rock reached out to grab the doorknob.

"Wait. You need to know something, Rock. The only way to stop Decker is by–"

That's when I saw it.

A car, blurred from its suspended animation state, suddenly rocketed to life.

Rock saw it, too.

A black car with several gun barrels pointing out the side windows.

There was no cover. No parked cars to duck behind.

"Rock!" I shouted. Too late.

He shoved me through the door and slammed it shut as the deafening sound of machine guns tore open the night.

"No!" I screamed, frantically trying to open the door. It wouldn't open. There was no door. It was now a wall.

"Stop gibbering. It's what you wanted."

A voice, coming from somewhere behind the door to my room.

The voice was easy to recognize.

It was mine.

The last words I was desperate to tell my detective echoed through my mind.

The only way to stop Decker is by killing you off.

I created Rock McGraw as a joke. He deserved better.

Anger rooted itself in my gut, then spread through my body until it reached my head, where it presented itself in a different form. A form, until this moment, I had not been used to.

Control.

The door to Decker's room looked like it had when I first checked in. Stained, but undamaged.

Until now.

I summoned the rage in my legs, lifted my foot and thrust it into the door just beneath the knob. The jamb splintered easily and the door burst open, the knob punching a neat hole in the drywall.

"We've got some unfinished business, you and I."

Decker never looked up. Never acknowledged my presence. He just stared at the screen in front of him and typed away.

"I'm working on a new series," he explained. "I gotta be honest; I didn't think I had it in me. I was having just a bitch of time coming up with anything new! Until you brought us here, that is. Yes sir, working in this crap hole really gets the juices flowing. Gotta hand it to you on that one."

I glanced around the room. There was no sign of the book anywhere.

"Where is it?"

"Where's what?"

"The book you stole. Where is it?"

I stepped around the desk, fists clenched. Ready.

He continued working. He wasn't just writing. He was writing over existing text. The words at the top of the page were right out of a Rock McGraw novel. Hard. Violent.

The words at the bottom described a much different setting. They were meaningful, nearly poetic in contrast. They were not the words of pulp fiction. They were the words of a great literary novel.

And they were being consumed.

I noticed something else. A thumb drive sticking out of the edge of the machine.

The book.

In McGraw's world – in my mind – it was a book, but here in the real world it took on a more modern form.

"Stop!"

"Candy from a baby."

He stopped working for a beat, long enough to finally make eye contact with me while he gestured at the words he was erasing.

"Only this candy ain't sweet. I mean, what's crap like this ever gotten us? A dead-end, working-stiff teaching gig and a pile of rejection slips, that's what! C'mon Decker – give the people what they want, man! The end of Rock McGraw. Can you imagine the sales? They'll be lined up around the block!"

"I'm not playing this game anymore Decker."

Decker ignored me and laughed, "Then we'll take a little creative license and bring him right back!"

I reached out and folded down the screen on the computer.

Decker stood, his back to the door, facing me. The movement was tricky; unstable. The empty bottle next to him explained why. I never felt more sober, more in control, than I did at that moment.

He squinted as he paused to think about the current situation before speaking.

"You know, I'm not sure why we haven't done the whole 'merge-thing' yet, but until we do, go sit down and mind your manners."

"I know why, Decker. It became clear to me when I first saw you sitting there. We haven't done the 'merge-thing' because you're not real. You're just a character I created. I thought that was the only way I could write the books. But I was wrong. Those books weren't bad. It was you who was bad. But I'm done with you. I don't need you anymore."

"Is that right? You're done with me, huh? Well I'm done with you!"

He fumbled for an object next to the computer. The fail-safe I had brought. The gun.

"Looking for this?"

I had it. Slipped it away while distracting him with the computer. He never noticed. He was just a drunk, after all.

He laughed.

"Go ahead! Shoot! You'll kill us both!"

"I don't think so."

Decker's rant continued.

"Shoot! Shoot and say goodbye! Goodbye Robert Decker! Goodbye Rock McGraw!"

"Hey Decker, remember what happens to low life thugs like you in Rock's world?"

The detective appeared behind him, the barrel of his automatic planted an inch from the back of Decker's skull. He spoke, his words a harsh whisper.

"Goodbye, you two-bit hack."

He fired.

And Decker was gone.

Rock McGraw put away his gun.

"Creative license?" the detective quipped, referring to his sudden resurrection.

"Guilty," I replied, smiling.

Then he turned and headed for the door.

"Hey!" I called out to him as I stepped to the computer and pulled out the thumb drive.

"Do me a favor."

He turned to look as I tossed the electronic device to him. In his hands it turned back into a book.

"Put it someplace safe, would you? I won't be needing it for a while. I'm working on another story first."

"Is that right? What's it about?"

"It's about a private eye and some unfinished business."

The detective nodded his acknowledgement. I thought I saw a grin, but it was probably just a trick of the light. Then he opened the door. Before he vanished into the shadows he said,

"Get it right this time. Or you'll be hearing from me."

The Dep Tank

A.A. GARRISON

Francis was ugly, though tall and strong enough that no one said so to his face. Thirty-three and perpetually single, he wore a candid homeliness, as one might look while popping a zit. He was, however, reconciled to this genetic injustice and it had failed to sour him, so much so that he made friends easily. One such friend was named Steven, and it was through him that Francis became acquainted with the tank.

Steven called him over, ecstatic, and was waiting at the door. "You gotta see this, man," the longhair said, looking stoned, though he wasn't. "Can take you to another world. Gotta see it."

Francis agreed to see "it" and was led through Steven's bachelor home and into the basement, where there awaited him a long half-cylinder reminiscent of a miniature quonset hut. It was metal and occupied two sawhorses, looking very strong.

When Francis showed no reaction, Steven said, "It's a dep tank." Then, when Francis remained silent: "A sensory deprivation tank." More silence. "You lay in it."

"And?" Francis said, implacable.

"And you *see* things," Steven enthused. "Can send you to a whole other world. I mean, not really, but ..."

Francis regarded the tank with a new eye, tracing its sleek white length. It reminded him of a giant pill capsule, and then, when he opened its hatch, a cheap coffin.

"Looks like a hot-water heater, don't it?" Steven said, still alone in his enthusiasm.

Francis supposed that it could look like that, too. The hatch was outfitted with two handles, one outside and one in. Also inside was a simple latch. The door creaked when moved.

"Wanna give it a go?" Steven asked.

Francis creaked the hatch and paced thoughtfully, as though it was a prospective purchase, and finally answered yes.

* * *

The preparations involved loading the tank with a solution of water and Epsom salts, then Francis divested himself and slid inside. It was a tight fit, as he was so tall, but he managed. It felt good, very womblike. Just achieving displacement, he was afforded a not unpleasant sense of weightlessness. He made himself comfortable and pulled shut the hatch, its rubber gasket completing the seal. He engaged the latch as an afterthought, with a *clink* that echoed a little.

The interior was dark as to if to define the word, and quiet too: the capsule was soundproof and Steven's basement was isolated to start with. The combination again evoked a coffin, now occupied. Francis tried to whistle, but it felt wrong.

After an uneasy few minutes of adjustment, he at last relaxed, the black silence spinning out. Steven had instructed him to, "just chill and let go," and Francis soon found himself doing so despite his lingering feelings of interment. He braced himself for when he started to "see things" and/or go to "another world."

Thirty minutes later, however, there had been no things seen, nor worlds visited. Francis's mind cleared so much that he remembered to get bread on the way home, but there was otherwise no discernable effect. He had just decided that being sense-deprived wasn't all it was cracked up to be, when there was a noise.

Though short and small, it was loud in the tank's hush. Francis had time to think it could be the shutter of a camera, when suddenly the tank felt as though it were falling, rendering his weightlessness complete. There followed an angry crash–like breaking glass mixed with splintering wood, or maybe wood made of glass–and Francis tumbled wildly, his neck whiplashed, and the water sloshed. The tank stilled as quickly as it had crashed, and Francis composed himself, the water equalizing around him. A muted tumult sounded from the outside world, something like screams.

Francis felt blearily for the latch, a task made heroic in the perfect dark. Doing so, he noticed his ears popping, as from an abrupt change in altitude. He lay still for a minute, dumbstruck, and the screams became foreign-language whispers, underscored by an electronic drone that could have been a TV. Once he found it, he slid the latch and cracked the door, flooding the chamber with a white light that shouldn't have been.

He creaked the door fully and Dracula'ed upright and the screaming reignited. His profoundly dilated eyes described only a blur of white and shape, like bugs drowned in milk, which slowly became a room that was not a basement, Steven's or otherwise. There were decorated walls and electric lights, a couch-like thing set before a turned-on TV. The TV displayed the static image of a frail blonde figure, with a score of compelling electronic music. Framed pictures depicted a bust of same face.

Another world, Francis thought, complete with Steven's burn-out intonation.

He looked around, palmed his eyes, looked again–and he was still there. He drunkenly traced the screams to a quartet of people-shapes cowering across the room, looking foreign for no ascribable reason. He started to climb all the way out, but his movement renewed the screaming. He remained in the tank, recumbent.

"Hello?" Francis called to the terrified family, unable to think of anything else to say.

The people only screamed. Francis kept mum, afraid to upset them further. He studied them instead, fascinated despite himself. There were two adults and two children, all blonde and pointing, faces bunched with an alarmed distaste. The children were crying and hugging their parents' legs, though the adults were no better off. Francis was struck by their similarity; he couldn't discern male or female in face or bearing.

The blondes gradually stopped screaming but came no closer, and for several minutes the two parties exchanged only looks. Francis stole a peek over the side of his vessel and saw that it rested atop a walnut coffee table, the glass top smashed wonderfully. Its presence satisfied the offensive crash that had pronounced his arrival.

"Sorry about your table," Francis said to the people.

They answered with a gasp that failed to become screaming. One of the two adults spoke then, and Francis understood not a word of it. The language held a sharp pronunciation suggestive of circumflexes and umlauts, almost Swedish, but in a staccato lilt that could have been African. The voice offered no clue to the speaker's sex.

"I don't understand," Francis said, now suppressing his own screams. Reality was making itself felt, clenching his guts and nipping his balls.

All four blondes ignored him. One, the androgynous creature that had talked previously, spoke to the other adult while indicating the connecting room with an air of command. The other promptly disappeared, footsteps smacking through the rooms.

Francis's back was complaining, so he again started from the capsule. At that, the remaining adult blonde pointed accusingly and spat more Afro-Swedish, which Francis took to mean *Stay there*. He resituated himself like a bad dog, and only then realized that the tank was clothing him; his fascination died off for good, replaced by a smothering fear. He rapped his fingers, scanning the room for any clothing-like articles.

Eventually the other adult reappeared, babbled to its spouse, and disappeared again, taking the selfsame children with it, their eyes glued to Francis for all their upheaval. Only the outspoken blonde was left, and he/she stared Francis with bald contempt. Francis couldn't blame it; he had, after all, crashed naked into its living room.

This pseudo-confrontation lasted for ten minutes and felt longer, the musical TV staving off silence. Then a kind of humming arose from outside, followed by closing doors and footsteps–like a car parking and unloading, Francis thought. Before he knew it, the living room was flooded with bodies, all blonde and identically featured, and clothed in loud red jumpers that demanded attention. The visitors stormed the room, danger in their demeanor, surrounding Francis's capsule in a tight half-circle. Each carried a funny white stick with a bulb on the end. None would look directly at Francis.

Again faced with a dearth of words, Francis said hello to the crowd at large. Instantly, a shudder passed through them, and one of the jumpsuit-blondes shouted more gibberish, indistinguishable from that heard earlier.

"I don't understand," Francis said. Déjà vu.

The blondes conferred amongst themselves, then one of the jumpsuits started forward, taking mincing steps as one might approach a rabid animal. The blonde tendered its stick, the bulbed end preceding him, and Francis eyed it in askance. He suddenly wanted out of this house.

After spying an open window feet away, he made his move.

Acting entirely on instinct, Francis feigned surprise and jerked his head left. When every blonde took the bait, looking at something that wasn't there, Francis cupped tank-water in both hands and lobbed it at the encroaching blonde. The blonde reacted as though dowsed with acid, dropping his stick and jigged in place, the arms working. He screamed what sounded like "Hi! Hi! Hi!" and beat at his wetted person. In one lithe, ballet movement, Francis clock-springed from the tank and dove headfirst through the yawning window, finding grass and sunlight.

Adrenaline screamed and he ran as never before, penis flailing angrily. The world was a sun-shot suburban locale, much like Steven's neighborhood, with mailboxes and sidewalks and a bisecting street. Francis dashed down the walk and deeper into this unbidden place, bare feet slapping the concrete, eyes dancing in their sockets. He passed more blondes and each ran screaming. He'd managed several blocks when he heard a familiar humming noise and turned to discover a car-like vehicle in pursuit, loud with flashing lights.

He ducked right and followed a street with more fenced-in houses and kempt lawns, driveways harboring vehicles similar to that in chase. Bumper stickers described that immaculate Aryan face he was coming to know: a button nose and blue eyes beneath a unisex coif of sun-colored hair. Many of the houses waved flags, also imprinted with The Face. All lawn gnomes were fair and blonde and sexually ambiguous. Francis ran faster.

Soon the flashing car was upon him, blondes visible inside it. The car stopped alongside, and Francis zigged right and through an ornamented lawn, careering into a cheerful maze of grass and fences. High-tempo footsteps and hurried words sounded from behind, a living tangle of their bizarre argot.

Francis hopped one fence, and then another, and a third, jumping in pogo escapements. He ran more and nearly cleared a fourth, but then ducked behind it, instead. There he rested and covered his mouth, allowing the blonde entourage to pass obliviously in the opposite direction. His body and lungs ached, pelting his brain with red pangs of disapproval. He had to pee, on top of it all. He pooled against the fence, wanting to stay for an hour or forever, breathing as hard as he could while keeping quiet. Then a door opened and closed, and a towheaded figure was screaming and running off, arms in a *Y*. Moaning, Francis stood and ran.

He scrambled back the way he'd come, into the street, and had started down the walk when he noticed the blondes' car, open and running. Francis tarried uncertainly over the curb, shifting on his stinging feet... then made for the car.

It was big and yellow, faintly van-shaped, and only when he saw that it lacked wheels did he realize it was floating. The open side-hatch invited him in, and the car proved empty of blondes. The driver's seat was heinously comfortable, suitable for sleep, and he stole a brief, orgasmic rest before attempting the controls. There were three knobs in the center console, along with a joystick-like contraption where the steering column would be.

Francis grabbed the joystick and eased it forward, and the car answered, gliding with the tacit smooth of butter on latex. Francis went "Woo!" and made the suburb blur past.

There were mirrors and he could see the blondes in them, crowding the curb and waving their sticks.

* * *

Francis found the hovercraft serviceable, if not enjoyable, and he navigated the streets with ease. One of the three knobs had closed the door, and another had killed the flashers. The third activated a radio that had spewed Afro-Swedish until he cut it off.

Several miles opposite the suburb was a small township, suspiciously quaint. There were brick buildings, signs he couldn't read, more wheel-less cars. All pedestrians seen conformed to the standard established earlier: blonde, androgynous, indubitably beautiful. The dress code was casual, tee-shirts and slacks predominating; many shirts showed The Face, doubling their wearers. The businesses promoted it too, windows dressed with dolls and posters and other merchandise in no way brunette. Further down was a memorial of some type, dominated by a large basalt sculpture that resolved into a giant head, repeating The Face in effigy.

"Ya'll are some vain sons of bastards," Francis said aloud, in the privacy of the car.

He cruised the pleasant/creepy streets and before long came to an intersection, at it a kind of single-bulbed stoplight. The light cycled between red, green, and yellow, as opposed to a separate bulb for each, and Francis hated it on principle. It went red and he stopped.

As he waited, a blonde child passed the car and saw Francis through the windshield. There was a distended second of fright, then the child pointed and screamed, a reaction to which Francis was becoming accustomed. The child's accompanying adult followed suit, and soon a respectable crowd was indicating the dark ugly man in the car, in the loudest manner at their disposal.

Francis said, "not again," and begrudgingly quit the intersection, the people scattering into nearby buildings, surely intent on reporting the incident to whatever authorities presided here. Sure enough, Francis got five blocks before a craft like his own devoured his rearview, its lights shouting. His first reaction was to run, but there was nowhere to run, so he pulled over anticlimactically and exited the car. He would've put his hands up if they weren't jacketing his genitals.

The other car stopped and birthed a five-strong crew of blondes, all in red jumpsuits and wielding the curious batons. As one blonde addressed Francis with an abusive flurry of language, another edged toward him, like before, brandishing its baton in a way Francis didn't appreciate.

For want of response, Francis went submissively prone, on his stomach with his hands at the small of his back. The blondes scuttled about, and soon Francis's hands were bound. It felt like some kind of glue rather than handcuffs, mating his palms together, but the effect was the same. He was then manhandled to his feet and consigned to the second car, the blondes giving him a berth. They turned from him with smooth scowls of revulsion, The Face exquisite even in disgust.

He hunched in the car for an uneventful few minutes, alone, before a blonde opened the side panel and leaned inside, extending a burlap sack. Francis caught a glimpse of the blonde's sour expression, that of one processing a dirty diaper, then the sack was over his head, night coming with it.

* * *

Francis spent his next hour being herded blindly around, through what he presumed was some sort of bureaucracy involving his arrest. There was a long drive in the hovercraft, then a stop at first one building, then another, a wealth of inextricable words exchanged at each. He was at one point fitted with a weird jumpsuit, which seemed to make itself over him rather than being put on, and he repressed a thank-you. It was in a third building that the sack at last came off.

Francis looked wildly about, finding himself in a pastel-colored cell. Two blondes were retreating warily to the door, sky-blue eyes fixed on Francis as they backed away as fast as they could do so. When they were out, the barred door thunked closed and a lock engaged. One blonde left. The other lingered beyond the bars, now relaxed, but not looking away.

"What?" Francis said abjectly. His fascination was long gone, replaced by a dismal detachment; the situation had exhausted his savoir-faire.

The blonde continued staring as though Francis excreted on newspaper, and then said something like "Hoedown lick-shits."

Francis shook his head, crumpled against the cold wall. It felt good; he was hot.

"Hoedown lick-shits," the blonde repeated, and put its perfect hands through a slot in the bars, patting them in a subdued clap.

It reminded Francis his hands were still bound, and he understood. He stood, backed to the bars, and slid his melded super-hand through. There was a spraying and his hand became two. He turned in time to see the blonde disappearing down the hallway.

The cell was a respectable size, with a bunk bed and a metal head and a washbasin, all remarkably clean. Several similar cells were visible outside, bayed into the wall like teeth, unoccupied. The jail was very quiet. Hours later, a guard brought a tray of bread and water. Francis had no way of knowing if it was the same one that had uncoupled his hands.

More time passed, and it soon felt like night. Francis was amazed to find that he was able to sleep.

* * *

He awoke to the unbound terror of remembering where he was. Then came a voice and another tray of food was scratching through the slat, delivered by a guard who wouldn't look at him. The blonde stared raptly down the hall, perhaps at something magnificent, and kept doing so until Francis took the food. The guard promptly made itself gone, and Francis ate greedily. He was very hungry.

The morning passed in the grueling fashion of time counted, then Francis had another visitor, this one as blonde and indistinct as the others except for a handsome black suit that projected seniority. The face knew neither blemish nor age.

Francis stood and the blonde spoke, three short words: "Home-freckly dick." The voice held a vaguely male intimation, enough for Francis to consider the blonde such.

Francis wagged his head and showed the blonde his palms, doing his best to convey ignorance.

The blonde surprised him by summoning two other, subordinate blondes from down the hall, one of them opening Francis's cell. Both carried bulbed batons used to gesture Francis out. He complied and the guards stood at arm's length, batons upheld. The head blonde started forward and Francis followed, his baton-wielding detail at heel.

After a labyrinth of squeaky tile hallways and more empty cells, Francis was led into a brightly lit room with a proper door. The four entered, the door closing behind them, and on a table at the room's center was Steven's sensory deprivation tank, open.

The head-blonde pointed a tanned, hairless finger and spoke a confusion of syllables that reminded Francis of the vomiting he'd heard. It looked in his direction but couldn't hold Francis's eyes, as if Francis had something on his face.

Francis interpreted this as *What the hell is this thing?* or maybe, *How did you get here?* He shrugged flaccidly. "Your guess is as good as mine, pal."

The head-blonde said more, waving his hands and looking irate, and Francis began tuning it out, wondering who would feed his dog. That's when he got an idea.

He coughed into the crook of his elbow, stealing a sidelong glance at the blondes by the door. They still held their batons at right angles, but now with limp, weak grips, like flag bearers in a parade. Francis saw his chance and seized it.

With crazed spontaneity, he twirled around, swiped the left blonde's baton, and jabbed its bulbed end into the blonde at his right. After a sizzling noise, Francis's victim disintegrated into a polite pile of ash, unmade before his eyes. The other baton clanged to the floor. There was an ozone smell.

Francis eyed briefly his new weapon, in both horror and wonder, then turned it on the two remaining blondes. They shouted in concert–"Freak-dee hole-cock!"–then raised their impeccable hands, passing nervous looks between Francis and his baton. Francis backed defensively from them, toward the open tank, periodically stabbing the baton to inspire distance. When he felt comfortable, he sheathed himself in the tank and pulled the door to, at once throwing the latch. He laid the baton between his legs, careful to avoid its disastrous bulb. There was still water inside.

After a heartbeat of silence, the tank erupted in banging and struggle, gales of Afro-Swedish as the hatch tugged futilely. Doing his best to ignore the tumult, Francis hugged his chest and attempted the ritual that had seen him here. He closed his eyes and chewed his lip and prayed to any god listening, the water splashing into a little squall. It was a long shot, but there was nothing else and he knew it.

Then the noise cut out, as if on a switch, and Francis again felt to be falling.

* * *

The tank landed with a mighty clang, like the conclusion of his last flight. Francis again tumbled about the chamber, and his first thought was the deadly baton, which he grabbed and steadied. When the world had gone still, Francis unlatched the door and swung it open. It was another few seconds before he opened his eyes.

Thankfully, there was only darkness, and the damp, old-magazine musk of Steven's basement. He periscoped his head from the tank and the room was as he'd left it, gloomily calm, disheveled with Steven's things. He climbed from the contraption with a groan of relief, holding the relic baton vigilantly from him. He loitered the basement for a recuperative hour, digesting his day-long adventure.

Eventually, clatter sounded from the house and Steven galumphed downstairs, looking wasted and ecstatic as ever.

"So, whaddy'a think?" he asked, coming to an abrupt halt. His smile evaporated, perhaps due to Francis's strange clothing and unhappy expression.

Without a word, Francis about-faced to the tank and touched it with the peregrine baton. There was a *bzzzt* and a flash of light, and the tank was a little log of gray ash.

Francis set the baton on a table and sat down, looking very tired.

I've got the Conch

BY KELLY M. HUDSON

When Janice slapped him a second time, it briefly flashed through Sean's mind that the conch might be cursed, but it was a momentary thought, because by then, a week into ownership of the giant sea shell, things had progressed too far to come back from. All he really knew in those moments was violence, hot and brilliant, as solid and sure as a gripped fist. And that violence was going to be directed at his girlfriend of three years, the beautiful and deadly Janice Murphy.

Was it only one week since Tom, his neighbor and enemy, had come to his doorstep and given him the conch as a peace offering? Tom, he of the barking dog and annoying kids and constant noise next door? Tom, two years younger than Sean's thirty, tall and handsome and dark-haired and with smoldering eyes? Tom, the guy who tried to bed Janice during a cookout the year prior and then acted like it was no big deal? How had he trusted that man with anything?

"Do you know what it is?" Tom asked, standing at the threshold and holding the box the shell was in like an offering of supplication. It was a regular old shoe box and Tom held it with rubber-gloved hands, the kind you use to do dishes with. He thought it must be some joke.

"A box?" Sean said.

Tom smiled and took the top off, revealing the shell.

"Ta-da!" he said. "Do you know what this is?"

"Uh, yeah. It's a conch," Sean said, rolling his eyes.

"But do you know who it belonged to?"

Sean stared at Tom like a parent catching a child in a lie.

"Let me guess, the King of Hawaii," Sean said.

"Don't be stupid, man," Tom said. "This belonged to William Golding. You know who that is, right?" Tom knew damn well that Sean knew who Goldming was; after all, The Lord of the Flies was part of his yearly curriculum as a high school English teacher. Sean taught it in his Novels class for Juniors and Seniors. That book was one of the few popular choices because of the violence. The kids always liked it, even if they didn't get it.

Sean shook his head. He had never heard of Golding owning a conch. Then again, he had never heard the man didn't, either.

"Sure, you know who he is," Tom continued. He was smiling now, the grin greasy and wide and Sean should have known there was something else behind that smile. Something sinister. "He wrote that book about the flies. And it's said it was all inspired by this conch he found when he was vacationing in Florida. I read this interview with him once where he talked about it, how the conch was sitting on his shelf and he was staring at it and the name 'Piggy' came into his head and like a flash the story was born." "I've never heard of that," Sean said. Tom was full of crap.

"Oh, it's true. He wrote the book in a hot streak, the words pouring out of him. When he finished, he put his mark into the shell, just inside the inner lip, so he'd always remember the day," Tom said. "Go ahead, look: it's engraved right in there." Sean, not exactly sure why he was humoring Tom, turned the big shell over in his hands and looked where his neighbor was pointing. Sure enough, carved into surface was the word "Piggy." It didn't prove anything, of course; anybody with a knife could make those marks. But there was something about it, something intriguing. Holding the conch in his hands, Sean sensed to the core of his being, despite his trepidations, the story Tom was telling him was true.

"I found it at this estate sale. Well, it wasn't really an estate sale, it was more like a police auction. Remember that rich prick, Ed Saunders, the guy who pulled that Ponzi scheme? They were liquidating everything he owned and I went, just out of curiosity. And when I saw the conch, I thought of you and I bid on it. I got it for cheap, too, because nobody knew what it was. But when I saw the word written inside it, I went on Google and sure enough, I found out all about it," Tom said. He was beaming now, proud of himself. "And then I knew for sure you should have it. I thought about how it inspired Golding and how maybe it could inspire you." Sean had been working on his own novel for over two years now.

It was a lovely little idea, about a guy who takes a spiritual trek to Nepal to find inner peace but ended up being coerced into a terrorist cell and fighting for the Taliban against Americans in Afghanistan. It was coming slowly, but everyone was sure it was going to be something special.

The novel had been the goal. When he got his Master's degree, he knew he could teach and so he did, getting a job at the local high school. This was to give him money to live on while he wrote in his free time. Once the novel hit, he could give up the teaching and write full-time. This was a great plan because it kept him near to his beloved Janice, the girl of his dreams, while she worked on her own degree. She was finishing her undergraduate work at the time he took the job and she was now into her first year of graduate school. She moved in with him when he started renting this house, about the same time he got the teaching job, and things had been pretty damned good between them. Oh, they had their fights like any other couple, but through and through, they were devoted to each other.

She stuck by him, even as his work on the novel grew less and less by the day. What used to be daily work became every other day had become once a week became once a month and now was once in a blue moon. Life piled up around him: bills, job responsibilities, spending time with Janice. Pretty soon, the novel was looking more and more like a dream and less and less like his future.

And so there was Tom, giving him this gift, which turned out to be a curse. Tom, the man he despised more than any other in the world. Tom, the asshole.

Sean grinned and thanked him and shut the door in his face.

He took the conch, his anger overriding the feeling it gave him to hold it in his hands, and placed it on the mantle over the fireplace in the living room. Janice came waltzing through at about the same moment, her eyes instantly drawn to the shell.

"Who was that?" she said. She had hair black as a raven and skin as bronzed as a shield. She was just under six feet tall and built like an Amazon, with naturally thick hips and breasts. Her eyes were black, like her hair, and they seemed limitless; he loved to stare into them when they made love.

Sean was six foot two and pretty sturdy himself, although his muscle came through working out when he could and not from any natural proclivity. He had sandy hair and gray eyes and his complexion was two shades lighter than hers. They made a good couple, complimentary to each other in nearly every way. He was going to marry her, he decided, once he finished the novel.

"It was the asshole," he said.

"Oh," her black eyes turned darker. "What did he want?" She plopped down on the couch and turned on the TV. She loved her afternoon soaps, and if there was one thing about her he could change, that would pretty much be it.

Sean thumbed towards the conch. "A present. To make up for everything."

Those black eyes settled on the conch and glittered in a way he never saw before.

"Oh, it's pretty," she said.

* * *

It took one day before the first argument. They were in the living room, standing in front of the fireplace, deciding on which restaurant they were going to. He wanted Italian, she wanted Chinese. There wasn't much middle ground there. The talk between them got heated, unlike it ever had before. For some reason, she grabbed the conch from the mantle and held it in front of her.

"I've got the conch," she said. "So I get the choice."

And for some other reason, that totally made sense to him, they ate Chinese.

A day later, another argument, this time over something he couldn't recall. This time, he grabbed the conch and held it aloft, a fire flowing from it and down his arms. He gripped it and offered it to the sky, like something for a primitive god.

"I've got the conch," he said. "So I'm right."

Immediately, Janice acquiesced.

Which brought him to the here and now, to the slap on the face, to the violence thrumming in his chest like an overburdened electrical circuit. Janice stood opposite him, her black hair streaked with gray and her black eyes bloodshot so deep that there was no whites visible. She looked like a demon from hell.

She gripped the conch with her right hand so hard it was bleeding.

"I've got the conch," she said, hissing the words from between her clamped teeth.

This time, the sting of his cheek and the anger in his heart overcame the vibe of the conch.

"I don't care," he said. He leapt forward and batted it from her hand. The shell flew out of her grip and slapped against the far wall. It did not break but instead tore a gash into the dry wall.

Janice gasped, stumbling back, the power in her gaze all gone now.

"How dare you?" she said, her voice a whine now, the keening of a kicked dog. "How dare you?"

She ran from him, fleeing to the bedroom he hadn't slept in for two nights now, slamming the door behind her. Sean stood still, glowering at her ghost. So much hot hate burned in him he didn't know what to do with it. Finally, after a few moments, the strength left him and he collapsed onto the couch, his bed for the last two nights, and wept. The tears were cold, ice cubes gone liquid, and sizzled from the heat of his face.

He cried until he fell asleep.

* * *

In his dreams, he remembered the first time they'd made love. It was their second date. They had gone out to eat and seen a movie and he was driving her back to that little apartment she shared with two other girls when she asked him to detour to the park. He smiled and said yes and then the dream blinked like a pair of eyes and they were on the ground, underneath an big old oak, and he was entering her for the first time. She cried out and whispered softly, and with each thrust he lost more of himself in her black eyes. When she came, she laughed.

That laugh made his soul sing.

* * *

When he woke the next morning, he was already late for school so he called in sick. His head seemed clearer than it had been for days. He felt as if he'd been drinking cold medicine that made him drowsy and filled his head with cobwebs, but now the sleep was gone and his mind was clean.

He hung up the phone and sat back, thinking. Things had been so terrible between him and Janice and they'd been bad for so long it felt like his only reality. He strained his brain, conjuring up happy memories: the times they went out, laughing and giggling; the moments spent alone, in bed, touching and bonding; and the times they were apart but longing for one another. Looking at them in his brain was like staring at a needle in the corner of the far end of a darkened cave. He could make them out, but barely. Like his dream they were fading, fog dissipating under a hot sun.

He wept again at this loss, feeling for sure those days and memories were gone forever now. And as he cried, through the prism of his tears, he spotted the conch, laying on the floor next to the wall.

It was the conch. That was the problem. It all started with Tom giving it to him. Somehow, Tom had fooled him into accepting this thing from hell and it was the cause of all their troubles. Fire burned in him. He was going to pick the damned thing up and crush it. That or throw it away. The quicker it was gone, the better.

Sean jumped to his feet and stomped over to the shell. He bent down and scooped it up, gripping it hard, pretending it was Tom's neck he was choking, and all at once he felt the anger leave. As he held it a comforting calm came over him, a feeling of control and peace.

"I've got the conch," he whispered.

Janice, standing in the kitchen and watching the whole time, screamed and launched herself across the room.

"I've got the conch!" he screeched as she crashed into him. Her nails raked his face and neck, tearing long, slender divots of flesh. His skin burned and he cried out, pulling the conch closer to his chest. But she was too quick for him, too savage. She clawed at his arm next, ripping skin and growling like a wildcat. Pain shot up his arm like lightning and he let go, the conch falling from his grip. She snatched it, holding the shell to her chest, and jumped off him.

"I've got the conch," she said, her voice cold, steady, and even. The voice of a sociopath.

Sean watched through tears as Janice scuttled away, clutching the conch and cackling.

* * *

A week later and the battle lines were drawn.

Sean hadn't been to work in days. His last call to them was his resignation. The principal sounded hurt but Sean could give a damn; that woman was nothing but a pain in his ass anyway. He gave his parents one last call, pretending all was right in the world, listening to his mother gossip about the people in their neighborhood. He'd been polite and gentle and when he hung up and said goodbye, he knew in his heart it would be for the last time. And yet, this did not bother him one bit. No, all he cared about was Janice and the conch; he had to have it. Come hell or high water, he would hold it once again.

He won it from her a couple of days ago, waiting patiently until she left her room to get some food from the kitchen. He jumped her, punching her so hard she spun in a complete circle, dropping the conch and collapsing in a heap. He laughed, plucked it up, and ran to the living room. Just holding it again gave him such a feeling of peace.

She stole it back a day later, sneaking in as he slept. She yanked it from his grip before he could react and ran. He chased her, cursing himself for being so stupid, and tripped over a wire she'd set up at the base of his bedroom door. He fell head-first into the hallway wall, breaking his nose and knocking himself out. When he woke, he was covered in his own blood and in so much pain he didn't really want to live any more.

The pain passed, and as it did, he plotted his final move.

It was two days later. Janice hadn't moved from her room. She kept the door locked and sealed. He couldn't peek under it because she kept stuffing towels into the crack, but he could hear her in there, doing things. Secret things.

He wondered what they were and hated her for it. He hated her for her laugh and her clothes and the way she always sighed when she slept next to him. He hated her for pressuring him all the time about the novel and for whining when she didn't get her way. Mostly, he hated her for having the conch and not sharing.

He would have shared. He knew it, in his heart. If he could just hold it for a few minutes, maybe an hour, maybe a day, he would cherish the feeling and then pass it on to her. But she couldn't be trusted. She would keep it forever now. She was a bitch of the first order, and she was giving Sean no choice but to break into her room and do whatever it took to get the conch.

Oh, how he wanted to touch the conch again.

His face, once full of fading youth and steadfast optimism, was now tight and narrow, the skin stretched like a beaten drum, red and angry. His eyes bugged out and his arms and legs were skinny. He couldn't remember the last time he ate. He didn't care. All he wanted was to touch the conch again, to hold it close to his heart.

He smiled, his lips cracked and painful, and thought about the last time he had it, in bed with him. The conch was more wonderful than a lover, closer than a god. It was all that mattered in this life and he'd be damned if some cunt like Janice was going to keep him from it.

Sean crept to the door. He was naked and stunk; pieces of old, dried feces stuck to his ass and the backs of his legs and dried urine stained his thighs. He didn't care, though. Personal hygiene didn't matter anymore. All that mattered was getting hold of that shell and never letting go again.

He held a spear in his gnarled right hand. It had taken him a day to fashion it. Something about the thought of holding a spear, a primitive impulse, felt so right to him. He'd gone into the front yard, found a fallen tree branch of some substance, and whittled one end of it until it was sharp enough to punch a hole in the living room wall. It was then he knew it was ready to use.

His plan was simple: bust down the door, charge in, spear the bitch, and get the conch. Nothing after that mattered. If he had the conch, he had it made.

Sean held his breath, turning the knob slowly. It was still locked, just like it had been the last time he'd fiddled with it. He put his ear to the door and listened. Nothing but silence. He'd done this four times a day since she'd locked herself in. Almost every time he heard nothing, but twice he did hear something. Once, he heard a slapping sound, like a wet towel whipped against the wall, and the other was a whisper. A "shick-shick." He had no idea what they meant. It didn't matter. He had the spear, and soon he would have the conch.

The conch.

Thinking of it brought tears to his eyes.

Sean backed-up until he was flush against the wall. He eyed the door, grinned again, and charged.

He smacked against it and bounced off, his teeth rattling from the blow. It jarred him and his whole body sung, like when he was a kid and hit a baseball funny with an aluminum bat. The way it rang up his arms was how his entire body felt for a moment. He thought of vomiting but pushed it back down. He would not be deterred.

Sean back-up and ran at the door again. He bounced off once more, but this time he heard the wood crack. Another couple tries and he'd be in there. He ran back and got ready, his breath coming hard and heavy.

The door creaked open on its own.

What was this?

He picked up his spear where he'd lain it on the floor and crept over to the cracked door. He peered in. Outside, it was mid-afternoon, and although he'd gone through and shut all the curtains so it seemed like night inside, Janice hadn't closed off her room. The shades for the sliding glass door that led to the backyard were wide open and sunlight flooded in. It was so bright it hurt his eyes.

Another reason to hate her.

Sean pushed the door open and jumped back, expecting some kind of attack. And he was assaulted, but not by a person, but a smell. It hit his nose heavy and thick, as wet as a rain shower.

Inside the middle of the room, filling it from wall to wall and as tall as he was, stood a mound of shit. It wasn't all made of shit; he could see there was lots of mud packed in there, with twigs sticking out like buried skeletons. And it had other things shoved into it, too. He could make out the bottom of their bed and a piece of the small chair they kept by the dresser. And sanitary napkins. Yes, pushed in at various spots were blood and mud covered tampons.

She had gone completely insane.

The stench was so strong he vomited. He couldn't help it. Stomach acids and bile exploded from his throat and splattered the wall next to the door. If she were going to attack, now would have been the time–but she didn't. Instead, Janice appeared from the other side of the mound, trudging up, naked as a lunatic, with wild eyes and a wide grin. Her hair was gone, chopped off by scissors, and what was left was sprawled over her skull like frenzied crabgrass. Her tits and legs were smeared in the mud and shit and the dark, thick patch of her pubic hair was matted with blood.

She held up her right hand.

"I've got the conch," she said.

It put Sean over the edge.

He charged up the mound, his feet and legs pumping furiously. He slipped and slid and was momentarily distracted as one of her used tampons slid between his toes. But he pressed on.

Janice slid back down the other side, cackling like a witch.

Sean reached the top of the mound, the high ceiling of the bedroom barely giving him clearance to crouch, and spotted her standing by the open, sliding glass door. She lifted the conch and taunted him with it.

"I've got the conch," she said.

He flung the spear as he leapt for her. He watched with crazed pleasure as the spear arced through the air and slammed into her stomach, slashing it open. As he fell face first towards the floor, he grinned in triumph, thrilled by his victory. The conch would soon be his.

The smile froze on his face when he saw that Janice had been doing a little stick-sharpening of her own.

Dotting the floor, like pungi sticks in some movie about Vietnam, were a dozen sharpened shards of wood. They were driven into the floor and jutting up like the broken teeth of a giant.

Sean plummeted, landing hard. He felt their bite only for a moment and then that pain disappeared into numbness. When he hit, he heard his body chunk against the wood and he thought of someone biting into an apple. This made him laugh.

Blood dribbled from his mouth as he giggled, impaled on four of the sticks. In front of him, Janice weaved for a moment, pulling the spear out of her stomach. Intestines flowed from the hole like water from a spigot. She tried to push them back in but it was too late, they were loose now, and, as if freed from a lifelong prison, they ran wild across the floor at her feet.

She fell next to him, dropping the shell.

With his last shred of strength, he reached out and pulled the conch to him. Its cold surface soothed the pure agony burning through his body.

Sean stared into his dead wife's eyes and let out a snarl of savage triumph.

"I've got the conch," he said.

* * *

They were found a day later.

Tom was the first on the scene, of course. It was his handiwork, after all, that had brought this wild disaster down on his neighbors. He sat and watched and waited, using binoculars and sneaking over sometimes, in the dead of night, to peer in whatever windows open to see through. His plan worked so much better than he ever could have hoped.

He hated Sean. He hated that prick with nearly every inch of his being. First off, the guy thought he was hot shit for writing a book. Yeah, like doing that made you something special. You and the other million people out there. Second, he acted like he was above everyone else. Sean wouldn't come to any of the barbecues Tom threw and he never got involved in all the neighborhood activities the rest of the block was a part of. No Neighborhood Watch, no Yard Sale Week, and no decorations for Halloween and Christmas. Allen Lane, their street, was renowned through the city as THE place to go each Halloween and Christmas to see some prime decorations. And Sean and his bitch of a girl would never, ever do anything to participate. How did that look, all these houses and yards decked-out in boughs of Holly, and the one house that wasn't was right smack dab in the middle of the block?

Ridiculous.

And then there was Janice. That girl was too big for her britches and thought she was way hotter than she really was. She was the straw that broke his back. When she turned down Tom—and he was TOM, for God's sake, not some shlub; he was a stud; no woman turned him down—she had done what no other babe on the block he was interested in had done. That couldn't stand.

So he went online. He looked for ways he could get rid of them, from infesting their house with mice to other, more deadly methods. Tom had served in Iraq and killed plenty a person in his day, so death was no big deal to him. None at all.

One day, after all his searching, he came across an obscure old article—an obituary, actually—about the last survivor of a crashed plane of Englishmen on some remote Pacific island. They were missing for over a month and when they were finally found, the five persons that remained alive were surprisingly robust for a hard-scrabble piece of land that had only a small stream and no other vegetation they could feed from. Nobody said much, although rumors flew wild. The rescuers reported finding a pile of human bones, just off the shore, dumped out there like they were trying to be hidden. Those bones never washed away and neither did the stories, until the day the last of them was on his death bed and made his confession. The five survivors had methodically hunted and killed the other twenty survivors. They killed them and ate them and were happy to do it.

The last survivor to die had carried a conch with him from the rescue as a memento. It was said that this story and the existence of the conch was what gave William Golding his idea to write The Lord of the Flies. Whether this was true or not, Tom didn't care. All that mattered was if Sean did and of course he would. Sean was so arrogant.

In any case, this conch was passed on to the dead man's niece and apparently some bad things happened when it was in her possession. She got rid of the shell, selling it to some pawn shop that burned down a week later. Only the conch survived the flames.

The shell became a legend, whispered about in old books on the occult and, later, on the internet. But each case was well-documented and each owner had some tragic story to tell before getting rid of the conch. Some threw it away, others gave it to charity. In every instance, the presence of the conch drove the people to wild madness. Eventually it ended up in the hands of a collector of odd objects, a man who sealed it in a glass case so it could be looked upon but never touched. This man, the guy who had the ponzi scheme and defrauded dozens, died a month ago and his estate was auctioned off. This was where Tom, after his research, found the conch.

It was a simple matter after that to break the glass and only handle the shell wearing rubber gloves. He carved the word "Piggy" in it to add extra authenticity.

And that sucker Sean bought every word of it.

Now Tom fetched the shell from Sean's dead hands, wearing the same rubber gloves to keep the conch from exerting its influence on him. He would pack it away in a box and seal it with tape and there would be no danger to him.

He smiled, plucking the shell and staring down into Sean's dead eyes. It felt good to show that punk who was boss. Now his only problem was what to do with the shell next.

He thought of Aaron, his manager in Accounting. Yes, Aaron was a real prick. Aaron might enjoy this little gift–and, hey, what did you know?–Christmas was right around the corner!

Tom whistled, exiting the house. He thought this conch was turning out to be alright after all.

Letter from Matt Nord, editor of Strange Tales of Horror

So, the sad thing is that this next story was supposed to be in the first Norgus Press anthology, Strange Tales of Horror. It was in the ToC, but through a huge oversight it didn't actually make it into the book, which I am ashamed to say was totally and utterly my fault. Patrick D'Orazio is and amazing writer, a great friend and a thoroughly forgiving guy, as he's agreed to let me present to you his story. So, in the theme of the book you hold in your hands, Look What I Found! It's Patrick's story!

VRZ

BY PATRICK D'ORAZIO

Parker shut the door and peered through the spy hole. No shadow crossed his vision, and he breathed a sigh of relief. Stepping back from the door, he slid three deadbolts into place and wiped the sweat from his brow. His breathing slowed as he waited, listening for sounds from the hallway. Hearing none, he turned toward the shadows of the apartment. The room was sparsely furnished with a small pressboard desk, a couch that'd been there when he moved in, and a cot he'd commandeered from Goodwill. It was as uncomfortable as hell, but Parker couldn't care less; he rarely slept anymore.

The thin man with the hollow cheeks and sunken eyes ignored the furniture and focused on the corner–or, more accurately, on the object that stood there concealed by a tarp. A nervous twitch of a smile formed on his chapped lips. He didn't bother activating the lights before he crossed the room.

Parker gripped the tarp with long, quivering fingers and tore it away. The cover was the only surface in the room that remained free of dust.

The VRID glistened in the moonlight trickling through a nearby window. It resembled a dentist's chair, with several stainless steel apparatuses dangling from above. Various tubes and wires ran from the side of the chair into a gaggle of routers and power strips. A control panel with a small monitor and keyboard sat beside the armrest, ready to be swiveled into place. The plush leather surface was the only part of the beast not made of metal. Even the overhanging headset that looked like it was on steroids reflected light off its silvery surface.

Parker had purchased the Virtual Reality Immersion Device back in '15, when a sliver of his soul was still intact.

* * *

He'd been an award-winning neurobiologist on the forefront of the virtual reality revolution. There were ramifications for VR in every industry, but its use in surgery was what intrigued Dr. Nathan Parker the most. He conducted experiments and surgeries using virtual emulations of the brains of patients with Alzheimer's, cerebral palsy, and even autism. He was able to delve deeper into the mysteries of those ailments than medical science had ever been able.

But it wasn't the medical applications of this new technology that had turned Nathan Parker into a VR addict. It was the stims being peddled illegally that had turned him into a full-blown tweaker.

The first stim Parker tried, a gift from a fellow doc, provided a sensation best described as a cross between an LSD trip and an hour-long orgasm. The VR hallucinations felt more real to Parker than the real world ever had.

Parker was approached by a few less-than-savory individuals not long after that. All he had to do was use his connections in the medical community to make sure a few select stims got into the hands of the appropriate people. In return, he would have access to more stims than he could imagine.

Parker tried to stick with stims that put him in a serene, peaceful setting like a remote beach or quiet woodland, allowing for an escape from the guilt he felt at becoming a pawn of the stim dealers, but as time went on his tastes grew racier.

At first, he dabbled with the narcotic and sex-fueled fantasies into which most people wanted to lapse, but soon even those were not enough. His brain demanded more and more perverse stimulation.

The first time Parker played at being an assassin, the rush from pulling the trigger on the high-powered sniper rifle felt like a religious experience. After that, his enthusiasm for the criminal and debauched grew until he was playing at being Caligula and Genghis Khan, among other notorious historical figures. Even that wasn't enough, as he grew jaded by the countless executions and rapes he committed in virtual reality. He needed more.

Ultimately, Diana took the kids and left. In his drug-addled state, Parker found it hard to care. That was when he got serious about his addiction and bought his very own VRID unit from the man who had gotten him into stim trafficking in the first place, Jericho Maltese. Jericho was more than happy to provide financing on one of the expensive machines to his best connection in the medical field. Parker knew it was a trap; he would be beholden to the thug forever after the purchase, but he had his priorities.

Three months later, Nathan made a serious error in the treatment program of a man misdiagnosed with depression, when in fact he was a full-blown schizophrenic. It took one virtual treatment for the patient to go completely mad. Before he could be detached from the machine and sedated, he'd torn out his eyes and was working on biting off his tongue. The good doctor was stripped of his medical license, the man's family sued everyone involved, and there was talk of criminal charges.

Before the state or Jericho Maltese could decide what pain to inflict on him for being such a royal screw-up, Parker cleared out his bank accounts and went into hiding. He no longer cared about anything except getting a fix. After a couple of years in the stim trade, Parker had enough contacts besides Maltese to acquire what he so desperately needed.

For a few months, things were fine. He would hustle on the street, selling stims he'd burnt through as he sought out more potent stuff. It was more miss than hit, but he managed to make some new connections that got him some freaky stuff on occasion. It was enough to keep him from going mad.

Parker knew Maltese was looking for him, and so were the police. Knowing his luck would eventually run out only stoked his hunger for more potent stims. He fell in with dealers far more sinister than Maltese on the off-chance they would offer him something on which he could drift away forever. It had happened before: tweakers would jack in and never return to reality.

That was all he wanted anymore–a way to escape.

* * *

Parker slid his hand inside the pocket in his worn leather jacket and caressed the stim the Bulgarian had sold him. A shiver of excitement cascaded through his body. The chip had cost him most of his available funds, but if what the man said were true, he wouldn't need money any longer.

"It'll set your world on fire," Ilian had said. Ilian had connections in Eastern Europe and the Far East, where some of the best stuff came from these days. If you wanted to be a rabid dog or a mythical dragon, Ilian could hook you up. He wasn't cheap, but the syndicate for which he worked was one of most powerful in the stim underworld. Their stuff was good, and as long as you paid, everything was aces.

This particular stim was fresh from the labs of a hacker out of the Ukraine know as 'Boris the Virus.' Before the VR revolution, Boris had spent time hacking military servers and robbing credit card companies blind over the net, but now dedicated his programming talents to making the most potent stims in existence.

"When I caught wind of this one, I knew exactly who to bring it to," Ilian had told Parker a week ago. "But it will cost you five times the normal price."

Slipping off his jacket and letting it drop to the floor, Parker slid into the comfortable seat of his VRID and swiveled the control panel in front of him. Sliding the stim memory stick into the slot at the side of the unit, he tapped on the keyboard. Then he moved the mouse to the appropriate icon and clicked.

A video image popped on the screen and made him jump. It was a skull with flaming red eyes. Its lower jaw slid open and the diabolical image laughed at Parker. The screen pulled back to display a cartoonish representation of the angel of death riding a pale horse. It came complete with sickle and cowering nubile feminine forms ready to be trampled by the Clydesdale-sized hooves. Abruptly, the screen was slashed in half, and the words *A Boris the Virus Original* appeared.

Rolling his eyes at the tacky logo, Parker clicked the mouse and got to a directory screen. He clicked "start" then pulled the headset down, ignoring the instructions that flashed across the screen in Mandarin, Italian, Spanish, Japanese, Arabic, English, and German. He already knew the drill. The helmet fit snugly on Parker's head, and he reached up to pull down the retractable cables with clips that attached to his index fingers. Clipping them in place and wrapping the Velcro around his wrists, he tapped on the screen a few more times before pulling the visor over his face, which sealed him in darkness. When Parker pressed a button on the side of the chair, the control panel slid out of his way and the chair adjusted until he lay flat. A quiver of excitement ran through him as the software counted down from fifty.

He waited patiently until the count faded. There was a slight vibration, a numbing sensation inside his head, a squawk of white noise, and then nothing.

Parker sat for a couple of minutes, hoping against hope this wasn't some sort of dud. It'd happened before: the software was incompatible with his unit's operating system or there was a coding error in the programming. But if that were the case, there should have been nothing, no introductory screens on the display, no countdown.

Uttering an inhuman growl, he ripped the helmet off. At the sight of his dreary surroundings, he cursed silently and tried to stand. The Velcro straps on Parker's wrists weren't tight, but as he pulled against the restraints he was yanked back into the chair. Hissing in frustration, he fumbled with the strips and clasps keeping his appendages in place. The ex-doctor felt a bit loopy, as if the stupid stim had stunned him before crapping out. Still, he managed to remove the Velcro and step away from the chair.

Parker yanked the memory stick out of the machine and stumbled drunkenly across the floor. He didn't bother picking up his jacket as he shoved the stim into his pocket and undid the locks on his door. The junkie's vision was hazy, and he found it difficult to manipulate the deadbolts–but that was not his main concern. Ilian had screwed him or Boris had screwed Ilian. Either way, this piece of crap program hadn't done anything but give him a bad buzz and make his stomach feel like a huge jungle cat was raking its claws across it.

Moving out into his hallway, Parker dragged himself along the grimy wall and toward the stairs. Fortunately, he lived on the second floor of the tenement and didn't have far to go to reach the street. Grabbing for the railing, he nearly tripped as he shambled down the steps.

A familiar odor invaded Parker's nostrils as he reached the first floor landing. Looking up, he let out a low moan as he saw his bum of a landlord standing outside his door.

To describe Parker's landlord as hairy would be an understatement. It was more accurate to say that Gerald Parsegian was a hirsute Sasquatch, standing well over six feet and weighing in at three hundred pounds. Many of his tenants theorized that much of his weight rested in the thick carpet of hair that spread down from his neck, crossed his shoulder blades, and kept going into the depths of the wife-beater he wore. Nuzzled deep in the recesses of a canyon formed by his copious man-boobs sat a gaudy gold crucifix. It looked like a ship lost in a sea of coarse, greasy chest hair. No one knew if the crucifix was a symbol of Gerald's religious devotion or something he wore to make up for the constant blasphemies flowing from his lips.

Gerald was in his typical gray undershirt and food-stained boxers, smelling like he'd bathed in garlic and sweat, a departure from his usual piss and onion combination. As he looked up from the newspaper he'd scooped up off his doormat, a grin formed on the ogre's face. "Ah, Mr. Parker, just the guy I wanted to see."

Parker tried to skirt around the overbearing zeppelin, but Parsegian stepped into the middle of the hall, blocking his route. The brute eye's narrowed as he looked his tenant up and down.

"Look, Mr. Parsegian, I'll get you your rent. I apologize for the delay, but I'm expecting some money within the next day or two. I promise you'll be the first person I pay."

Parker tried looking apologetic as he spread his hands in front of him. His tongue felt strange as he spoke, still tingling from the aftereffects of whatever Boris had put into that craptastic stim. He ran it across the top of his mouth and watched the smelly monstrosity in front of him offer up a skeptical look.

"What in the hell is wrong with you, boy? Cat got your tongue?"

Parsegian moved forward, crowding Nathan until his back was against the wall. The buzzing inside Parker's head was getting stronger, and all he knew was that he needed to get past this giant lump of shit and find Ilian.

Snorting with disdain, Gerry Parsegian leaned in as the former doctor continued to backpedal. The foul stench coming off of the man was overwhelming, and the fiery agony in Parker's gut was getting worse. He was worried he would heave chunks into his landlord's bushy, crumb-encumbered mustache if he didn't get the hell out of there.

"I always knew you were a tweaker, Parker. I can see it in your eyes: you're a goddamn addict!"

"Look, Mr. Parsegian, I don't have any idea what you're-"

"Quit mumbling, boy, and speak English!" Parsegian yelled, spittle flying from his lips.

Parker was at a loss for words, not sure why the fat bastard who smelled like a trash compactor was ignoring what he was saying; but as he stared up at the man, he felt a cold resolve come over him.

Without understanding why, Nathan Parker reached out toward his landlord, his hand grasping, his mouth gaping. All he could see was the enormous pores on the man's face, swimming in a greasy confection. The desire to touch that skin shot through him like a thunderbolt. A ham-like fist swatted at Parker's delicate fingers, knocking them away.

"What the hell is wrong with you, boy? Are you so strung out you don't know what you're doing?" He snapped his fingers in front of Parker's eyes, as if trying to wake him up.

Parker didn't blink as a primal surge of desire crawled up from the base of his spine. He could no longer feel the buzzing in his head or the torturous pain in his gut. All he could sense was something approximating the lust he'd discovered upon reaching puberty. It was a brushfire inside his head. But it wasn't directed toward some woman. It was, inexplicably, directed toward the fat sausage fingers dancing in front of his eyes.

With a burst of strength of which he hadn't realized he was capable, Parker snatched at the fingers fluttering oh-so-tantalizingly close to his mouth. He wrapped his surgically skilled digits around them and pulled them toward his waiting teeth.

Gerald Parsegian was no wimp. His hirsute forearms were nearly Popeye-sized, and he'd won his fair share of scrapes in his time, but he had no time to react as his fingers were dragged into the mouth of the lunatic tweaker standing in front of him.

There was a sickening crunch as Nathan Parker's pearly white incisors bit clean through the first two knuckles of Gerald's index and middle fingers. As a gush of blood sprayed Parker's face, Parsegian's jaw dropped.

That was when Gerald Parsegian did something he hadn't done in over thirty years: he screamed like a baby. As he struggled desperately to wrench his hand back, he was stunned at the strength with which the bony tweaker gripped him. As he tugged, Parker moved forward, his crimson-stained maw opening wide to take another bite out of the stumps of the two fingers he'd already decapitated.

Pulling back harder, the lumbering man stumbled as Parker retained his inhumanly strong grip on his wrist. As they teetered toward the floor, the remains of the victim's fingers wriggled and danced on Parker's tongue.

As they landed with a thud that echoed down the hallway, the back of Parsegian's head slammed against the concrete floor. Parker didn't notice, absorbed as he was with the remaining fingers on his landlord's hand.

The gush of blood that squirted from the ragged wounds was a wondrous elixir, and the hairy skin surrounding the delectable finger bones, manna from heaven. Parker had no real comprehension of what was happening or what he was doing—all he knew was that for a very long time, he'd felt more dead than alive and now felt vital and real again. There was no guilt or remorse for what he was doing as he pushed the stumpy hand away, spitting out the denuded bones. He ripped at the cotton material covering his landlord's voluminous gut. This was it: perfection. All the dull layers of civilization and technology swept away in an instant. What remained was the primitive, fierce desire to feed.

Ignoring the shag rug of hair on Gerry's gut, Parker sank his teeth into the soft belly flesh and tore off a long, thick strip of skin, setting off a geyser of blood. He bathed his face and neck in it, letting his clothes soak up the wondrous juice as he dug into the wound he'd made on Parsegian's belly. He tugged and tore at the layers of skin and fat, eager for the sweet meats underneath.

He almost missed the screams emanating from inside Parsegian's apartment. Looking up, Parker saw Millie, Gerry's wife, standing a few feet away, her face locked in a grimace. She wore the flower-print housecoat that was as much her standard attire as the wife beater was for her hubby. Nathan didn't see any curlers, though they were usually in by this time of night. Instead, her thinning crown of drab brownish-gray hair clung limply to her scalp.

As Parker looked up from Gerald, his hands buried deep in the man's abdomen, there was an itch at the back of his mind that hinted that he was doing something that might be construed as *wrong*–though for the life of him, he couldn't understand why.

Rising to his feet, Parker moved toward Gerald's spouse.

"Hi, Millie. It's great to see you again! You're probably wondering what I'm doing to Gerry," he said as he moved through the doorway of her apartment. Parker shook his head and laughed. "It's a really funny story. I think you'll get a kick out of it."

"Get away from me! What have you done to my husband? Oh my God, Ger! GERRY!" Millie screamed as she retreated into the apartment. The dimensions of the Parsegian's home were similar to Parker's, but with the lights on and with a woman's touch, it had a far cozier feel to it.

"I like what you've done to the place. It's really swell, a lot nicer than mine," he said with a grin as Millie screamed even louder.

Millie turned and pulled open a drawer. Parker increased his speed, desperate to get to her. He knew she would understand once they were able to sit down and speak rationally about things. He wasn't greedy; she could have a taste of good ol' Ger as well. Parker knew that, given the chance, he could *make* her understand.

He reached for Millie's shoulder, and she turned and thrust an eight-inch-long butcher knife into his gut. The blade slid in clean, all the way to the hilt, and Parker stumbled back, shocked at the brutality of the assault. Millie remained where she stood, watching in horror as Parker's blood-drenched shirt became a darker shade of red around the wound.

Parker pulled the knife free and let it drop to the linoleum tile. He felt a bit miffed that Millie had not allowed him to explain his actions before rudely trying to eviscerate him. At the same time, he realized there was no pain emanating from the gaping wound in his belly.

Knowing this wasn't the time to screw around pondering imponderables, Parker sent his fist crashing across the bridge of Millie's nose. There was an audible crack that he felt more than heard over the loud squawk coming out of the woman's mouth. As he followed her to the floor, Parker realized he might have broken a finger or two with that punch, but he couldn't feel that pain either.

As he leaned in, ignoring her feeble fists as she tried to keep him at bay, Dr. Parker smiled. Millie's throat had always intrigued him for some odd reason. The woman was thick set, but her neck was long and slender. Perhaps it was the pale, delicate skin or the fact that it was the only part of her physique that didn't repulse him. But as his teeth sank into her esophagus and her screams turned into garbled, weakened protests, he understood the fascination: Mrs. Parsegian's neck was delightful. It smelled of clean and powdered linen, with just a hint of perfume that tantalized and teased the taste buds. As her hyoid bone snapped free of the ligaments holding it in place, there was a single shining moment when Nathan Parker was deeply and profoundly in love with Millie Parsegian. Crunching on the bone and delicate flesh, he looked down at her adoringly as her hands flew to the gaping hole in her throat. A gush of blood and vomit shot past her clamped hands as Parker leaned forward again and let his mouth burrow into one of her eye sockets.

Millie's protests grew feebler as Parker heard moaning behind him. Rising up, he let her eyeball roll around in his mouth for a moment. He'd tried scooping it out of her skull with just his tongue, but when that didn't work Parker cheated and used his fingers to pop it out.

Swallowing the juicy tidbit whole, he called out to Gerald, who was stumbling back into the apartment.

"She's all yours, man. She got a little rude, but I think we've come to an understanding. I hope you don't mind."

Gerald's only response was to moan in excitement as he spotted his dying wife on the floor. The lumbering oaf looked a little out of it, but that wasn't too surprising. Part of his small intestine dangled from the hole in his abdomen, and the landlord was working hard not to stumble over the wet, squishy tendrils swinging back and forth with every step he took.

Parker gave one last look down at Millie and sighed. He wouldn't mind getting to know her better, but he was starting to remember why he had left his apartment in the first place. He needed to pay Ilian a visit and give him a piece of his mind.

Stepping out of Gerry's way, Nathan let the big man pass. He gave him a hearty slap on the back as he walked to the door. "You two lovebirds have fun, ya hear?"

Moving onto the landing, Parker heard another scream from down the hall and swiveled his head. All he could see was a door slamming shut, which he ignored as he shambled toward the entrance of the building.

As he pushed the doors open and walked out onto the sidewalk, a cascade of screams bombarded him from all sides. The streetlights' glow gave passersby an eerie look as they recoiled from him. Their screams echoed through his head in a way he found irritating.

"Okay folks, you don't all need to freak out at once. Sheesh!"

Apparently, the words didn't have the calming effect Parker hoped for as more screams cascaded down on him. Raising his hands to his ears, he growled and tried to focus on the person closest to him. He was going to have to rattle a few cages if they didn't shut the hell up. The buzzing sensation in his head had returned, and his stomach, despite being filled with Parsegian goodness, clenched and sent a pain through him as though someone were slicing thick chunks out of it with a razorblade.

Parker spotted a young woman pushing a stroller and howling like a banshee. She was attempting to cross the street to get away from him. Even her mewling brat was chiming in, and it was clear they needed to be taught a lesson about respect. There was no good reason for their screams when his head already felt like it was about to burst open like a rotten melon.

He was shocked when the woman was able to dodge underneath his outstretched hand as she pushed the stroller off the curb and guided it between two parked cars. There was another blur of motion as a man ran by and distracted Parker, who tried grabbing for him. *Someone* needed to pay for all the rude screaming.

"Parker! Holy shit, Parker, what the hell?"

Parker recognized the voice and whipped around, trying to find the source of the heavily accented words. Spotting the man he'd been heading out to see, he raised his hands in excitement.

The Bulgarian was decked out in one of his many track suits. It was the blue one with white piping that had to be Ilian's favorite. Just like Parsegian, Ilian wore a gold crucifix that bounced against his chest as he strode down the street.

"Oh man, Parker," Ilian said in his thick accent, adding a few extra letters to the ex-doctor's name, "what have you done?"

"Nothing much, old buddy, but I think you have some explaining to do about this piece of crap you sold me," Parker spat out as he reached inside his pocket to pull out the bad stim.

The buzzing faded again in Parker's head as he approached the Bulgarian. In the past, he'd been timid around Ilian, knowing the man could have him killed or would do it himself if the former doctor gave him any reason to, but Parker was feeling strong tonight. The thug wasn't going to intimidate him anymore.

A look passed over Ilian's face, one that Parker hadn't seen before. As he shambled closer, he tried to discern whether it was regret or frustration, but he couldn't be sure—and he realized he didn't care. "I want my money back, and I want a product that actually works, you two-bit hood!"

Ilian reached inside the zippered front of his jogging suit and pulled out the Makarov he carried with him everywhere. Parker had seen the pistol several times. Ilian showed it to everyone he dealt with, telling them it was his good luck charm … and bad luck for anyone who crossed him.

"I'm really sorry, Parker. I just found out what Boris did to that stim. I was coming to try and stop you from jacking in … I *am* sorry."

That was all Nathan Parker heard before the muzzle flashed and he felt something like a stiff punch to the chest. It caused him to slow, but when there was no other sensation, he gritted his teeth and bore down on Ilian.

There were two more thunderous blasts from the gun before the slender ex-doctor slammed into the burly Eastern European, driving them both to the ground.

As Ilian battered Parker with the butt of his pistol, the stim junkie's fingers scratched deep furrows in the dealer's face, causing him to scream out in pain.

"*I'm* not sorry, Ilian, not one little bit!" Parker screamed before taking a jaw-stretching bite out of the Bulgarian's shoulder.

There was a whirlwind of feedback and a high-pitched screech as he moved his assault to Ilian's ear. As he tore through the cartilage, he felt a shift in his position and was suddenly flat on his back. He was lying on a cushiony-soft surface profoundly different from the concrete sidewalk outside his apartment. The world had gone dark, as if everything had fallen away or he'd been tossed into a sensory deprivation tank.

Parker would have been shocked by the mind-shattering transition were it not one he'd experienced before.

There was a ripping sensation and the Virtual Reality helmet came free from Parker's head. He had to blink several times to adjust to bright lights in his apartment.

Standing over him was a face that wavered in and out of existence a couple of times before it came into focus. Parker didn't recognize the pockmarked visage or the broad, flat nose until he heard the ugly man speak.

"It's been a while, Doc," said the gruff-voiced man whose bulk blotted out the bright glow of the halogens mounted in the ceiling.

Parker gave the man a weak smile. "Jericho. How're tricks?"

The rabbit punch caused Parker to gasp and was quickly followed by a hand to his throat.

Jericho Maltese was a slab of beef, a knuckle-dragging bruiser who'd ascended to the highest ranks of the criminal underworld, but still liked taking out the garbage every now and then. This was one of those times. The squeak coming from Nathan Parker's mouth brought a smile to his face.

"It seems you got yourself into a bit of trouble with the medical boards, huh, Nate?" Jericho tightened his grip around Parker's neck. "Then you hit the road and didn't even leave a note for me, your best buddy in the whole wide world."

Parker struggled momentarily, but stopped as he realized he was stuck. As he settled down, the gangster's grip loosened slightly. When it did, and he was able to breathe again, Parker's head began to clear.

It was obvious that the stim he'd gotten from Ilian *had* worked. There wasn't any blood dripping off of his shirt, and while the taste of raw meat and viscera lingered in his mind, it wasn't on his tongue. The only pain Parker felt was that inflicted by the thug gripping his throat.

Jericho's bulbous head was directly in front of him, and the stim dealer's eyes narrowed as they evaluated the strung-out doctor.

"Nate, my boy, I am trying to figure out what to do with you. You had so many great contacts in the medical field, but after your screw-up, I doubt any of those uppity pricks would be caught dead associating with you anymore."

Jericho shook his head, disappointment scrolling across his face. "And it's not even that, so much. It's that you took off on me, tried to run, took my machine and a lot of the money I'd staked you with, just to hole up in this stink pit."

The gangster finally relinquished his hold on Parker's neck and turned away from the VRID unit, waving his hands in frustration. "You bolted just so you could hide out in this piece of crap? The least you could do was head to some tropical island and made it challenging for me to find you."

Taking a few steps back, Jericho slipped the silenced revolver out of his jacket as he heard Parker slide off of the VRID with an odd grunting noise.

"Sorry, Nate. It was fun while it las-"

He didn't get out the rest of his comment as he raised the gun just in time to be plowed into by Parker.

Jericho had not been expecting the blow, but had far too much experience with desperate men to be caught off guard by the assault. Parker had been stupid enough not to go for the gun, instead driving his shoulder right into the big man's gut.

The blow was surprisingly powerful from the man who couldn't weigh more than a hundred and forty pounds sopping wet. Enduring the attack actually made Jericho's thick legs wobble.

As the wiry man jumped on the gangster, he realized the tweaker was growling at him. He slammed the butt of the nickel-plated .357 down on the side of the doc's head, but the blow didn't faze the lunatic as Parker wrapped his arms around Jericho's neck and ripped a chunk of flesh out of his face with his teeth.

Jericho roared in pain as his flesh tore. Slamming the butt of his gun on the top of Parker's head again, he felt a gush of his own blood splash down the front of his suit from the scratch on his face. Even with the solid blow he'd landed on Parker's noggin, the tweaker refused to relinquish the grip he had around the gangster's neck.

Jericho pointed the gun at Parker, realizing the bastard wasn't going to stop biting and clawing at him, at least not before his Brioni suit was totally ruined. But as Jericho aimed the gun at Parker's head, he felt teeth sink deep into his neck. His eyes went wide with surprise as he tumbled to the floor.

The last thought that went through Jericho Maltese's mind was that he should have realized a doctor would know exactly where to bite someone so he would bleed out quickly.

Five minutes later, the buzzing inside Parker's head had stopped and his stomach felt gloriously filled with blood and meat once again. The arterial spray from Jericho Maltese's carotid had coated a ten-foot radius around the remains of his neck and pretty much every square inch of Nathan Parker. He had gnawed on the thug's neck but also did a number on his face, since he was too impatient to dig through the expensive silk suit the lunkhead was wearing. After tasting Millie's eye during his latest tour of virtual reality and the delightful burst of juice when it popped between his teeth, he had to sample Maltese's as well.

But as Jericho's corpse started to cool, the bloodlust simmered and Parker came back to a more rational state of mind. He had a lot of questions about what was going on, but had no answers. Echoes of the desires instilled in him while he was on the chair must still have been resonating in his brain. Sure, Jericho had planned on killing him, but the idea of turning cannibal to defend himself would never have crossed the doctor's mind an hour ago. Now it didn't seem like such a bad idea.

The buzzing sensation returned, and Parker's stomach lurched just like before. With a wistful look at Jericho's corpse, he moved to the door of his apartment. The taste of the gangster's cold, dead flesh had lost its allure. He needed something fresher.

Just before he stepped out into the hall and pulled the door shut, Parker thought he saw Jericho's body begin to twitch. Ignoring it, the tweaker hummed something tuneless and wondered if his landlord were home. The rent was due, and it was time to pay up.

Author Bios

A.J. French has appeared in Abandoned Towers, The Absent Willow Review, Short Story.Me!, Black Lantern Publishing, This Mutant Life, theDF_underground, Fantastic Horror, Sex and Murder, Black Ink Horror, and Golden Visions Magazine. He also has stories in the following anthologies: Ruthless: An Extreme Horror Collection by Pill Hill Press with introduction by Bentley Little, Deep Space Terror, By Mind or Metal, Novus Creatura, and Pellucid Lunacy edited by Michael Bailey.

Alex Azar is an author born and raised in New Jersey. After attending a technical school for two years and taking every English course offered there, he knew writing was not only his passion but his future.

Allan Izen lives on the Windward side of Oahu. He frequently strolls on the beach watching the wealthy at play.

Ben North resides in the Blue Mountains in Australia with his partner, Glenda. He thinks transgressive writers should have benign biographies.

Berry Rosenburg was born in London in 1943 and moved to Australia in 1970 after completing a PhD.
He has been involved with creative writing since 1975. He started with poetry and moved up the literary scale to horror fiction. He can be Googled.

Brandon Cracraft lives in the historic district of Tucson, Arizona with his partner and a black cat. His short stories have appeared in several anthologies including Monster Party and Attack of the Fifty Foot Book. He has also written plays, screenplays, and articles. His fiction is set to appear in the comic book anthology, Life After the So-Called Space Age.

D.G. Sutter is a writer, editor, and recluse living in Western Massachusetts. His work has thus far appeared in the anthologies "Seasons in the Abyss" and "Alienology: Tales from the Void", which he also edited. Future stories are to appear in forthcoming collections from NorGus Press, Twisted Library Press, Wicked East Press, and Coscom Entertainment. You can keep up with him at www.dgsutter.wordpress.com.

Dale Elster is an author and homebrewer living in Auburn, NY. His first published short story, "The Isolation Method," can be found in the NorGus Press anthology entitled, "Look What I Found." Find Dale on Facebook, or follow him on Twitter.

Jeffrey A. Angus lives in the Finger Lakes region of New York with his wife Bonny. He loves crafting tales for people to enjoy. He has been published in a number of books and his poems and stories range from the macabre to the humorous. Visit Jeff on Facebook or his website at www.sttales.com.

Jeremy Bush is a carpenter living in western New York with his wife. He has flash fiction forthcoming in Daily Flash 2011: 365 Days of Flash Fiction, The Journal of Microliterature, Cup of Joe: Coffee House Flash Fiction, and Strange Tales of Horror.

Joshua Ramey-Renk is a freelance writer currently living in Dublin, Ireland. When not writing, he can be found in a pub with a roaring fire buried in a book with a pint or a cuppa near to hand. Not surprisingly, this is also where he can be found when he IS writing. Visit him on the web at www.writereadrant. wordpress.com.

Jutter Caine has published short stories in Dark Gothic Resurrected, Indigo Rising, Look What I found Anthology, and Twisted Tongues and has written two books of poetry under the name Sir Christopher Stewart through Author house "A Knight's Grotto" and "Rebecca".

Kelly M. Hudson grew up in the wilds of Kentucky and currently resides in California. He has a deep and abiding love for all things horror and rock n' roll. He has had about two dozen short stories published in various anthologies, most of them zombie stories for Living Dead Press. He has also had work published by Comet Press and Pill Hill as well as a couple of online zines that are now defunct and one called Dark Fire which is still up and running. He has a zombie novel currently released under Living Dead Press as well as a self-published novel available on Amazon.com via the Kindle. All of his work can be found on his website www.kellymhudson.com.

Ken Goldman, former English and Film Studies teacher and affiliate member of the Horror Writers Association, lives on the Main Line in Pennsylvania and at the Jersey shore. His stories received seven honorable mentions in The Year's Best Fantasy & Horror and appear in over 575 publications in the U.S., Canada, the UK, and Australia. His book of short stories, "You Had Me At ARRGH!!" (Sam's Dot Publishers) remained an all-time top ten best seller at the former Genre Mall from October 1997 until its closing in March 2011, and Damnation Books published his novella "Desiree" in June 2010 (downloadable eBook, with print and Kindle editions available on Amazon.com). Ken's story "The Devil, You Say" appeared in Strange Tales of Horror, edited by Matt Nord.

Lachlan David is a native of California who currently resides in Phoenix, Arizona. He has been writing for his personal entertainment for many years and is excited to take on the challenge of writing for publication.

Marc Sorondo lives with his wife and daughter in New York. He has had work published by Pill Hill Press, Post Mortem Press, Northern Frights Publishing, Blood Bound Books, and Wicked East Press.

Matt Nord lives in Central New York with his wife, Karen, two sons, Jacob and Judah, and daughter, Jordan. He is a fledgling horror writer with several credits under his proverbial belt, including several short stories published by Pill Hill Press, Static Movement Press, NorGus Press, Living Dead Press and Library of the Living Dead Press as well as stories to be featured future anthologies from Wicked East Press. His most ambitious project to date may be the collaborative novel he is currently spearheading with 18 other authors, and will hopefully see published before his baby girl graduates college.

Nicholas Conley is a 21-year-old writer from California, who has also resided in Arizona, New Hampshire and North Carolina and enjoys spending his free time exploring the open road in search of new experiences. His work has been published in the anthology The Coffee Shop Chronicles, Vol.1, as well as such venues as Short Story Library, Microhorror, NVH Magazine and Gravediggings. More information can be found on his website, www.nicholasconley.com.

Patrick D'Orazio resides in southwestern Ohio with his wife, Michele, two children, Alexandra and Zachary, and two spastic dogs. A lifelong writer, he only recently decided that attempting to get published might be a better idea than continuing to toss all those stories he's been scribbling down over the years into a filing cabinet, never to be seen again. Over twenty of his short stories appear or will be appearing in various anthologies from a wide array of different small press publishers. He has dipped his toes into a variety of genres, including horror, science fiction, fantasy, erotica, Bizarro, western, action-adventure, apocalyptic, and comedy. Beyond the Dark is his latest novel, and the final book in the Dark Trilogy. It is preceded by the novels Comes the Dark and Into the Dark, both of which are also available through the Library of the Living Dead Press. He will be releasing all three books, plus another book of short stories in an ebook release entitled "The Dark Trilogy: Revised, Expanded, and With Additional Stories." You can see what Patrick is up to via his website at www.patrickdorazio.com or over at the forums at www.thelibraryofthelivingdead.com.

Rick McQuiston is a forty-two year-old father of two who loves anything horror related. He has had over 200 publications so far and recently started his first novel, a zombie tale tentatively titled "To See as a God Sees." He has written four anthology books and one book of novellas, which are available on Lulu and Amazon. He is also a guest author each year at Memphis Junior High School, and is editing and contributing to an anthology of Michigan authors called "Michigan Madmen". His website is many-midnights.webs.com.

Somewhere in southern California lurks a creature by the name of **Robert Essig**. This beast is known to have a macabre fascination with horror and is fortunate to implore an imp of whom whispers dark delicacies to him in the night. Robert's fiction has been published in Bards and Sages Quarterly, Night Terrors, Tales of the Talisman, Hungur, and Withersin amongst others. He is the editor of Through the Eyes of the Undead (Library of the Living Dead Press). Visit him at: robertessig.com.

Robert Freese is the author of the zombie novel Bijou of the Dead. His most recent short stories have appeared in CD Publication's In Laymon's Terms, the Norgus Press anthologies Strange Tales of Horror and Look What I Found, the Pill Hill Press anthology Daily Bites of Flesh 2011: 365 Days of Horrifying Flash Fiction and the charity anthology The Undead that Saved Christmas: Vampire Edition. His first scripted comic appeared in the charity anthology The Undead that Saved Christmas Volume 2. His collection of horror stories 13 Frights will be released in 2012 by StoneGarden.net Publishing.

Sean T. Page is author of The Official Zombie Handbook (UK), out in July 2010 through Severed Press and of the zombie-fighting website ministryofzombies.com. Has clocked up numerous short stories, has an over-active imagination and a Lovecraftian interest in the bizarre.

Steve McGuire lives and writes out of Portland, Oregon. He is married to Harmony Ray. He enjoys reading and writing about the scary and the strange.

Suzanne Robb has stories in current and upcoming anthologies, Coscom Entertainment, Pill Hill Press, Wicked East Press, Static Movement, Library of the Living Dead Press, Living Dead Press, Library of Fantasy, NorGus Press, Panic Press, and hidden Thoughts Press. She is also a member of Collaboration of the Dead, a novel being written by several writers, each contributing a chapter or two. In her free time she reads, watches movies, plays with her dog, and enjoys chocolate and Legos.

Thomas Scopel has written numerous articles for "American Chronicle." Has had an article reprinted in a Canadian Newspaper, translated into Russian, and used in a national podcast. Has been both a correspondent, as well as a feature writer for the Daytona Beach News Journal. He has been published in The Dark Fiction Spotlight, SNM Horror Magazine, Lit Fest Magazine, Suspense Magazine, and various websites. He has an AAS in Design Engineering Technology,and lives in Ormond Beach, Florida. He can be reached through his website www.thomasscopel.com.

William R.D. Wood lives and writes in Virginia's beautiful Shenandoah Valley from an old farmhouse turned backwards to the road. He was born in South Carolina, grew up in the US Navy, and has spent a fair amount of his life fixing things. His *fiction* can soon be found in titles from M-Brane SF/Hadley Rille Books, Sword and Saga Press, and Library of the Living Dead, among others. His *truth* can be found closer to home. http://writebrane. blogspot.com/.

www.ingramcontent.com/pod-product-compliance
Lightning Source LLC
Chambersburg PA
CBHW070808180626
46818CB00001B/160